THE BEST PLACE

May you find your own
Best Place!

Tyler R. Tichelaar

THE BEST PLACE

a novel

Tyler R. Tichelaar

Marquette Fiction
Marquette, Michigan

THE BEST PLACE

copyright © 2013 by Tyler R. Tichelaar

Marquette Fiction
1202 Pine Street
Marquette, MI 49855
www.MarquetteFiction.com

ISBN-13: 978-0-9791790-7-5
ISBN-10: 0-9791790-7-6

Library of Congress Control Number: 2013906589

This is a work of fiction. All of the characters, names, incidents, organizations, and dialogue in this novel are either the products of the author's imagination or are used fictitiously.

Printed in the United States of America
Publication managed by Storytellers' Friend
www.storytf.com
Printing managed by Globe Printing
www.GlobePrinting.net

To the memory of Irene Watson

who never ceased to find inspiration in life
and pass it on to others.

Acknowledgments

Thank you to:

Diana DeLuca, Rosalyn Hurley, and Jenifer Brady for reading drafts of the manuscript and for all their invaluable feedback and suggestions.

The Writers Ink group, for listening to me read passages from the novel and talk about Lyla ad nauseam at our meetings.

Larry Alexander, for his cover design and the interior layout of the book.

Jack Deo of Superior View for the colored postcard image of the Holy Family Orphanage.

All my readers, who keep asking me, "When's the next book going to be out?" You make me feel it's all worthwhile.

"How strange life can be. At seventy-eight, you'd think that you'd stop being surprised, and something like this happens, and it's as though the world had only just begun."
— Rosamunde Pilcher, *September* (1990)

PRINCIPAL CHARACTERS IN *THE BEST PLACE*

The Hopewell Family

Heiki Toivonen – father who goes to Karelia, Finland during the Great Depression

Elizabeth Hopewell – his wife who takes back her maiden name from shame when people find out her husband has moved to a Communist country

Jessie Hopewell – their oldest daughter, adopted by Thelma Bergmann

Lyla Hopewell – their youngest daughter, who ends up in the Holy Family Orphanage, which marks her for life

Orphanage Inhabitants

Bel Archambeau – a young orphan, later Lyla Hopewell's best friend

Charlie Greenway – an older orphan who likes to pick on Bel

Janet – an orphan

Sister Euphrasia – a nun whose duties include finding employment for orphans who leave orphanage

Sister Perpetua – a nun in charge of dormitories at the orphanage

The Mitchell Family

Roger Mitchell – oldest sibling, deceased at time of the novel

Mary Mitchell – middle sibling, a former schoolteacher, now blind

Florence Mitchell – youngest sibling, a stubborn, ornery woman

The Whitman & Goldman Family
Bill Whitman – Lyla Hopewell's ex-boyfriend, now very ill
William Whitman III – Bill Whitman's oldest son
Jason Whitman – Bill Whitman's middle son
Alan Whitman – Bill Whitman's youngest son
Gil Whitman – Alan Whitman's son
Annette – Bill Whitman's second ex-wife and mother to his children
Eleanor Goldman – Bill Whitman's sister, age ninety-three and going
    strong
Lucy Goldman – Eleanor's oldest daughter
Maud Goldman – Eleanor's youngest daughter

The Vandelaare Family
John Vandelaare – trustee of the Robert O'Neill historical home (great-
    nephew to Bill Whitman and Eleanor Goldman
Wendy Vandelaare – John's wife, member of the women's group
Neill Vandelaare – John and Wendy's son
Tom Vandelaare – John's father
Ellen Vandelaare – John's mother (Bill Whitman and Eleanor Goldman's
    niece)

The O'Neill Family
Robert O'Neill – famous local novelist, now deceased, Lyla Hopewell's last
    employer before she retired
Eliza O'Neill – late wife of Robert O'Neill

The Dalrymple Family
Bea Dalrymple – wife to the late Joseph Dalrymple, who was first cousin to
    Bill Whitman and Eleanor Goldman
May Dalrymple – Bea's granddaughter; the child of an American soldier
    who died in Vietnam and a Vietnamese mother; raised by her paternal
    grandparents in Marquette; member of the women's group; owner of
    May's Antiques
Josie Dalrymple – May's teenage daughter

Other Characters
Frank Jarvi – John Vandelaare's former college roommate

Sybil Shelley – part-time employee of The Pancake House, part-time employee at May's Antiques, member of women's group, writer for *The Mining Journal*

Diana – member of the women's group

Mr. Hampton – the Mitchell sisters' lawyer

Matthew Newman – storeowner who hires Charlie Greenway when he leaves the orphanage

Norma Juntunen – Finnish American involved in the Finn Fest 2005 celebrations

Mike Koski – Finnish descendant from Duluth who attends International Finn Fest in Marquette

Paul Lehtimaki – Finnish descendant at International Finn Fest

Brad – Paul Lehtimaki's cousin who also attends International Finn Fest

Joan – Brad's wife who accompanies him to International Finn Fest

Viola – resident at Snowberry Heights

Gloria – resident at Snowberry Heights

Minnie – resident at Snowberry Heights

HISTORICAL PERSONS REFERENCED IN *THE BEST PLACE*

John Voelker – Upper Michigan author of *Anatomy of a Murder*

Dorothy Maywood Bird – Upper Michigan author of *Granite Harbor*

Carroll Watson Rankin – Marquette author of *Dandelion Cottage*

Phyllis Rankin – Carroll Watson Rankin's daughter, longtime librarian in Marquette

Imogene Miller – daughter of Carroll Watson Rankin

Monsignor Louis Cappo – pastor of St. Peter's Cathedral

Mary Dwyer – church lady at St. Peter's Cathedral

Pauline Kiltinen – chair of Finn Fest 2005

Mr. Pearce – employee at the Union National Bank

Carl Pellonpaa – TV host of *Finland Calling*

Chapter 1

It's the Saturday of Memorial Day weekend, and I've just put my feet up after mopping the floor so I can read *The Mining Journal*—not that there's much in it worth reading when you live in a small city like Marquette, Michigan, but I at least have to check out the obituaries. I've only turned halfway to them when the phone rings.

"Goddamnit!" I shout.

Since I spent my working life on my feet, I still feel guilt whenever I sit down during the day. That guilt grows when the phone rings—it's like it wants to torment me, telling me I don't deserve a rest—you know what they say about the wicked. The jury's still out on whether I qualify, but the way my life seems to go, God must think I am.

But thank God anyways for the cordless phone. I've got one right beside my chair so I don't have to run to the kitchen like I used to, but I'm still angry that I can't get a minute to relax.

"Hello," I says, wondering who it could be. I know there's that Caller I.D. people have nowadays, but hardly anyone ever calls me other than Bel, so it'd be a waste of money to have it. I can always just hang up if it's a telemarketer.

"Is this Lyla?" asks a frail sounding woman.

"Yeah," I reply, wondering who it is. My first thought is maybe it's my sister, Jessie; I keep hoping she'll call, but I know it's ridiculous to wish for it. I haven't talked to her in more than forty years, and I doubt she'll ever want to talk to me again. Hell, I don't even know for sure if she's still alive—I mean, she would be seventy-nine now. Sometimes I think about getting a computer just so I can do a search for her—I hear there's all kinds of personal things you can find out about people that way. Hate to think what's on there about me—hopefully nothing bad, or not any of my personal information like bank numbers or anything, but I guess if there was any of that, I'd have had my bank account wiped out by now—or more likely, whoever looked at my account would just laugh since I hardly have anything in there except for the few days right after my Social Security check comes in.

"Lyla, it's Eleanor—Bill's sister."

It takes me a second to place the name, but to cover my not knowing it right away, I says extra-friendly, "Hi, Eleanor. How are you?"

I'm almost as surprised to hear from her as I'd be to hear from Jessie. I haven't talked to Eleanor in years, other than to say hello if we bump into each other at Walmart or Econofoods. We sure never talk on the phone.

"Lyla, I have some bad news," she says. I wait, not knowing what to say. "It's Bill," she says, confirming my suspicions.

"What's wrong?" I asks when she doesn't say more. He must be dead is all I can think, and she's trying to break it to me softly.

"I'm sorry," she says, sounding distracted. "It's been a long day, and I've been so worried."

"What's wrong with him?" I asks again.

"He's in the hospital. He had a heart attack this morning. I suppose it's wrong for me to call you since it's been so long, but I know how much you cared about him, and—"

"It's okay, Eleanor. I'm glad you did," I says, though I'm not so sure I am. "Is he going to be okay?"

"I don't know. I've been here with him all day. He called me at six this morning. I don't know why he didn't just call the ambulance himself. I had to yell at him to get him to hang up the phone so I could call 911, and then my daughter Lucy drove me over here—we actually beat the ambulance. Lucy stayed with me until she had to go to work—I don't know why after all the years she's put in at that office she still has to work Saturdays, but it was her one Saturday of the month, so she couldn't stay with me. Anyway, they say he's stable now. I was just allowed into his room. He's sleeping but he looks terrible. I don't think he even knows I'm here, though he's opened his eyes a couple of times and looked my way, but not like he recognizes me, so I just keep sitting here and talking to him and holding his hand. I—it's just terrible waiting, and I can't get ahold of anyone else, so I thought maybe—"

"What about his boys?" I asks when I can get a word in. Those boys never did give their father the attention they should—then again, I don't know that he ever gave them the attention he should.

"I can't get ahold of Jason, but William said he'd call and tell him. William didn't want to come until we knew more. He's busy with some big work project he has to get done over the weekend—like that should matter when your father's in the hospital. So I called Alan, who said he'd be here right away, but it's an eight-hour drive from downstate. I was going to call Ellen—you remember her, my niece, but—well, I thought—"

"Eleanor, are you telling me you're there by yourself?" I asks, and while I'm trying to sound concerned, I also start to feel anxious about what I'm thinking of doing, but I know it's what she wants—why she called me.

"Yes, but Alan will be here by suppertime, and Lucy will come back to pick me up after she gets off work. I just don't want to leave Bill alone."

"You need your rest too," I says, trying to calculate in my head how old she must be now—at least ninety, if she's a day. "You're not young anymore," I says. "You don't want to wear yourself out."

"What else am I supposed to do?" she asks. "He's my brother, the last one I have, and my baby brother at that, even if he is eighty-five now. When he told me he had chest pains this morning, I hoped it was just indigestion—he ate an awful lot last night when I had him over for supper. He even had two pieces of the cake I made."

"You shouldn't be there alone, Eleanor," I says, still wondering what gave her the idea to call me, but from her broken and frantic tone, I feel sorry for her, so before I even know what I'm saying, I says, "I'll come down and keep you company."

"Oh, I—well, I didn't expect you to do that, Lyla."

Well, why else did she call me then? She obviously thinks I still care about Bill enough that I would want to know that he's sick, even though we broke up so many years ago; it's clear she wants me to come down there and see him.

"Well," I says, wishing I could think of a way to get out of my offer and yet kind of wanting to go, "it might take me an hour or so to get there. I don't drive, so I'll have to ask my friend Bel to give me a ride, but I'll be there as soon as I can."

"Oh, thank you, Lyla. Just an hour or so would help so much, and then Alan or Lucy will be here, and it would be nice to catch up with you again. You know I always thought Bill made a mistake when he broke up with you."

I didn't know that—which is why I'm surprised she's called me, but it's nice of her to say so after nineteen years.

"Okay. I'll see you soon, Eleanor."

"Thanks, Lyla. Bill might still be asleep when you get here, but then maybe we could go have a snack in the cafeteria or something and have a little chat."

She sounds like she's inviting me to a tea party—Eleanor always did have some class about her—even though she's divorced—not that anybody cares about that kind of thing these days, and she was divorced a long time ago—not long after World War II ended Bill told me—but knowing Eleanor, I'm not sure she ever got over the stigma of it. It always made her seem a bit delicate or even wounded to me, knowing how her husband mistreated her and then abandoned her and her daughters when they were still little girls.

"Sure, what's his room number?" I asks. She gives it to me and then I says, "Okay. I'll see you in a little while, Eleanor. Goodbye," and I hang up the phone.

I set *The Mining Journal* back on my end table, put down my chair's footrest, and then dial Bel for a ride.

"What do you wanna go up to the hospital to see him for?" she asks when I explain what's going on.

"I just feel bad for Eleanor is all," I says.

"She's got all kinds of family. She doesn't need you up there too."

"Are you going to drive me to the hospital, or aren't you?" I asks, not wanting to waste time arguing with her.

"Of course I will," she says. "I just don't know why it's so important to you. I'll be ready in five minutes, but I think you're making a big mistake, Lyla."

I think I am too, but I'm not going to admit it to her. "I'll be waiting down in the lobby for you," I says. "Thanks."

As soon as I hang up the phone, I asks myself, "What the hell are you doing going up to the hospital to see him?" I go in the bathroom to fix my hair, trying not to feel anxious; instead, I try to focus on how Bill must be suffering. "Poor, Bill. He needs comforting now. He needs to know I don't hold any grudges." But the truth is that I'm the one seeking comfort. It's so stupid of me to go at all—like he's even remotely part of my life anymore. I've told myself so many times that I'm over him. It's silly when we only went out for three years, and now something like six times that many years have passed. Sometimes a whole year can go by without it upsetting me, but then I'll see a sad movie, or someone at Walmart who looks a little bit like him, and it'll all come back to me, making me feel in the dumps again like we just broke up yesterday.

I never have figured out why I feel so bad about it. Probably because it's the only real serious long-term relationship I ever had. All the time we went out, I kept hoping he'd ask me to marry him—I mean, by then I was well into my fifties and him over sixty, though I didn't think he looked it—he was always such a handsome man—I figured at our ages he'd ask me so he didn't have to spend the end of his life alone, but I guess he chose to do that instead 'cause I never heard anything about him dating any other women after me.

I guess I chose to be alone after that too. I mean, I could have gone looking for another man. Living here in Snowberry Heights, I've known a few men who were interested—but they all just looked like shriveled up old raisins. Back in the day, I had quite a few men looking at me. I had a good round figure, the kind that men used to like before the girls started looking like skinny little birds. But I never met a man who wanted to be serious with me so I stayed away from most of them. There were only one or two, like Scofield, who were really decent men, and I couldn't have them. And then when Papa came home and moved in with me, well, I was thirty-five then, and after taking care of him for eleven years until he died, I was so worn out I didn't have much sex drive left in me—not until I met Bill anyways. I thought then I'd found a man mature enough to love me. Should have known better since he'd been divorced twice—but I figured we were each other's last hope at that point, so we'd be stable. Only, he didn't see things that way.

And then it all ended over something stupid I said that I didn't even mean. You would have thought he'd take my side, but he just went ballistic on me, which made me think he'd been looking for an excuse to break up all along.

Though I still think it was that son of his, Alan, who was the real problem. He never did like me. He was still living at home—end of his senior year of high school—when Bill started dating me. Then Alan went to go live with his mother because he didn't like me being around. He was probably just going through a stage, but Bill blamed me anyways—he needed someone to blame, so he didn't have to look at how he'd been a bad father, and I was the scapegoat he picked. I understand all that now, but it still hurts.

I've always been a tough broad, but hell, I've got feelings too. I want to be loved just as much as the next person. No one's ever understood that or given me a chance to show I can love them. Not my mom, my sister, damn Miss Bergmann, not Scofield, not Bill, not no one. Even Papa, much as I loved him, though I know he was too broken to give it back after what the damn Russians did to him, so at least I can forgive him for that. I suppose the rest of them all had their reasons too, but they could have at least tried. Papa at least tried by going to Karelia to find us a better life—it just didn't work out the way he had hoped—especially when all those years we thought he must be dead. So it was the least I could do to make his life comfortable in the end. I guess I can understand Mama too—she couldn't help it that she died. I know she must have had a hard time of it after Papa left for Karelia and didn't come back. I was too young to understand then, but now that I'm older, I can imagine how embarrassed she must have been to have people think her husband abandoned her when he actually couldn't contact us because of the Russians. I feel bad for both of them. They at least tried to be good parents—Jessie never tried to be a good sister—no one else ever tried to be good to me either, except Bel, of course. She at least tries to be a good friend, though she's a headache to deal with a lot of the time.

It's all so long ago now. Even with Bill, it's so long ago. But I still feel like a little girl wanting someone to love her. I wish to hell I could get over having that feeling.

"Suck it up, Lyla," I tell myself, looking in the mirror to fix my makeup. "You don't want Bill to see you looking like a mess."

I go grab my purse and coat and tell myself, "I'm just going for Eleanor's sake. She was always nice to me, and she shouldn't have to be at the hospital by herself. I'll just stay for an hour, just long enough so she won't feel all alone."

"I can't believe you want anything to do with that man after the way he treated you," says Bel the minute she sees me. She's in the lobby, already waiting for me when I get there. Since we both live in Snowberry—her apartment's on the floor below me—we tend to bump into each other in the elevator a lot when we go somewhere together, but not today. "And after all these years, why would you even care about him anymore?" she asks.

"I don't," I says, walking right past her and out the door because I don't want all the snoopy old ladies in the building to hear my business. "I just feel bad for Eleanor. She's up there all alone until Alan can get here."

I march to the car and wait for her to catch up with me.

"I know you, Lyla," Bel says, coming up behind me to unlock my car door and then hitting the automatic lock button so she can get in on her side. "You better not be thinking about getting involved with him again," she says as she gets in the seat beside me.

"Don't be ridiculous, Bel," I says, putting on my seatbelt. "He's in his eighties now, and I'm no spring chicken either. Why would I be thinking of that?"

"You must be if you're ready to run off and take care of him at a moment's notice," she says, starting up the car.

"Put on your seatbelt," I tell her. I always have to remind her about everything.

She snaps together her seatbelt and backs out of the parking lot in a way that makes me just know she's not going to let it go.

By the time she's pulled the car onto Fifth Street, I can't stop myself from saying, "It seems to me that when Charlie was sick at the end, even though you'd left him years before, that you were all set to take care of him."

"That's because I'm a good person," she says, "and I was married to him for many years, and being an orphan like us, you know he didn't have no one else, and besides, I was codependent. That was before I knew about codependency, so I felt all guilty and obligated to take care of him since, after all, I had left him when he was down. So how could I say that I wouldn't take care of him? I'd do it again today if I had to, and you know he was sick. Of course, if I could do it all again, I'd have never married him. That's where I went wrong. But you weren't never married to Bill so don't go making a fool of yourself by chasing after him now."

"Hmmph," I laugh. "I can hardly chase after him if he's lying in a hospital bed and hooked up to a bunch of tubes. And where you went wrong was letting Charlie get you pregnant when you were hardly more than a kid."

"Still, Lyla," Bel says, "we both know how Bill treated you, so don't act like it don't matter now just because he's sick."

"Well, can't I at least figure I'm a good person to go and see Bill rather than bearing him a grudge?"

"Not if you're really trying to worm your way back into his affections," says Bel, "and I think that's what you're trying to do."

"Jesus Christ, Bel! I'm not trying to worm my way into anything. I just feel bad for Eleanor being there by herself. She's all alone at the hospital until Alan can get there from downstate."

"You're not going to stay until Alan shows up, are you?" she asks.

"I don't know," I says. "He's driving all the way up from downstate. I don't imagine he'll get here until suppertime. I'm sure I'll leave before then."

"Well, you better leave before he does show up," says Bel. "I know how you two always butted heads."

"Yeah, well, Alan is grown up now, Bel. He was just a teenager back then."

"Whatever," she mutters, sounding like a teenager herself.

By now we've gone all the way up the steep hill of Fifth and turned onto Ridge. After her comment, I don't feel like talking to her about Bill any more, and I don't feel much like making small talk either, so I don't say anything for a minute or two, but by the time we turn off Ridge and onto Fourth, she's come up with a new topic.

"I've been thinking about joining another group," she says.

"Another group? Isn't AA enough?" I asks.

"No. I've got other problems besides alcohol," she says, "and anyway, I've been going to AA for so long I need to try something different."

"Haven't you tried just about everything there is?" I can't even remember all the groups she's gone to—Codependents Anonymous, Al-Anon, some sort of grief therapy group, and one I think was called Rainbow Recovery—I thought anything with "rainbow" in it was for gay people but she told me it wasn't—and then there was something like the "When Life's a Bitch" group—that probably wasn't the name of it, but it was something like that. You would think, after all these recovery groups she's been going to for decades, that by now she would have recovered, but she says that's not how it works—that you don't ever recover when you go to recovery—I've given up trying to figure out why they call it recovery then—it all sounds like a racket if you ask me. But I know better than to ask her again how it works because she's explained to me about a gazillion times how alcohol is a disease, and so is everything else wrong with her—codependency, love addiction, and on and on, so she has to keep going to her meetings 'cause they're like medicine and the disease will take over again if she doesn't. Honestly, I think these recovery groups are the addiction that just replaced her alcoholism. So, really, I don't know why I'm even surprised that she wants to join another group.

"It's a new group," she says. "It's for women to get together and talk about their lives. I think it'll be good 'cause sometimes with the other groups, I think having the men there sometimes keeps us women from saying what we need to say."

Not having gone to any of these groups, I wouldn't know, so I don't say anything.

"Since it is a group for women," she goes on, just like I knew she would, "I thought maybe you'd like to come with me."

"What? Are you crazy?" I asks. "Why would I want to do that? I don't have any issues with drinking and stuff like that."

"No, I know, Lyla, but sometimes it's good just to find people you can talk to about things that are bothering you—everyone needs to talk to somebody sometimes."

"Bel, you've known me for over sixty years. When have I ever talked about what's bothering me?"

"That's the problem with you, Lyla," she says. "You can't keep everything bottled up. It's not good for you."

"I'm seventy-seven and healthy as a horse," I says. "So keeping things bottled up sure ain't hurting me. It's no good talking about troubles. You just have to deal with them and move on in life."

"Well, it's like this thing with Bill," she keeps on, making me realize her talking about this group wasn't her changing the subject but her roundabout way to keep telling me how to live my life. "Maybe you have some mixed feelings or guilt or something that's making you want to go see him."

"Yeah, sure I do. Isn't that obvious?"

"Well, then you can go to this group to talk about those feelings and try to make sense of them."

"Bel, if I ain't made sense of them after all these years, some women's group isn't going to help me, and besides, I don't think my relationship problems are anyone else's damn business."

"Well, but I've shared mine with you," she says, "and you know it helped me a lot, especially after I left Charlie, and then later when he got sick and I had to take care of him in the end."

"Yeah," I mumble, remembering how she drove me crazy back then, even more than she does now—my phone was ringing off the hook at all hours back then 'cause Charlie was dying and she was feeling all kinds of guilt for having left him. Thank God she was never dumb enough to get married a second time 'cause I don't think I would have survived it.

We turn onto College Avenue now, and in another minute, she's driven me up to the hospital entrance.

"Just think about going to the meeting, Lyla. It won't hurt you," she says as I undo my seatbelt.

"Okay, I will," I says just so she doesn't keep nagging me in the emergency drop off lane when another car might need to let someone out.

"When do you want me to come back for you?" she asks.

I look at my watch. It's nearly three o'clock and Alan'll probably show up around five, and Bel is right—I don't want to be around when he gets here.

"How about four-thirty?" I says.

"Okay. I'll be here then," she says.

"Thanks," I says and get out of the car.

After I go through the sliding glass doors, I take the escalator up to the next floor, walk across the skywalk to the next elevator, and finally go up to the room. They sure don't build these hospitals for old people; they're so big and inconvenient—it's almost like they design them purposely to send us old people into cardiac arrest from all the walking we need to do—probably their way to make some extra bucks—thousands of bucks, 'cause God knows healthcare costs have gone through the roof.

And all that walking only gives me more time to get nervous about seeing Bill. I'm kind of hoping he's still asleep, but doing better of course, and I wonder what I'll say to Eleanor when I see her. Why'd she have to call me? What was she even thinking? And what am I thinking to be going to see him?

After I find the room, I slowly peer around the half-closed door, and the first thing I see is a young couple I don't know standing over the bed, but then I see Eleanor sitting next to it, and Bill, who looks awful—all pale and wrinkly and gaunt—lying there with oxygen tubes up his nose. Since the other patient's bed is empty, there's nothing to block their view of me, so they all—except Bill whose eyes stay closed—see me right away. For a minute, the young man and woman and I exchange glances, and then Eleanor, like the sight of me has finally registered in her brain, says, "Lyla, you came. Thank you." She stands up, carefully unwrapping her hand from around Bill's, and comes up to hug me as I take another step toward the bed.

"Hi, Eleanor," I says, allowing her to lead me toward the bed. "How's he doing?"

"He's not very responsive, but the doctor says he's stable," she replies.

"I thought you were here by yourself," I says, not knowing what else to say and wishing she was.

"Oh, this is my great-nephew, John—my niece Ellen's son—and his wife, Wendy."

"Hello," I says.

"It's nice to meet you," says the girl.

"Hello," says the guy. "We met years ago, although you probably don't remember me. I was still a kid then."

I just nod. I don't remember him, and I think it strange he would remember me. If he was a kid back then, I must have made some impression on him, or else he's heard stories about me. I can just imagine how Bill's family talks about me.

"Do you want to sit down?" Eleanor asks me. There's a chair next to hers so I go ahead and take it since John and whatever the girl's name is were already standing anyways when I got there, and I am a lot older than them—I'd guess neither one is much over thirty.

"Aunt Eleanor," says the young woman, "John and I are going to go get something to drink. Can we bring you some coffee or something?"

Eleanor looks at them for a moment like she can't seem to grasp what the girl just said. She turns back to Bill before it registers and then she says, "I'm sorry. It's been such a long day and I'm tired. Coffee might perk me up some."

"Okay. Do you want cream or sugar?"

"Oh no, I drink it black. And make sure it's decaf," she says.

I don't know how decaf is going to perk her up. John must agree with me since he makes a face at the word "decaf."

"Can I get you anything?" the girl asks, looking at me. I think she's forgotten my name too.

"Coffee's good," I says, "only I do want cream and sugar."

"That's my kind of answer," says John, smiling.

"We'll be back in a few minutes," says John's wife, and then they leave the room.

"I'm so glad they came," says Eleanor. "Do you remember John?"

"No," I says. "He must have just been a little kid when I was going out with Bill. How is he?"

"Oh, he's very happy," says Eleanor. "I'm so glad he married Wendy. She's such a sweet girl, and it's so funny how they met—she's actually a distant cousin of some sort, though I can never remember exactly how— somewhere back on my father's side of the family I guess. Don't they make a sweet couple? They already have a little boy and are expecting another child in a few months."

"That's nice," I says, not having noticed the girl was pregnant, and not really caring since I'd meant, "How is Bill?" So I asks instead, "Has Bill woken up at all?"

"Just opened his eyes a few times," Eleanor says. "I don't think he's really aware of what's going on. Oh, he scared me so badly. He called at six o'clock this morning, and when you hear the phone ring at that hour, you just know something is wrong. I'm often up by then, though, and the girls are usually up by six-thirty or seven to get ready for work—even though it's Saturday, Lucy went to work this morning, so it didn't make any difference. I usually try to go use the bathroom before them, just so I don't have to hold it while they're in there. At my age, I have a hard time sleeping. Although Bill knows I'm usually up early, he's not a very early riser. He never calls me before eight o'clock so when the phone rang so early, I knew something was wrong."

"Why did he call? Did he know he was having a heart attack?"

"Oh, yes, his voice was all panicky, and he said he was sweating really bad. He wanted one of the girls to drive him to the hospital, so I yelled for Lucy, but then when he said he was having chest pains, I told him to go take an aspirin and sit down and that I would call the ambulance. Then once I got ahold of 911 and they said the ambulance was on the way, I had Lucy drive me to the emergency room. The ambulance hadn't even gotten to the hospital yet when we got there. That had me really worried, but I guess they wanted to make sure he was stable at home first. Oh, I've never been so scared in my life. Not even when my brother Henry had his accident or anyone else in the family died. I think it just shocked me so much because, poor Bill, he really has no one else but me. His boys are all far away, downstate and in Wisconsin, and—well, there's the Dalrymples across the street—do you remember them? My cousin Joseph's wife and her granddaughter and great-granddaughter, but they're not the same as close family like a child or a sister, so I know I'm the one he depends on—he's still my baby brother, no matter how old we are."

I'm losing track of who she's talking about and starting to wonder what good it's doing me to be here. I don't remember Eleanor running her mouth like this before, but of course, she's a lot older now—so are we all—and she is worried. And so am I, but I still don't see what good it's doing me to be here. It's not like Bill knows I'm here or anything. I should have waited until he was better—a day or two at least.

And then just as I'm thinking I shouldn't have come and Eleanor starts fretting over whether Bill's house is clean enough for Alan to stay there, Bill's eyes open. At first, I barely notice it until I find he's staring at me, and then before I know it, I'm looking him straight in the eye, and thinking how strange it is that Eleanor's more caught up in talking than in paying attention to her brother. But I stop thinking when Bill's eyes start getting wider and wider like he's surprised to see me, and I know my fate has come as a low rumbling, grumbling sound rises up from his throat.

Like everything's in slow motion, Eleanor turns at the sound of Bill trying to speak. She adjusts herself in her seat when she sees his eyes are open, and then she squeezes his hand and says, "Bill? Bill, can you hear me? Oh, please, Bill, say something."

He looks at her for a moment, and then his eyes come back to meet mine. He raises his eyebrows and lifts his head to get a better look at me. When I give him a smile, his eyes get even bigger. "Hello, Bill," I says, trying to sound friendly because I don't know what else to do.

Suddenly, his head snaps back toward Eleanor, and then, in words that sound like a wounded animal shrieking, he shouts, "Jesus Christ, Eleanor! What the hell is she doing here?"

He's so loud that I jump back in my seat. And Eleanor gets all tongue-tied and starts stumbling over her words. "Bill, it's Lyla. She came to see how you are. She was worried about you."

Before I can say anything, the nurse comes into the room. I think she must have heard Bill shout.

I want to crawl into a corner. I just can't believe that the first thing he says to me after all these years is so cruel.

Eleanor says something to the nurse and Bill grunts a little and mumbles something. Then as the nurse checks Bill's vitals, Eleanor says to me, "Oh, Lyla, don't take it personally. He's doped up on all kinds of drugs and not thinking straight. People aren't in their right minds when they wake up like this in the hospital; isn't that right?"

She turns to the nurse, looking for reassurance, but the nurse only says, "He seems okay. I'll go get the doctor to check on him. He doesn't seem to be in any pain."

Bill's hand reaches up like he's going to pull the oxygen tubes out of his nose, but Eleanor stops him by grabbing his hand. "Bill, honey, you have to leave those in. You're in the hospital. You had a heart attack, remember? Just try to relax."

"How can I relax when I'm in the hospital?" he growls.

"I know you're not comfortable, but they're going to take good care of you," Eleanor replies. "The doctor says you're lucky that the ambulance brought you when it did. And the nurses have been so nice. And everyone is praying for you. John and Wendy are here—they went to get coffee, but they'll be back in a minute, and Lyla's here to see you, and Alan is on his way."

"What did you go call him for?" Bill barks.

"Well, he's your son. He cares about you."

"What about Jason and William?"

"Well, they told me to stay in touch with them to see if they need to come."

"I'm in the fucking hospital," Bill says. "What do you mean, 'if they need to come'?"

"Don't upset yourself, Bill," Eleanor says. "They love you. Now just try to rest."

"I wish you hadn't called Alan. He's almost the last person I want to see right now," he says, staring back at me.

I'm not stupid. I know he's not happy to see me. I figure I had better leave than keep upsetting him with my presence, but still, I stay in my chair—probably because I'm also feeling a little angry at him—even if he is sick. I can understand if he doesn't want to see me, but he doesn't need to be so blunt. You would think he'd soften a little toward me considering I cared enough to come see him.

"Here you are, Aunt Eleanor," says the young lady, reentering the room. "Oh, Uncle Bill, you're awake!"

"How are you feeling, Uncle Bill?" John asks, stepping into the room behind his wife.

Bill just stares at them.

"He's tired," Eleanor tells them, taking the coffee from the girl. "Thank you, dear."

"Thanks," I says as John hands me a cup.

"Are you feeling any pain, Bill?" Eleanor asks.

He shakes his head. Then he closes his eyes.

"Are you just tired?" asks Eleanor.

He tilts his head an inch and then breathes deeply.

"We should let him rest," says Eleanor.

The nurse returns now and says, "The doctor will be here in a couple of minutes. The hospital's visitor policy is only two patients to a room, and he really does need to rest."

"I can go sit in the waiting room," John offers.

"No, I should go anyways," I says, quickly getting up.

There's no point in my being here. I'm not wanted and I don't know why I even came. It was just plain stupid of me. I should have listened to Bel, not that I'll tell her she was right 'cause then I'll never hear the end of it.

"Oh, Lyla," Eleanor says. "I'm sorry you came all this way, but I guess he should be left to rest now."

"Thanks for coming, Lyla," says the girl to me, having picked up my name from Eleanor using it. "It was nice to meet you."

"You too," I says. I still can't remember her name, though I know Eleanor told me more than once. It's something weird. I think it's Windy, like that old '60s song, but I'm not sure so I better not venture to say it.

"I'll call you later, Lyla," says Eleanor, "to let you know how he is." She sets her coffee on the bedside table and stands up. Before I know it, she's hugging me again. "Don't pay any attention to what Bill said. He's not himself right now, you know. You come back in a day or two and he'll be happy to see you."

"Thanks. I'll see you all later," I says, hoping I never see any of them again.

Still clutching my coffee cup, I walk out of the room, nearly bumping into the doctor as I step into the hallway.

"Excuse me," I says. The doctor thinks he's too important to apologize, or else he's really just concerned about going to see Bill. Funny—I'll bet the old coot outlives me. He's stubborn enough.

I walk to the elevator, wishing I'd never come. I look at my watch and see it's only been half an hour since Bel dropped me off. I could call her to come pick me up early, but then she'll just say, "I told you so." I'll sit in the lobby or check out the gift shop—and think up what to tell her in the meantime—maybe just that Bill was asleep all the time I was there.

What a wasted afternoon this has turned out to be. And what an ignorant man Bill is. I don't care what Eleanor said about him not being in his right mind. He never was one to mince words. I knew he wouldn't want to see me, so why the hell did I come in the first place? If he had wanted to see me, he would have contacted me sometime in the last nineteen years. Who did I think I was kidding?

And why the hell do I have to be so damn stupid as to let it matter so much to me after all these years? Here I am, seventy-seven years old. You'd think I'd have learned something about men by now. When am I ever going to get smart?

Chapter 2

I go sit in the hospital lobby and wait for Bel. I know it'll be a long time before she shows up, so I sit in a comfy chair by the escalators and pick up the copy of *The Mining Journal* that I didn't get to read at home. I figure then I'll have time to do other things later. It's Memorial Day weekend so I was thinking about making potato salad this afternoon, even if I don't have a picnic to go to. It'll probably be too cold for picnics anyways, but I always get a hankering for potato salad around this time of the year.

I start reading the story in the paper about Finn Fest coming back to Marquette—it's going to be an international Finn Fest this year, combining the U.S. and Canadian events I guess. Finnish people from all over the world come to these events. The last one in Marquette was nine years ago in 1996. I remember thinking I should have gone last time, but I didn't. About all I saw of it were the blue and white chairs that were painted and arranged all around town. Well, I probably won't go this time either, though this'll probably be the last time I get a chance. It's not likely it'll come back to Marquette again in my lifetime.

But it's not really Finn Fest I'm interested in. It's trying to find some way to distract myself so I can pretend it doesn't hurt as much as it does—I mean, the way Bill yelled at me. What an asshole he was—medication and heart attack or not. I come all this way to see him, not knowing why I should or what I think I'll get from it, and then he acts like that.

Finally, I see Bel's car pull up and go outside.

"So?" she says, wanting to know how it went, but I don't say much. Just that Bill was sleeping so I talked to Eleanor a little. I don't mention John and his wife since I don't figure it matters that they were there, and the less said about my experience the better. I'm expecting Bel'll rake me over the coals with questions and just give me grief about going to see Bill at all, so to change the subject before she gets started, I says, "I saw that article about Finn Fest. Eleanor had the paper with her so I read it there."

"You should go," Bel says.

"Maybe," I says, "but what do I know about being a Finlander?"

"Well, at least you know what your roots are, Lyla; that's more than I know. I don't even know for sure that my last name was Archambeau—for all I know, the nuns may have made that up since I went to the orphanage when I was a baby. I wish I did know for sure. Anyway, I bet your dad would like it if you went to Finn Fest."

"My dad's been dead over thirty years—I doubt he'd care."

"You don't know that," she says.

"Well, I'll think about it," I says, though I don't plan to.

"About that women's group, Lyla," she says. "I double-checked and they meet every Wednesday."

"Oh, jeez," I think, not that I have anything else to do on Wednesdays, but I'll be damned if I'm going to spend every Wednesday sitting around and listening to a bunch of women talk about their problems. I don't know why Bel's even asking me because she's gone to plenty of other meetings by herself. I wonder what put the idea into her head that I should go to this one.

"I can't go this Wednesday," Bel says before I can think what to say, "because I'm going to the doctor that day, but we can go next week."

"What are you going to the doctor for?" I asks, hoping that if I change the subject, I can avoid going to the stupid meeting altogether. "You were just at the doctor's last week. What do you need to go for again?"

"It's just a—a checkup," she says.

"Well, what did you go for last week then?"

"That was the foot doctor, remember?"

"No it wasn't," I says. "It was your regular doctor. Since when have you had to go to a foot doctor?"

"Well, my ankle was bothering me last week."

I just roll my eyes. My feet hurt all the time—that's what happens when you work as a housekeeper for other people for fifty-plus years, always standing on your feet, but you don't see me going to no foot doctor.

"Oh," is all I says, not really in the mood to argue with her, though I don't know why she's lying to me about going to the foot doctor, or why she thinks she can get away with it. I've never known her to go to a foot doctor in her life, and that's saying something since I've known her since 1938.

"So anyway, we can go to that meeting the Wednesday after next," she says.

"Well," I says, "I'll have to let you know in case I have anything else planned."

"What do you mean you'll have to let me know?" she asks. "What else would you have planned?"

"That's why I have to let you know. I don't know if I have anything else planned. I'll double-check my calendar."

"Lyla," she moans, and I see her roll her eyes like she knows I'm just trying to get out of going. I guess I can't lie to her either. She knows I don't write things down on the calendar—I don't have so much going on that I'm going to forget something; even at my age, my memory is pretty good.

By now we're back at Snowberry. I'm glad to be home because I'm irritated that I went to see Bill at all, and Bel is starting to push my buttons and make me cranky.

"All right, I'll see you later," I says after we've gone up the elevator and it stops at her floor.

"All right. Bye," Bel says, stepping out of the elevator.

Once I'm back in my apartment, I keep beating myself up for going to the hospital. Even making potato salad doesn't take my mind off it. When Eleanor doesn't call me that evening, I tell myself that she realized it was a bad idea to call me at all. But another part of me figures she's just busy or tired, and maybe fussing over her nephew Alan coming up to visit.

The next day—Sunday—I go to Mass at St. Peter's, and then I come home and putz around the house, not doing much at all, because I keep thinking back to when I was dating Bill. It was so long ago now, but we did date for three years, about 1983 to 1986—seemed like a long time then. He just happened to stop me on the street one day when I was walking home from work. I could see he'd already had a couple of drinks, but he was so good-looking—I'd thought so for years whenever I saw him around town—that I didn't let a little alcohol on his breath stop me from saying yes when he asked me out, and we were a couple from then on. I kept thinking he'd eventually want to marry me, but I should have known better. He didn't even want me spending the night at his house, and he wouldn't stay over at my place. He said it was because of his son, Alan, and it might have partly been that, but Alan only lived there the first year we were together before he got his own place, and I don't imagine Alan being there stopped Bill from having women over before that. He never said so at least, and I thought it was better not to ask him, but his family hinted plenty to me that both his wives divorced him for running around on them. He moved into his mother's house right after she died and he got divorced for the second time, and I guess he then had a string of women before he met me, which was just about the time Alan decided to go live with him.

Alan was the reason Bill and I broke up—and maybe the reason why our relationship never got to where I wanted it to go. Bill's two older sons, William and Jason, were already out of the house, but Alan was still in high school. He had lived with his mother after the divorce, but then his mother remarried, and she and her husband were moving out of the area. Alan didn't want to leave in the middle of his senior year so he moved in with Bill while he finished school.

That boy didn't like me from the start. As soon as we met, he was obnoxious and rude to me. The first time I went over to his father's house, Alan said to me, "So you're my dad's latest bimbo."

"Hey," Bill told him, "don't talk like that." I wasn't too happy that Bill didn't say more to him—didn't stick up for me more. Granted, Alan didn't say much to me after that, but he made it clear by his tone and the way he'd roll his eyes at me that he couldn't stand having me around.

Once Alan started going to Northern Michigan University, he moved into an apartment with some of his friends. I hardly saw him after that, but when he did come over to his father's house—which was hardly ever since they never got along—he would still pretty much ignore me.

Bill didn't pay any attention to the situation, but then when Alan's brother William got married, it all came to a head. By that point, Bill and I had been dating for three years—the longest I'd ever been with any man—and there had only been Scofield before him anyways, and that was twenty years before. I was still hoping that Bill would ask me to marry him. That spring I had even helped him to repaint the living room, and he had asked me to help him pick out new curtains for the kitchen, so I figured he wanted to make the house nice for me before we got married—I thought we'd live in his house rather than my little apartment.

So we went to William's wedding and the reception at the Northwoods Supper Club. About a hundred guests were at the reception, and I was feeling pretty awkward about going since I knew Bill's ex-wife Annette was going to be there. I'd never met her, but I'd heard she was an attractive woman, and I knew she was several years younger than me. And it didn't help that I'm just not the fancy kind of person who would go to the Northwoods—that's where the lawyers and doctors and other people I cleaned houses for would go to eat. I would have felt real awkward bumping into any of them, not that Bill's family had lawyers and doctors in it, but there were other dining rooms besides the one where the reception was held, so I had no idea who I might see.

But I managed all right at first. I had been tempted to invite Bel to go with me, but I was really Bill's guest, and the two of them never got along anyways, so I felt like Bill was my only ally there. I was so sure Annette would look down her nose at me, but she didn't even seem to notice me—I'd say she ignored me on purpose except that Bill never bothered to introduce me to most people, and he pretty much ignored me himself all during the reception, so at first, I doubt she even knew who I was, though she might have guessed if she saw me sitting next to him in the pew at the First Baptist Church during the wedding—not that we were there long—the service didn't last more than twenty minutes—it sure wasn't like a Catholic wedding where at least you get your money's worth. The ceremony was over before I knew it, and then Bill and I went back to his place and he took a nap in front of the TV until I woke him up to go to the reception.

As soon as we got to the Northwoods, Bill went off to talk to his friends—didn't say a word to me the rest of the evening. I didn't see him say much to his sons either, though, so I shouldn't have felt neglected. Of course, it was Eleanor who made me feel welcome. She insisted I sit with her and her daughters during the meal—Bill went and sat with his brother and sister-in-law, Henry and Beth—who was Miss Bergmann's cousin. When I saw Bill go through the food line and then go sit with them, I went the other way, so I guess maybe it wasn't his fault, but he should have known I didn't want to sit with Beth. We always kind of avoided each other—I don't know that she was stuck up, maybe just shy, but after three years of basically avoiding each other while I was dating Bill, I didn't see any point in changing it, and if I did sit with her, I knew she'd ask me about Jessie, and talking about my sister, who I hadn't spoken to in over twenty years, was the last thing I wanted, so I was relieved when Eleanor called me over to sit with her and Lucy and Maud.

Alan was one of the groomsmen so he sat up at the bridal table. Everything seemed like it was going okay through the meal, and despite how nervous I was, I didn't even slop on my dress. The speeches were made and then the dancing got started. Lucy and Maud, who were in their forties and had never married, were telling me about when they used to babysit for Bill's boys and what a handful they had been.

At some point, Alan must have been standing behind me, but neither Eleanor nor I saw him. Eleanor was saying something about how Bill's sons had actually been pretty well-behaved until their parents got a divorce, and then how Annette had spoiled the kids to make up for the divorce.

And then I opened my big mouth.

"I'm surprised by that because she looks like she's too full of herself to bother with her kids," I said. "From the way she's dressed, she looks like she's quite the hoity-toity show off type."

Before Eleanor could reply, Alan appeared at my side and said, "Don't you talk about my mother like that!"

He said it so loud that even people on the dance floor turned to look. He must have started drinking early that day because I'm sure his voice sounded slurred when he said it, but that didn't matter—that the whole room heard him say it is what mattered.

"Shh, Alan, you're making a scene," Eleanor said, but he didn't care.

"I'll make a scene if Lyla's going to run her mouth off," he snapped.

"Alan, sit down and behave yourself," said Lucy. She tried to grab his arm and pull him into a chair, but he jerked away.

"You have no right to be talking about my mother like that," he said to me, "and especially at her son's wedding. You're not even part of this family."

"I didn't mean your mother any disrespect," I said.

But now Annette had walked over. "What did she say?" she asked Alan.

"She said you're an overdressed snob and a terrible, selfish mother, so it's no wonder Dad divorced you," Alan replied, exaggerating in a real nasty voice.

"Oh, did she?" said Annette. "Well, at least my clothes fit me. I'm not wearing some tight blouse to show off cleavage so fat and old no one wants to see it."

That wasn't at all fair. My cleavage was barely showing, so, although I wanted to crawl under the table, I said, "You're just jealous that you don't have any to show off." I knew it was a mistake as soon as I said it because now everyone was staring at us.

"You better leave," Annette said. "This is my son's wedding, and you're not going to ruin his day."

"Bill invited me," I said, "so I have every right to be here."

"Get out!" she shouted.

"Shut up, you bitch!" I yelled back, finally losing my temper. I'd thought that word many times about different women, but I think that was the first time I ever used it to anyone's face. I was shocked myself by how loud I said it. I remember the whole room going quiet for a minute. And then I wondered if she was going to pull my hair or throw food at me or something like Joan Collins would have done to Linda Evans.

But what happened next was worse. Bill came over and said, "Lyla, you can't talk to her like that."

He was actually taking the bitch's side! I was speechless.

"Come on, Lyla; we're leaving," he said, and then he grabbed my arm, practically yanking me out of my chair.

It was all I could do to grab my purse as he dragged me toward the door.

"Why are you defending her?" I yelled, trying not to trip in the high heels I'd bought just for the wedding while everyone watched us head for the door.

He didn't answer until we were in the parking lot, and then he said, "She's the mother of my children, and this is our son's wedding, so she doesn't deserve to be badmouthed today."

"But I didn't do anything!" I said.

"I know you're not the smartest broad, Lyla," he said, "but to badmouth Annette at her son's wedding...that's really stupid."

"Bill, I didn't say what Alan said I did. I—" But I shut up, not wanting to get Eleanor in trouble too, though she and Lucy and Maud had started it.

"Actually," he said, "I'm the stupid one. Stupid enough to think I could bring a broad like you out in public to a decent occasion like my son's wedding. You ain't fit to associate with decent people like them."

"Just a minute now," I said. "What do you mean, go out in public with you? We go out to eat together all the time, and bowling too. What's wrong with you, acting this way? I didn't say anything worth getting so fussed up about."

He stopped beside the car, turned to look me in the eyes, and said, "The question is, 'What's wrong with you, Lyla?' You don't have any common sense, or common decency for that matter. I can't believe I ever went out with you."

"Oh, Bill, come on. After all this time, now you're saying such things. I can't believe—"

"It's over, Lyla," he said. "You've pissed me off one too many times. Get in the car. It's over."

I couldn't believe he would act this way. I knew he was ornery and all, but he'd never been downright mean and unreasonable like this before.

"Where are we going?" I asked. I was actually starting to fear he was going to do me bodily harm. After all, the Northwoods was on a back road in the woods. He could easily hurt me, bury me somewhere back there and no one would find me for days.

"I'm taking you home so you can't embarrass me anymore," he said, getting in the car.

"But we can't leave. It's your son's wedding," I said, but I got in the car anyways since he said he'd take me home rather than do me in. And I knew there wasn't any way I was going to go back into that room now, even if he did calm down.

"I'll come back after I drop you off," he said, starting up the engine.

I don't remember what I said after that. I probably didn't say anything. I just remember the tears running down my cheeks. He didn't even offer me a Kleenex when I started to cry. It was getting dark by then, and I was grateful for it because I could just imagine what a mess I looked like.

"I can't believe you're treating me this way, Bill," I said, "after all the time we've spent together."

"Quit whining," he said. "I can't believe you didn't know it was coming. You've been getting on my last nerve for a long time now."

I didn't know how he could say that. It made me start crying worse, but he just drove me back to my apartment, all the way muttering under his breath about how stupid he had been ever to ask me out. By then, I was trying not to cry so I could stay calm enough to talk to him before he threw me out of the car.

When we got to the house where I rented a floor, he practically flew into the driveway before he slammed on the brakes, just to show how mad he was. Then he turned to me and said, "Get out!"

"Bill, please?" I begged, putting my hand on the door handle but not opening the door.

"Just shut up," he said. "There's nothing to say. Christ, even the sex wasn't worth listening to your constant griping and your stupidity."

"I'm not stupid, and I've gone out of my way to be good to you," I said, hardly able to hold back my tears.

"You are stupid. You don't know shit about most things. Didn't they teach you anything in that damn orphanage? No wonder your mother died and your father abandoned you, and your sister won't have anything to do with you. You're just a leech is all you are, and you've never learned when to keep your fat mouth shut. I'm so sick of listening to it yapping all the time. I don't know how anyone could ever put up with you."

I didn't know what to say to that. I remember I turned my head to the window, not even able to look at him. I felt like he had hit me below the belt, and how that wasn't even fair since I wasn't a guy. Finally, when he just glared at me and didn't say anything else, I opened the door. But before I got out, I said, "Bill, I'll call you tomorrow when you're calmed down, and then we can talk it out."

"There's nothing to talk about. I don't want you calling me or coming over to my place again."

"But Bill—you're overreacting. I—"

"It's no good, Lyla," he snapped. "You've been pissing me off for a long time, and tonight was just the final straw. I've had it. It's time to move on."

"Bill," I said, groping for any way to convince him not to do this to me, "I can understand if you still have some feelings for Annette. I don't hold it against you; it's just that sometimes I get jealous."

"Hah! you should be jealous," he laughed. "You ain't half the woman she is no matter how big your tits are. Just get the hell out."

"But, Bill—"

"I said, 'Get the hell out!'" He lunged at me, and it frightened me so much I nearly fell onto the ground as I tried to get out of the car.

I wasn't going to let him hit me. That's where I draw the line with men. I'd never let a man abuse me, and I wasn't going to start now, not for Bill or any man. I'd always known he had a temper, but I had never really been afraid of him before. Now I could see that for whatever reason, his anger toward me had been building up for a long time.

"Okay. I'm going," I hollered, and I slammed the car door shut. His car tore down the street before I could even find the key to my apartment.

That was the last time I spoke to Bill until I saw him lying there hooked up to all those tubes in the hospital. I had waited a good week for him to call and make things up to me, but he never did. Of course, Eleanor called me about a week later when she must have figured enough time had passed that it was clear we weren't going to make up right away. When she told me how sorry she was, I just started bawling on the phone. I told her I couldn't understand him, and she said no one had ever understood her brother, least of all the women he'd been involved with. I felt like an idiot saying so, but I couldn't help telling her how much I loved Bill. "He's probably the only man I've ever loved. If I knew it was going to end like this, I would have left him a long time ago. I just thought he was the one. I thought we'd get married, even though it's been three years and he's never asked me. Eleanor, it's just—I don't know; I just thought finally that he was the one."

I don't remember much of what Eleanor said to me, except, "I just never have understood Bill. He's so different from the rest of my family." I know she felt bad about it all, like she bore some of the responsibility, because Eleanor is the kind to feel guilt and take on others' problems, but it wasn't really her fault.

Looking back, it disgusts me how pathetic I acted, begging him not to break up with me, and crying on the phone to Eleanor. What had I been thinking to go up to that hospital and just make a bigger idiot out of myself? Perhaps Bill was right—I was stupid.

Whether he gets better or not, I'm not going to visit him again. I just need to quit thinking about him. Eleanor should have known better than to ask me. Even if he died, I don't think I would go to the funeral. I have more respect for myself than that. I don't want anything to do with him, or any of that Whitman family. Life's too short to be doing things I don't really want to do, or to keep dwelling on something from the past that I can't change.

I'm just glad it's all over now. No more, Lyla. You're not going to think about it no more.

Chapter 3

The only part of Sunday that's very cheery for me is suppertime when Bel comes over and we have our picnic in my apartment. She brings a Jell-O salad she made and I boil hot dogs and we eat those and the potato salad, and then we watch old movies. Bel's an old movie fiend. I admit they don't make movies like they used to, but I'm not crazy about them like Bel is. Neither of us will go to the movie theater anymore. All they make is trash these days. We decided after we saw the cast from *Dirty Dancing* on *Oprah* that we weren't going to support Hollywood any more. That movie—well, I only saw the scenes they showed on *Oprah*—but my goodness, it was like having sex with your clothes on. I'm not paying to watch that crap.

Not long before that, I had bought Bel a VCR, and a few years later, I got one for myself, so since then, we've just rented movies, and cable TV got going in Marquette too somewhere around then, so we started watching AMC—that Nick Clooney host is quite the looker. I'd take him over his son any day—that boy is just too oily looking to me. Anyways, Bel knows everything about every old movie star there is, and she can even remember going to see all those old films for the first time in the theatre, but somehow, the stories just don't stick in my head like they do in hers.

So after supper, we watch *Summertime* with Katherine Hepburn and Rossano Brazzi. I have a hard time getting into it. I mean, I know he's a handsome Italian and all, but I heard later how he got into trouble for drug dealing—I just can't separate the movie stars from their personal lives like that. I figure it's a good thing in the movie that Kate doesn't stay with him—she probably sensed he'd be trouble in the end. I have to admire that about

Kate—she could always hang on to her independence.

And then at eight o'clock, the movie ends and Bel says she has to go home and wash her hair, and I think, that's the most fun I'll have all Memorial Day weekend, but Bel's only just stepped out of the door when my phone rings.

No one ever calls me except for Bel, and I know she couldn't have gotten back to her apartment that fast, so right away, I'm afraid it's going to be Eleanor calling me about Bill. I'm almost tempted not to answer it, but of course, I do.

I'm surprised when it's a man's voice on the line.

"Is Lyla there, please?" he asks.

"Ye-es," I says, wondering what he's trying to sell. "This is her."

"Hi, Lyla. This is John Vandelaare, Bill Whitman's great-nephew—I saw you at the hospital yesterday."

"Oh yeah," I says. "Is Bill okay?"

"Yes, he's stable now I guess. The doctor told Aunt Eleanor he's lucky he got to the hospital when he did, but he seems to be past the worst now. Still, they're going to keep him in the hospital for a few days to watch him. Alan got here just after you left so that's a relief for Aunt Eleanor."

"That's good," I says. "I'm glad he's doing well and that Alan is here—it's too much for Eleanor to have to worry about taking care of him at her age."

I feel like I'm forcing out the words—I mean, I'm glad Bill is doing well, but I can't help thinking it's weird that John would call me.

"Yes. The doctor says the worst is over," he says, "so she's not as frazzled as she was yesterday when you were there."

"That's good," I says, not knowing what else to say, and not wanting to talk any longer. I figure I might as well go wash my hair too. "Tell your aunt I'm glad he's doing well."

"I will," says John, "but the real reason I'm calling is that I don't know whether you realize I'm the person in charge of the Robert O'Neill Historical Home, but Aunt Eleanor told me you used to be the O'Neills' housekeeper."

"Oh," I says, a bit surprised. "Yes, I was. That was my last job before I retired. I worked for the O'Neills for fifteen years."

"You know his house is now open for tours, right?"

"Yes, I read that in *The Mining Journal*, oh, quite a while ago. I guess your name didn't ring a bell, though. You inherited the house, didn't you?" I asks. "I didn't know the Whitmans were any relation to the O'Neills."

"No, I didn't inherit the house," John says. "I've basically been given care of the house for my lifetime, so I get an income from the estate, but it's more like a paycheck in exchange for managing the estate's affairs—I keep the house open for tours, and I oversee decisions about the rights to Mr. O'Neill's novels. I just helped to get his autobiography published last year."

"Oh," I says. "That's good. I'm glad he's still remembered. I don't think I ever did read one of his books—I'm just not much of a reader, but he was a good, kind man. I wouldn't want him forgotten."

"No, neither would I, or a lot of people," John says. "That's why I'm calling. Wendy and I would love it if you would come over for dinner and share some of your memories with us. We'd be thrilled to have you tell us about what the house looked like when you worked here and how it changed over the years, or any little history you know about it or any of the things in it that belonged to the O'Neills. We want to put together all the information we can, including interviewing anyone who knew the O'Neills, so stories aren't lost."

"Oh," I says. "Well, I don't know what help I could be. I mean, it wasn't that long ago I worked there—I retired in '98—it can't have changed that much."

"No, but you worked here a long time didn't you?"

"Yes, since I don't know, the early '80s, so fifteen or maybe sixteen years at least."

"You must have known the O'Neills really well then?"

"Yes, I guess you could say that. I was just their housekeeper, but they were really good to me. Better than just about anyone else I ever worked for. I figured I was lucky that the best job I had was at the end of my working years when the work was getting harder on me."

"Will you come over for supper then tomorrow night?" John asks.

"Well…" I says, trying to think of some excuse. I really don't want to get more involved with the Whitmans, but having dinner with John and—Wendy, I think he said her name was, which is a lot better than Windy like I thought it was—isn't the same thing as going to visit Bill. Bel will try to tell me it is, but it's not. It's more like it's for the O'Neills, and they were always good to me. "Well," I says, half-wanting and half-not-wanting to go, "I don't go out much at night, and—"

"Aunt Eleanor told me you don't drive," John says, "but that's no problem; I'd be happy to come pick you up and drive you home. I see from your address in the phone book that you must live over at Snowberry Heights, so it's no problem—that's not far away. It'll just take me a few minutes to run over and pick you up."

"Oh," I says, thinking how I didn't plan anything for supper tomorrow night—I had my hot dogs and potato salad picnic tonight with Bel. And they do seem nice, this John and his wife. "Well, okay," I says, and after a second, I add, "I would like that" just in case I don't sound very enthusiastic.

"Great. How about I come pick you up around 5:30 then?"

I tell him that would be fine and that I'll be downstairs in the lobby watching for him. Then I asks, "Do you want me to bring anything?" I hate asking that because I don't have hardly any food in the house, and it'll mean having to ask Bel to take me out to get something tomorrow, but I asks anyways because it's the proper thing to do.

"Oh no," he says. "We'll take care of everything. Just bring yourself and your stories of the O'Neills. That will be more than enough."

When I hang up the phone, I says to myself, "Damn it! What the hell am I doing going over there for supper? I'm not one of them—I don't belong with those people. I'm not in the same class as them. What do they want to be involved with someone like me for? I mean, I've been in that house thousands of time when I worked for the O'Neills, but nice as they were, I worked for them. I don't want to be getting involved with the Whitmans or whatever John's last name is." But then I reason with myself. "Calm down, Lyla; they just want to know about the house. It's not the end of the world. I'll go over there and tell them what I remember about the O'Neills and that'll be the end of it, I'm sure. It's not like a young couple like them would want to be friends with an old lady like me, otherwise."

I tell myself to shut up and quit babbling and to go wash my hair before I get too tired to do it. Here I've stayed busy all day trying to keep my mind off Bill, but no matter what I do, the universe seems like it wants to thwart me now. I try to divert myself by thinking about what kind of food I could bring over tomorrow night 'cause I don't feel right about going over there empty-handed, but if I asks Bel to take me to the store tomorrow, then I'll have to tell her why I need to go, and I can just hear what she's going to say about my getting involved with Bill's relatives.

"Quit worrying about Bel," I tell myself, like her opinion has ever really mattered to me. As I wash my hair, I try to focus on thinking about the O'Neills and any little stories I can tell John about them. It would be good to see the inside of the old house—it's been maybe seven or eight years now since I retired from working there—the last job I had, and the only one that was full-time where they were the only people I worked for at one time. They were some of the best people I worked for too. I felt bad when Mr. O'Neill died not too long after I quit working for him. I'd have stuck it out longer for his sake if I had known his time on earth was so short. Then again, he was ninety-four or something when I retired—but he was still getting around good then. I was afraid he'd live to be a hundred, and I knew I didn't have it in me to keep working that long. And then he died rather sudden I seem to remember. Well, it won't kill me to go over there. It's just a few hours at the most. It'll be over before I know it.

I manage to calm myself down and watch the 11 o'clock news before going to bed, but once I do crawl under the covers, the dread starts to creep up on me and I sleep real restless like, having weird dreams I don't remember until I wake up in the morning feeling like the sky is going to fall on me if I get out of bed. I just dread the thought of going over to the O'Neill House that evening and trying to find things to tell those young people, and I dread the thought of spending all day dreading the evening. But finally, I drag myself out of bed and tell myself there's no point in wasting the day dreading something since it's not even eight o'clock in the morning yet, and I've got nearly ten hours before I have to go over there for supper.

I get up and go to the bathroom, but the second I sit down in there, the phone rings. It never fails to ring at the worst times. I wish I was like those rich people who can afford to have phones installed in their bathrooms. I should just make it a habit always to bring my cordless phone with me into the bathroom.

I stop tinkling and stand up, pull up my underwear enough that no one will see anything through the window in the next room—even though I'm on the eighth floor—grab the cordless phone, and make my way back to the toilet to sit down. As I answer, I try not to make too much noise so the person on the other end won't hear me doing my business.

Of course, it's Bel.

"What took you so long to answer the phone? I figured you'd be up by now," she says.

I'm still feeling kind of down after last night, and I ain't had my coffee yet, so the last thing I need is her getting on my case first thing in the morning about something so silly as how long it took me to get the phone. I know she says I'm her best friend and all, so I should appreciate her, but there are days when I can't help thinking that I'd have picked someone else for a best friend if I'd had a say in it. But I guess the Lord decided to bless me with her—even if she does act like she has a bit of a screw loose now and then.

"I just got up," I says.

"I thought we were going out to breakfast and then to the cemetery this morning?"

I don't say nothing. Why does she feel the need to call me before eight o'clock? She knows I don't like going out before nine o'clock for breakfast—not before I've had my coffee and used the bathroom.

But I try to stay calm and just says, "Yeah, we are."

"Okay. Just checking," she says. "I've been feeling kind of forgetful lately. Too many things going on I guess."

Since I haven't had my coffee yet, I'm in no mood to ask her what she means by "too many things going on." What the hell? She doesn't have anything to do except harass me most days.

"Okay. I'll see you down in the lobby at nine," I says and hang up the phone.

Well, I am glad she remembered about the cemetery because I completely forgot about it. But God forbid she would ever forget about Charlie—he's been dead for something like thirty years—right after Papa died—I think that's when he died, or was it before Papa? Anyways, she acts like they're still married, despite all the drunken binges and other grief he put her through, plus the dozen years or so they were separated before he came back home to die.

I finish using the bathroom and then go make myself a cup of coffee to tide me over until I get to the restaurant. I'm grateful she didn't call me earlier really. She has a terrible time driving in the dark, but now that it's summertime, being Memorial Day and all, it's daylight at like six in the morning, and she's ready to go sooner than later. And she's willing to haul me around, so I shouldn't complain, considering I never did own a car or learn to drive.

Anyways, I'm glad we have plans today because it'll take my mind off Bill and going to supper at the O'Neill House tonight.

Only, when I get in the car, the first thing Bel asks is, "What are you doing tonight?"

I wasn't going to tell her, but she'll get it out of me now.

"I have plans," I says.

"Plans? Doing what?"

"Going out to dinner."

"Who with?" she asks, all surprised, like I don't have anyone but her to go out to dinner with.

"John, Bill's great-nephew. Him and his wife invited me over. They're living in the O'Neill House. It's a historic home now, you know, and open for tours, so they want me to come over and tell them about the O'Neills and my memories of the place."

"Oh," she says. Then she's quiet for a minute, making me think she's bored with my answer until she says, "Lyla, you're not using this O'Neill House thing as some kind of excuse to get to see Bill some more are you?"

"Bel!" I says. "God, no, why would I do something crazy like that? I don't even want to go. They invited me. I'm only going out of respect for Mr. and Mrs. O'Neill."

"So you aren't going to see Bill again?"

"Not if I can help it," I says.

"Well, you sure were fast to go see him the other day."

I bite my tongue, remembering that I didn't tell her what Bill had said when he saw me. "No," I says. "I just don't see the point in seeing him again. I mean, I'm sorry he's been sick, but that part of my life is over now."

"That's good. I don't need to see you crying over him anymore."

"I didn't do no crying over him," I says.

"Well, you sure were grouchy for a long time after you broke up with him."

"And I'm going to get a whole lot grouchier if you keep talking about it," I says. "It was nineteen years ago. It's all water under the bridge now. Slow down and pay attention to the road. I want to get to the restaurant in one piece."

Not that she's going fast. I just say that to change the subject. If anything, she drives too slow, even stops at green lights, fearing they're going to turn red—someday someone's going to rear-end her for it.

"I just don't want to see you hurt by getting involved with someone who's no good for you," she says, stepping on the gas enough to go twenty. I don't know why I didn't learn to drive. I'd do a better job of it than her.

"Why are you worrying about me?" I says. "You're the one who was fool enough to get married. I never made that mistake."

"You don't have to be so cranky with me, Lyla."

"Well, I only had one cup of coffee so far this morning," I says.

"Well, still," she says.

"I don't like digging in the dirt either," I says to change the subject. "You know I'm no gardener."

She looks at me and rolls her eyes. "Fine," she says. "I'll plant the flowers."

"No, I'll help," I says as she pulls into the parking lot for The Pancake House. "I just need more coffee first."

The Pancake House is our favorite restaurant and everyone there knows our names. It's about the only place in Marquette to get breakfast other than Tommy's since the Big Boy burnt down. I guess they're going to rebuild the Big Boy, but they're sure taking their sweet time about it.

After we place our order—pancakes for her, she always gets pancakes, while I usually get eggs and sausage—she says, "So, what are you doing tomorrow?"

"I don't know," I says. "Why?"

I hate the "So, what are you doing tomorrow?" question. It's so unfair. I know it means that she wants something and isn't just asking because she's interested in what I'll be doing. When she pulls that, I don't know whether to tell her what I'm doing, or to admit I'm not doing nothing, or to come up with some fake things I'm doing just so I don't have to do whatever it is she's holding back on telling me she wants me to do. Only, I can't tell her I'm doing such important things that I can't cancel them without being caught in a lie if I do want to do what she wants me to do. I should probably just tell her to quit asking me that unfair question, but if I tried to explain to her what's wrong with it, she wouldn't get it anyways. Like I said, she's got a bit of a screw loose sometimes.

"I was hoping," she says, "that maybe you'd go to my doctor's appointment with me."

"Yeah, I can do that," I says. See, why couldn't she have saved the "What are you doing tomorrow question?" and just asked me if I'd go with her to her doctor's appointment? I mean, I've gone to doctor's appointments with her lots of times and never complained about it, so what's the big deal?

"It's at eight in the morning," she says. "I hope that's not too early. We can go out for breakfast after. It'll only be an hour at most."

"Eight a.m.?" I groan. There's another morning where I won't get my coffee. Not that I can't get up to have coffee a little early. It's just, I don't feel right if I don't have a bowel movement in the morning, and I can't seem to have one unless I have two cups of coffee first, and I know my body isn't going to be up to doing that before eight o'clock no matter how many cups of coffee I have.

She doesn't reply to my moan. I guess she's distracted thinking about her doctor's appointment. I don't ask her why she's going. I'll find out soon enough tomorrow when we get there. I focus on drinking my coffee. Then it hits me.

"Bel, you told me on Saturday that you had to go to the doctor on Wednesday."

"I do," she says.

"But tomorrow is Tuesday."

"No, it's not."

"Yeah it is. It's Memorial Day today."

"Yeah, today's Tuesday and tomorrow is Wednesday," she says.

"Bel, Memorial Day is always on a Monday."

"Oh, I forgot," she says, looking kind of pale like she's embarrassed. She's done a lot of stupid things in her life, so I don't know why she'd be so embarrassed over something as simple as messing up what day Memorial Day is.

"So is your appointment Wednesday or Tuesday?" I asks.

"It's Wednesday. I told you that before."

If I hadn't just had another cup of coffee, I'd be seeing red now. She's so looney she's starting to confuse me.

The rest of breakfast is mostly taken up with talking about where we'll go to buy flowers and what kinds to get and for whose graves.

When we leave The Pancake House, we go over to Wright Street and then down to Meister's Greenhouse to buy our flowers. After that, since Holy Cross Cemetery is the closest, we go there first. Everyone's buried there except my parents—Bel's Charlie and their daughter, and then the Mitchells, my sort of surrogate family. And sometimes we'll put a flower on Sister Euphrasia's grave. I'd never have given her a flower while she was alive, but it was Bel's idea a few years ago to do it when we stumbled on her grave, and I've softened some as I've gotten older. Couldn't stand the woman when she was alive, but I was just a kid then, so what did I know? I still don't think she was a nice woman, but she did her job as a nun I guess, and I have to admit that if I had to be in an orphanage, I should be thankful that she was there to keep an eye on all of us kids.

Bel parks near Charlie's grave and then we get the flowers out of the trunk and I help her carry them over to the tombstone. Charlie's dates are written on it, of course, and Bel's got her name there too.

Charles Greenway 1926—1976
Bel Greenway 1930—

It would give me the creeps to have my name on a stone like that, but I guess it was cheaper to have it done then than later. It kind of gives me the creeps to think she plans to spend all eternity with him too. If I were her, I'd have spent the money on a stone for their daughter, but they didn't have it when she died, and for whatever reason, Bel's never done anything about it since.

It hasn't been thirty years yet since Charlie died. I thought it was a year or two sooner because Papa died in '74 I remember. So many years have gone by now, though, that I tend to forget what happened before what, like whether Charlie died before or after Papa came home, but apparently, it was after. And he was only fifty—died a few days after his birthday. It's hard to believe he died that young, considering he was two years older than me, so I've always thought of him as being older, and now here I've outlived him by twenty-nine years.

Bel gets down on the ground and starts digging with a spade to plant the flowers. I can't bear to watch her do it; I just don't understand her devotion to that man after how he treated her. I can kind of feel sorry for him the way he died of liver cancer, but all that drinking brought it on him. I can even kind of understand that she put up with him as long as she did since he's the only real family she's ever known, but I can't understand how she can stay so devoted to his memory. It's just not right. Kind of sick—maybe not as sick as those women in India who throw themselves on their husbands' burning bodies, but maybe the American equivalent to it. If they'd burned Charlie that way, well, I'm not sure I would have put it past Bel to do something similar.

Just so I don't get sick from listening to her—she's been known to talk to him too while she's planting flowers—I wander around looking at the other stones, at all the people who are dead now that I used to know or at least knew of. I bet I know more people now who are dead than are alive. It's a scary thought. I recognize about half the surnames—and if not the people buried there, I know people who must be their relatives. Marquette's a pretty small town after all. Bel will take me later to plant flowers where the Mitchells are buried—way over on the other end of the cemetery—but I have to admit I find it kind of funny when I just happen to come to where the O'Neills are all buried. Not just Mr. and Mrs. O'Neill—Robert and Eliza—but a whole slew of their relatives. There's a Kathleen O'Neill with another Robert O'Neill—I think those are Mr. O'Neill's grandparents, and then there's a John O'Neill and Louisa May O'Neill, and then next to the grandparents on one side is a Carter, and there's Smiths and Hamptons on the other. They must all be related somehow. I know Mr. Robert Hampton, the lawyer in Marquette, was something like a nephew or cousin or something to Mr. O'Neill. I wish now I had paid more attention when Mr. O'Neill would tell me about his family. He was always talking about them, but I never really listened much—I didn't understand then how he could be so interested in all his ancestors since I didn't really know anything about my own.

I can't help thinking, though, how funny it is that I happen to stumble across Mr. and Mrs. O'Neill's stones today when I've never noticed them out here before, and then I find them the same day I'm going over to their house for supper, for the first time since I quit working there. According to the stone, they'd both be over one hundred now. They were old even when I started working for them, but it just seems like yesterday I was polishing their silver and cooking their meals, so it's hard to believe it's now been seven years since Mr. O'Neill has been gone and even more for Mrs. O'Neill. It makes me realize how it probably won't be much longer for me now before I'm in the same place as them.

I'll be buried here in Holy Cross Cemetery. That's one thing I never told anyone, not even Bel, I don't think. I have a plot next to the Mitchells. I don't know why it was, but the Mitchells bought one plot more than they needed, and when Miss Mary died, I told the sexton that that other plot was for me; he didn't even ask if I was family—must have just assumed it, so he put my name on it in his book; I figured that was the least the Mitchells could give me, and poor as I was, I didn't know how else I'd ever afford a grave. Only, I wish when Miss Florence had been buried, we'd have put her next to her brother rather than Miss Mary because now I'll end up spending eternity next to Miss Florence. But at that time, I didn't know I might want to be buried with them. Well, I suppose when we all get to Heaven, we won't care where our bodies lie, and more importantly, if God is good like they say, then Miss Florence won't have any reason to be ornery like she was on earth. Not that in the end I really did mind her.

I do feel kind of bad that I won't be in Park Cemetery with Papa, but by luck, the spot next to Mama was never taken so I was able to put Papa next to her so he's not alone there. I kind of wonder if the Mitchells' other spot was for Mama, but who knows. Park Cemetery is a lot nicer cemetery than Holy Cross, but it being the Protestant one and Holy Cross being the Catholic cemetery, and me being Catholic—even if I was made so against my will, I'm too old to become a Lutheran again now—Holy Cross is where I'll be buried.

"Lyla, can you bring me some water?" Bel shouts to me, so I go back to where she's making a mess of herself, getting dirt all over her pants, and pick up the bucket and go find a water faucet. Enough thinking about the dead for one day. I mean, I'll go put flowers on the Mitchells' and my parents' graves, but that's enough thinking about death. I may be seventy-seven, and I'm not saying I really have anything in life worth living for, but neither am I ready yet to give up the ghost. I'm not sure why not, other than that maybe I have a little of Miss Florence's orneriness in me, but I'm just not ready yet.

Chapter 4

By the time I get home, it's nearly noon, and since I'm still feeling full from breakfast, there's no point in having lunch. I don't have anything else I have to do the rest of the day, but I'm so nervous about going out tonight that I can't sit still. I go to use the bathroom and decide I need to clean the bathtub, so I go change into my around-the-house clothes, and then I start scrubbing away, and once I get started on the bathtub, then I have to do the whole bathroom, and then I figure I might as well just do up the dishes I didn't do for the last couple nights because when you live alone, you only do them every few days—there's no point in doing them constantly—but there is a stack of them from when Bel and I had supper last night. I can just imagine what the O'Neills would think of me if they saw how messy my apartment is. "How did we ever let her clean for us?" they'd say. Well, maybe the O'Neills wouldn't say that, and probably not Mrs. Marshall either, but some of those others I worked for would. Miss Florence sure would. She wasn't too happy with what I did to keep the house clean for her, and that was when she was half-blind in one eye and couldn't even see most of the dirt, but she still managed to complain. God, I'd have pitied anyone who worked for her when she had her full eyesight.

But none of my former employers would probably understand that I spent so much of my time keeping their houses clean that I didn't have much energy left to clean my own. I mean, when you clean house Monday to Friday, you don't much feel like doing it on Saturday and Sunday—those are supposed to be days off. And no one pays you to keep your own house clean. But now that I live alone, every once in awhile the old cleaning bug bites me and I get whipped up into having to clean. So this afternoon, I get so busy scrubbing and washing that you'd think I was the one having the party at the O'Neill House tonight—I did always go all out to straighten it up for them. Mrs. O'Neill would even hire a couple extra girls to come in and help me every year when she had her annual Christmas party.

After I finish the dishes, I get started on cleaning the refrigerator, but I'm only halfway when I realize it's almost five o'clock, so I shove everything back in and go get ready. By now I'm starting to feel sleepy, partly from having worked all afternoon, but more I imagine from some reluctance to go. I wish I could call John and his wife to say I'm sick, but then they'll just want to reschedule for another time. I feel like I need a nap more than a dinner out, but I said I would go, and they do seem like a nice young couple, and John sounded excited on the phone, so it's not like I want to disappoint them—it's just that I don't want to get involved with Bill's family again.

"Oh, I hate trying to figure out what to wear," I grumble as I look with disgust at everything in my closet. I finally decide on a dress—I've always been a dress person, though I'm afraid they make me look like an old lady now, but I am an old lady now, and my tastes are from the era when I was young—when people still knew how to dress—the '40s and '50s. I pretty much gave up on dresses during the '60s and '70s, but now that I'm old, I guess I feel sentimental about wearing them again. Somehow they're like a safety blanket. I've noticed the younger people treat you with more respect when you're wearing a dress—or at least I imagine so. And I'll bring along a sweater. It's still only May and a bit chilly in the evenings. The high today was only supposed to be 54. Darn chilly for Memorial Day weekend in my opinion. Couldn't have had a picnic outside if I had wanted to. Even inside the house it's bound to be cold—the O'Neill House is so big it always was a challenge to heat, and these young people always have the heat turned down a lot lower than is reasonable; they never think about how us old people get cold, so I'd better wear my sweater, and I'll put my spring jacket on over it.

I hope I'm not underdressed, but then I hope they realize I don't have money like them. I'm probably fussing too much about it. But I wish I could remember what they had on when I saw them at the hospital—probably jeans—that's all the younger generation ever wears these days. But the O'Neill House is pretty fancy. I don't think Mr. O'Neill ever said anything when I'd wear slacks to work, but I felt like he must disapprove. Mrs. O'Neill wore fancy pants suits all the time when she was older—but then, she had a flare—could carry off the pants like an eighty-year-old Katherine Hepburn, but me, I'm more like what Fanny Brice would have looked like if she'd lived to be my age. Though I'd rather look like Fanny Brice than that Britney Spears tramp—that's for sure. I wonder if we women wearing pants in my generation are responsible for the liberties that followed. Sure we might have worn pants, but we didn't burn our bras, and God forbid we ever would have thought about running around like these young girls today with their toeless shoes, their belly buttons hanging out, and tattoos all over every inch of their bodies. Hussies and white trash—that's what we would have called them in my day—and floozies too. What are their mothers thinking to let them look like that? I didn't even have a mother when I was their age to look after me, but I had enough common sense not to do anything as stupid as all that. Even the trampiest girls I knew back then wouldn't be caught looking like the girls today.

Well, I decide on a skirt instead of a full dress. And a nice blouse. Not my fanciest—I don't want to overdo it because it might look tacky, but standing in front of the mirror, I think I look good enough, though with this sweater over my shoulders, I feel a bit like an old lady, but I am seventy-seven now. I keep thinking I'm only fifty-eight or something—keep thinking it's some year like 1982—time goes by so fast you forget how old you are when you get old. One day you're thirty-two and then an eyewink later you're gray and insisting on your senior discount at Beef-a-Roo.

Five minutes before John's supposed to arrive, I put on my coat and go down the elevator so he won't have to come into the building looking for me. Then I stand by the door and wait. The lobby is quiet, which is just fine because I don't like the other residents knowing my business, and they're not so much friendly as wanting to gossip about me usually. Well, maybe I've been a bit stand-offish toward them, but I don't need some minister's widow or some doctor's old battle-axe looking down her nose at me. It was Bel's idea to move into this place, not mine. My old friend Mary Dwyer used to live here and I'd come visit her once in awhile, so I thought it'd be a nice place, but for the most part, I've kept to myself since moving in.

John pulls right up to the door and gets out of the car to come and find me. He's a gentleman at least—not like his great-uncle. Bill would have just sat out there and beeped his horn at me. When John sees me open the door, he stops and smiles and says, "Hello," and then he turns and opens the passenger door for me. Of course, when you're in your thirties, you must think seventy-seven is old and that people my age need help getting in and out of cars, but I appreciate the attention anyways. I don't often have a man open a door for me.

"How are you, Lyla?" he asks as I get in the car. "I'm fine," I says as he pulls out the seatbelt for me to grab. After he shuts the door, he goes around to his side and gets in. He makes sure I get my seatbelt buckled; then he pulls the car away from the curb and says, "I'm so excited to have you come and tell us what the O'Neill House was like when you worked there."

"Well, it really wasn't all that long ago," I says, "so I don't imagine it's that much different."

"That's all right," says John. "I'll appreciate anything you can tell Wendy and me. I'm sure you have all kinds of stories you can tell us about the O'Neills. You know, Mr. O'Neill apparently took a shine to me at the end, but I didn't really know him that well. I wish I had. Sometimes I don't feel right that he let me stay in the house like he did."

I can't help thinking, "Too bad he didn't leave the house to me," considering how many years I put in working for the family. Not that they didn't pay me good, but I did more for them than this young man did.

I don't know what else to say to John. I don't feel much up to making small talk with someone I don't know, and if I were better at saying, "No," I never would have agreed to go, only I am kind of looking forward to seeing the O'Neill House again. I hope the whole night isn't as awkward as this moment. We're silent until we've driven a few blocks, and then John says, "We've been lucky with our weather so far. Winter ended kind of early this year, right with Easter, and even that was pretty early—end of March."

"Yeah," I says. "I like spring, but now that May's almost over, it's going to start getting hot and I don't like hot weather."

"No, I don't either," says John.

Then I asks the question I'm dying to ask, just because I'm nosy. "So just how did you get to own the O'Neill House? I don't remember you ever coming over to see Mr. O'Neill when I worked there, and I think you said you're not a relative."

"No, it's because I'm a writer," he says. "I did visit a couple of times, but it must have been your day off or something when I came with my grandpa once for lunch; he and Mr. O'Neill knew each other—my grandpa apparently did some work on the house—fixed the porch anyway—and I guess he and Mr. O'Neill went fishing together a few times. But then I didn't visit again until just before Mr. O'Neill died. I was more surprised than anyone by his will, but I didn't really get the house. It's in trust with his estate. He just appointed me as trustee for life—I guess you'd say—so I would have a place to live and I could write. He apparently saw something in me because I was a writer, and he thought I had the potential to write some great books about Upper Michigan, so he wanted to give me some financial security while I did it. So, no, I'm no relation to the O'Neills. But the funny thing is—and Mr. O'Neill found this out even though I didn't know myself—the house actually belonged to my family before it belonged to the O'Neills."

"I thought most of you Whitmans had money," I says. "I mean, you're related to the Bergmanns, right? And they had money."

"Oh, no, the Whitmans were always fairly poor. It was the Henning family who built the house and had money. That was generations ago, though. It's a long story. It might be easier to explain to you once we get to the house. Then I can show you the family tree."

"But you're related to the Bergmanns, right—Thelma Bergmann I mean?"

"Oh, well, my grandma's maiden name was Bergmann, and she married my grandpa, Henry Whitman."

"That's right," I says. "Your grandma was Beth Whitman and she was Thelma Bergmann's cousin, right?"

"Yes," he says. "I imagine you knew her since you dated Uncle Bill."

I don't reply. I remember how Beth Whitman used to pretend not to see me when we would pass each other in the store or on the street. She always was stuck up, just like her cousin. But I guess the Whitmans aren't too much like the Bergmanns—not stuck up at least. Eleanor was always good to me, and while I can't say Bill was exactly good to me, for some reason, I did love him in a way, but...no, I'm not going to start thinking about him again. It's too late now.

"Did you know Thelma Bergmann?" John asks.

"No, not really," I says. "She adopted my sister, Jessie, but once that happened, I didn't see either of them much."

"Oh," says John. "I've heard something about that I think. Why was she adopted?"

"My parents died," I says. That's not exactly what happened, but it's easier than explaining what happened to my dad. "Miss Bergmann was my sister's piano teacher so she adopted her, but no one wanted me. Miss Bergmann, even though she had no right, she had me stuck in the orphanage."

"Oh," says John. "That's terrible, Lyla. That must have been hard for you."

I don't say nothing, just kind of nod.

"I always thought the orphanage was so interesting," John says. "Someday I'll have to write a novel about it. I should interview you about it sometime."

"Don't bother," I says. "It would make a crappy story. I wasn't very happy living there."

"No, I imagine you wouldn't be," he says.

We have an awkward moment of silence while I wonder whether he thinks less of me for saying "crappy," though I don't think this younger generation gets easily shocked over four-letter words like people did in my day.

"I hope you like lasagna," he finally says. "Wendy makes a great lasagna."

"I like a free meal anytime I can get one," I laugh, but as soon as the words are out of my mouth, I realize how pathetic they must make me sound. "I enjoy lasagna a lot," I add, "though I haven't had it in forever because it's just too much work to fix for just me."

"I understand. I lived alone for years and never cooked," says John, "but I'm sure glad to have a wife who does."

We're driving down Ridge Street now, and in another minute, we pull into the driveway of the O'Neill House. It doesn't look any different than it did when I worked there—seems like just yesterday, though it's been about seven years now. I always felt bad that I quit when I did since Mr. O'Neill passed away just a year or so later. If I'd known he had so little time left, I would have stuck it out longer—after I quit, he had some college students coming in to help, but who knows what kind of care they took of him? I never understood why neither of his children or any of his grandchildren came to stay with him near the end, or why he didn't go live with them, but he said Marquette was home and his son and daughter lived out in California or somewhere like that. Still, I would think they would want to see him more often. Young people are just too busy for old people, I guess. I'm surprised John and Wendy even want to be bothered with me.

As I get out of the car, I realize again how old this house is. It's a great big sandstone mansion built back in the 1860s I think Mr. O'Neill used to tell me. But now it doesn't seem that old to me, considering I'm well over half its age myself.

"It feels funny coming back here," I says. "Like no time has passed at all."

"Well, we're very glad you have come," says John, as we walk to the front door and he holds it open for me.

I've hardly stepped through the door when I'm confronted by a little boy standing in my way.

"Hi," says the kid. He must be about three since he's walking and talking and standing there staring at me rudely.

"Hi there, buddy," John says to him. "Can you step out of the way so we can get in the door?"

He steps aside, but he's still staring at me.

"Lyla, this is my son, Neill. Neill, this is Miss Hopewell."

No one's called me Miss Hopewell in thirty years. What's up with that? You'd think John was as old as this house. Most young people aren't all that polite anymore.

The kid didn't get his manners from his dad. He's still staring.

"We named Neill after Mr. O'Neill," John says.

"That's nice," I says as he takes my coat and hangs it up. "How many kids do you have?"

"Just Neill right now, but Wendy and I are expecting another."

"That's nice," I says again. I suppose I should say, "Congratulations" and ask if it's going to be a boy or a girl, but I figure I'll be stuck having the same conversation in another minute with his wife, so I might as well hold off. I can't say kids interest me all that much anyways. I never wanted any myself—in fact, I could never figure out why anyone would. I had a couple housekeeping job offers I turned down just so I didn't have to deal with them—old people were more my speed, at least to work for. They might be ornery or need a little help getting around, but they weren't going to jump all over the furniture or track up the floors right after I mopped.

"Go ahead and sit down in the parlor," John tells me. "I'm sure Neill will entertain you. Just give me a minute and I'll go check on Wendy."

"Okay," I says, not at all thrilled to be left alone with the staring three-year old. Ignoring the kid, though I can hear him pattering after me, I step into the parlor. For a moment, I feel déjà-vu when I see the fancy old antique sofa, and then all kinds of memories, even smells, come back to me. Mrs. O'Neill had loved this front parlor with its satin furniture. Some of it she told me dated back to 1920 when she'd had the room redecorated not long after she inherited the house from her first husband—he died in World War I if I remember right, and he was some sort of cousin to Mr. O'Neill—which I guess is how she knew Mr. O'Neill and ended up marrying him later. I never did dare to sit on that sofa while I worked here, but I'm not young anymore and it's very inviting. I'll be careful not to get it dirty. I wonder if Mrs. O'Neill's spirit is watching me as I sit myself down on it. I just hope I can get back up. At my age, you never know if you'll ever get up again once you sit down.

Once I am down—and the sofa's very comfortable even if it is older than me—I realize the kid didn't follow me into the room. Fine with me. It is kind of sweet, though, that they named him after Mr. O'Neill—I guess it's the least they could do after he left them the house, or however he did it—I don't really understand the whole Will & Trust thing John tried to explain to me.

I about half-expect Mrs. O'Neill to come through the door and catch me sitting on her sofa, not that she'd say anything. She was always such a sweet lady—what a real lady should be—gracious and kind—that I never could bring myself to sit on the sofa from fear it might upset her. I don't know how to say it, but she was one woman you always did your best for, not because you were afraid she'd jump down your throat if you didn't, but just because somehow she always brought out the best in you. I always knew she appreciated me—Mr. O'Neill did too. I wouldn't go so far as to say I looked forward to cleaning their toilets and washing their dishes, but I got to feel responsible for them, especially Mr. O'Neill after Mrs. O'Neill passed away. Mrs. O'Neill was agile until the end even though she was in her eighties, but by the time I came along, things were getting to be a bit much for her. She'd had hired help all her life except a few years during the Great Depression, but she said I was a harder worker than anyone else she'd ever had. I felt terrible leaving Mr. O'Neill with those college girls when I finally retired. I felt like I was betraying Mrs. O'Neill because I know she trusted me to look after her husband, but after all those years of being on my feet, I just didn't have the strength to keep working much longer, not when Mr. O'Neill seemed like he was going to live to be a hundred and maybe even outlive me.

"Wendy says we'll be ready to eat in a few minutes," says John, coming back into the room and carrying Neill, who I didn't even notice had left and who now won't even look at me. "Neill's being shy," John adds. "Can I get you something to drink?"

"No, I'm good," I says, not daring to drink anything while sitting on Mrs. O'Neill's sofa from fear I might spill.

"So, is the house much like how you remember it?" John asks.

"This room is," I says. "Mrs. O'Neill loved this sofa. I'm almost afraid to sit on it. She bought it not long after her first husband died when she decided to remodel."

"Really? That's wonderful. We knew it dated to about 1920 but not how it came to be here. That's the kind of information we want to hear."

"Didn't you say this house was historical now—I mean like historically preserved for tours or something? Don't you worry your little boy will wreck something?"

"Wendy and I don't let him downstairs unless we're with him and keeping an eye on him. We basically live upstairs—we kind of have our own apartment up there, even with a little kitchenette, but we entertain company down here. Many of these older homes in this neighborhood have been divided into apartments, so it's actually kind of strange that this one wasn't, but we treat it like it is upstairs, like we live in a big apartment—it gives us privacy, too, so we don't have to clean up during the tours or have to worry about tourists tripping over Neill's toys. We used to spend a lot more time downstairs before Neill was born, but we have to be careful like you said since it's a historical home and many of the antiques date back to the 1800s. But, of course, we wanted to entertain you down here since we want you to tell us about the home and what you remember about it."

"Well, I'm not sure what all more I can tell you," I says. "I mean, it's not like I was here that long. I think it was something like 1982 to 1998 that I worked here. Not any of the earlier years."

"That's a lot longer than we've been here or than I knew the O'Neills," says John. "In fact, I think I only met Mrs. O'Neill once. Wendy never met either of them, so we appreciate any information you can give us. We'll give you the tour after dinner so you can tell us more. We've updated a few things or tried to restore them to how they were, but we have some things we're not sure about so maybe you can help us with those."

I just nod. It kind of makes me feel good being here, though I already feel like I'm running out of things to say.

"Honey, we're ready!" Wendy calls from the kitchen. "Can you come help me pour the drinks?"

"Coming," John calls back. "Come on into the dining room, Lyla. I'll put Neill in his booster seat and then maybe you could just watch him for a minute so he doesn't make any messes while I help Wendy get all the food on the table."

"Okay," I says, but what does he think I am, the kid's babysitter? I put my hands on the sofa's arms to give myself a push up, which turns out not to be difficult since the old sofa is a lot firmer than you might expect.

I follow John into the dining room where Wendy is putting a bowl of salad on the table.

"Welcome, Lyla," she says. "We're so excited to have you here. John's been talking about nothing else all day. He gets so excited to meet people who knew Mr. O'Neill."

"Thank you for having me," I says, not used to being treated like I'm a celebrity.

"It's our pleasure," says Wendy. "I'm sure that, having been the O'Neills' housekeeper, you know things about them that their family members didn't even know. All the gossip and stuff like that, right, Lyla?" She winks at me and then goes back into the kitchen.

John's got Neill in a booster seat now and he hands the kid a little stuffed animal to play with while he raises his eyebrows at me as if to say, "Keep an eye on him" before he goes in the kitchen.

Feeling annoyed and ignoring the kid, I reply to Wendy by saying, "The O'Neills were real good people. I doubt they had any secrets or that either of them ever did anything really bad in their entire lives."

"Well, maybe some of their guests then. I'm sure you could tell us some stories about them," she calls from the kitchen.

"Well," I says, feeling funny to be in the dining room and not the kitchen. "They weren't ever ones to speak ill of other people—except—"

"Ye-es," says Wendy, grinning in anticipation as she returns with a pan of lasagna to set on the table.

"They never had a problem with talking about Mr. O'Neill's Aunt Carolina. They were always saying, 'What an odd old thing she was.'"

"Oh," laughs John, coming back with a gallon of milk to fill all our glasses. "I guess we know a lot about Aunt Carolina. She's mentioned in Mr. O'Neill's autobiography."

I tell John I'll just have water and then he pours the drinks, gets me water, and he and Wendy sit down. Despite the stuffed animal, the kid just sits and stares at me all this time. As Wendy starts to dish out the lasagna, John asks, "Did you get a chance to read it, Lyla?"

"What?" I asks.

"Mr. O'Neill's autobiography."

I shake my head, not sure how to answer at first, so John keeps talking.

"It just finally came out a year ago. I had a lot to do in twisting the publisher's arm to produce it, and I worked hard at editing it to get it in a publishable state. Mr. O'Neill always did like to write by hand and his handwriting was pretty hard to read in his later years. And he didn't quite finish it—he left some fragmented parts—but I think it reads smoothly."

"No, I'm not much of a reader," I says. "What's it about?"

"Well, it's his autobiography, the story of his life," says John, "so he talked about growing up in Marquette, his family, getting married to both of his wives."

"Did he mention me in it?" I asks.

"No. He only got up to writing about where he married Mrs. O'Neill— the second one. That was in 1934. I don't know if he really wanted to end it there, or he just ran out of steam. A lot of the book reviewers and critics were disappointed that he didn't talk more about his later years once he became really famous or about writing all of his books, but I think it's a charming book in and of itself. It's called *The Only Thing That Lasts*. You must have seen it in the stores. It should have made the *New York Times* bestseller list, in my opinion, but I guess Mr. O'Neill, although he was one of the twentieth century's great American authors, has fallen out of favor now."

"I'll have to look for it," I says politely. I don't read anything but *The Mining Journal*, but I might be interested in reading that since it's a book about someone I knew—not that I ever read any of Mr. O'Neill's other books.

Wendy's got my attention now as she starts dishing out the lasagna. "Oh, it looks wonderful," I tell her when I see all the cheese dripping out from between the pasta and how thick and filled with meat it is. It's been a long time since I've had a real home cooked meal like this.

"Thank you," says Wendy. "John is really fond of lasagna, but I don't make it too often since it's so much work, especially with Neill always keeping me busy."

"Lyla, we don't even know what the O'Neills ate regularly," says John. "What kind of food did they usually serve, or what did they like to eat?"

"Oh, I don't think they ever had lasagna," I says. "Usually more traditional meat and potato dishes. They liked pasties, and Mr. O'Neill being so Irish could never seem to get enough of boiled dinner, corned beef, that kind of stuff."

"Hmm, I never thought about boiled dinner," said Wendy. "We've been thinking about having a period dinner here—a fundraising event or something like that in conjunction with the history museum or a book club or something—but we've always planned to do Victorian type meals, like something the Hennings who first owned the house would have served, but maybe we could have an Eliza O'Neill meal—something she would have made instead."

"Well," I says, "I don't know that Mrs. O'Neill ever did much cooking. I did it when I was here and I think except maybe for a few years during the Depression, she always had help. The O'Neills did love to have dinner parties, especially with their family members, and they were really close with the Hamptons. And then they'd have local people over too—people like John Voelker or Dorothy Maywood Byrd or Mrs. Miller and Phyllis Rankin—you know, people who wrote books—Mrs. Miller didn't but she was some writer's daughter I guess—Phyllis Rankin was her sister."

"Hah, the literati!" laughed John. "I love it. The Rankin sisters' mother was Carroll Watson Rankin who wrote *Dandelion Cottage*; she lived down the street by the Episcopal Church. I wish there were more literati around so I could invite them over myself. I belong to the U.P. Publishers and Authors Association, of course, but we're so spread out across the U.P. that we hardly see each other. Wouldn't it be fine if Marquette had its own circle of literati?"

I have no idea what he's talking about and the lasagna is awful cheesy anyways, so I don't say much else.

"After we eat, Lyla," says Wendy, "we'll have to give you a tour of the house, so you can see what we've done with the place. Or maybe, you'll end up giving us the tour, telling us more about it."

"I can tell you how hard it was to clean," I laugh.

"It still is," Wendy smiles. "I worry so much about everything getting ruined—even the things Mrs. O'Neill did to redecorate after she inherited the house from Aunt Carolina are vintage pieces after all these years."

"The dusting was the worst," I says. "I used the vacuum hose a lot of times to try to reach things what with all these high ceilings and some of that old woodwork on the doors, and even a lot of the old cabinets are a lot of work to keep clean. I even used to polish the silver."

"It sounds like you had your hands full."

"Well, when they had dinner parties, they would usually have someone in to help me. They were always entertaining up until just before Mrs. O'Neill died. I think I honestly was lucky because they were both about eighty when I came to work for them—Mrs. O'Neill, she was about three years older than

Mr. O'Neill. And at their age, they couldn't see the dirt so well anymore, and I was pushing sixty then, so I couldn't quite either, so we got along just fine. They were real good people, always appreciative, so I did the best I could for them. They were a lot better than most of the other people I worked for; I can tell you that. You wouldn't believe some of the stories I could tell you about the others I cleaned house for."

Wendy laughs and then asks, "Where else did you work?"

"Oh lots of different places—I cleaned houses for fifty years of my life or more. I never really wanted to be someone's full-time maid so I didn't work for too many of the super rich people, but rather, I came in a day or two a week for lots of families. The O'Neills were one of the few that I worked for full-time. I started out just coming in to help them a couple days a week, but when their other housekeeper left, Mrs. O'Neill asked me to stay full-time, and I liked her more than some of the other people I worked for, so I agreed. She wasn't afraid to help out with the cleaning either. She was spry right to the end. I don't think she needed my help so much as she wanted the company and was worried that if something happened to her, Mr. O'Neill wouldn't have someone to look after him. And then after she died, I sometimes used to spend the night here because I was worried about him falling or something. He usually had a college student come in to do that, but I filled in plenty of times because you know how unreliable some college students can be. It got to be too much for me, though, taking care of this big house, so I finally had to retire, though I'd stop in once a week or so when I could to make sure Mr. O'Neill was being looked after properly. This one time when I came over, I ended up telling off this girl because she wasn't getting the dishes clean. She quit after that, but I didn't feel bad. I wasn't going to let anyone neglect Mr. O'Neill after he and his wife had been so good to me."

"I'm sure he appreciated everything you did for him," says Wendy. "I bet Mrs. O'Neill was glad to know she left him in good hands."

And suddenly, I find myself staring at my lasagna and getting all teary-eyed. I didn't realize I missed him so much until then. After Papa, Mr. O'Neill was the only man who had ever really been good to me.

"Are you okay?" John asks me. "Do you want a Kleenex?"

"No, I'm all right. I just—I just miss him. He was old enough to be my father, but see—I never really had a father—I mean, not as a girl. I did later when my papa came back home and he lived with me for several years before he died, but Papa wasn't really in his right mind then."

They both look embarrassed when I look up at them, like they don't know what to say and don't want to pry into my private life. I told John earlier that I went to the orphanage because my parents died, but I guess he doesn't notice I fibbed about both of them dying. It's not that I meant to lie; it's just so hard to explain to people so they'll understand about what happened to Papa. It's still unbelievable to me to think how he went to Karelia during the Depression when it belonged to Russia, and that he ever escaped from the Communists and made it back home—he never really did tell me how he got away—the look on his face always said it was too scary for him even to think about, much less talk about.

"Did you always clean houses, Lyla?" Wendy asks. "Or did you do other work too?"

"No, I was pretty much always a housecleaner. The nuns found me my first position, so I guess I just stuck with it. Miss Bergmann tried once to send me to secretarial school, but I wasn't interested in it. I never did like gadgets like typewriters or see the point in shorthand, so I dropped out the first semester. She was mad about it and said she'd never help me again, but I didn't care. I wasn't going to spend my life trying to please her."

"She means Thelma Bergmann, my grandma's cousin," John tells Wendy.

"Oh sure," Wendy says.

"My sister was adopted by Miss Bergmann," I tell Wendy, "but she didn't want me. I had to go to the orphanage instead."

"Oh, you poor thing," says Wendy.

"Why didn't she adopt you too?" John asks.

"I've spent most of my life trying to figure that one out," I says, but as soon as I says it, I hear the whining tone in my voice, so I quickly add, "First job I did was to go work for the Mitchell sisters. Mr. O'Neill actually knew them when he was a boy. I went to work for them though during the War. Miss Mary, she was a sweet old lady, but Miss Florence was as mean as they come."

"Oh, the Mitchells are mentioned in Mr. O'Neill's autobiography too," says Wendy.

"Sure," says John. "Mr. O'Neill wasn't too fond of Florence, but of course, he was just a boy then."

"I told Mr. O'Neill one time how Miss Florence always used to snap at me," I says, "and he told me, 'Lyla, she's always snapped at everyone. You took it too personally. She was just an old fussbudget and a deeply unhappy woman—that was no fault of yours.' That meant a lot to me 'cause I was only fourteen when I went to work for the Mitchells. When they didn't like me—well, Miss Mary did, but I think she liked everyone—but Miss Florence, well, I had already figured out that Miss Bergmann didn't like me, and the Sisters at the orphanage weren't all that crazy about me, so when Miss Florence didn't like me, well, I—well, it didn't make me feel very good you know."

"You poor thing," Wendy says again; she sounds almost like she wants to pat me on the head to console me. I feel sort of like little Neill there, having his mother kiss his boo-boos. But I don't remember anyone ever kissing my boo-boos.

"I can't imagine growing up in an orphanage, and then having to go out to work at fourteen," says John. "It makes me realize how lucky I was growing up."

"You were lucky," I says. "The orphanage wasn't that much fun."

"Oh, honey," Wendy says. "Neill's about to make a mess."

I look over and see he's got a handful of lasagna, which he tosses on the tablecloth before John can stop him.

"Hey, buddy," John says. "You're supposed to eat that, not play with it."

"He just wants attention," says Wendy. "He's not used to us having company and not being the center of attention."

John picks up the lasagna and puts it on his own plate.

"He's got sauce all over his clothes too," I says, seeing despite a bib, the kid has smeared it on his shirt. "That'll be a pain to clean."

"Oh, well," says Wendy. "That's what it's like to have children. He'll grow out of it eventually, although now we have another one on the way."

"Congratulations," I says, figuring she'd eventually get around to talking about babies. "When are you due?"

"We expect her about September 1st," Wendy says.

"Her?" says John.

"John wants a boy," Wendy says. "He grew up with a brother and thinks Neill should have one too, but I want a girl. We decided not to find out but to be surprised. Either way, I'll be glad to have another. I was an only child and always wanted a sister."

"Do you want seconds, Lyla?" John asks as he tries to get Neill to hold his face still while he wipes it off. The kid still hasn't said, "Boo" to me, but at least he's quit staring now.

"Oh, no. I'm stuffed," I says, "but it was delicious."

"I hope you saved room for dessert," says Wendy.

"Oh, well, not right now. Maybe in a little while."

"Wendy made a chocolate mayonnaise cake," John says.

"It's not fancy," Wendy says, "but John likes it. It's one of his comfort foods—it was his Grandma Whitman's recipe."

"That's nice," I says, thinking how thrilled his grandma would be to have me eating her cake.

Wendy stuffs the last bite of lasagna into her mouth before she says, "Well, I'll get these dishes out of the way and then we'll give you a tour of the house. That'll help you walk off some of dinner, and then when we come back downstairs, you'll have room for dessert."

"That sounds good," I says.

John has got the kid cleaned up now and releases him from his high chair. The kid instantly disappears, though I'm not sure where he goes.

John excuses himself and helps Wendy carry the plates into the kitchen.

"Can I help with the dishes?" I asks.

"Oh no, we have a dishwasher," says Wendy. "The O'Neills didn't have one, but we had one put in since we figured we'd be hosting special dinners and other events here."

I think how Mrs. O'Neill never would have bought a dishwasher. She would have thought it a waste of money, but I don't say anything.

I wait while they finish clearing the table and then Wendy comes and wipes it down with a dishcloth. John has apparently gone out another door in the kitchen because a minute later he comes from the hall with Neill perched on his shoulder. "We're going to give Miss Hopewell a tour of the house now, Buddy," he says to Neill. "Do you want to help? You can show her your room and all your toys."

Great. Checking out the kid's toys is exactly what I want to do.

In a second, Wendy has joined us and we start the tour. The house is actually pretty much the way I remember it since John moved in just a year or two after I quit working for Mr. O'Neill. A couple things are different, either from needed renovations or pieces of art work or furniture John and Wendy pulled out of the attic because they want the house to look as historical as possible, they says.

One thing they make a big deal out of showing me is a giant family tree chart I never saw before. It's right on a wall in the entry hall where they can use it to tell the house's history when the guests first come in for their tour. "We had this family tree specially made," John says. "You see, my and Wendy's ancestors first built this house. It's rather complicated, which is why we need the tree. Mr. O'Neill found out I was descended from the Hennings who built the house, which I think is partly why he wanted me to look after the house. I'm descended from Gerald and Clara Henning's daughter Agnes. After Clara died, Gerald married Sophia Brookfield, who was actually the sister to another of my ancestors. Gerald and Sophia's daughter Madeleine was Wendy's ancestor."

He's already got me confused, but he must not notice the look on my face because he keeps on explaining everything. Wendy is just smiling, obviously very proud of the family tree.

"Wendy and I," John continues, "are fourth half-cousins on the Henning side of the family, and fifth cousins on the Brookfield side of the family."

"Really?" I says, thinking it kind of weird that cousins would marry. "Have you known each other all your lives then?"

"Oh no," says Wendy. "My great-great-grandmother Madeleine Henning Carew ran away from home and settled in Montana. It was when I was researching her family tree that I found out she came from Marquette so I came here to do research and that's how I ended up meeting John. The history museum gave me his name. Genealogy brought us together, but I fell in love with him because he's so sweet and handsome."

John starts blushing like a schoolboy—you would think he'd be used to how his wife feels about him by now.

"That's romantic," I says, and I guess it is—but I still think it's a little weird that cousins would marry each other.

"We have the Smith and O'Neill family tree depicted here too," says John, pointing to the chart on the wall. "The Hennings sold the house to Mr. O'Neill's Aunt Carolina and her husband, Judge Smith. That's how it got passed down to the O'Neills eventually, and now it's sort of come back into the Henning family. It's all been quite serendipitous really."

"Uh huh," I says, not having a clue what 'sarandiptous' means.

"Well, we'll have to show you the upstairs now, Lyla," says Wendy. "I want you to see our apartment we've constructed up there. It's quite spacious."

"Show Elmo, Mommy," says Neill. Of course, she agrees and I get dragged into his room first where I have to "Ooh" and "Aah" over a bunch of toys, including a red stuffed Tickle-Me-Elmo, which I recognize from TV commercials.

"Thanks for being a good sport, Lyla," Wendy says when we finally get out of the kid's room and I know it's safe not to worry about tripping over any more play trucks or blocks or the fifty other toys the kid has. I never saw so many toys. If you put all the toys I and all the other kids in the orphanage had together it wouldn't come to that many—and ours were mostly all hand-me-downs—even the ones we got for Christmas most of the time.

I get to see John and Wendy's room and the little living room and kitchenette they have, and their bathroom, of course. And there's the upstairs rooms that are open for the tours, including the O'Neills' bedroom—I bet Mrs. O'Neill wouldn't like that; she was pretty private about those things—and the bedroom that belonged to Mr. O'Neill's Aunt Carolina as well as the one that belonged to Madeleine—that's Wendy's runaway ancestor, although I always knew it as the O'Neills' son Bernie's old room. It's actually all really nice. They've put new wallpaper in Aunt Carolina's room but its restoration stuff Wendy says—it looks new, but it's the Victorian pattern they found beneath some other wallpaper so it's looks just like what the old lady put in when she remodeled the house in 1877, Wendy says. At least, I think that's what year it was—I can't keep all the dates straight that they keep talking about.

"Well, it all looks very nice," I says as we start back downstairs, and it does look nice since a lot of it was just closed up and never used when I worked here because the O'Neills said they didn't need all that space once their kids were grown up. "I think the O'Neills would be very pleased," I adds just as we hear the doorbell ring.

"Oh, who could that be?" asks Wendy. John picks up Neill, who's been following us around, throws him over his shoulder, and runs downstairs to answer it. "John, be careful!" Wendy shouts to protest his running down the stairs with the kid, but he's already at the front door. Wendy and I follow him at a slower pace.

"These stairs didn't seem so high when I worked here," I says to Wendy. I'm about to tell her how Mr. O'Neill told me that him and his first wife used to slide down the banisters when they were kids, but then John yells, "Frank! What are you doing here? Why I almost didn't recognize you at first."

"It's the beard," I hear the man I assume is Frank say, "and I've gained a few pounds."

"You look great," says John. As I reach the bottom of the stairs, I catch just a glimpse of them releasing each other from a hug, with Neill still half-hung over John's shoulder.

"Come on in and meet my wife," says John. "Wendy, this is Frank. You know, my college roommate."

"Frank?" says Wendy, stepping past me. "Of course, John's told me all about you."

"Then you'll probably be kicking me out in a minute," he laughs.

"No way," John says, patting him on the back and looking pleased to see him.

Now that I'm all the way down the stairs and can get a good look at him, I see that Frank's a pretty big man. Maybe six feet or a little more. He's about John's age—mid-thirties, but far more muscular and sturdy looking. Very attractive if not for one of those silly goatees like the young men all seem to have these days. He's got on a V-neck blue T-shirt that's about skin-tight. Men never dressed like that in my day—but then, neither do I know any men who had bodies like his in my day.

"Oh, I'm sorry," says John. "Lyla, this is Frank. Frank, this is our friend, Lyla."

"Hello," says Frank.

"Hello," I says. "It's nice to meet you," but I'm more focused on being surprised that John called me their "friend."

"Come on in, Frank," says Wendy. "We just finished supper, but we were going to have dessert out on the porch."

"Dessert? Sounds good to me," he says.

Dessert sounds good to me too, but out on the porch? It's like fifty degrees outside. Good thing I brought my sweater. I'll probably need my jacket too.

"Yeah, and then you have to tell us what you're doing here. I haven't seen you in so long," says John. "Why didn't you tell us you were coming to Marquette?" He finally sets down Neill, whom I've been expecting all this time to see fall.

"Everyone go out to the porch and I'll bring dessert," says Wendy.

"Do you want help?" I asks her.

"Well, sure, Lyla. I have a tray, but with the coffee, it'll be a bit much to carry. Neill, you go with your father."

"I got him," says Frank, picking up the kid like he's just a pillow and tossing him up toward his shoulder. "Hi, kid. We'll have to get acquainted. What's your name again?"

"Neill," the kid says.

"Well, I'm Uncle Frank."

"Hi, Uncle Frank. Do you like Elmo?" the kid asks as Frank walks off with him.

The kid won't say a word to me, but he'll spit out whole sentences for "Uncle Frank." Well, I didn't want to pay attention to the kid anyways.

"Mrs. O'Neill always had someone serve for her," I says, following Wendy into the kitchen and thinking I'll at least get back her attention. I hate when people drop in without calling first. It's just rude. I wouldn't have come if I'd have known John and Wendy would be having other company. "Not that Mrs. O'Neill was above doing it herself," I says, "but it was all about style with her. She wanted everything to be nice and pleasant to make people feel special."

"I wish I had known her," Wendy says as she takes a chocolate cake out of the refrigerator and sets in on the counter. "She must have been quite a lady."

"Yes, I'd say she was the last true lady I knew. There were plenty who acted like ladies when I was young," I says, "but something changed about the 1960s or so you know. Women quit wearing gloves, then hats, then even dresses. The world hasn't been the same since. People just don't have the manners they used to. Now the girls even show off their belly buttons like they think we're in India or something."

I stop myself, wondering if I've said too much—Wendy's young—she probably doesn't agree with me, but she just laughs and says, "Yes, I know. No one says oops anymore when they're passing their gas—whatever happened to class?"

We wouldn't have mentioned passing gas in those days either, I want to tell her, but I don't. It's all true though—I saw those young tramp girls hanging out one night in front of that Mattrix place on Washington Street. I'm not usually out that late, fortunately, 'cause I'm afraid to know what other things might be going on in this town. Yeah, I spent my time with Bel hanging out in Remie's back in the day, but that was before the hippies and the punk rockers took over the country. I don't know what the girls are thinking anymore the way they act and dress.

As Wendy cuts the chocolate cake and places it on paper plates, she says, "You'll have to show me later which dishes Mrs. O'Neill used for different occasions. We have all her china. Some of it is quite old and chipped, so I think it must have belonged to Mr. O'Neill's Great-Aunt Carolina, but we didn't want to get rid of anything because it was so historical. Maybe she told you the history behind some of her pieces?"

"Well, I'm not sure. If she did, I don't remember," I says. "That looks like a really rich dessert."

"Oh, probably," she says. "I didn't even think of that because John has such a sweet tooth. Will it be too much for you, Lyla?"

"No, I'll eat it. As long as I have a little coffee to go with it, it'll be fine. It is decaf, right?"

"Yes, we always have decaf in the evening when we serve coffee. Aunt Eleanor won't drink anything but decaf, so we have to be prepared for when she comes over. I think we're ready now."

She's scrunched four paper plates of cake and forks on a tray. "The one with the extra cake," she says, "is mine so I can give Neill some. If you wouldn't mind carrying that out to the porch, Lyla, I'll follow with the coffee and cups."

"All right," I says. I make my way out to the porch and somehow manage to open the door while holding the tray.

"Thank you, Lyla," says John as I set it on a wicker tea table.

"Wendy's coming with the coffee," I says.

I don't know where John put my coat when we got here, but I still have my sweater on so I take my dessert and sit down, and for a minute, I listen as the men talk to each other until Wendy comes with the coffee, with Neill trailing behind her. I don't listen that closely, but I gather Frank is planning to move back here, and John confirms that when Wendy returns.

"Wendy, Frank is moving back to the U.P. to be near his daughter, Delta. Her mother's gotten a job in Marquette, so Delta lives here now, and Frank's going to find a place in Marquette too—isn't that wonderful."

"Oh, that's great, Frank," says Wendy. "It'll be like old times for you and John, and John could use a good friend. He spends too much time worrying about this old house and me and his writing. It'll be good for you both."

"I've just felt guilty being so far from my daughter," says Frank, "especially now that she's becoming a young woman."

"How old is she?" asks Wendy as she pours and serves the coffee to everyone.

"Thirteen. Almost thirteen-and-a-half," says Frank.

"My," says Wendy. "She'll need her dad around to give her advice on how to fend off all the boys."

"Frank will know all about that," laughs John. "He gave the girls a lot of trouble in college."

"Well, you can't blame the women for liking me when I have this smoking bod." Frank smiles and pulls his arm forward to flex a gigantic muscle. I have to admit I'm impressed by it, though I don't like his arrogance.

"You haven't changed any," John laughs and rolls his eyes.

"Are you seeing anyone now, Frank?" Wendy asks, having finished pouring the coffee and now taking Neill from Frank and placing him in a chair next to her so she can feed him his cake.

"No-o, no, I haven't for a while. I've just been busy taking care of myself I guess. How about you guys? I remember John writing and saying you inherited this house or something like that. I looked up the address in the phone book and couldn't believe it when I saw it."

"No, we didn't really inherit it. We're more the caretakers," says John, "and it's quite a job, let me tell you."

"Well, what else do you do?"

"John writes, and we both take care of the house," says Wendy. "We have tours and other events here, and John's busy overseeing Mr. O'Neill's legal affairs—publishing deals and that kind of stuff, and I have my hands full with little Neill, and we have another baby on the way."

"Another one? Well, congratulations," says Frank. "Boy or girl?"

"Boy," Wendy says at the same time John says, "Girl."

"We've actually decided not to find out until it's born," Wendy says.

"How old is this one?" asks Frank, pointing at the kid.

"Three," says John.

"He's adorable," I says, not because I think he is but because I feel left out of the conversation so it's something to say. Okay, I admit I do feel a little bit of a soft spot for the kid since he's named after Mr. O'Neill. In a few years, I probably won't mind him so much, not that I expect I'll be still coming over here in a few years.

"Man, Wendy," says Frank. "This is some cake. I'm going to have to go home and do a hundred sit-ups and run around the block to burn it off."

"Where's home?" John asks. "You haven't said where you're staying."

"I'm not sure yet," says Frank. "I have an interview tomorrow so I just drove up today. I'll have to go find a motel later."

"No, Frank. You'll stay here," says John.

"Oh well," says Frank. "Not if you have a family—I mean kids and all; I don't want to be in the way, and plus, you have company."

"I ain't company," I says. "I'm just an old lady they're being kind too."

"Lyla used to work for Mr. O'Neill," says Wendy, "so we invited her over to tell us what the house was like when she knew him."

"Who's Mr. O'Neill?"

"You know, Frank," says John. "The man who set me up to have this house—the author. I wrote and told you all that."

"Oh yeah, when you sent me your wedding invitation or something."

"John was really disappointed you couldn't come to the wedding," says Wendy. "He wanted you to be his best man."

"Well," Frank says, "I had a lot of stuff going on then—sorry."

"It's okay," says John. "My brother did fine. In fact, I think he was really touched that I asked him."

"How is your brother?"

"Okay, I guess. He lives in Duluth now."

I'm getting bored. So's the kid, apparently, because he's done with his cake now and curled up into a half-upside down ball in his chair. I feel like doing the same thing. I didn't come over here to watch old friends catching up, so I figure I'll just finish my dessert and go; thankfully, my coffee is now getting cool enough to drink. Hopefully, John will take me home then. I can always say I'm old and tired—they'll understand. But I did come to talk about the O'Neills, so I says, "Mr. O'Neill loved to sit out here. He was a real nature lover. Loved to look at the lake and trees and flowers and everything. He used to tell me stories about the Hundred Steps that went down to the harbor right by here too."

"Yes, they were just over there," says John pointing across the yard. "You can see everything from this porch. The ore dock, the lake, the harbor, most of the downtown buildings, and yet you feel secluded and safe from the rest of the world because you're so high up and the house reaches back farther toward the ridge than many of the others on the street."

"I've always thought it was so relaxing out here," I says. "It doesn't make you feel dizzy like the view from my apartment. I'm on the eighth floor, and I've got a great view of the cathedral, the lake, and the ore dock, but everything looks so small from up there."

"I always thought it must be a lot of fun though to live in a senior home," says Wendy. "Like being part of a community."

"Yeah," I agree, but it's not really like that. There's a few women I talk to there, but mostly I keep to myself. A lot of those old broads look down on me I think, though what with their dentures falling out and the spots on some of their dresses that they can't see, they shouldn't talk. Old age is the great equalizer, that's what I think.

"Anyone home?" calls a man's voice, followed by the man himself appearing from around the house. "No one answered when I rang the doorbell, but I saw cars in the yard."

My heart drops. It's Bill's son, Alan! He's the last person I want to see, except maybe for Bill. I knew I never should have come over here. I'd get up and make an excuse to leave right now if I hadn't been driven here. If I were ten years younger, I'd walk home. But as soon as John stands up, I can see I'm stuck while he plays host.

"Alan," he says, going halfway down the porch steps to welcome his cousin. "It's good to see you—although I wish it were under more pleasant circumstances."

"We're so sorry about your father, Alan," says Wendy. "How is he doing?"

"Thank you," he says, coming up onto the porch. "He's doing better, I think. At least, he's stable, but he looks pretty weak. It sure gave me a scare when Aunt Eleanor called me."

"I imagine," says Wendy. "Have you eaten supper?"

"Yes," said Alan.

"How about a piece of cake? We have plenty."

"Oh, it looks terrific," he says, eyeing what's left of Frank's piece. Frank set it aside after only eating a couple bites. Apparently, Frank is watching his boyish figure. If I were twenty years younger, I'd be watching his figure too.

"I'll be back in a minute with a piece for you," says Wendy, returning inside.

"You look tired," John says to Alan, who sits down in a chair across from him and next to Frank.

"Yeah, I am," Alan says, "but I just didn't feel like going home alone, and if I went over to Aunt Eleanor's, I'd just have to listen to her worrying—besides she was up at the hospital with me for half the day anyway, so I thought I'd come visit my cousin."

"Do you still live around here, Alan?" asks Frank.

Alan turns and looks kind of funny at him, like he's surprised that Frank knows his name, but then he says, "Frank Jarvi? I didn't know you still lived around here. John never told me."

"I just moved back," says Frank. "Just got into town today."

"Oh," says Alan. "How about that. I just got here Saturday night. I live downstate, but my dad's in the hospital so I came up. I'm staying at his house for who knows how long—until he's well I guess, although I'm doubtful whether he'll ever be well again."

"Alan's father, Great-Uncle Bill, had a heart attack a couple of days ago," John tells Frank.

"Oh, that's too bad," says Frank.

"Here we are, Alan," says Wendy, returning with his piece of cake.

"Thank you," he says.

"Would you like some coffee too?" she asks.

"Sure," he replies.

"How about you, Lyla?" Wendy asks me. "Do you need a warm up?"

"Sure," I says. I'm ready to go home but I can't expect John to take me right now when his friend and his cousin have both just shown up. At least the coffee will keep me warm, though it isn't as cold out here as I expected. It will be cold as soon as the sun starts going down, though.

As Wendy goes back inside for the coffeepot, I realize Alan is looking at me like he's trying to figure me out, and then I see recognition cross his face—I expect his look of surprise to end in some nasty comment, but instead, he says, "How have you been, Lyla?"

"Oh, you know," I says, like we're just making everyday conversation. "I've got the regular aches and pains for my age, but I'm still chugging along."

"Alan, did you know Lyla used to work for the O'Neills?" asks John. "We asked her over to tell us about what she remembers of the house when she worked here."

"Aunt Eleanor tells me you came up to the hospital Saturday to see my dad," says Alan.

"Yes," I says, uncertain how he might feel about my visiting Bill.

"Aunt Eleanor told me he kind of snapped at you. I'm sorry. He wasn't quite himself," says Alan.

"Oh well," I says politely like I'm dismissing it. But Bill was himself. I shouldn't have expected anything more from him, though I won't be rude and say so to his son.

Alan must be close to forty now I guess. He's all grown up, a man, not a boy anymore—he was only nineteen or twenty I think when me and Bill broke up. At least he's being polite now, though I doubt he likes me any more than he did back then.

"Aunt Eleanor said it was a great comfort to her to have you there with her, Lyla," Alan says. "I wish I could have gotten here sooner."

"How long do the doctors think your dad will be in the hospital?" I asks.

"They don't think Dad can ever go back home. Turns out he had a stroke too. He can't even get out of bed right now. At the very least, he's going to need some physical therapy. I'm afraid I may have to send him to a nursing home."

"Oh, no," says Wendy. "He's been doing so well up until now. He's always been very active for his age."

"I know, but he is eighty-five," says Alan. "Even if he gets better, I'd be afraid to have him living at home by himself anymore. We'll just have to wait and see. I have a couple weeks of vacation time coming so I can stay and try to get it all sorted out."

"That sucks, though," says Frank, "having to use up your vacation time like that."

"Well, school will be out next week and then my son can come up to stay too."

"So you and Gil will stay at your dad's house then?" asks John.

"Yes. That way if Dad can come home, I'll be there with him to watch him, but I somehow don't think that's going to happen."

"What about your brothers, Alan?" Wendy asks. "Are they coming up?"

"I don't know—maybe next weekend to visit, but not to stay. They have their families and their jobs to keep them busy. I guess, not being married, and not having full custody of my son, I'm the only one who can spare the time. If it wasn't that Gil's mother is downstate, I'd probably just move back up here so I could keep an eye on my dad. I kind of miss living up here anyway—I don't have any real family or friends down there that give me any reason to stay. At least I have relatives up here."

"I'm moving back," says Frank. "My friends back in Milwaukee can't believe I'd move back up here—they think this is a hick town, but my daughter lives here with her mom and stepdad now so I don't have any other choice if I want to be near her."

"What do people in Milwaukee know?" says John. "I'd rather live here than anywhere else in the world."

"We aren't that much of a hick town," says Wendy. "We're important enough that President Bush came up here to campaign last summer."

"That's not saying much," says Alan. "He's a bit of a hick himself."

"What do you mean—just because he's from Texas?" asks Frank.

"Just—well, maybe 'hick' isn't the right word, but backwards anyway."

"Backwards, how?" Frank asks. "His family's loaded."

"I mean," says Alan, "all that family values talk. All those conservative values—it's not being conservative—it's being narrow-minded and discriminatory. Especially the Republican stance on gay marriage. How are two people loving each other and committing to a relationship going to threaten a married man and woman? It's ridiculous. Republicans—they say they're all about freedom, but then they're trying to regulate our bodies and sex lives. I can't believe this country was dumb enough to reelect him."

"Yes, I don't agree with that either," says Wendy. "We voted for Kerry. John and I—well, you know how interested we are in genealogy—so don't be surprised but we found out that John's related to him."

"To Kerry? How's that?" Alan asks.

"He's descended like we are—I mean, you and me, Alan," says John, "from Thomas Dudley, the second governor of the Massachusetts Bay colony."

"Never heard of him," says Alan.

"Neither have I," I says, laughing. I never did put too much stock in family tree stuff.

"Well, Clara Henning," Wendy explains, "was descended from Thomas Dudley's daughter, the poetess, Anne Bradstreet. Clara is John's great-great-great-grandmother—not mine though, so I guess I'm not related to Kerry except by marriage to John. I'm descended from Gerald Henning's second wife, Sophia."

"You're right though, Alan," says Frank, no more interested in the family tree stuff than Alan or me, "who is Bush to tell people what to think about gay marriage or anything else? After all, the man's a recovering alcoholic so he should understand about 'There but for the grace of God go I.'"

I'm about to say, "But being gay just ain't natural," but I decide to keep my mouth shut. You can't tell these liberal young people anything these days, and sadly, the country's going to pot because of their ideas. It's bad enough there's girls with their bellies hanging out walking down Washington Street. Not that I know that the Republicans are much better—they're only for the rich, and I've never been rich so how am I suppose to identify with them?

I just hate to think where this country is headed, though I'll hopefully be gone before it gets too much worse. No one has any respect for what is right or wrong anymore. Maybe the nuns in the orphanage were strict, but they taught us what was what—so even if I didn't always do what was right, I felt guilt when I didn't. Today, I wonder if people even have a conscience anymore.

Alan shakes his head over Frank's comment but he doesn't say anything else. After a few seconds of silence, Frank says, "I better get going. I'll need to find a motel to stay in tonight. I just wanted to stop in to say hello and let you know I was in town."

"What do you mean you'll find a motel?" says John. "You'll stay here. I'll help you go carry in your luggage."

"Oh, no," says Frank. "I couldn't impose—you have Neill, and the tourists coming through the house, and—"

"So what? Old friends are always welcome," Wendy adds.

"No, no offense," says Frank, "but—well, you know me, John. Children make me uncomfortable—even my daughter still does—and this place is just a bit too fancy for me. I'd feel out of place and in the way."

"But you can't go to a motel," said John. "It might take you weeks to find an apartment."

"Why don't you come and stay with me?" Alan says, surprising me—after all, it's not his house but his father's that he's staying at.

"I thought you didn't live here?" says Frank.

"No, but I'm all alone staying at my father's house," says Alan, "and I could use some company to distract me from worrying about him. And my dad's not much of a housekeeper so you don't need to worry about making a mess."

"I don't want to impose," says Frank.

"You wouldn't be imposing. You'd be doing me a favor, so I don't sit around and mope all evening."

"Well, it would beat staying in a motel," says Frank, "but, hopefully, it will just be for a day or two. If I get the job I'm interviewing for tomorrow, I'll be able to rent an apartment right away. I do have some money saved up."

"Well, if you get sick of him, Alan," says John, "send him back here."

"Deal," says Frank. "Don't worry. I'll be coming over often."

"Alan, your dad wouldn't mind your having company in his house?" I can't help asking. I know how Bill would react.

"What he doesn't know won't hurt him," says Alan, "and it's just for a few days anyway." His voice doesn't sound irritated, but he gives me this look like I should mind my own business. I should have known better than to think he's quit hating me, just because he's grown up enough to know how to be polite.

"Well, I'll buy my own groceries," says Frank, "and it'll just be until I can find my own place."

"I should probably get going too," Alan says. "I'm pretty exhausted. Do you want to follow me over there, Frank? It's just across town in North Marquette."

"Sure," says Frank. "Thanks for the dessert, guys."

"Our pleasure," says Wendy. "We'll have to have you over often now that you've moved back. I'm sure you and John have a lot to catch up on."

"Yeah, we sure do," says Frank. "The stories I could tell you about this guy."

"Not as many as I could tell about you," John laughs, and then he stands up and follows Alan and Frank down the porch steps as he says, "You don't know what you're getting yourself into living with this guy, Alan. It's not pretty."

"I seem to remember," says Frank, "that Alan had a bit of a wild side himself back in the day. I remember many parties at his house."

"Yeah, well, that was before I had a son," says Alan. "I'm a lot quieter now."

"Well, we'll have to do something about that," laughs Frank. "I never let having a daughter stop me from having fun."

"Well, thanks again, Wendy, John," Alan says, stopping to look back at us on the porch.

"You're welcome," says John.

"It's good to have you home, Alan," Wendy replies.

"John, you got yourself a good one here," Alan says. "She acts like she's always been part of the family; I feel like I've known her my whole life."

"Well, actually, I always have been part of the family, you know," she says.

"That's just too weird for me," says Frank. "Cousins marrying I mean."

"We're fourth half-cousins, hardly a connection at all," says John, "but somehow, I think Madeleine Henning planned it that way."

"We sometimes wonder whether her ghost haunts the house," Wendy smiles. "I'm not sure a ghost can haunt a place where the person didn't die, but if she were going to haunt anywhere, we think it would be here. It just feels like I was drawn back here by someone. It's definitely home."

"And you've made it into a beautiful home," Alan replies.

"It's good to see you again, Alan," I says to be polite. I almost add, "Let me know how your father is doing," but I manage to stop myself. It's long been over between me and Bill. If he can't even go back home now, there's no point in thinking we could have a relationship. And I'm not going to sit around a nursing home to take care of him, even if he does decide to forgive me.

Frank and Alan go down the porch steps and around the house. John follows them to the corner of the house, waves goodbye, and then comes back up on the porch to sit down.

We all sit in silence for a moment, staring out at the sun starting to go down. I look at my watch and see it's already nine o'clock. John gets back up, opens the door to the house, and flips on the porch lights. They instantly add a nice warm glow to the moment. John sits back down and we all kind of breathe in the peace and quiet of the moment until John breaks it by saying, "Why didn't Frank call to let me know he was coming? And why wouldn't he stay here? We have the room, and he barely even knows Alan."

"I think he isn't comfortable with our being a family," says Wendy. "I mean he probably feels odd seeing his best friend from college married and with a house and a family, especially when he doesn't have any of that. I think he's kind of a drifter, not the settling down type; I don't know him but I just get that sense. Alan seems a bit like him—no wife, just a child from a broken relationship. I guess maybe they feel they can relate to each other."

"I don't know," says John. "I think he was kind of rude not to stay. Then again, Frank always was..."

He doesn't finish his sentence, but I can tell he's remembering less than positive things about his old friend—sort of like how I've been feeling about Bill. Sometimes you want to like someone, but the reality is different. All these years, I've built up Bill in my mind as my great love since he's the only man I ever had a serious relationship with, and I've been beating myself up for spoiling it, but now, after how he treated me the minute he saw me at the hospital—well, I realize I'm better off without him. Bill could be charming when he wanted, but it was all an act mostly, just to get what he wanted from you—I saw him turn on the charm to plenty of people he didn't really care about. I bet Alan's the same way—I got that sense by the way he acted all polite but then shot me that 'Mind your own business' look. I knew he still had a temper. The less I see of that family, the better—though I do like John and Wendy, and they can't be blamed for their relatives.

"I can see, John," says Wendy, "why you've always said the girls were taken with Frank. But it's strange to think he was your best friend in college—you seem so different."

"Yeah, we are," says John. "We just happened to be assigned as roommates in the dorms. I didn't pick him for a friend—he just kind of latched onto me really and I put up with him—well, that sounds mean. He does have his good points, but—I wonder how much he'll even bother with me now that he's moved back here. I've barely heard a word from him in the last ten years. I mean, he wouldn't even come up here for my wedding, so I really don't expect much."

"Maybe we should fix him up with your cousin," says Wendy.

"Who?" John asks.

"Julie?"

"Who's Julie?" I asks. "Another Whitman I don't know?"

"No," says John, "she's the daughter of my dad's brother, my uncle, Roger Vandelaare. He's moved to Marquette since his wife died, and so Julie's decided to move here too, but I don't think fixing Julie up with Frank would be a good idea."

"Why not?" Wendy asks. "She's pretty and she's pretty stable. She might be a good influence on him."

"I just don't think my best friend dating a family member would go over very well. Frank isn't the most stable person in terms of relationships."

It's quiet for a minute, and then Wendy says, "Neither is Alan from what I've heard."

"No," I can't help but add because I'm kind of irritated with him. "Alan was kind of a wild partier when he was in college from what I remember—I think he dropped out of school more than once." I know I shouldn't say anything, but the boy does rub me the wrong way—he always acted like I wasn't good enough to go out with his father—like his father was such a catch anyways.

"It was that Sheila that Alan hooked up with in college," says John. "She was the wild one—nothing but trouble. And then just as soon as she had his baby, she dumped him and married another guy. Poor Alan moved downstate just to be near his son without her even giving any thought to their son getting to be near his father." John just shakes his head and then says, "I guess I'm lucky. Not everyone can find the happiness I have." He gets up and steps over to kiss Wendy.

Their affection makes me uncomfortable so I turn and stare over the porch railing where I can see the Lower Harbor, all lit up now—the ore dock and the boats in the marina. It's the end of May—summer is here. I made it through another winter. I wonder how many more summers I'll have left. Not that it matters. I always think I should have some fun when summer arrives, but I never do.

"Are you cold, Lyla?" Wendy asks.

"No," I says, trying to hold back a yawn, "but I should probably get home. It's getting late."

"Yes, and I should put Neill to bed," says Wendy, "but I'm glad you came. Let me send you home with some of the leftovers."

"Thanks," I says, standing up so I can follow her into the kitchen. "I won't turn down leftover lasagna."

"I'm sorry our time together got interrupted," she says as we walk into the house. "We'll have to have you over again. Maybe we could get out a tape recorder and John could interview you about the O'Neills."

"That's a great idea," says John, who has collected the plates out on the porch and now followed us inside. "And I want to interview you about living in the orphanage too."

I'm not sure I want to come back to visit, but they're so nice and polite that I don't want to hurt their feelings, so I says, "Sure, we could do that."

John goes back out on the porch to bring in Neill, who's now groggy and just half-awake enough to stare at me again from his father's arms while Wendy finds an empty Cool Whip bucket to stick my lasagna in.

Five minutes later, I'm in the car and John is driving me home. He's kind of silent, and I sense it's because he's still kind of irritated by his friend Frank. We exchange a few comments about the warm weather and summer coming and then he drops me off at the door of Snowberry.

"Thanks again," I says. "Tell Wendy what a good cook she is."

"Thanks, I will," he says. "I'll give you a call and we'll do it again sometime."

"Okay," I says, hoping he doesn't. Then I go inside and up the elevator.

By the time I get up to my apartment and put the leftover lasagna in the refrigerator, I'm yawning. It's been a long day and I go get ready for bed right away.

I wonder whether John and Wendy really will invite me back over. They're nice enough, but I don't want to be involved with Bill or Alan. Somehow, I seem to be getting involved anyways. I feel kind of frustrated too—maybe just because I'm tired—and maybe it's because after seeing the old house again, I kind of miss the O'Neills. They were always good to me, but I was the hired help, so there always was a line between us. John and Wendy act like they want to be my friends, but I don't think that would be right. Nothing good can come from mixing with your betters, I think, and then I wonder where that idea came from. It's a stupid, old-fashioned idea, something Miss Florence probably would have said to me, but I guess it's true. John and Wendy are young and educated, and they apparently have a lot more going for them than I ever did. I have no business being involved with such people. It's no different than Miss Bergmann, or the Mitchells, either. Nothing good came from being around those people—just disappointment—only the O'Neills were really decent to me.

But even so, I do like John and Wendy. You can see they love each other and are happy to be a family. If there were more young people like them, I wouldn't think the world is going to pot.

You're just old, Lyla, I tell myself. But I'm not just old. I'm a pessimist and I've had good reason to be. There's no point in being hopeful or excited about making young friends. It can't last. They're just polite, like Alan; they can't possibly want to have anything more to do with an old lady like me. They're probably at home now talking about me, maybe laughing at the old lady who had to wear a sweater on Memorial Day.

By the time I crawl into bed, I'm grateful the day is over. Tomorrow I won't have anything to worry about like I did today.

Chapter 5

The next morning, I go with Bel to her doctor's appointment, but it isn't until we're in the car and on the way that she tells me where we're really going.

"I'm going to go see a shrink, and I don't know if I might be upset after talking to him so I just wanted you to come along in case I'm a basket case and can't drive home."

What the hell is she thinking? She knows I don't have a driver's license. I can't drive her home if she's a basket case, but I bite my tongue and instead asks the more important question.

"Oh," I says, "what made you decide to do that?" I can't help thinking she should have seen a psychiatrist a long time ago, though I don't know why she wants to start now.

"I just think I need to talk to someone about my problems," she says.

"Well, you tell me your problems all the time," I tell her. Hell, she's been telling me her problems for years and years. She'll usually go on and on about them too, but at the end of the day, I come away feeling good that she wants to talk to me, and whenever I think I've got problems, well, rather than having to whine to her about them, there she is as a reminder to me that some people have it worse—not that our lives have been that different—it's more that Bel just hasn't handled life as well as I have, but then for whatever reason, God just didn't make her as tough as me.

"I need an educated opinion," she tells me. "I mean, a professional one, from someone who understands about how the mind works."

"Bel," I half-laugh, "I doubt anyone will ever understand how your mind works."

"I'm serious, Lyla. You know, it's about my drinking mostly. I mean, yeah I quit years ago, but you know drinking is just a way to mask your symptoms—to hide deeper problems. I've always been afraid of looking deeper, but now, well, I just have my reasons, but I need to talk to someone who can help me."

I can hear she's pretty desperate—sort of like how she sounded after Charlie died from being an alcoholic and she realized she had better clean up her act if she didn't want to join him in the grave. I'm proud of her actually—I don't think she's had a drink in about thirty years now. But I also know it's possible she could fall off the wagon at any time. Still, after all these years, why does she need to go to a shrink now?

"Bel, after all these years, why a shrink now?" I asks.

"I just have things I have to cope with," she says.

"Like what? You've been doing fine for years now with not drinking."

"Well, but lately I've been feeling emotional, and I don't want to be too upset to drive myself home."

"Well, I can't drive you home, Bel. I don't even have a driver's license."

"Well, maybe you can calm me down enough to drive later."

I doubt that. I can feel my blood pressure rising just by listening to her. I swear her mind doesn't work right sometimes.

"Bel, you're fine, you know. I mean, I know all about your drinking problem, growing up in the orphanage, having an abusive husband. That was all years ago. You're fine."

"Sometimes, Lyla, I need to talk to someone who doesn't know all that about me, to get a new perspective, and—and—well, there's things about me, Lyla, that you don't know."

"Oh, really?" I says. "Bel, I've known you since you were eight years old. There's nothing about you I don't know. I think you just like the drama; when you solve one problem, you have to start making up new problems 'cause you don't know how to live without them."

"You're a real piece of work, Lyla Hopewell," she tells me. "Here I try to share something personal with you, and you just mock me."

I admit that what I just said didn't come out all that nice, but it's real early in the morning and I woke up late so I barely had one cup of coffee this morning. I'm hoping they'll have some at the doctor's office.

"I'm just saying," I says, "sometimes you let your problems get out of hand. You make them bigger than they are."

"Well, that's better than repressing them like you do. You always pretend you've got it altogether, but I know better."

"Yeah, I have problems. Who doesn't?" I says, "but I just don't get the point of whining about them like everyone does these days. I don't see how that helps anything."

"Hmmph," she says. I know I upset her, but she knows better than to argue with me before I've had my second cup of coffee. It's just my nature to be a little crabby in the morning. I'm trying to fight the cloudy fatigue feeling from not having had enough caffeine yet. I look over at her, trying to think of something to say to lighten the mood when I can see she's got tears coming down her cheek. Oh jeez, here she goes with the mushy stuff.

"I love you, Lyla," she says. "You're my best friend, but sometimes I wonder why. Sometimes you don't treat me like you love me."

She pulls the car into the medical center's parking lot and finds a parking place while I try to figure out how to reply to what she just said. All I can think to say is, "You know, I didn't have my second cup of coffee yet so I'm still a little crabby," but that sounds kind of lame since something really is bugging her, even if it's just in her head.

Finally, when she turns off the car, I open my door and says, trying to sound serious, "Let's go in now and get you the help you need."

She doesn't say anything back, but we get out of the car and walk into the building.

"I'm sorry if you don't think my problems are legitimate, Lyla," she says to me, ignoring that people in the hallway might overhear her. "We just have different ways of dealing with things is all. That doesn't mean one way is the right or the wrong way."

"No, I guess not," I mutter, spotting a coffee shop area as she stops to look at a map and then leads us upstairs. I figure I'll come back here to get my coffee if the shrink doesn't have coffee in the waiting room.

We go upstairs and down a hall—I don't know what the suite number is and Bel doesn't tell me, so I just follow her until she stops at a door and opens it. I look over her shoulder and spot a coffeepot on a little table in the reception area so I immediately head over to it while Bel goes up to the receptionist to let her know she's there. The coffee doesn't look too fresh, and all they have is powdered cream, but it's better than nothing—I'll even put up with the Styrofoam cup. After a minute, I throw away my stir stick and go sit down next to Bel to wait. She looks tense, but I don't say anything to her. I won't encourage her to air her business in the waiting room—even if we are the only ones there—it's none of the receptionist's business anyways.

After a minute, the receptionist comes out into the waiting room with a clipboard for Bel to fill out. She hands it to her, then asks, "Is this your sister?"

"Sort of," says Bel.

"I'm her friend," I says. "I'm moral support."

I think it's kind of funny that I say that, but neither the receptionist nor Bel says anything back.

"Lyla is my best friend," says Bel. "She's the closest thing I have to family. We grew up together in the orphanage."

"Oh my," says the receptionist. "That's interesting. I've always wondered what it must have been like to grow up in there."

"Trust me; you don't want to know," I says.

After a minute, Bel has her papers signed and she hands the receptionist back the clipboard.

"If you'll just follow me, Mrs. Greenway," she says to Bel, "I'll take you in to see the doctor."

"Okay," she says.

I watch her get up and follow the receptionist through a door. Then I look around and see there's nothing good to read in the reception room.

A minute later, I look over and see the receptionist sitting behind her little sliding window. For a moment, we make eye contact but she kind of gives me a smirk. Maybe she thought I was rude the way I said, "Trust me; you don't want to know." But she doesn't really. People say things to you like they want to know about growing up in the orphanage, but they don't want the truth. This woman, she thought it was "interesting." I don't know what's interesting about it. People act like they think it was some kind of glamorous adventure, but it wasn't.

The only good I can think of that ever came out of my being in that orphanage is that I met Bel there. Yes, she drives me crazy and has since the first day I met her, but what she's lacked in smarts she's made up for in loyalty. She has plenty of irritating habits, but I've been looking after her all these years so I know that's not going to change now.

The coffee tastes like crap and gets cold fast so I pour myself another cup and add extra sugar and cream to kill the taste. Then I pick up a copy of *Good Housekeeping* because it's that or some science magazine that'll be over my head or some dirt bike/motorcycle thing. It's hard to pick between them since, after all the years I cleaned other people's homes, good housekeeping is about the last thing I care about. After looking at a couple stupid recipes, I find I'm just flipping pages without seeing anything. I can't help thinking about the orphanage now that it's in my head. I don't think about it in too much detail usually, but I guess it's always there, kind of just stuck in the back of my mind all the time, but today I can't help wondering what Bel's latest problem is, and it makes me remember my first day at the orphanage, the day I met her, back in 1938.

I was mad as hell to go to the orphanage. Papa was gone—God knows where really—Mama had said Karelia, wherever that was—somewhere in Finland or Russia—I'm still not all that sure where it is today, and Mama wouldn't talk about it back then. Jessie told me when we were older that Mama was ashamed that Papa had left us to go there and she didn't want to go live in Russia anyways, but supposedly, Papa had gone to get settled and then was going to send for us—only he never did and for all we knew then, he could have been dead. And then Mama died.

Before Miss Bergmann stuck her nose into our business, Jessie and I went to live with our neighbors, the Powells, for a few weeks. I know Mrs. Powell meant well, but her son Ned was a little monster. I swear he punched me in the arm at least three times every day that I stayed there, and when I finally slugged him back, Mrs. Powell locked me in the closet for what seemed like hours; of course, she never punished her son.

I don't know why Mrs. Powell even took us in—she clearly thought we were beneath her, but maybe she thought it was her Christian duty. She told Jessie and me that our cousin was coming from Minnesota to adopt us—that she had written to him—Jessie had found the address for the cousin among Mama's things. But then I think the cousin changed his mind, so Jessie somehow maneuvered it so Miss Bergmann would adopt her—you would think Jessie'd have put in a good word for her sister with the old lady, but no, my sister was never anything but selfish—always looking out for herself, always trying to make herself seem better than me by telling me what to do, and she liked to act superior too, just because she was taking those damn piano lessons from Miss Bergmann, though from the way she would bang on that old piano Mama had and hit wrong keys all the time, she couldn't have even gotten herself a job playing in a honky tonk joint back then. She must have gotten better though 'cause Miss Bergmann sent her to some fancy music school later, but so what? She should have been looking out for her little sister—the only real family she had left—not sucking up to her music teacher, but the only person Jessie ever thought about was Jessie.

When Mrs. Powell told us Miss Bergmann would be coming the next day to pick Jessie up, she told me to pack my bags too. When I asked her where I was going, she just said Miss Bergmann would explain everything tomorrow. And when tomorrow came and I asked Miss Bergmann where I was going—I remember it like yesterday 'cause those words were such a shock to me—she told me, "Lyla, I've been asking around to find you a family, but I haven't had any luck. I'll keep trying, but for now, we're going to take you to the orphanage. You'll like it there. You'll have lots of other little boys and girls to play with."

"'Like it there'?" I remember thinking. "Is the old lady crazy?" That's what I wanted to ask her, but I didn't say a word. I was only ten and didn't know too many swear words yet. I'd have liked to have used a good one on her right then if I had dared, but I knew it wouldn't do me no good. She wasn't going to do anything to help me so there wasn't any point in getting mad at her. I just sat in the back of her car with my arms crossed, my lips pouting, and feeling like I wanted to rip the isinglass curtains right out of her back windows just to show her, but since it was snowing out—it was in February—I didn't because it was already cold enough in the car.

When we pulled up to the orphanage, Miss Bergmann told Jessie to wait in the car while she took me in. I remember her saying, "We'll just be a minute," which made me think she wanted to get rid of me as fast as she could, and that's about all the time she did stay too. Jessie didn't even get out of the car to give me a hug, and Miss Bergmann didn't think to suggest it. Jessie was probably too busy thinking about how she'd have a room of her own once she got to her new home rather than having to share one with me.

Miss Bergmann pulled my suitcase out of the back seat, set it on the ground, and shut the door. Then she picked up the suitcase and tried to take my hand, but I yanked it away. She made an annoyed face, said, "Come on," and started up the orphanage's front steps. Since I didn't have a better option, I followed her up to the top step where a tall nun in a black habit stood with the door open. When we got close, the nun stepped out onto the porch.

"Hello, Miss Bergmann," she smiled. "This must be Lyla. Welcome to your new home, Lyla."

I glared at the nun since she was Miss Bergmann's accomplice—I didn't know that word then, but I sure knew they were in it together and she was another adult going to tell me what to do.

"I'm Sister Euphrasia," she said, "and I'll make sure you're comfortable here, Lyla, and have everything you need."

"I brought her things, Sister," said Miss Bergmann, handing my suitcase to her. "Poor thing didn't have much in the way of good clothes since her parents were so poor, but I bought her some new underwear and stockings. I trust she'll take care of them, and if she needs anything else, I'll do what I can. You just let me know."

"You've already done more than your share, Miss Bergmann," said Sister Euphrasia, "and we appreciate it."

"Jessie and I will come by to visit you some time soon, Lyla," Miss Bergmann then said to me. They did come visit too, about three months later. That's how much they cared for me. I saw them at Christmas, and for the first year or two, on my birthday, and then they forgot about that too.

"Come, Lyla. I'll show you your new home," said Sister Euphrasia, turning around and still carrying my suitcase.

"Goodbye, Lyla," Miss Bergmann said. I thought I heard just the slightest bit of guilt in her voice and I was glad for it. But the guilt is probably why she stayed away, rather than it working to my benefit. Not only was she nosy, but she was a coward too—her and my sister were perfectly suited for each other—both selfish and too cowardly even to admit it.

Sister Euphrasia took my hand, and oddly enough, I let her, hoping Miss Bergmann was still watching and would see it as a slight. Then I walked through that orphanage door and it shut behind me, blocking me from the real world for the next four years—from the time I was ten until I was fourteen when I was forced to go out to fend for myself.

I remember Sister leading me down the hall to an office. We passed a couple nuns in the hallway who simply bowed their heads to us; a little girl was being led by one, but she turned her head away from me, looking ashamed like maybe she was in trouble for something, and the stern look on the nun's face only confirmed that. The nun even glared at me when I looked at her.

After a minute, I was led into an office where Sister Euphrasia told me to take a seat in front of her desk. She then shut the door behind us and took a seat across from me.

"Lyla," she said. I can remember it like it was yesterday the way it's all coming back to me. "I don't have to tell you why you're here. I'm sorry that your parents died. But you have to make the best of it now."

"They didn't both die," I said to her, "just my mom."

"I know it's hard for you to lose them, but you must face reality."

"My father's not dead," I insisted. "He went to Finland. He'll be back though."

She looked confused and shuffled some papers on her desk. When she finally picked up one, she stared at it for a minute.

"That's right. I'd forgotten about that. Well, you can't hope that he'll be back, Lyla. It's not very likely you know. The Communists might do anything to him. It's best for you to accept that you're an orphan now, and while I know that isn't a pleasant thought, and I'm sorry for your loss, it also means that you're not special in any way. Almost all the children here are orphans whose parents have died, or at least, their parents can't afford to take care of them. In any case, don't expect to get any special treatment because your parents have died. We can't treat you special here because the outside world won't treat you special when you enter it."

I didn't know what to say to that. I hadn't asked for any special treatment. I just wanted to be treated like my sister—but I supposed having a rich lady adopt you was special treatment.

"We have a schedule here and there are things expected of you," said Sister Euphrasia, sternly peering over her glasses at me, "and that includes being on schedule. You'll get up with the other children, get dressed, and eat with the other children. You'll do your chores, go to school, and go to bed as expected of you. We won't tolerate any spoiled behavior. I understand you have a bit of a habit of acting spoiled, but we won't tolerate that here. Is that understood?"

"Yes, ma'am," I said. I understood, but I didn't like it. Right from the start, I could see Sister Euphrasia and me were getting off on the wrong foot, and I didn't have much hope we'd ever see eye to eye—even if I did grow up to be as tall as her. I wasn't trying to be difficult back then, but I probably did end up being more difficult than I needed to be since she obviously expected me to be difficult. I mean, kids will act the way adults want them to act, and even though she said she wanted me to be good, I think she expected me to be difficult, so I guess I tried not to let her down.

"I've seen your grades from school, Lyla," Sister Euphrasia told me while looking back at her papers. Then she looked up to peer at me over her glasses. "Suffice it to say, I am not impressed. Your teachers say you are stubborn and lazy. You need to know that I expect you to work harder while you're here. You have no one but yourself now to depend on in this world, and you'll have to work hard if you want to amount to anything and be able to take care of yourself when you're older. If you're lucky, someday you'll make a good wife and mother, or perhaps you'll even find a religious calling like myself, or you—"

"I don't want to be no nun," I said, "and I don't want to be married or have kids, either. Husbands can't be depended on. That's what Mama said after Papa left."

"I will not tolerate your interrupting me!" Sister Euphrasia snapped. "Your future success will depend a lot on your learning some manners."

"Sorry," I said, but I wasn't. What right did she have to tell me what I should grow up to be? But she apparently thought differently 'cause she started telling me when I should get up, when to go to bed, and on and on about the chores. You'd have thought I was joining the army or something. I don't know when I stopped listening to her, but eventually, she got up from her desk and opened the door and another nun came in.

"Sister Perpetua, this is Lyla," Sister Euphrasia introduced us.

"Hello, Lyla," said Sister Perpetua, slightly bowing to me with a smile. "Welcome to Holy Family."

"Hello," I said, sizing her up. She looked nicer than Sister Euphrasia. She was too, I would later find out, though a bit ditzier.

"Lyla," said Sister Euphrasia, "Sister Perpetua will show you where you'll sleep, and then you can go outside and meet some of the other children before suppertime."

I got up from the chair, but I didn't say anything, though I appreciated how Sister Perpetua kept smiling after I'd had to deal with Sister Euphrasia's sternness.

"Poor thing," said Sister Perpetua to Sister Euphrasia. "It's always difficult to adjust."

Sister Euphrasia didn't reply, just told Sister Perpetua where my bed would be, and she then turned to me and said, "I hope you'll be as happy here as can be expected, Lyla."

"Thanks," I said, afraid she'd lecture me for being rude otherwise.

"Come, Lyla," said Sister Perpetua. She reached for my hand, but my reflex was to hide it behind my back. "Is this your bag?" she asked, looking at my suitcase next to the desk.

"Yes," I said.

"Very good," she said, picking it up by the handle and heading out the door. I followed behind her, and in another minute, I began to find my way through the maze of hallways and rooms that made up Holy Family Orphanage—my home for the next four years—I remember Sister Euphrasia telling me it would be four years because when I turned fourteen I'd have to leave and go out to work in the world—but fourteen seemed like a lifetime away at that point.

Sister Perpetua led me up the stairs and to a big dormitory room lined with beds. "The girls sleep here," she said. "It's nothing fancy, but it's a warm room and the girls all get along well together. Your bed is over here." She led me almost to the end of the room to a bed. There was a trunk for me to put my clothes in, which didn't take long to do. Sister let me put my suitcase under my bed. I was embarrassed that it took so little time to put my underwear and three dresses away, and part of that was what Miss Bergmann had bought for me. Later, though, I'd find out that lots of the other girls came here with even less than that.

Sister showed me the washroom and then took me downstairs to see the schoolroom.

"You have some time before supper," she said, "and it's a pretty warm day for February. Since you still have your coat on, would you like to go outside where the other children are playing and meet some of them?"

"I guess," I said, shrugging my shoulders. She had a kind voice, rather like my mother's, so I almost would have rather stayed with her, even if she was a nun, than play with the other kids, but I followed her outside.

We went back down the big steps into the front yard where a couple of the younger girls were building a snowman. "Girls, this is Lyla. Lyla, this is Belinda and Janet."

"Hi," said Belinda. "You can call me Bel."

"Hi," I said.

Janet just stared at me without saying anything.

"Well, I'll leave you girls to get further acquainted," said Sister Perpetua, abandoning me to these strangers.

Belinda didn't look like she knew what to say to me. Janet started packing snow up into a mound.

"That's not how you make a snowman," I told her. "You need to roll it."

Janet didn't look up or even act like she heard me.

"Roll it?" Bel asked.

"Yeah," I said. "Haven't you ever made a snowman before? Here, I'll show you."

I reached down to pick up some snow and make a snowball. Then I knelt down and rolled it in the snow and kept rolling it until it grew into a giant snowball. I kept moving farther away from them, with my back to them, as the snowball got bigger and harder to push.

"Go away!" screamed Bel.

I looked back, wondering why she was yelling. Two big boys, older than me at least, were standing over her and Janet. One of them gave Bel a push.

"Go away yourself," he said. "We want to play here. No girls allowed."

"Yeah," said his friend. "No girls allowed!"

"We were here first," said Bel, but Janet took off running around the side of the building.

"I don't care," the first boy said to Bel. "You know this is boy's territory. Girls play on the other side."

"No, we were here first," Bel insisted.

"Get lost!" he shouted, and this time he pushed her hard, down onto the ground.

That was it. I jumped up from where I'd been crawling on the ground to roll my snowball. I ran over and helped Bel to get up.

"Who's this?" the boy asked.

"It's Lyla, my new friend," said Bel, on her feet and brushing snow off her coat.

"Well, what's good for Bel is good for Lyla," he said, and he stepped over, planning to give me a push, but before he could do that, I kicked him right in his nuts.

To this day, I don't know how I knew to do that. It was just some sort of automatic reflex, but he immediately bent over; he looked like he wanted to howl in pain, but he was too out of breath to do anything but collapse on the ground and roll up into a ball.

"Hey!" screamed his friend in shock. I just looked at the friend, daring him to try anything. In a second, he'd run up the front steps and disappeared into the orphanage.

"What'd you do that for?" cried the bully, still on the ground, tears running down his face.

"Because you're a bastard, that's why!" I said.

He just lay there, clutching his privates and looking up at me like a wounded animal.

"Do you think that makes you tough, you little shrimp, picking on girls half your age?" I asked him. "I'll kick you in the nuts again if you ever lay another finger on Bel or any other girl. Do you hear me?"

He didn't answer. He was still laying on the ground trying to catch his breath and clutching his nuts, like that was going to help protect them now.

"That girl, Sister!" I heard his friend holler from the top of the steps.

By the time I looked, Sister Euphrasia was down the steps and running over to us. At the same time, I became aware that several other children were surrounding us because they must have heard the bully's screams.

"What's going on here?" demanded Sister Euphrasia.

"The new girl kicked Charlie in his business," said the tattletale friend.

Sister Euphrasia looked from the tattletale to me and then to Charlie, who was still rolling around on the ground. I saw Sister's eyes grow big as she looked down to where Charlie's hands were clutched in the most inappropriate place imaginable. She drew in her breath, silently shrieking, then screamed out a man's name, and in a second, some sort of janitor appeared.

The janitor rushed over, picked up Charlie, and brought him into the building. Then Sister Euphrasia stepped up to me. I glared at her, just daring her to tell me I did something wrong, but rather than speak, she grabbed me by the ear and dragged me toward the building. I tried to pull away, but she only tightened her grasp until I felt her fingernails digging into my earlobe. With tears springing to my eyes, I struggled to keep up with her until she got me to the steps. Then she sort of flung me down into a sitting position on them.

"Lyla Hopewell, it's your first day here and you've already started causing trouble. What do you have to say for yourself?"

"I was trying to protect Bel," I said. "He pushed her down in the snow. He was trying to boss us around. I'm not going to let no boy treat a girl that way."

She just looked at me, surprised by my words—surprised I'd be so hotheaded and say so much.

"Belinda, are you okay?" she asked. Bel had walked over to the steps to see what was going to happen. "Uh huh," she said.

"Go back to playing then," Sister told her before turning her attention back to me. "As for you, Lyla, I already warned you that I'm not going to put up with your troublemaker behavior. This is your final warning. Now go up to your room and wash up for supper, and if you ever kick a boy in his business again, you won't like the punishment I'll dole out to you."

I shrugged my shoulders and went in the building. I was actually surprised she was letting me off so easily. I thought she'd take a ruler to me. Maybe she didn't know what to do about a girl kicking a boy in the nuts—I doubt she'd ever had to deal with that before.

I went upstairs like I was told. None of the kids in the hallways or on the stairs dared to look at me. Luckily, I remembered how to get back up to the dormitory where my bed was. A couple girls were in the dormitory room now, playing on the floor, but I just ignored them and went into the washroom. I didn't know what I had to wash up for—I wasn't dirty, but I ran my hands under the warm water anyways since they were cold from playing with the snow. Then I took off my coat and laid it on my bed, not knowing what else to do with it. I was just about to turn around to go back downstairs, figuring it was time to eat, when I heard footsteps running after me and a voice shouting, "Lyla!"

It was Bel.

"Oh, Lyla, thank you," she said. "I hope you didn't get into too much trouble. But I'm glad you kicked Charlie like that. He deserved it."

For the first time that day, I cracked a smile that grew until I felt myself grinning from ear to ear. And Bel started laughing and I joined her. After a minute, she said, "We better go down for supper. Don't leave your coat on the bed or the Sisters will scold you. I'll show you where to put it."

"Thanks," I said, following her to a closet. She took my coat and hung it up. Then she took my hand and led me downstairs. "This way," she said.

I felt like pulling back my hand. I wasn't used to people touching me. Even Mama hardly ever touched me. I didn't like it. But Bel meant it kindly enough. It wasn't like she did it to control me like Miss Bergmann or Sister Euphrasia had when they tried to hold my hand.

By the time we were down the stairs, the other kids were gathering for supper so Bel introduced me to a bunch of them, though I knew I wouldn't remember all their names. A few of them said things like, "You're the one who kicked Charlie" or "I hear you gave Charlie a good one" or "I hope the next time you kick Charlie that I don't miss it." But then Sister Perpetua and another nun I didn't know yet appeared and hushed everyone before ushering us into the dining hall.

Once we were seated, we all had to bow our heads in prayer, something I wasn't used to doing. When Papa was still at home, we all used to go to the Lutheran church together, but Mama quit taking us once he was gone. We never prayed at meals. This praying stuff was strange. The sister talking was asking God to teach us to be thankful, but I didn't feel thankful about anything. I felt out of place, and once our heads were back up and the food started being passed around, I just felt irritated with all the noise and commotion. Eventually, I would get used to it, but that first day, it felt overwhelming.

I don't remember much else from that day like what we ate or what we did after supper—probably chapel and prayers and maybe some playtime I imagine. Funny, I can't really remember what our daily schedule was either after all these years. But I do remember what happened that first night after we went back upstairs and the lights went out.

I was laying there on my back, wondering if I'd ever get used to that place. I had heard the nuns praying and talking about God, but it was easy for them—they were nuns, all holy and stuff, I figured, never bad like me. Sister Euphrasia had said I was stubborn and spoiled, and I knew I was stubborn, but I'd never been spoiled. You have to have rich parents to be spoiled. But I knew I had always been whiny and bossy around Jessie, although I didn't really know why. It's not that I didn't want to be good—just that no one had ever given me a chance to be. The nun at supper had said we were supposed to be grateful and thank God for what we had, but I felt like God couldn't like me very much if He let Mama die and Papa leave us and now even my own sister didn't want to be around me. What did I have left to thank God for?

I just felt sorry for myself, and the thought of the next four years in the orphanage didn't make me feel much hope for the future. I was angry a lot at night while I lived there, thinking about how Jessie must be sleeping in a nice comfy bed with a fluffy pillow and a new teddy bear that Miss Bergmann probably bought for her. One time—it must have been Jessie's birthday or something, so Miss Bergmann let me come over to visit—I got to see Jessie's room; she had so much—fancy bedspread, fancy curtains, and nice furniture. It seemed like she had more toys than half the kids in the orphanage put together—Miss Bergmann had bought her tons of dolls—and Jessie had the nerve then to tell me how she didn't even like them because she was too old to play with them.

Anyways, that first night, I was just laying there in bed, feeling sorry for myself, when I heard Bel, who happened to have the bed next to mine, whisper to me, "Thank you again for standing up for me, Lyla."

"You're welcome," I said.

"You sure did kick Charlie hard. I don't think he'll ever pick on me or any girl ever again."

"I hope not," I said. "I don't like when boys are mean. It just got me riled up, I guess, the way he was behaving."

"Well, I just thank you," Bel whispered. I didn't say anything back. But then after a minute, she said, "Lyla, does...will...will you be my friend now?"

Had I known then what I know now...oh, I'm just being mean thinking that just because she was so irritating in the car on the way here. I know she has a lot of good points, even though being her friend hasn't been a bed of roses, that's for sure.

Anyways, when she asked me to be her friend, I didn't know what to say. I didn't have any friends—never had really. All the kids at school had always been snotty to me—or maybe I was snotty to them, but either way, I didn't know what a friend really was. Still, I figured in this place maybe I'd need one since it wasn't like school where I just had to put up with the other kids for a few hours and then could go home. So, I said, "Sure." That's all I could think to say.

And then I heard her moving around in her bed, and then she was standing next to my bed and starting to crawl into it. Not knowing what to do, I moved over so she didn't sit on top of me. Then once she was in bed, she put her arms around me and hugged me tight and said, "Thanks, Lyla. I—I'll be the best friend I can ever be to you. I promise. I'll do anything I need to so I'll be your bestest friend. I've really wanted a friend."

She cuddled her head into my nightgown sleeve and I could hear her sobbing.

Oh jeez, I thought. I didn't bargain for being friends with a crybaby. "Do you have a handkerchief to blow your nose?" I asked her.

"I'm sorry," she said, and I could hear her trying to suck her snot back up her nose. "It's just, I never had a sister or nobody special. Some of the other girls, they remember their parents and talk about their moms or their big sisters. Even though their moms or sisters died, at least they had them. I never had that. You're the closest thing I've ever had to a real friend, Lyla."

"That's all right," I said. "You're not missing out on anything 'cause I've got an older sister who got adopted, and she's never cared about me."

"Is that why you did it, Lyla? Because you know what it's like not to have anyone look out for you?"

"I guess so," I said.

"Your sister can't be very nice or smart," she said. "I don't see how anyone could not care about you, Lyla. You're nice, and—and I think you're pretty too."

"Thanks," I said, surprised. Even Mama had never really told me I was pretty. Once when one of the neighbors had said I was pretty, Mama had just said, "Don't tell her that or it will turn her head" and then Jessie had said, "Too late for that. Lyla's already stuck up." I kind of liked now that someone thought I was pretty.

Bel moved a little bit, no longer hugging me but still cuddling up against me. "Lyla?" she asked.

"What?" I whispered.

"Can I sleep here for a little while? Sometimes I have bad dreams at night, but I feel safe with you."

"Okay," I said, "but we better go to sleep before the nuns hear us."

"Okay," she said. "Good night, Lyla."

"Good night," I said.

I rolled over and turned my back to her, and she cuddled up against me. I didn't like it—it made me feel hot and uncomfortable, but after a few minutes, I could hear her snoring, and then she rolled over to the other side of the bed.

When I woke up in the morning, I was all alone. She'd gone back to her bed. It was a good thing 'cause I'm sure she'd have been in trouble if the nuns had caught her.

That was—sixty—yeah, sixty-seven years ago, and Bel and I have been friends ever since—even when I wasn't so sure I wanted her around. Though

I admit most of the time I haven't minded it. She's done her best to be a good friend to me, and considering my personality, I guess she's the best I could do for a friend, so I can't complain too much.

Now that I've had my coffee, nasty as it was, I decide I'll be nicer to her on the way home. Much as I hated the orphanage, sometimes I realize it calms me down to think about it. Makes me grateful I'm not there anymore. Whenever my life gets tough, I realize it could be worse—I could still be stuck there, so I should be thankful. I'm a lot better off now than I was back then.

Chapter 6

When she comes out of the office, Bel doesn't say anything to me about her appointment with the shrink. I wait until we're out of the building for her to say something, but she doesn't.

Finally, on the way home, I asks her, "So, how'd it go?"

"Fine!" she snaps.

Obviously, it didn't go fine, but I'm not going to get her upset when she's driving.

She usually tells me everything, and usually far more than I want to know, so it has to be pretty bad if she doesn't want to talk about it.

I imagine the shrink told her she really is nuts, which is what I would have expected, but she's been nuts all her life, so I don't know what the point is in trying to fix things at her age.

When we get back to Snowberry, she still doesn't say anything until we get into the elevator.

"Are you going up to your apartment?" I asks.

"Yeah," she says, so I push the button for her floor and mine, and when she gets off on hers, I says, "Okay. I'll see you later."

I feel like I should have asked her what was wrong and whether she wants to talk about it, so I call her up about ten minutes later to see if she wants to come over for lunch, but she says, "No. I have leftovers in the fridge that I have to eat."

"Okay," I says, wondering why she doesn't ask me to help her eat the leftovers. But if she wants to be moody, let her, I figure.

I call her again just before suppertime, but this time she tells me she's not hungry, so the heck with her. I don't know what her problem is, but she should have gotten over it years ago after all those AA meetings she's gone to. I'm not going to let her attitude problem ruin my night. She'll probably feel better in the morning anyways.

So I have supper and watch some TV and read *The Mining Journal* and go to bed.

When I hear the telephone ring, my bedside clock says 3:12 a.m. Only one person ever calls me at that hour. It was when I realized these calls were starting to become a habit that I bought a cordless phone to put by my bed. I'm not one to waste money on all the latest gadgets, but it was worth it not to have to jump out of bed to answer the phone.

"Hello," I says.

"Lyla, it's Bel." Like it could be anyone else. "You asleep?" she asks.

"Nah, just lying here trying to sleep," I lie.

"I've been thinking a lot about going to that women's meeting tomorrow," she says. "And it's making me kind of nervous."

"Yeah, well, I imagine so, but it'll be fine once you go. It's the waiting that's hard." That sounded pretty good, I think, considering I'd completely forgotten about agreeing to go to the women's meeting with her.

"Yeah, but I can't get my mind off it. I can't sleep, and since I didn't eat supper, now I'm hungry."

I knew it was one of those calls. About once a week, she calls me late at night, worried about something, and at least once a month, it means we have to go somewhere. I don't mind that much though. I like pancakes.

"I could use a little snack," I says. After all, by the time she gets done talking to me, I probably won't fall back asleep and will just get up to make breakfast anyways.

"Really? I was afraid you'd be angry with me calling."

"Nah, I'm kind of hungry. I know I grumble sometimes, but I don't really mind going once in awhile."

"Aren't you tired from having been out the night before last and then getting up early yesterday morning to go to the doctor with me?"

"No, and I can't sleep either," I lie. I mean, at least she's talking to me now. She doesn't get silent unless something is really bothering her, so I'm glad whatever it was is over. Maybe she'll tell me now, or tomorrow at the women's meeting.

"Okay. I'll call for a pick up and then meet you down in the lobby," she says.

"Okay. I'll be ready."

I hang up the phone and then crawl out of bed. It's funny when you get old how time doesn't matter that much. I never would have gone out to breakfast at four in the morning when I was working, but now, what else do I have to do? I can come home and have a nap before we go to the women's meeting at noontime.

I mind even less now that The Pancake House opened up. I never cared for the Big Boy's pancakes, just their French toast, but after the place burned down, I didn't know what Bel and I would do. But not only did The Pancake House open, but it'll send someone to pick you up 24/7 if you want a ride so you can go eat there. Of course, Bel has a car, but she doesn't see that well at night, and why waste gas if the restaurant is willing to pick us up?

It doesn't take me long to dress and then I head downstairs. Bel is already down there waiting for me. After a minute of sitting quietly in the lobby and stifling a couple yawns, we see the car pull up. Sybil, our regular driver, gets out to open the doors for us like we're a couple old ladies—well, we are but we can still open our own doors. Still, it's nice that she's friendly. She's a pretty girl too, so I don't know what she's doing driving a car around in the middle of the night to pick up old ladies so they can go have pancakes. I'm surprised she doesn't have a husband, but then again, maybe she's smart not to.

That possibility doesn't stop Bel from starting in on Sybil before we've even pulled out of Snowberry's parking lot, just like she always does.

"Sybil, I'd think a pretty girl like you would be out on a hot date at night," says Bel. "Or down there at the Mattrix doing the Macarena."

"They don't do the Macarena anymore," Sybil laughs. "They haven't for years."

"Well, breakdancing then, or whatever you young people do now," says Bel. "I don't understand why you don't have a young man yet. How old are you now?"

"I'm twenty-eight," says Sybil.

"Twenty-eight and still single with all that beautiful hair of yours," says Bel, shaking her head. "Why, I'd already been married half my life by the time I was your age. I don't understand you young independent women who don't get married."

"Don't listen to her, Sybil," I says. "I'm seventy-seven, and I still haven't found the right one, and chances are, if the right one ever did exist, he's dead now anyways."

"Oh, I don't worry about it," says Sybil. "He'll come if he's meant to."

"Well, I think you need to go out and find him," says Bel. "Otherwise you never will. He should have shown up by now."

"Oh, Bel, leave her be," I says.

"I'm just too busy right now," says Sybil.

"Yeah, but I forget," I says. "What do you do besides drive us to breakfast at 4 a.m.?"

"I write for *The Mining Journal*, and I help out my friend May at May's Antiques."

"Oh, yeah, I've been down there," I says, "but not as a customer—to get rid of stuff I didn't want anymore."

"I didn't know you wrote for the paper, Sybil," says Bel. "You should have lots of advantages then to meet cute young guys—like you could interview a strapping young firefighter when a house burns down, or a police officer at an accident, or some successful young lawyer who's opening his own practice. Lots of opportunities."

"That wouldn't be professional, to hit on the guys I interview," says Sybil.

"If you want to find a husband, sometimes you have to break a few rules," says Bel. "And you're too pretty for any fellow to mind if you hit on him."

"I don't know," says Sybil.

I give Bel a good poke in the leg so she'll quit bothering the girl. I don't know why Sybil's still single, but I know how I hated people getting on my case about being single. I don't see what the big deal is if she doesn't get married. Sex is overrated anyways—it feels good for a few minutes, but then you're stuck with some man wanting you to feed him and iron his shirts and keep his house clean while he burps and farts and acts like a pig. And then if he gets you pregnant, well, you might as well figure your life is over then. Forget it. I've known a lot of women who got married and later wished they hadn't, so I count myself lucky. And I don't know why Bel still expects women to rush into marriage like she did when she ended up marrying a drunk who hit her. If people would just look around, they'd realize a lot of people never get married—the Mitchells never did—not one of the three of them—or Mary Dwyer that I worked with at the cathedral—or any of those old nuns from the orphanage—or the O'Neills' daughter, Helen, or me for that matter.

"Thanks for the ride, Sybil," I says as we pull into the restaurant parking lot. "We'll see you later."

"You're welcome. Just let the waitress know when you want me to take you back. I'll be helping in the kitchen in the meantime, unless I get a call for another pickup."

"You cook back there too?" Bel asks.

"Yes, I help out a little."

"Any woman who can cook should have a man—these days, most of the girls your age couldn't make toast, so you're a real catch, Sybil," Bel keeps on. "You just have to get yourself out there so you can get caught."

"Yes, I suppose you're right," Sybil says. "Anyway, just tell the waitress when you're ready to have me take you home."

"Okay. Thanks, Sybil," I says, getting out of the car.

Once Bel is out too and we've both got the car doors shut, I says to Bel, "Why can't you leave her alone?"

"I just want the girl to be happy," she says.

"Like you were married to Charlie?" I snap as I open the restaurant door.

We're the only people in the place—one reason I like it here early in the morning. Nothing I hate more than worrying about someone else overhearing my conversation, and with Bel, you never know what she might say that will embarrass you.

"Hello, ladies," says the waitress. Unlike Sybil, she doesn't know our names yet, though she's seated us a half-dozen times. She leads us to a table and we sit down. She gives us water and asks if we want coffee—it's only four o'clock in the morning so of course we want coffee if we're going to stay awake to eat our meal. You would think by now she would know that, but she asks us every time anyways. She goes off to get the coffeepot while I open the menu, but before I can even look at the specials, Bel says, "So how'd it go with that young couple at the O'Neill House? You didn't tell me yesterday, and I didn't want to ask in the cab since it wasn't any of Sybil's business."

Hmm, she never thinks not to put her nose in Sybil's business though.

"Fine," I says. "They're real nice people, but I don't have anything in common with them. I find it kind of trying to be around married people, especially young ones with little kids."

"How many kids do they have?"

"One, and one on the way," I says.

"Boy or girl?" she asks.

"A boy—he's two I think—they don't know what the other one will be. They named him Neill for Mr. O'Neill."

"Oh, I bet he's adorable," says Bel.

"I guess. All he seemed to do was stare at me a lot." I decide not to tell her how the kid took to Frank, or that Alan showed up—some things aren't any of Bel's business.

"You know what your problem is, Lyla?" she asks me.

Oh God, here we go! But I have to stay in suspense about what my problem is because the waitress picks that minute to come back with the coffee.

"Are you ready to order?" asks the waitress.

"No, we need another minute," I says.

"Your problem, Lyla," says Bel once the waitress is gone, "is that you had a family so you miss it too much, and that's why you're so hostile to families; you can't handle being around one because it gives you pain. But for me, I never really knew a family growing up, so I can only see them as a blessing without all the hurt."

"I'd think never having known a family would be worse," I says.

"No. The only bad part is that Charlie and me wanted one so bad and Lilybelle—well, you know I had those women problems—but I've always thought if I'd given Charlie a family like he deserved, he wouldn't have drank so much, and—"

"Stop blaming yourself," I tell her, seeing she's about to turn on the waterworks. I figured it was coming—that damn shrink brought all that crap back up for her, like she needed to think about it again. "After all those years of going to AA and counseling on and off, you should know better by now," I says.

"Well, I'm sure that having lots of children would have made Charlie happier. He never did hit me until—"

"I know," I says, "but if Lilybelle hadn't died, something else would have triggered his anger. You know, Charlie probably had that post-traumatic stress syndrome they talk about now, only no one knew about it back then. That's why he drank."

"Yeah, I suppose," she says. "He did have nightmares now and then about the war."

"See, and if you'd had all those kids you talk about, why you'd have been a lot more miserable, trying to raise all of them with a drunk for a husband, and what if he'd slapped up your kids like he did you?"

"Oh, Charlie never would have done that."

"Bel, you don't know that because you didn't have any kids around to see if he would. And even so, with him drunk and hitting their mother, don't you think those kids would have ended up with a bunch of mental and emotional problems? Trust me, Bel; it's a blessing you didn't have any more kids. What would you want to bring them into this screwed up world for anyways? And now you'd be worrying about them and your grandkids, and what with the terrorists and anthrax in envelopes and war and crazy people blowing up buildings and stuff, what do you want to put people through all that—think about it. We're just lucky we're old and will be dead soon before that sulfide mining they want to do up there near Big Bay pollutes all our air and freshwater. I hate to think what the world's going to be like in another fifty years—I'm just glad to think I'll be dead by then."

"Oh, Lyla. You don't really believe all that do you? You don't have to be the voice of doom all the time. Happiness is possible."

"I don't know how you can believe that after all what you've been through," I says. I'm not sure I believe everything I'm saying, but she's got me all worked up now and the lack of sleep is starting to get to me. The coffee must be cooled off enough to drink, though, so I take a sip of it.

"We've had our tough times," says Bel, "but we've had good times too. Even in the orphanage, we had good times—we had a roof over our heads and people to care for us. We didn't have to fend for ourselves."

"We did once we turned fourteen."

"But even then, the nuns found places for us."

"Yeah," I says, rolling my eyes. "It was like going out of the frying pan and into the fire—that's what it was like for me going to the Mitchells. At least you had Charlie, drunk though he was, to look after you. I had to fend for myself, and it sure the hell wasn't easy."

"You had me, Lyla. I've always been a good friend to you."

I breathe through my nose to stay calm. Then I swallow the whole cup of coffee, hot though it is. I'm going to need a whole pot to keep my temper once she starts telling me what a great friend she is. Anyone with a grain of sense could see I've done far more for her over the years than she's ever done for me. Sure, she drives me around now and then, but after all the crap I put up with from her when she was a stinking drunk, and the crap I put up with from her husband, and all the long whining phone calls I listened to when she started going to AA—she doesn't even come close to having made things even between us by taking me grocery shopping now and then.

"I mean," she says, "at least you always had me for a friend—more like a sister really."

"Don't say that," I says. "You know how I feel about sisters."

"You should get over that," says Bel. "Not every sister is like Jessie."

"You know I don't want you mentioning her," I says as I see the waitress heading our way again. "Just decide what you want for breakfast."

"What can I get for you?" the waitress asks.

"I think Lyla needs some eggs sunnyside up and a coffee cup that's not half-empty," Bel mutters.

"Is the coffee okay?" asks the waitress, looking confused.

"Just fine," I says. "I'll have two eggs, over medium, with bacon and toast."

Bel, who thinks she's still a kid, gets the strawberry waffle with whipping cream on it—and I know she'll put plenty of syrup on it. At four in the morning, it'll be a wonder if she doesn't feel sick later. I swear she eats like a teenage boy sometimes.

Once the waitress is gone, Bel can't let the matter drop.

"You always forget the good times we had, Lyla—I mean when we were in the orphanage."

"I'm thankful," I says, "that I survived living there, but there weren't no good times—not when I had to help take care of those stinking cows. Not when I had almost no privacy. Not when I had to get up at ungodly hours to go to Mass and they forced me into being a Catholic. Even now, I think I still go to church because of all the guilt they shoved down my throat."

"Oh, Lyla. Get over it. You like going to church. No one makes you go."

"I am over it," I says. "I know it's in the past and can't be changed, and I'm not that upset about it anymore, but you're always bringing it up like we had some kind of idyllic childhood. That's what I can't get over. How you can hang onto some romantic version of your life. I think you're the one who needs to get over it."

"Lyla, I know life is hard. Believe me. And I know your life has been as hard as mine in a lot of ways, but focusing on what's wrong doesn't help anything. I just try to remember the good times and forget the bad."

I don't say anything but just inhale through my nostrils. I don't know why, after so many years, that she still pushes my buttons—and she knows how to do it, too—and I've never learned how not to let her. Maybe I do need to go to this woman's meeting, but if it's to talk about your problems, it won't do me much good since she's one of my biggest problems—or, well, maybe not a problem, but she sure is a major frustration in my life.

We don't say much else until the food comes. Then I can tell she's excited. Bel always gets excited by food—it's like she's a wound up music box when she eats because it always sets her to talking too much.

"For example, Lyla," she says as she drenches her strawberry waffle in maple syrup just like I knew she would, "you don't seem to think being in the orphanage was a good experience for you, but you met me there—you have that to be thankful for."

I take a bite of my eggs and says nothing.

"And," she goes on, "another advantage of being raised in the orphanage is they taught us what good work ethic is. You have to admit that."

"They worked us to the bone," I says. "We were always mopping and dusting, or out there milking a damn cow or something."

"Yes," says Bel, "but you learned your trade that way."

"What trade?"

"You learned how to keep house, and I'm sure it was good training for a lot of the girls, including me, for being a wife and taking care of a house."

What the hell is she talking about? Her apartment is a mess.

"And it made you a living all these years," she says.

"You think I should be thankful to the orphanage that I got to spend my life being a housekeeper?" I asks. "You make it sound like they sent me to charm school."

"Well, with your attitude, Lyla, sometimes I wish they had."

I can't help laughing at that. Me at charm school. Can you see me walking around with a book on my head?

Bel sticks a gob of whipping-cream-and-maple-syrup-covered-strawberry-waffle in her mouth.

"And my love of movies came from the orphanage. Remember all those movies we used to get to watch?"

"Yes," I says. "How could I forget? You acted like Shirley Temple was your personal friend or something the way you talked about her all the time, and all those silly singing cowboys."

She's right, though. She has a love for movies and it must have started in the orphanage. But she's been weird about that too. Back in the '80s when they invented the VCR, I thought it would be the best gift in the world for Bel, so I went and bought her one for Christmas.

And VCRs weren't cheap back then, let me tell you. I paid four hundred dollars for that thing, and now you can get them at Walmart for something like sixty bucks. It wasn't cheap, that's for sure, but the O'Neills had given me a Christmas bonus, and I figured it would save me money in the long run what with the price of movie tickets becoming so high, not to mention the snacks.

But when I gave it to her, what did she say?

"What do I want this for?"

"Well, so you can watch movies," I told her. "You can watch them on video and not have to pay as much as at the theater, and plus, you can watch them over and over instead of just waiting for them to come on TV."

"Yeah okay," she said after a minute, but she didn't seem too excited about it.

"Look what else I got for you," I said. "*The Wizard of Oz.* You'll have to go out and rent more movies, but I knew this was one favorite of yours I couldn't go wrong on buying."

Her face kind of lit up for a moment then.

"Thanks, Lyla," she said.

A week later when I was over at her place, I saw she had the VCR all hooked up and *The Wizard of Oz* was sitting on top of the TV.

"Are you enjoying your VCR?" I asked her.

"Oh, Lyla," she said, "I wish you had never bought me that thing."

"Why?" I asked.

"Well, it must have cost you a fortune, and it just kind of ruins the movies for me."

"What do you mean?" I asked.

"Well, *The Wizard of Oz* used to be special. I mean, I'd wait all year for it to come on television, but now, here I own it so I can watch it all I want. I've watched it three times this week, and now it doesn't feel special anymore."

"You just watched it three times, so no wonder," I said.

"No, I don't know if I'll ever watch it again. It isn't magical if you can't look forward to watching it. Now it's just—well, just ordinary."

"Well, go get some other movies—*Gone With the Wind* or *It's a Wonderful Life* or something."

"Oh, no, Lyla. Those are favorites too. I can't have them all ruined for me."

I had to bite my tongue then. I was about to offer to take the VCR back, or just take it home for myself, but I figured she'd come around eventually, only she didn't.

"So, can we go to the movie on Saturday?" she had the nerve to ask me then. "I want to go see *The Color Purple*."

"But why spend the money?" I asked. "We can wait until it's on video and then rent it for a dollar and watch it here rather than paying $3.50 per ticket each and a small fortune for popcorn and pop."

"But, Lyla, I don't want to watch it in my living room. It's not as magical as watching it in the movie theatre."

"Well, you go if you want, but I'm not wasting money on the movie theatre anymore when I can watch movies on video." I didn't want to go see that movie anyways—that was before anyone even knew who Oprah Winfrey or Whoopi Goldberg were.

But I ended up going with her—we always went to the movies on Saturdays, so I figured if I didn't go with her, I'd be sitting home alone because she was stubborn enough to go by herself. So I went. And that was one of the toughest movies I ever had to sit through—a real tearjerker. The end was a killer for me—those sisters being reunited like that after years being kept apart. Not that happy endings like that actually happen in real life, but sometimes I wish they did.

Fortunately, *Dirty Dancing* came out not long after that, so I convinced her that all the movies were becoming trash and we just rented old ones after that.

"Lyla, don't you ever enjoy anything?" Bel asks, pulling me back to breakfast in The Pancake House.

"Yeah," I says as I watch her stuff more strawberry waffle into her mouth. "I do."

"Well, I don't know what it is then," she says. "You're always grouching. You're lucky you met me at that orphanage because I sure wonder sometimes who else would put up with you."

"Thanks a lot," I says. "No one asks you to put up with me. You can leave any time you want."

"More coffee?" asks the waitress—waitresses always know how to show up at the worst moment.

"Yes," says Bel. "Lyla definitely needs more. She's still cranky this morning."

"I need to use the restroom," I says, and I get up to go to the Ladies' Room. "I should have stayed home," I mutter to myself. I probably am still tired and cranky. I don't know why she's getting to me today, except that maybe after seeing how happy John and Wendy were together—and knowing I'll never have that—not at my age—and well, whatever.

After I flush the toilet, look in the mirror, and see I do look crabby, I tell myself to try to be more pleasant and I go back to the table. Bel is right. She does put up with me, despite all my orneriness, and I know I can be pretty ornery at times. I'm probably lucky that she's dumb enough to put up with me. I'm not that mad at her—it's thinking about *The Color Purple*—that's what got to me because I never got what Whoopi Goldberg got in the end. Never got what John and Wendy have. Just never got, period, I guess, dumb as that sounds.

When I get back to the table, I notice a couple college kids have come into the restaurant. They're sitting close enough to overhear Bel and me, so I figure I better be easier on her now.

When I sit down, she's focusing on chasing a bit of strawberry waffle around her plate with her fork, trying to soak up all the whipping cream and syrup on it that she can.

"Bel," I says, deciding to play along with her game. "I do remember one fun thing from being in the orphanage."

"What's that?" she asks.

"When we used to play nun and priest. Do you remember that?"

"Yes," she laughs, "only, you were always the heathen the rest of us had to convert."

"Yeah, or that one time we were playing and Charlie was the priest—can you imagine that—and he said I had demons in me and he was going to exorcise me."

"I don't remember that," says Bel.

"Well, it happened," I says.

"I'm sure it did," she says.

"But I guess it didn't work too well," I says.

"No, I guess not," she smiles. "But I haven't given up on you yet, Lyla. God'll make a nice person out of you, yet. I'm sure of it."

Chapter 7

I come home from breakfast and stay up until about 6 a.m., long enough to digest the food. Then I doze off in front of the TV6 morning news. When the phone ringing wakes me up, Regis and Kelly are on TV, so I realize I better go get ready for the women's meeting as soon as I'm off the phone.

When I hear Eleanor's voice, I think I should reconsider getting Caller I.D.

"I hear you had a good time at John and Wendy's house the other night," she says.

"Yeah, they're really nice people," I says.

"They were delighted to have you. They were really pleased with the stories you told them about Mr. O'Neill."

"Oh, well, I don't know that I told them much worth knowing, but it was good to see the old house again."

"Alan mentioned that he stopped in while you were there. He said he couldn't believe how you don't look like you've aged at all since you went out with Bill."

I can't imagine Alan saying something like that, or why he would even mention me. He probably didn't. It's probably just Eleanor trying as usual to play the peacemaker.

"That was nice of him," I says to be polite. "I can't believe how grown up he looks."

"He'll be forty this year; can you believe it?"

"Where does the time go," I says to humor her.

"I'm glad he went over to see John and Wendy. He's been so worried about his dad, and I think it helps a lot that his friend Frank is going to stay with him for a while. He needs a friend at a time like this. Poor Bill. I don't know what's going to happen to him. Alan is afraid to go back home anytime soon since his dad is so bad."

"How is Bill?" I asks. "I've been meaning to call and ask you."

"He's stable, but the doctor doesn't think he'll ever be able to go home again. His heart attack was a lot worse than they first thought, and I guess he had a little stroke too."

"Oh no," I says, feeling bad for Bill despite his orneriness. "Does that mean he'll have to go to the nursing home?"

"I'm afraid so," says Eleanor. "I don't know what Alan's going to do. Bill should be near his sons, but I don't think he'll agree to move downstate or to Wisconsin. If he's here, I could go visit him every day, but I'm not getting any younger. Alan or one of his brothers should be looking after him now. Still, I hope they don't move Bill to a nursing home near one of them and then I never get to see him again."

"I don't blame you," I says. "It's hard when kids move away from home and have to worry about their parents."

I've never had to worry about any kids, but I know how Papa worried me all the time, even when I just left him home alone while I was working. I was always afraid he'd fall and break his hip—and that was back in the days before people had lifelines or you could call 911—or worse, that he might burn down the house while I wasn't there. In the end, he just went in his sleep—maybe the only truly kind gift God ever gave him.

"Lyla," says Eleanor, real serious suddenly, "will you come back up to see Bill? I think he'd like to see you."

I don't know what to say. I've never been good at saying "No," but I'm not going to put myself through that experience again.

"I don't think he wants to see me," I says. "I think it's better I stay away."

"He didn't mean what he said the other day, Lyla," Eleanor insists. "He was just surprised to see you is all, and he was on all those drugs the doctors were giving him. He didn't know what he was saying."

He knew what he was saying—I know he did. But I just says, "Yeah, I know, Eleanor, but whatever was between us is over with now. I think it's best to let the past rest."

"I'm sorry it's this way, Lyla. I've always been fond of you, you know. Bill's wives, well, they both were a bit problematic. They had real attitude problems—putting on airs and such. Not like you. I liked that you were down to earth. I thought maybe Bill would finally settle down with you, and for a while, it seemed like he did. I don't think he ever cheated on you with anyone else while you were dating. I'm not sure any other woman, not even his wives, could say that."

I know she's trying to make me feel better but I'm not willing to let her. It's not like his not cheating on me deserves a medal or something—it's just what a decent man should do. I take a deep breath, and then say the best thing I can. "Bill certainly had his issues, and I'm real sorry that he isn't doing well, but he has you and his sons and his nephews and nieces. He doesn't need me."

"Well, Lyla," she says. "I hope you and I can still be friends."

"Sure, Eleanor; we've always been friends," I says, and it's true I've always wished Eleanor well, but considering that I've barely spoken to her in the nineteen years since I dated Bill, I don't imagine we'll have much contact in the future.

"I'll have to have you over for lunch sometime soon, Lyla," she says.

"Sure, that would be nice," I says, cringing at the thought. "But I better go now. I promised to go with my friend Bel to an appointment, and she'll be here in a few minutes."

"Okay, Lyla. Take care of yourself," she says.

I hang up the phone and sigh loudly. Then for just a minute I feel sad. I think Eleanor is either losing it or getting really lonely and scared in her old age—after all, she's got to be over ninety now. I guess if she does invite me over, I'll go; it can't hurt so long as I don't have to see Bill, and I won't if he's going to a nursing home. I don't want to see Alan either, but if he did say something nice about me like Eleanor said, then maybe that wouldn't be so bad either. Eleanor just caught me off guard the other day when she called about Bill. Maybe I have what they call "unresolved grief" after all these years, and that's what made me go to see him right away, but deep down, I know he was never right for me. He never treated me all that well. I know I'm not that much to look at, and I don't have any money or education or anything, but I was always good to him. Still, we were two very different people. I'm lucky it worked out the way it did.

"Quit dwelling in the past and go and get ready," I says to myself. Bel will be here any minute now, and I have to put on a positive face since I'm going with her to that women's meeting. I'm not looking forward to it, but it can't be any more awkward than being around Bill and his family, that's for sure.

I'm just about ready when Bel knocks on the door.

"Are you in a better mood?" she asks.

"Yeah, I took a little nap," I says as we walk to the elevator.

We don't say anything else until we're out the door and getting in the car when she says, "Thanks so much, Lyla, for agreeing to go with me."

"It's okay," I says.

"Maybe it will help you too," she adds.

"Don't start that," I tell her. "I agreed to try it once, but if I don't like it, I won't go again."

"All right, all right, but I do appreciate you going with me," she says. She was all mopey and depressed yesterday, and kind of argumentative in the middle of the night, but now she's being real nice; you never know with her. Well, I guess mostly she's nice, just a bit dingy, but last night she was argumentative the way she tried to tell me what "my problem" was, so I'm glad her attitude has improved now.

I don't even know where this meeting is, but I don't bother to ask. I figure she knows, and when we pull into the parking lot of St. Paul's Episcopal Church, I have my answer.

"I'm kind of nervous," she says as we get out of the car.

"You've been going to AA for years," I says. "What's there to be nervous about?"

She doesn't answer me but just says, "It's in the chapel." And then we go inside and find the chapel and enter.

A couple women are already there; they're young—maybe thirty at the most. They nod their heads in greeting, and Bel asks, "Is this the women's group?" One of them says, "Yes, welcome." And then as we walk into the room and we can see each other better, the other one says, "Hello, Bel and Lyla."

For a moment, I wonder who the heck would know us here. Turns out it's Sybil—The Pancake House cab driver. Oh jeez. She's a nice girl, but do I really want her to know all my crap?

"Sybil, it's so great to see you!" says Bel.

We sit down, and before we can say anything else, the door opens, and what do you know? In comes Wendy.

"Goddamnit," I says under my breath. Is every woman I know in Marquette going to show up?

Wendy looks a bit surprised to see me too, but she just nods hello and sits down across from us.

"We usually have more people than this come," says the woman whose name I don't know that I'm sitting next to.

I just nod. The less people the better as far as I'm concerned.

But then one more comes in, this Chinese-looking broad, just as Wendy says, "Welcome, everyone. Shall we get started? Let's begin by giving our names—first names are all that are required, remember, and we don't repeat each other's names outside of the meeting. We maintain anonymity so the meeting is a safe place for sharing."

I'm glad to know about the anonymous part. That means whatever I says won't be repeated by Wendy to Eleanor so she can tell Bill—not that I plan to talk about Bill since there's no point in it.

So anyways, we go around the little circle we've made and say our names. "I'm Wendy. I'm Sybil. I'm Diana. I'm May. I'm Bel. I'm Lyla." When it's my turn, I feel like adding, "and I don't want to be here," but I don't because Bel is my friend after all so I'm here for her.

"First, let me give a little background information on our group since we have new people today," Wendy says. "Lyla and Bel, we decided to call our group the Women's Table because this is a place to discuss issues affecting us as women, although anything that is bothering you is free to be discussed, but we talk about things like women's health issues, pregnancy, being a mother, being a wife, work, relationships, religion and spirituality, all those sorts of things. We started about two years ago, and how we began is that after I gave birth to my first child, I was suffering from post-partum depression. I felt I needed other women to talk to, and at that time, May expressed to me how she was having problems knowing how to talk to her daughter who was just starting to have her period, and whom she was raising as a single mother; after we talked for a while, we thought about forming our own group for women. There are a lot of other support groups like the ones built around the Twelve Steps such as Alcoholics Anonymous, Codependents Anonymous, Al-Anon, all those, but we didn't want anything quite that formal or subject-specific. We're kind of like a coffee clutch, but we follow a similar format to those groups when we do our sharing, and we don't allow crosstalk. We just each say what we need to say and witness what each other has to say. And we're open to having any women come. In fact, we're happy to have both of you, Lyla and Bel, because so far we haven't had anyone come who's much more than early middle-age, so we'll appreciate the wisdom you have to share."

Wisdom to share? She doesn't know us very well. These women look like they have their stuff together. I mean, I know Sybil's gone to college and she must be really smart because she writes for *The Mining Journal*, and Wendy seems polished and smart. I don't know the other two, but I remember Sybil saying she works for May, the Chinese-looking woman who owns an antique shop. Bel and I don't have anything that good going on in our lives. I was just a housekeeper and Bel a wife and later she had some different odd jobs, but nothing impressive. I'm starting to feel intimidated by them now and wishing I hadn't come. And after all the years Bel's gone to Alcoholics Anonymous, you would think she'd have had enough of these kinds of meetings anyways.

When Wendy finishes her spiel, Sybil reads from a book called *Affirmations for Women*. The reading says something about how women often feel like they have to do everything—be a wife, mother, sister, daughter—and take care of their families, but they have to remember to take time for themselves too. I suppose that's true for most women, but for me, I pretty much never did anything but make time for myself, except for the years I was taking care of Papa and, of course, when I was working. I guess taking care of an aging parent is a woman's issue, but it's been thirty years since I had to do it, so no point in bringing it up here.

After Sybil finishes reading, everyone together says, "Thank you, Sybil," which kind of creeps me out a little.

"All right then," says Wendy, after the reading. "Since Lyla and Bel are new, it might be nice if we kind of introduce ourselves and talk about why we started coming to this meeting for their sakes, as well as anything else we feel called upon or need to share. We'll have a moment of silence, and then if someone feels called upon to share, she may do so."

Everyone goes silent. Some of them sit with their eyes closed. The silence makes me uncomfortable. If we're going to have a meeting, we should get on with it. I stare at the chapel's big stained glass window, wishing someone would speak. I've heard it's a Tiffany window. It's really pretty but kind of blended-like—not as sharp as the windows with people in them at St. Peter's.

"I'm Diana," starts the one I don't know anything about, "and I'm a sexaholic."

And now I know more about her than I ever wanted to know. Jesus

Christ! Don't young women today know what's supposed to be private?

"Only there aren't any Sexaholics Anonymous meetings in Marquette," she continues, "so I decided to start coming here, and I feel comfortable here, although I'm not sure it's helped me stay away from sex. I try to control my sexual urges, but sometimes I find I just can't help myself. But it's good to have people to talk to who don't judge."

I want to ask her just how much sex she's having since she's willing to share about it, but I got from Wendy's introduction that I'm not allowed to be interrupting or asking questions. And I suppose if I did ask, I'd come off all judgmental, though I can't imagine she doesn't think we're all judging her.

"I'm a beautiful young woman," Diana continues, "and so the men really like me, and there are just so many hot guys around, especially at the college, and especially now that it's summer. The beach is full of them, and they're all so hot, and since I'm older than them, they all think it's a big notch in their belts to do me—not that I'm that old, but the college boys think I am. I get hit on all the time, and sometimes I just can't help myself. Only, it's not really that I want sex. I keep thinking maybe the next man will be the one who will love me, but just when things start to go well, I get scared and break it off, or run, so I've hardly had sex with the same guy more than three or four times, except for my husband, of course.

"Anyway, most of you know my story. But there's one guy I do really like, and I think I hurt him really bad when I told him I couldn't be with him. I told him I was married, which is true, although we've been separated for a while now, and this guy told me he didn't even care because he was in love with me. I've had guys tell me that before, but a lot of the time, it's just to get into my pants, and I don't even usually tell guys I'm married, but it helps once in awhile when I need to get rid of a guy.

"Anyway, a few weeks ago, my husband told me he wants a divorce. He knows I've cheated on him in the past—though he thinks it was only once—and he forgave me, but now he found out I was seeing this one guy I really like. I don't know how I feel about it—his wanting a divorce. I don't even know that I love my husband. I don't know how I feel, except scared that maybe I'll end up all alone and never be able to be married to just one man. And though I'm careful, I worry about catching some disease too, and worse, not knowing I have something and then giving it to others—I'd feel terrible about that. Except maybe if I gave it to my husband because he's a real prick to tell you the truth. Sometimes I think I run around on him just to get back at him (although I had a lot of men before him too, not that he knew that). I don't think he ever loved me—my husband—I think he just saw me as a trophy wife or something because I'm so attractive and my family is pretty well-off—but then I realize that's just me sometimes making an excuse for what is really a serious problem I have.

"But I do like this other guy, and although I told him I was married and he said he didn't care, I told him I didn't want to see him anymore. But then when my husband went to see a lawyer about the divorce, I saw this guy again and told him how I was getting divorced, and he said he wanted to marry me then. Now I don't know what to do. I think I do love him, but I'm also afraid of really being loved, and afraid of hurting him because he's so cute and sweet, and—I'm just scared. I never wanted to hurt anyone, and this guy is so nice that I'm afraid I won't be able to control myself if I marry him, and I might then end up cheating on him and hurting him. And sometimes I think I'm getting better, but today, I just feel terrible, kind of hopeless."

She starts crying. Wendy hands her the box of Kleenexes. She wipes her eyes and tries a couple times to say something more but finds she can't, so after a minute, she says, "That's all. Thanks."

"Thank you, Diana," everyone says. And then after a few seconds, like nothing embarrassing has happened, Sybil starts talking.

"I'm Sybil. And I don't want to jinx things, but I just feel really good today, kind of hopeful. But like Diana, I'm also kind of scared. You see, I met this guy recently, and I really like him."

Oh God, Sybil too! What is wrong with these women that all they can talk about is the men they like? We might as well be at an overnight pajama party for teenage girls. But Bel will be happy to know Sybil's found a guy finally—I hope Bel keeps the confidentiality thing and doesn't harass Sybil about it outside the meeting.

"I've gone out with a few guys in the past," Sybil says, "but most of the guys my age, at least when I was in high school and college, all seemed so childish and even the guys around my age—I'm twenty-eight now, still seem like they'd rather just party or fool around with a girl than have a serious relationship. This guy's quite a bit older than me—he's thirty-nine, so that's, what? Eleven years older. But I like that he's older because he's mature, and he's good-looking, even kind of sexy considering his age. He has a little boy—well, not that little—he's twelve. And well, I just really like him. I only just met him a few days ago, but I'm hoping to see more of him. I just feel like we really hit it off, and so I feel hopeful, and maybe like I'm finally ready to settle down with the right guy. I know it sounds silly; I hardly know him really, but I don't know how to explain it—I just have this feeling like he's the one and we've known each other forever, and I've never had that feeling before. I knew a lot of girls who would say things like that when I was in high school, but I never felt that way before until now.

"It's hard to explain," she continues after taking a few seconds to breathe, "but I—well…there are some things about me I don't like to share with people—that I don't trust other people with knowing about me. I guess I've always had trust issues, or maybe abandonment issues is more accurate—I know they're based on my parents dying when I was only twelve. My grandmother raised me then, and she was a great substitute parent, but I kind of wonder sometimes if the reason I'm interested in an older man is because I'm looking for a father figure since I lost mine so early. But he's nice and I don't see anything wrong with dating a mature man. I've only seen him twice, but—I just feel this powerful connection to him, like I've known him before. And he's going through a tough time right now—in fact, he just came up here to care for his father who is really sick, and I think that makes me codependent toward him, wanting to care take of him. I haven't even met his son yet, but anyway, I just have this crazy feeling he's the one. I can't explain it. Anyway, we're going out again on Friday night, so I'm really hoping this time it will work out. I don't know if he's the one, and I know it's too soon to tell, but I'm not sabotaging myself this time by convincing myself it can't work. I kind of feel like maybe I've finally grown up emotionally so that I'm ready to take a risk, and also that this time I found a guy who won't be so much of a risk, so that makes it easier too, so just wish me luck or say a few prayers for me. Thanks for listening."

"Thanks, Sybil," everyone says. I see them all smiling at her, hoping she has found the love she wants. But I feel kind of sorry for her, remembering what it was to be that young—twenty-seven I think she told me she is; my goodness, that was half a century ago for me. I hope this guy does work out for her because I know what it's like to spend a lifetime hoping for that special one and never having him arrive.

When I hear Bel clearing her throat, I know it's time for the trouble to start.

"I'm Bel, and I'm an alcoholic."

I've been friends with Bel most of my life, but still, whenever she opens her mouth in public, I can't help but be afraid of what's going to come out of it.

"I know," she says, "how these meetings go 'cause I've gone to AA meetings before, which means that, yes, I'm a recovering alcoholic. I haven't had a drink in nearly thirty years. I finally quit after taking care of my ex-husband—drinking killed him, and he's also the one who got me started with drinking. And I understand that drinking is just a crutch—something people do as a way to hide their pain and real issues, although I don't know exactly what those issues are for me, although having been an orphan and growing up in the orphanage, and then marrying an alcoholic and abusive husband is a big part of it, but I realize you never figure it all out because I've been trying to for years. Lately, I've been feeling depressed about some things, and I just don't feel like AA is enough or the right program to help me with them so that's why I'm here instead. I just want to see if coming here will help. And just for the record, I want to say that I'm seventy-seven years old, and I'm angry that after all these years, all of these issues still bother me so much, and then more issues show up in my life."

She starts to cry. I hate when she does that. I s'pose she wants me to hug her, but I'm not going to in front of all these strangers.

Wendy hands Bel a Kleenex. "Thanks," Bel says and blows her nose. Then she says, "Thanks, I'm finished…oh, except that I brought my friend, Lyla, with me 'cause she's my best friend and she and I grew up together in the orphanage, and I think she has some issues to work through too."

"Thank you, Bel," the rest of them says. "Thanks, Bel," I add, wishing I could reach over and slap her.

Then the Chinese-looking one named May gets started.

"Bel," she says, "I just want to say first that I'm glad you're here, and I can kind of relate to you being an orphan because my dad died in Vietnam before I ever knew him. He was an American soldier killed in the line of duty, and my mother was Vietnamese and they fell in love while he was there. Somehow my mother managed to get us to the United States where we came to live with my dad's parents, but then my mom died while I was just a little girl, so my grandparents raised me. In fact, my grandma is still alive and I live with her and my daughter, so although I had my grandparents, I kind of know what it feels like to be an orphan—at least not to have your parents, and it wasn't easy either that I looked so different from everyone else. I think I look more white than Asian, but maybe I just want to think that. I've always struggled with my identity, and my daughter doesn't make it any easier. I had her when I was young—early when I was in college, and her father didn't stay with us. He was white, and I thought we were in love, but his parents never approved—he was from Grosse Pointe, and the family had money, and they were maybe just too white, if you know what I mean. And that's the problem. I was trying too hard to be white, and I know that now and I accept that I'm half-Asian, but I mean, I wasn't raised that way. My grandparents meant well, but they didn't know anything about Vietnam. They only knew it was the terrible place where their son had been killed, and they would never talk about the war.

"Anyway, about being an orphan. I try to keep that in mind because my daughter, Josie, she grew up without a father. Only, she's so into being Asian and I didn't grow up that way. I guess I'm just not that interested—I've tried to assimilate into being American; multiculturalism didn't even exist when I was growing up in the 1970s and '80s. I wanted to be like everyone else, and I tried to like what I thought I should like—what white people like. I'm past having to think that way now, but it's still with me—I still like those things, and my daughter despises me for it—saying I'm trying to pass as white. My grandma makes a point of remembering things like all the china dolls I had as a little girl and how I loved them. I still had some of them when Josie was little, but one day in a rage, Josie smashed one of their faces in, and she's threatened to do the same with my bone china that belonged to my great-grandmother, Harriet Dalrymple. It's so beautiful with little pink flowers, and I know Great-Grandma never had that much money so this china of hers—I think it was even her wedding china—was her pride and joy; it's nearly a hundred years old now. I never really knew my great-grandmother. I was just a toddler when she died, but I think it's special to have something that belonged to her, but Josie just rolls her eyes over it and calls me names like 'Fancy Miss' and 'Little Miss White Girl' and 'Queen Mother.' I just don't know how to talk to her. I don't know why my own daughter has to mock me like that, and she won't listen to me. She even makes fun of the fact that I own an antique shop—even though it's what feeds her and keeps her in her new clothes. She keeps saying I like to collect 'white people's old junk.'

"She really was a sweet girl when she was younger, and I kind of encouraged her when she started expressing an interest in the Vietnamese side of her family because some kids at school made fun of her for having slanted eyes when she was little, so I tried to show her how cool it was to be Vietnamese, and I helped her with a class project on Vietnam when she was maybe in fourth grade or so, and so the other kids started to think it was cool that she was different. So cool I guess that now she has to reject the American, white side of her heritage.

"We got along fine until this last year when she started high school, and now she seems to hang around with a wild crowd, and although she was a freshman this past year, she's hanging out with the junior and seniors, and I don't like that. I'm so afraid she's going to get herself into trouble with some older boy. I started buying her birth control because I was so scared and she doesn't listen to me anymore. My grandma was angry at me about that, saying I was giving her a free card to go out and have sex, but what can I do? I love my daughter, but I can't just tie her up in her room. Grandma says she's just going through a phase, but I don't know. She kind of scares me the way she acts. It could be years before she grows out of this phase, and I'm really afraid it's not a phase. I don't want her to get involved with some boy and get pregnant and mess up her life like I sort of did. That's all."

Wendy hands May a Kleenex since she's starting to snivel too. I wonder if it's some sort of requirement to cry at these meetings. If it is, I'm leaving.

"Thank you, May," everyone says.

Boy, I thought I had problems. At least I was smart enough never to get myself pregnant. Thank God for that, especially since I never had any maternal instinct anyways. I just can't imagine having a child, being responsible like that for someone else. I had enough to do just being responsible for myself all these years. Kids are unreasonable, just like May said—you don't know what they're going to do, so how a mother keeps her sanity while raising one is something I'll never understand. Life is hard enough just trying to make money to feed yourself.

"I'm Wendy," Wendy then says, "and for the sake of those of you who don't know me well, I'll just say a little about my past. I grew up out West but moved here when I met my husband. I love it here, and I love my husband dearly. We have a little boy and we're expecting another child. My life is pretty perfect, at least most people would think so, but life is never quite perfect.

"It felt like everything was just meant to be, though, when I came here and met John. It was just the strangest thing, like I was coming home. Like I was meant to do it, although sometimes it felt like maybe I was trying to complete something for Madeleine, my great-great-grandmother—like I was living out something for my ancestor that she didn't complete, because she was from here but had left and never come home again. Anyway, how John and I met was I was doing genealogy research at the museum here, and the museum put me in touch with him, so I discovered we were distant cousins, and well, luckily, we were distant enough that we could get married. We felt a real bond right away, and it was like being in a jigsaw puzzle where all the pieces finally came together. I feel it's so special to live in the house that my ancestors lived in and to find a man I can love and who seems to understand me, even finishes my thoughts for me."

Why is she whining? She has the perfect life—the fairytale and Prince Charming and everything it sounds like. What the hell can she possibly have to complain about? I saw how her husband treats her and looks at her like he's crazy in love with her. I wouldn't have taken her for a whiner, but she must be if she has anything to complain about.

"But while I love the house and our history and everything," Wendy says, "sometimes having that kind of connection to the past makes you feel like you're not quite you but just an extension of your ancestors, and at other times, it makes you feel more complete and whole and better because you know precisely who you are because of your ancestors.

"So, I guess that's all I have to say. I've gotten a lot out of coming to these meetings. I'm long past the post-partum depression I felt after my son was born and we started this group, and I think I'll be a lot better able to cope after my next child is born as a result. It just helps a lot to have other people to talk to, and I hope, Lyla and Bel, that you'll at least come to a few of our meetings to try them out and see how coming to them might help you. I've just found it's a lot easier to talk to people you can trust. Thank you everyone."

"Thank you, Wendy," everyone says when she's finished.

And then it's silent.

Everyone has shared except me. I suppose it's my turn but I don't say nothing.

The silence is uncomfortable, and I don't even know where to start so I don't. I don't want to talk, and I can't think what I would say if I did. Bel pretty much said it all for me anyways.

"I'm Sybil again," Sybil says.

I didn't know you could talk twice, but it's fine by me if she wants to take my turn. "I just want to say that I can relate to Wendy. My family has lived here a long time, and I have a manuscript one of my ancestors wrote about living here in the 1800s. It's fascinating, and I've actually shown it to Wendy's husband, John, and he thinks I should publish it. But I'm a bit nervous about it because of some of the things it reveals about our family. Anyway, I—well, I am afraid, but I also feel like my past, or my family's past or something, is pushing me forward. Like my ancestors want me to do something more for them. It's just a weird feeling, so I can relate to how Wendy feels. I don't know if I'll publish that book or not. I don't think I'm quite ready to yet. That's all. Thanks."

"Thank you, Sybil," everyone says.

And then we're back to silence. We wait and we wait, and no one says anything. I look around, and most of them are sitting there staring at the floor, but they're all smiling and looking content. "Can we go now?" I want to ask, but I figure Wendy's in charge so she'll let us know the protocol.

"Lyla, do you wish to share?" Wendy asks.

I don't want to share. I'm not going to share. I—

"It's fine if you don't," Wendy says. "And if anyone else wants to share again they can. We want everyone at the meeting to share or not as they feel comfortable doing."

No one says anything else. The silence is killing me, so I figure I might as well say something because it beats just sitting here.

"I'm Bel again."

Shit! Before I could even open my mouth. She better not talk long. I want to go home.

"And I really appreciate the welcome I've received here today," Bel says. "I've been to AA like I said, but there are just some things a woman needs to talk about that she doesn't feel comfortable sharing when there's a man in the room. I can feel how much you women have already bonded, and I hope I'll be able to add value to your meetings. I'm not a mom, and I haven't been in a relationship with a man for years. I'm actually divorced, although my ex-husband is dead now, so I feel more like a widow, and I think I said he died from his alcoholism because he wouldn't get help, and that really scared me. That's why I started going to AA and I can't say enough about how much it helped me, so I just want to say that I hope you all really appreciate what you have here. It's because people care enough to reach out to each other and help one another that so many people have managed to overcome their problems and live fulfilling lives. I've seen it happen many times, and I know if I didn't have my AA meetings, or my good friend Lyla here to talk to, I might not be here today, so I just want to say that I look forward to continuing to come to this group, and I'm grateful to be here and I hope you all appreciate how special this group is. Thank you."

"Thank you, Bel," everyone says.

And then Bel gives me a "Say something" look. I'm feeling a bit trapped, like she got me to come because she thinks it will help me more than her. She's accused me before of having anger issues because of my past, which I think is ridiculous. There's no point in my obsessing over the past. Sure, I've had plenty of reason to be angry, but it doesn't do any good, but since she keeps staring at me, finally I do say something, just making it up as I go without knowing what will come out of my mouth until it's said.

"I'm Lyla, and I also appreciate everyone letting me come and listen to all of you. It—well, I guess it kind of makes me feel like I'm not alone in the world. Life is kind of hard at times. Well, more than kind of. I can't say I've had an easy life. Bel and I, well, we were in the orphanage together, but—well, she has been my lifelong friend as a result—even though she's been a drunk..."

Immediately, I wish I hadn't said that, not because it's not something I couldn't have said to Bel, but because the rest of them might think it's mean of me, though I don't know them well enough to really care what they think.

"So anyways," I says, finally finding words to continue, "I guess I appreciate that, and I've lived long enough I suppose that I—well, I wish since you're all so much younger than me that I could tell you everything that happens in your lives has a purpose, but I don't know that. My life doesn't seem to make much sense to me actually. God and I—well, we kind of have a strange relationship—I get angry at Him a lot, but I try to be good and do what I think God wants me to do, but I have a naturally ornery and rebellious nature. That's why, when my parents died, the woman who adopted my older sister didn't adopt me—at least, that's the reason she gave me, and well, I've pretty much held a grudge over not being adopted all these years and...um...and..." I know I better stop before I get myself in trouble. The last thing I want to do is to start crying. "I guess that's all. Thanks."

I clamp my mouth shut, but no one acts like they know I almost lost it; they just say, "Thank you, Lyla."

There's a few seconds of silence that make me wonder if they don't know what to say because I made such an idiot of myself. I hope they'll all keep their mouths shut about it when they leave like they promised.

"Well, I think we've had a very productive meeting today," says Wendy. "It helps when new people come. It helps to give us new perspectives on life. It reminds us how far we've come, and it helps us to reach out to one another rather than to isolate ourselves. Thank you all for making this meeting work. Let's close now with the serenity prayer."

Everyone stands up and forms a circle. Bel stands up, and then I stand slowly. Bel grabs my hand and pulls me into the group, and then Diana, the sex addict, takes my other hand—I hate to think what her hand was doing earlier today considering what she said. I'll have to use a lot of Ivory soap on it later.

Then they all say a prayer. It must be standard at these kinds of meetings 'cause I can hear Bel reciting it. Everyone knows it, and I know I've heard it before, but I don't know the words by heart so I says nothing.

God,
Grant me the serenity
To accept the things I cannot change;
The courage to change the things I can;
And the wisdom to know the difference.

Then I feel both Bel and Diana squeezing my hands.

"Thanks, everyone," says Wendy, and we finally let each other's hands go. We start to collect our coats, but there's a lot of chatter among everyone, and Wendy makes a point of saying it's good to see me, and all the women are thanking Bel and me for coming and asking us to come back again, and I just nod and smile and think I won't be back because it's all too awkward, though Bel keeps saying things like, "Definitely, we'll be back," and "See you next week." Damn her, why does she always think she has to speak for me?

It's such a relief when the two of us are finally back in the car.

"So, what did you think?" Bel asks me as she puts on her seatbelt.

"They're nice, but some of them are pretty screwed up, especially that Diana woman."

"Judge not lest ye be judged, Lyla," says Bel.

I don't say nothing. I just sit while she starts up the car and pulls out of the parking lot.

"You did well in there, Lyla," she says as we head for home.

I feel like she set me up, and I don't like it. "If I knew it would be that awkward," I tell her, "and that I'd have to say something, I never would have gone."

"But you did say something," she says, flashing her idiotic smile at me, "and next time won't be so bad."

I don't want there to be a next time. She knows that, but she has to push anyways by asking, "Will you come next week too?"

"We'll see," I says, just because I'm in no mood to argue with her. I'll tell her "No" in a few days, after I think about it and have cooled down enough. She should know me well enough by now anyways to know that "We'll see" means "No."

"It always helps to have someone to talk to," she says. "I know I'd be lost if I didn't have you to talk to, Lyla."

"Yeah, I know," I says. "That's what you told everyone."

Chapter 8

After a couple days, I still haven't decided if I'll go back to that women's meeting. They think talking about their problems will help them, but it seemed to me like all they were doing was just talking, not fixing anything—especially that sex addict girl; she admitted she's still going out and having sex, so what good is the meeting doing her?

As far as I'm concerned, talking to God is the only talking that's going to do you any good. I mean, most people can't fix their own problems, so what good does it do to tell them about yours? Not that talking to God has gotten me very far, either, except that one time when I just about lost it—the day I tried to make up with my sister after Miss Bergmann died. Jessie was so nasty to me that day that I went to the priest in tears asking him to go try to talk some sense into her. Instead, he told me to pray the rosary. I thought he just wanted to get rid of me when that was his answer, but I didn't know what else to do, so I walked home praying the rosary like he said, and when I got home, there was Papa standing on my front doorstep, just like God had answered my prayer—well, maybe not my prayer to have a better relationship with Jessie, but at least to have some family.

Of course, that was forty years ago, and I'm not sure God has answered a single one of my prayers since, but if it worked once, it could work again. Even if He doesn't answer, the nuns used to tell me that He always listens. Not many other people listen to me. Not even Bel most of the time, and considering God stuck me in this mess of a life I have, listening to me is the least He can do.

I guess I'm thinking about God on Friday because it's my one day a month I go to help with cleaning at the cathedral. I'm kind of sick of it, but it's harder and harder to find young people to help, and the ones who do couldn't clean properly if their lives depended on it. I've been helping to clean there for years now, ever since my old friend Mary Dwyer asked me to help out. That was right after Papa died. I didn't go to church hardly at all while I was taking care of him, but then I started to think about going back, and when I saw Mary downtown and she asked if I'd help, well, I figured maybe I could work off some guilt that way, get some points with God for being away from church.

So I said yes. It wasn't hard because Mary was real nice. She was nearly twenty years older than me, so I just let her take the lead and followed her around with the dustcloths or the mop bucket and did whatever she said we needed to do, whether it was dusting a statue or wiping down a pew.

Mary used to clean the church all the time and she was also the sacristan I think they call it—I'm not sure exactly what that means, but I know she did things like wash the chalices and launder the priests' robes. Mary's been dead for years now, but I'm still here. Now I'm the old lady telling the younger women what to do. I keep thinking I should quit, but I go every month when it's my turn and never do get around to saying I'm too old to do it anymore, though I sure feel it when I'm done.

I don't mind so much, though, when I get to clean the chapel. It's smaller and more peaceful than the bigger church. Of course, I worry about disturbing the people who are always in there doing Perpetual Adoration of the Eucharist, but they're just silently praying and don't pay me no mind, and I try to be quiet while I wash down the pews and dust.

It sounds kind of weird, but I feel kind of like I have a friend there in the chapel—no, not Jesus, even if the priest says he's present in the Blessed Sacrament, something I've never really understood. No, my friend is one of the angels in the mosaic in the front. It's a picture of Jesus and four angels— two of the angels are kneeling and one looks like she's greeting the Lord, and then there's the pouting one. She's in yellow, and she's got this sort of scowl on her face. She's got her hands together in prayer, like she's trying to play the role, but she's not looking at the Lord and she doesn't look too excited about seeing Him, and her dress kind of hangs around her waist so you can just tell that she's a bit on the chunky side. Even her wings don't look like much compared to the other angels because she's kind of tucked away in the corner of the picture. I often think if I ever get to heaven, that's the kind of angel I'll be. She just doesn't look like she fits into heaven, but she's there anyways.

"God accepts all kinds," Mary Dwyer used to tell me, and I guess that means even the cranky ones like me.

Tonight, I have a couple of helpers, but they leave while I finish up in the chapel. Earlier, Bel had wanted me to go to supper at The Pancake House, even though I'd told her half a dozen times it was my night to clean at the church, so finally, I told her we could go when I finished. By then I'd be tired and need a good meal to perk me up. Bel said she'd have Sybil come pick me up in the cathedral parking lot at ten o'clock.

I finish up just a couple of minutes before ten. Since I'm in the chapel, I have to walk back through the main church and then the gathering space to get to the parking lot. So, trying not to disturb the perpetual adorers too much, I collect my stuff and quietly open the door between the chapel and the church.

When I enter the church, it's completely dark inside except for a couple dim lights and candles glowing in front of the statues along the two side aisles. As I start down the side aisle, out of the corner of my eye I see in front of the statue of Mary and her mother St. Anne, a woman holding out her purse. She looks kind of short, but I figure she's just elderly. But as I get closer, I see it's not an old lady but a Chinese-looking teenage girl. And she's stuffing the candles into her purse!

I'm so shocked I holler out, "Hey, you can't...!"

For a moment, she turns to look at me. Then she runs toward the back door.

"Stop thief!" I yell and run around the pews to chase her.

I know I won't catch her so I try to take in all the details—short black hair, a jean skirt, and I see the hate in her face before she turns to run.

"What's wrong with you, stealing from God's House?" I shout as she disappears out the side door.

There's not a lot more I can do. By the time I get anywhere near the side door, she's gone through the gathering space and I just catch a glimpse of her opening the door to go outside. I know she'll be down the block before I even get to the door, but I move as fast as I can. When I get to the door, it's dark out. Even with the streetlights on, she's hidden away in the shadows somewhere. I step outside into the warm June night but even after searching both ways, there's no sign of her.

Just then I see a car pulling into the parking lot. It's Sybil and Bel. Quickly, I open the front passenger door and hop in.

"Lyla, you always sit in the back—" Bel says but I cut her off.

"Quick!" I holler. "Drive around the block! A teenage Chinese girl just ran out of the church. She stole some candles. If we hurry, we can catch her!"

"What?" Bel says.

"Go, go!" I yell. "We can't let her get away with stealing from the church."

"Which way?" Sybil asks.

"I don't know," I says as she heads toward Fourth Street and turns right to circle the cathedral.

"Lyla," says Bel, "it's not Sybil's job to be part of a police chase."

"It's okay," says Sybil as we turn onto Rock Street and go around the back of the cathedral.

"I don't see anyone," says Bel, "and I'm starving."

"When did you see her do this, Lyla?" Sybil asks as I keep my eyes glued to the road ahead.

"Just as I was leaving the chapel. She couldn't have gotten out of the church more than a minute before me."

"How old was she?" Sybil asks.

"Oh, maybe fourteen I'd guess. She had short black hair and a jean skirt on and a big black purse to stuff candles into. I was so shocked that I didn't know what to do except to yell, 'Stop thief!'"

"Juvenile delinquent," muttered Bel.

"You said she looked Chinese?" asks Sybil.

"Yeah," I says. "Should we go to the police?"

As Sybil turns the car onto Fifth Street, she says, "I doubt the police can do anything about it."

"There can't be many fourteen-year-old Chinese girls in Marquette," I says.

"No, I suppose not," says Sybil. I look over at her, wondering why she gets so quiet. Maybe she's thinking of writing about this for *The Mining Journal*. Then she'll want to interview me and I'll get my name in the paper. But she has this weird look on her face. "I don't think we should go to the police," she says. "She's just a kid really; we don't want to give her a police record if she's just a first-time offender."

"Let's just go eat," says Bel.

"No, make a bigger circle," I says. "Go down to Washington and then up

Third. Make like a three or four block circle. She can't have gone that far."

"Lyla," says Bel, "for all we know, she might live in one of these houses along here and already be hidden somewhere."

"Don't listen to her," I tell Sybil, who is now driving past Snowberry and up to Washington. For a minute, I think she's just going to take us to The Pancake House, but then she turns toward the lake instead and we go down to Third. There are people wandering about downtown, but they all look like college kids hitting the bars.

We don't say anything as we make a big circle. Sybil goes all the way down South Third Street to Fisher and then over to Fifth again, but we don't see a thing, so finally, she goes back down Fifth to Washington.

"We aren't going to find her," says Bel. "It's too late now."

"No, I guess not," I says. "I wonder whether I should call and tell Monsignor Cappo about it."

"I wouldn't," says Sybil. "What can he do about it?"

"Maybe she goes to St. Peter's," I says, "so he might know her and can call her mom or something."

"Lyla, wouldn't you know her if she went to St. Peter's?" asks Bel.

"No," I says. "If I knew her, we wouldn't have to chase her 'cause I could just call her mom. Besides, lots of people go to Mass on Sunday that I don't know since I go on Saturday."

"Well, Chinese people aren't Catholic anyway," Bel says. "They're Hindu or something."

"Finns aren't usually Catholic either," I says, "but I am. She could be a convert—or at least her parents. Though, I think she must be a heathen if she's stealing from the church."

"I don't think there's anything we can do about it now," says Sybil, turning onto Washington and heading west. "I'll just take you to The Pancake House."

"Sorry, Sybil," I says. "I didn't mean to waste your time."

"No big deal," she says.

"I'm starving," says Bel.

"Well, you should learn to eat at a reasonable time rather than dragging me out at all hours of the night," I says, feeling perturbed with her whining when I'm trying to stop a crime.

"You two," Sybil laughs. "You're the only customers we have your age who go out for pancakes late at night."

I don't say anything. I realize I'm kind of shaking from the shock of the crime I witnessed and a little out of breath since running like I did after the thief isn't something I do anymore. I take a deep breath as we sit at the red light at Seventh Street. But then just as the light turns green, I look up the hill and see the Chinese girl walking up it—she's almost clear as day in the streetlights.

"Stop. Quick. There she is!" I yell.

"What?" asks Sybil, looking where I'm pointing, but she's already driven halfway past Harlow Park.

"Turn around," I says. "She's going up the hill on Seventh. She's almost at the top. Hurry and we can catch her."

Sybil turns to the right once we're past the park, and she makes a circle around the block to get back to Seventh. By that time, I can't see the girl anymore because she must be over the crest of the hill, but I'm sure we're going to catch her this time.

"Lyla, this is crazy," Bel says.

"Shut up," I says. "How do you think God would feel knowing you care more about your strawberry waffles than stopping people who steal from His house?"

I don't see the girl when we get to the top of the hill until I look toward Park Cemetery, and there she is going inside its gates.

"There, there!" I yell as Sybil drives past the gate. "Back up!"

But Sybil's afraid someone will rear-end her car, so she goes all the way down to the next block, pulls into a driveway, and turns around. The gate for cars to go into the cemetery has already been closed for the night, but I can see the smaller walking gate open. That must be how she got in.

"Stop there, in front of that little gate!" I holler.

"Lyla, Sybil can't park on the road here," says Bel, but Sybil pulls up to the curb, and in another second, I'm getting out of the car.

"We can't chase her on foot, Lyla!" I hear Bel say as I head through the gate, not shutting the car door so the girl won't hear it slam. I wish Bel would shut up before the girl hears her.

I spot the thief in a few seconds over by the edge of the lily pond. I don't think she heard us pull up to the cemetery. I walk toward her in the dark as quickly but quietly as I can, thinking maybe I can grab her and get her back to the car. I am bigger than her after all, and hopefully, Sybil is close behind me. But when I'm not more than twenty feet from the girl, she turns and sees me.

For a moment, she just stands there, maybe frozen in fear.

"What the hell do you think you're doing, stealing from the Church, young lady?" I yell at her.

She doesn't move as I get closer, which makes me wonder if it's not her—maybe the dark is tricking me and I'm looking at a statue or a gravestone, but then when I'm only maybe ten feet from her and thinking I can grab her by the collar of her jean jacket, she steps forward, and says:

"Fuck off, Grandma!"

I almost freeze for a second. No one speaks to me that way. It really ticks me off. I lunge forward to grab her, but my foot slips on the grass. She darts off as I start to fall. Next thing I know, I've slid right into the pond.

"Lyla!" I hear Sybil scream as my head goes under.

The water is cold and a real shock to my system. The bottom of the pond isn't deep, but it's all soft and mucky so I have a hard time trying to push myself up. Finally, just as I give up trying to stand and begin to kneel in the muddy bottom, I get my head above water and hear Bel screaming. And then Sybil's at my side, helping me to stand up and dragging me to the shore.

"Are you okay, Lyla?" she asks.

I'm all soaking wet, and though it's too dark for me to tell, I just feel like I must be full of mud and pond scum and maybe have a lily pad stuck in my hair.

"That damn girl!" I shout. "Yeah, I'm okay. Here I try to do something good like stop someone from stealing from a church and this is what I get."

"You got it because you were acting stupid," says Bel, now standing over me on the pond's edge.

"Shut up," I says.

Sybil helps me to stand up and get back on the grass. I lean on her while I take off one shoe and then the other and drain the pond water from them.

"Where'd she go?" I asks.

"Who, the hoodlum?" Bel asks.

"No, Mary Poppins," I says. "Who do you think? Is there any other way she can get out of the cemetery?"

"She could probably climb over the gate in the back," says Sybil. "It's not much more than three feet high."

"She's long gone now," Bel says, sighing. "Lyla, give it up. We better get you home so you can change into some dry clothes before you catch a cold.

It's not that warm out tonight."

"All right," I says, still leaning on Sybil, who takes my arm and walks me to the car. I could walk myself but my shoes are all soaked and squeaky and I'm afraid I'll slip so I let her hang onto me like I'm an old lady.

We get through the gate and back to the car, and then I says to Sybil, "I don't want to get your car all wet."

"It's okay," she says. "The seats are leather anyway."

Bel and I get in the back this time. When Sybil gets in the front, she starts laughing.

"Lyla, you should have seen yourself when you fell, the way you threw up your arms and nearly did a somersault. I'm surprised you didn't break something."

I don't think it's all that funny so I just says, "Well, the water and the mud in the pond are soft."

"Now that I think about it," says Bel. "You did look hilarious, Lyla! I was scared when I saw you fall, but now it's funny."

"You'd have won if we had filmed it and sent it to *America's Funniest Home Videos*," Sybil laughs as she pulls the car back onto the road.

And then, despite how wet I am, I can't help laughing either. I mean, here I am a seventy-seven-year-old woman, taking the law into my own hands, chasing a Chinese girl halfway across Marquette and through a cemetery for stealing church candles.

"I don't know what I was thinking," I finally says. "I just—I was in such shock that someone would steal candles from a church that I just went ballistic."

"It's okay," says Sybil. "It made the evening interesting."

"Bel," I says, "I'm sorry we didn't get to The Pancake House. Are you really starving?"

"It's okay," she says. "I'll manage."

"Should I wait for you to change, Lyla?" asks Sybil. "I can still take you to The Pancake House."

"Sure, if you don't have to pick someone else up," I says.

"No, it's a slow night so far," Sybil says.

So we go back to Snowberry. Bel and Sybil say they'll sit in the car and wait for me. Thankfully, no one sees me walk through the lobby and ride up in the elevator all sopping wet. I don't move as fast as I used to, but in about fifteen minutes, I come back downstairs looking relatively decent again, and

I bring a towel back with me to soak up any water I got on Sybil's car seats. Then Sybil takes Bel and me to breakfast at nearly eleven o'clock.

Like I haven't had enough frustration for the night, as soon as we get back in the car, Bel says, "So, Sybil, I guess you must have been surprised to see us at your women's meeting."

"Well, I didn't expect it," says Sybil, "but I was happy to see you."

I wonder. Sometimes I bet Sybil must think we're a couple of wackadoos; I mean, like she said, we're the only old ladies in Marquette who go to The Pancake House in the middle of the night. Anytime we see other people there, they're usually college students, trying to sober up after eating at the bar all night, or people who work nights and just got off their shifts.

"So, how's it going with that boyfriend you were telling us about there?" Bel asks Sybil.

"Oh, okay I guess. I haven't seen him much the last few days. But we have a date tomorrow night after he gets home from picking up his son downstate."

"How old's his son?" I asks.

"Twelve I think," she says.

"Wow," I says. "He must be a lot older than you then."

"Yes," she says. "He's thirty-nine."

"That's not that old," says Bel.

"Well, but it's an age difference," I says. "How old are you Sybil, like twenty-seven?"

"Twenty-eight," says Sybil.

"Eleven years ain't all that much," says Bel. "Charlie and me were four years apart."

Eleven is a lot more than four, I think. Sometimes I wonder if Bel can really do math.

"So you haven't met his son yet?" I asks, more curious than I usually am.

"No. I probably will tomorrow, though," says Sybil. "The thought makes me nervous. I mean, it's not like I'm even really his girlfriend yet."

"Well, it's good you're meeting his son right away," says Bel, "because once you get the kid to like you, the boyfriend will want to keep you around. You should bring the kid a little present or something for that reason."

"Oh jeez," I says to Bel. "Sybil can't be bribing a kid to like her, and she just said she's not even sure how much she likes the kid's father yet."

"Oh, I do like him," Sybil says. "I really like him. It's scary, but I do."

That's right. I remember what she said about him now at the women's meeting. I've heard girls talk like that before. She's definitely smitten. And that usually means trouble.

By the time we get to The Pancake House, Bel is complaining that she's starving again so we say goodbye to Sybil and go in to eat. Later when Sybil drives us home, it's after midnight, and Bel is kind of sleepy so none of us are very talkative.

When I get home, though, I can't sleep, so I lay there in bed thinking about Sybil and her boyfriend, and how exciting it must be to be in love like that, and then I remember how smitten I was with Bill at first. Despite how he acted when I saw him last, I hope he's doing okay. It's been a few days so maybe I should call Eleanor to ask her. As I drift asleep, I envision myself going up to the hospital to see him again, and telling him I still love him, and how sorry I am that we stayed apart all these years, and then I imagine him asking me to come live with him and take care of him now, and I'm willing to do it.

I get weak and lonely like that at night sometimes. But in the morning, my sanity has returned. No man is worth it, least of all Bill.

Chapter 9

I come down with a cold over the weekend, probably from falling in that damn pond, and it's pretty bad all the next week so I don't make it to the women's meeting. Since I can't go, Bel goes alone, and then she comes by later to check on me. When I asks her if Sybil said anything about her date with her new boyfriend, Bel tells me, "Lyla, you know those meetings are confidential. I can't tell you what anyone else says."

"But I'm part of the group," I says.

"It doesn't matter," she says. "You weren't there and you've only gone to one meeting, and how do I know you'll even keep on going? If you want to know about Sybil's boyfriend, you'll just have to ask her yourself, and besides, she didn't even mention him today."

Sometimes, Bel is a real pain in the ass.

I stay in the house all week with a stuffed up head and a runny nose. By Sunday, I can't stand staying cooped up any longer and the cold's just about over so I go out with Bel for breakfast just like we always do on Sundays.

This morning she decides she wants to go to the Tiroler Hof—I don't really care where we go for breakfast—it's eggs and pancakes and coffee no matter where you go for breakfast; it's all the same—but she always wants to go somewhere different each week except on our middle of the night runs 'cause only The Pancake House is open late enough for those.

I meet her down in the lobby and we head off to the restaurant. It may seem like she never shuts up at times, but other days, because we see each other so much, there just isn't much to talk about, so we're silent as she goes south on Fifth, turns left onto Fisher, and then onto Champion and over the bridge. I don't go in that direction much anymore, and I'm not even thinking about it until Bel says, "Isn't that the house where you used to work?"

It takes me a second before I look down Jackson Street and see the Mitchells' house.

"Yeah," I says.

"They were a couple of old ladies, weren't they? Isn't that the first place you worked after the orphanage?"

"Yeah," I says. "The Mitchell sisters, Miss Mary and Miss Florence."

"That's right. You've told me about them; they're the ones whose graves you put flowers on, but you've always said they were kind of old and ornery, weren't they?"

"Well, Miss Florence was kind of ornery, but well, she was really just set in her ways."

"Kind of like you," laughs Bel.

"What do you mean?"

"You're kind of ornery, Lyla, but once someone gets to know you, they know it's all just an act to protect yourself."

Sometimes it ticks me off that Bel knows me so well, or at least that she thinks she knows me, but what she says does make me wonder if I am like Miss Florence—if maybe that's where I get it from.

"I wasn't trying to be mean," says Bel when I don't say anything for a minute.

"No," I says. "I know. I was remembering about living there. It was so long ago now, back during the war, that it's hard to believe it ever happened."

"That was a long time ago," says Bel.

That's all that's said about it, but it's enough to trigger something in me that keeps me thinking about the Mitchells for the rest of the day. I don't know that I ever thought about it before, but I guess I am a lot like Miss Florence, and maybe I shouldn't be so surprised, considering. I didn't notice it then, but people say you find yourself saying things your mother said when you get older, and now I'm, well, I'm probably five or six years older now than what Miss Florence was when she died, so I maybe shouldn't be so surprised if I sound like her at times, though I wish I had taken more after Miss Mary.

Either way, working for the Mitchells beat living in the orphanage, and I find myself replaying my memories of the time I spent with them all that afternoon after I get back home from breakfast.

It was the day after my fourteenth birthday that Sister Euphrasia called me into her office. I wasn't too thrilled to go talk to her since we'd never gotten along that well, but I knew that call meant she was going to get me out of that place finally, so I wasn't going to complain.

So once I was sitting down in a chair across from her desk, Sister Euphrasia said to me, "Lyla, you're fourteen now, and I'm sure you know what that means."

"Yeah, it means I have to leave. To go find a job," I said. "I'm looking forward to it."

"I hope you are grateful for the time you have spent here."

"Yeah," I said, trying not to show how excited I was to get the hell out of the place, "but I just want to be independent."

"Well," she sighed, "I guess I should be glad you aren't like some of the kids who would be content to stay here forever."

I didn't know what kids those would be. Some of the kids, Bel included, liked the orphanage better than others, but I couldn't imagine any of us really wanted to stay there, though there were some who decided to become nuns or priests as a result of growing up there. To me, that was just like... well, like being stuck in a rut or something and afraid to leave home—like you could call an orphanage home. Some of them even talked about coming back after they finished at the convent or seminary to work in the orphanage later—crazy.

"I'm ready to go, Sister," I repeated.

"That's good, Lyla. I've found you a position to help get you on your feet. Two elderly sisters who need you to help look after them."

I must have grimaced a bit at the thought of old people because Sister Euphrasia looked straight at me and her brow got those deep furrows in it like when she was irritated, and then she snapped, "Lyla, we expect you to behave like a young lady and make a good impression when you go out to work. Remember, you are representing this orphanage, and people in the outside world will expect us to have raised you properly. Do not let us down."

"Sister," I said, "everything ain't the way that you nuns—"

"*Isn't*, Lyla. *Isn't* the way."

"*Isn't*, but that's another example of what I'm trying to say. Everything isn't the way it is here in the orphanage. Out in the real world, people don't talk to each other with the kind of respect we do here."

"Be that as it may, Lyla, we are called as Children of God to make the world a better place. When you leave here, you go forth as a representative of this orphanage, and I expect you to represent us well. After all, we've fed and clothed you for four years, and now we are making sure you have a home to go to so you can get a start in life."

"Yeah, so's I can be a servant," I said.

"We are all servants, Lyla, servants of the Lord. Remember, even Christ was a servant to others. He did not find it belittling but an honor to wash his own disciples' feet."

No matter what happened, I could guarantee I wouldn't be washing no one's stinkin' feet. Christ chose that sacrifice he made, but I wasn't going to make a choice like that. Actually, I knew I didn't have a lot of choice in the matter. There was no point in arguing because I didn't have anywhere else to go except wherever Sister Euphrasia sent me. Better to go take care of old folks than to stay where I was—I could always look for something else in the meantime.

"Sister, I know about how the first shall come last and all that," I said, trying now to be agreeable, but she must have thought I was mocking her or something 'cause she said, "You are a rude young lady, Lyla. I don't think I've ever known a more difficult young lady—at least not in this orphanage."

"I don't mean to be difficult, Sister. It's just, you have to understand that I don't like it here. You can't expect me to."

"To be honest, Lyla, I don't expect much of you at all," she said. "I wouldn't even send you to the Mitchells if they weren't so desperate, so I'm hoping they'll put up with you. I don't know anyone else who would. Here's the address."

She handed me a slip of paper for an address over on Jackson Street in South Marquette, only a few blocks away really.

"Okay," I said.

She shook her head, making it clear she was frustrated with me. I could see it was her way of dismissing me, so I got up and started for the door.

"Ten o'clock tomorrow morning, Lyla. That's when I expect you to be there. You better pack your things tonight so you're not late. You'll at least want to try to make a good impression your first day."

"Yes, Sister," I muttered, closing her office door behind me.

Of course, Bel insisted on helping me to pack, like I needed it. It took all of ten minutes to pack the few clothes I had, my toothbrush, hairbrush, and not much else.

"Lyla, I'm going to miss you so much," Bel said halfway through, and then her tears started flowing.

"I know," I said.

"You won't forget me, will you?"

"How could I ever forget you?" I said, and then so she'd quit bawling, I tried to change the subject. "Besides, I'm only going a few blocks down the road so you won't even know I'm gone."

"But I won't get to see you every day. We won't get to share secrets, and I—I don't know what else to say because it hurts so bad."

"It's okay," I said. "You'll be out of here in a couple years yourself and then you'll be glad for it just like I am."

"Will you wait for me, Lyla?"

I looked at her, wondering what the hell she meant.

"I mean," she said, "you won't move away or anything, right? And when I get out of here, we'll be friends again, right?"

"Sure," I said.

"Maybe we could rent a room together in a boarding house or something, or even find a place where we do housekeeping together."

"Maybe," I said. "We just have to wait and see. Whatever's meant to be will be."

Then before I could brace myself for it, she flung her arms around me, hugging me tightly, and declaring, "Lyla, you're my best friend!" She hugged me until I didn't think she was ever going to let go of me.

She was sobbing into my shoulder while I patted her back. I didn't know why she was so crazy about me; as far as friends went, she could have done better for herself; granted she was a bit flaky, but she didn't deserve a cranky thing like me for a friend. Still, I was glad I'd had at least one friend in the orphanage. I didn't know what I'd have come tomorrow.

"What's all the blubbering about?" asked Janet, who was about the only other girl Bel was friends with and whom I tolerated for her sake. Soon, Janet was followed by several other girls, all come to get ready to wash up for supper. When Bel told them I was leaving tomorrow, they all started talking excitedly about how they wanted to get out of there themselves and then they wished me well and said they'd miss me. It was all a little overwhelming for me really because I hadn't realized they all liked me that much, and really, I don't think they knew it themselves until it was time for me to go. All through supper even, they kept talking to me about what they'd do when they turned fourteen and could leave, and saying how lucky I was, and asking me to promise to visit and tell them all about it, which I promised to do to be polite, but there was no way I was ever going to set my foot back in that place ever again. I'd had it with all the sadness we all felt over not having families, and all those strict nuns telling me what to do. I'd put up with it for four years and that was enough for any girl to take.

But that night, I have to admit I felt a bit sad about leaving—or at least scared since I didn't know what to expect next. Looking back now that I'm an old lady, it seems like my whole life has been that way—thinking, or at least hoping, that the grass will be greener whenever I get to the next stage in my life, only to find that it ain't.

And it sure wasn't greener when I got to the Mitchells' house, although it was just early spring and all the snow hadn't melted yet. I wouldn't say being with the Mitchells was worse than the orphanage, just different, but certainly, it wasn't like what I had imagined. Hell, they barely even had grass—they had let the place start to fall apart so much, but I'm getting ahead of myself.

The next morning, after more hugs and tears from the girls, and especially from Bel, and even all the nuns, Sister Euphrasia gave me a rosary to remember her by. My first thought when she handed it to me was to throw it in the road as soon as I was out of sight of the orphanage, but I guess I was too scared of being sacrilegious to do that. In fact, I've still got it now after all these years and I've even used it a few times. Sister Euphrasia and I never did see eye-to-eye, but in the end, I guess I've come to understood that it wasn't so much that she didn't like me as she just wanted me to be prepared for the real world. Too bad she didn't know nothing about the real world herself since she lived in a convent or the orphanage her whole adult life. But I suppose she did the best she knew how. Come to think of it, she probably figured giving me that rosary was her way to keep her hold over me even when I was out of her sight.

The Mitchells lived in South Marquette. I remember what a long walk it seemed like to their house that first day.

From the orphanage, I walked down Fisher Street to Champion and crossed the bridge. I was a bit scared about the bridge because I'd heard about the gangs that often had their rumbles there—the working people lived in South Marquette and the bridge was the dividing line in the town. I'd even heard that one time in a fight, someone was thrown over the bridge and killed, and that had to hurt since it's not a bridge over water, just over a valley. But I was lucky that day because it was still morning, so maybe it was too early for anyone to want to rumble yet.

Anyways, once I got over the bridge, I walked just a couple blocks down Champion and then turned and walked to Jackson Street. When I found the right address, I saw the Mitchell sisters lived in a big old house, one of the oldest in Marquette it looked like—not so much 'cause of how it was built as because it didn't look like it had been painted in decades. (Later I'd find out that their father built it soon after he came home from fighting in the Civil War, and then he raised three children who all grew up but never married. I would be working for his two daughters—old maids, whose old bachelor brother had recently died.)

It was an awful warm day for late March, and it didn't help that I was wearing my winter coat since it wouldn't fit in my suitcase. We were all walkers back in those days and even more so with the war on and gas rationing—it must have been 1942 I guess—so I didn't think anything of hiking that distance, but I was sweating like nobody's business by the time I got to the house, and though my bag didn't contain much, just having to lug it along with me wasn't much fun as my sweaty palms gripped its handle and I kept changing hands so I could wipe the sweaty one on my dress. I must have been a sight by the time I got to the house with the sweat soaking my hair and dripping down the back of my neck. But I couldn't do much about it, just wipe the sweat from my face with the sleeve of my blouse and then go up the front steps to the porch and knock on the Mitchells' front door.

I remember how frustrated I felt standing there waiting and waiting for someone to answer that door.

I kept waiting for someone to look out the window or ask "Who is it?" at least. But there was no response so I knocked again, and then again, all the while getting more nervous and wondering why no one answered, and what was I supposed to do if no one did? I sure as hell didn't want to go back to the orphanage.

"Didn't Sister Euphrasia tell them I was coming this morning? Or are the old ladies dead inside?" I muttered to myself, thinking I'd probably stay even if they were dead—it would be better than going back to the orphanage.

Finally, when I knocked the fourth time, I heard an old lady inside hollering, "Florence, someone's at the door!"

But again, nobody came to the door. Then I thought to try the doorknob, but it was locked. Nobody in Marquette locked their doors! If they got hurt, how the hell did these old ladies think anyone would get into the house to help them? By now, I was getting really irritated, and I could feel the sweat dripping down inside my bra. "Damn it," I said, wiping my boob with my sleeve.

"Watch your tongue, young lady!" snapped a voice. I looked in its direction to find a wrinkled up old lady gaping at me from the side of the porch. She must have just come from around the backyard.

"What do you want here?" the old lady demanded.

"I'm Lyla Hopewell," I said. "I'm from the orphanage. Sister Euphrasia sent me here to work for the Mitchell sisters."

"I didn't know they taught young ladies to swear at the Holy Family Orphanage. I'll have to talk to Sister Euphrasia about that," she said. "And if you're going to work for us, you'll need to use the back entrance. Come on."

She motioned to me with her head and disappeared around the side of the house. As I walked across the porch to the side steps, I already knew she and I weren't going to get along any better than me and Sister Euphrasia had.

"Let me show you where you'll stay," said Miss Mitchell—I still didn't know which one she was—as I joined her and we walked around the house and I avoided the patches of snow still on the ground. I assumed that meant she was going to take me in the back door, but instead, we headed across the lawn to a little building in the backyard.

"This is the old servants' house. We always had help until my mother died," said Miss Mitchell. "Then we figured Mary and I could take care of Roger, but Mary left all the work to me since she had to go and teach school." At this point, I figured out it must be Miss Florence I was talking to. "It's a bit musty. I didn't have time to straighten it up for you—if I had time to do things like that, I wouldn't have had to hire you, so you can just straighten it up at night or on your day off. I imagine you'll want all of Sunday off, and since it is the Lord's Day, I won't argue over it, though I may have to change that if Mary or I get sick and need you. Anyway, considering the dormitory room I know you slept in at the orphanage, I'd say these are pretty good accommodations—especially for one as young and inexperienced as yourself."

She stopped talking long enough to give me another look over, and I took the opportunity to look her over too. She wasn't as old as I had thought—at first, I'd have guessed she was eighty, but she was probably closer to seventy, and she looked strong, from stubbornness—at least that's how I remember thinking she looked, or maybe I'm remembering how I came to view her later. Probably all that I really decided about her that first day was that I didn't like her. I didn't like the way she flared her nostrils and looked down her nose at me, and I didn't like the tone in her voice when she spoke to me like I was stupid, or a troublemaker, or both.

"Yes, ma'am," I said to her, if only to get her to stop staring at me. "I'll get experienced fast."

Then she turned her attention to the door and inserted a key in it, which made me remember how the front door had been locked too. These women weren't letting anyone into their homes or their lives without caution—that's probably why they were still old maids. Though later, I found out I was being unfair to Miss Mary, who was usually at the mercy of her sister's rigid ways.

Miss Mitchell opened the door and we went inside. It didn't look like anyone had lived in there since before the first war. Everything was old-fashioned and the curtains were faded from the sun, but I saw there was a table and a stove and a little sofa along the wall, and through the doorway I could see the bedroom.

"There's a working bathroom back there. Mother insisted on it. She didn't think the whole neighborhood needed to know when someone went outside to do their business, not even the servants. Old Mattie and Jake were like family anyway—they worked for us for over twenty years, from the time my brother and sister and I were little children until we were adults. Jake passed on just before Mother, and then in the end, though Mattie wanted to stay useful, we more took care of her than she of us. She passed away the year after Mother, and we've been alone ever since, just my brother and Mary and me. Roger died last year, and Mary's been going blind for the last few years until now she can barely see a thing so she decided it was time I get some help. Not that I couldn't still take care of this house all by myself," Miss Mitchell said, throwing back her shoulders to show how strong she still was, "but we have the money so I don't see why I should have to slave away the last years of my life. I've worked hard enough all my days—you don't know much if you don't think watching over your aging parents and then your older brother and sister isn't working hard. We didn't have all these modern conveniences back in those days. I used to rise with the dawn to churn the butter, feed our chickens, do the washing, whatever needed to be done, so don't you think you can get away with slacking off like a lot of these young girls people hire."

When I didn't reply, she said, "We always had a married couple working for us—Jake and Mattie as I said—we thought they were more steady, not like the hired Irish or Finnish girls some of our friends had come in. You couldn't rely on them. I hope you're not lazy like that, Lyla."

I didn't like the way she was acting like she was my boss, though I guess she was, so I just said, "No, Miss Mitchell. I'm a hard worker." I figured I was a hard worker even if Sister Euphrasia thought I was obstinate. Being stubborn never stopped me from doing my chores; some of the other kids were lazy, but I didn't want to live in a pigpen even if I had to help milk the cows and clean the bathroom myself for all those slob girls.

"It's Miss Florence," she replied. "My sister is Miss Mitchell since she's the eldest. I'm only Miss Mitchell in the sense of your referring to us in the plural as the Miss Mitchells."

I nodded my head. I thought about saying, "Yes, Miss Florence," but decided that was too "hired girl" sounding for me, or maybe too much like them negro slaves in the Shirley Temple movies.

"I see you didn't bring much with you," said Miss Florence, "but I suppose that's the way it is with orphan children. No matter, it won't take you long to get settled. You look like you need to wash your face. You're perspiring all over. Go ahead and clean yourself up and then you can come inside and fix lunch for us."

"Yes, Miss Florence," I said, never having fixed anyone's lunch in my life.

"You're welcome," she said, though I hadn't said, "Thank you." Obviously, she thought she was doing me a favor by taking me on. I didn't like her at all, but I held my tongue because the last thing I wanted was for her to send me back to the orphanage. I thought maybe I could look for another position while I worked there, one that the nuns wouldn't have their hands in so I'd be free from them once and for all.

Miss Florence marched back to the house. I watched her go through the back door, and then I set down my stuff and decided I'd put it away later. I didn't want to be accused of dawdling and have Miss Florence snapping at me again. When I got in the little bathroom, I felt grateful for the first time to be there because of the clean towels and washcloths. I took out a washcloth and washed off my face and then the sweat under my armpits. The water was cold and didn't run out of the pipes very well, but it was better than sharing a dormitory with a bunch of girls.

When I felt I was presentable again, I walked across the backyard and to the house, opening the back door and stepping in. I found myself in a little sort of pantry room and then stepped into the kitchen. There was a lady sitting at a table who said, "Is that Lyla?"

"Yes," I said, stepping forward and finding the other old lady sitting at the kitchen table with her back to me.

"I'm Mary," she said. "I'm glad to have you here. My sister and I so need some help, and we hope you'll like it here with us."

"Thank you," I said. She didn't turn around to look at me, which I thought was kind of odd, but then I remembered as I walked around to see her face that Miss Florence told me she was blind. Even so, she had a big colander in front of her and appeared to be snapping peas, and doing a pretty good job of it too.

"I hope you like peas," she said, "because we have plenty of them in the garden."

"I do," I said, adding, "especially fresh from the garden, not cooked."

"That's how I like them, though Florence always wants to cook them. We certainly have an abundance this year. I can't do the gardening much anymore, but I do like snapping the peas and doing whatever I can."

"It's nice you still can do things," I said.

"Come closer so I can see you better," she said. "I can see just a little, shadows mostly, so I know where you are, although I can't see the details."

I did as she said, walking around to the other side of the table and facing her.

"You look like a big girl, sturdy and strong I mean. Florence will like that. She likes to pretend she can do everything, but I finally convinced her to get us some help by claiming I needed company and shouldn't be left alone. Then I wouldn't be such a worry to her when she had to leave me to go do the shopping and such."

"Are you ready to fix lunch, Lyla?" Miss Florence asked, suddenly coming into the kitchen from the dining room.

"I suppose," I said.

"You *suppose?*" she snapped. "We don't suppose here, young lady. Either you are ready to learn how to work or you're not."

"I'm sorry, ma'am," I said, though I could feel my blood starting to boil. "I'll try to answer better next time."

"We don't *try* here either, Lyla. We do or we don't," she said.

I tried to think what to say back—something that sounded better than what I really wanted to say back, but Miss Mary saved me by saying, "I would so love some of that chicken from supper last night. We could make cold chicken sandwiches, Florence. Doesn't that sound good, Lyla?"

"Yes," I said. "I'll be happy to do that." I wouldn't be, but saying it sounded good.

"All right," said Miss Florence. "I'll show you where everything is and my system for arranging things."

I followed Miss Florence and listened to her explain to me where everything in the kitchen and pantry and even the icebox was, and then she showed me how to make a sandwich properly, like I couldn't have figured that out on my own. I might not have liked being told what to do, but I was a quick learner so she didn't seem too irritated with me. Every once in awhile, Miss Mary chimed in with a comment to distract Miss Florence when her or my ire would get up. I liked Miss Mary already; I could see she'd learned how to handle her sister. She was going to be my best friend here, that was clear. I knew Bel wouldn't like me thinking that, but well, Bel wasn't here, was she? And I knew then how the world worked—Bel would have forgotten all about me by the time she got out of the orphanage.

After lunch, I washed up the breakfast and lunch dishes. Miss Florence informed me the breakfast dishes were to be done right after breakfast, but she hadn't been able to do them that day because she was busy tidying up the servant's house for me. Then I spent the afternoon helping Miss Mary with the peas and Miss Florence with the canning. I learned Miss Florence's schedule—which days to dust, to wash the laundry, to scrub the floors—and about a hundred other things, and I'm not exaggerating. That woman had housecleaning down to such an art and a precise schedule that it would make modern multi-taskers quake—and it was all hard labor in those days—we didn't have no dishwashers, not even a refrigerator; the vacuum cleaner they had was an old Hoover that was older than me and didn't pick up enough dirt to make an anthill, a clear sign that even when modern things came along to help them, the Mitchells weren't ones to take up with them.

By the time supper was over that day and I did up those dishes as well, I was exhausted and hoping to get the evening to myself, expecting I'd spend it exhausted and sleeping in my new servants' quarters, but as I wiped the last dish, Miss Mary called me from the parlor.

"Lyla, come and sit with us for a while and listen to the radio."

I wasn't interested in listening to the radio, but I went ahead, figuring I shouldn't be unfriendly my first night there.

Miss Mary was sitting and just beaming while music was coming out of the radio, just like it was the greatest thing that had ever happened to her to hear it. Over time, I would notice that she took great pleasure in what pleased her ears. Miss Florence had her head down over her knitting; she didn't even look up until Miss Mary said, "Go ahead and sit down, Lyla, and keep us company."

Miss Florence was in a rocking chair and Miss Mary in an armchair on the other side of the room. I'd soon learn those were their respective chairs, so I took a seat on the sofa. That's when Miss Florence looked over at me and said, "Do you have any work to do?"

"I finished the dishes," I said. "Is there something else I need to do?"

"She means needlework," said Mary.

"No, I don't do none of that," I said.

"Didn't the nuns teach you to knit or tat or crochet or anything?" asked Miss Florence.

"No, ma'am," I said. "I mean, we were taught to knit, but I wasn't no good at it."

"I can see they didn't teach you very good grammar either," she said. "Hopefully, we'll be a good influence on you. Tomorrow night, I'll teach you knitting. I assume at least you can darn your socks?"

"No, I never have," I said.

She made a "tsk" sound.

"It's okay, Lyla," said Miss Mary. "You're only fourteen, aren't you? You have lots of time to learn."

"I don't know," I said. "One of the Sisters used to tell me I'd be better off becoming a nun because no man in his right mind would want me to take care of his house."

"Well," said Miss Florence, "somehow I don't imagine you'd make a very good nun."

"You don't need to be a wife or a nun, Lyla," said Miss Mary. "But we will help you learn to take care of yourself so you can be independent."

"You won't learn independence unless you learn to work hard," said Miss Florence. "Idle hands are lost time and money—which is why even at night when we're sitting down, we're still busy—not Mary so much now that she can't see anymore—but there's nothing I hate more than sitting still and being idle."

"It's been a long day," said Miss Mary, "and Lyla has lots of time to learn everything she needs to know around here. She told me earlier she knows how to milk a cow so I'm sure she can do just about anything else she needs to."

Miss Florence just returned her attention to her knitting, but her brow made her look like she was doubtful that I'd be a good learner.

We sat quietly and listened to a couple songs on the radio, but then when a commercial came on, Miss Mary, just out of the blue, said to me, "Lyla, whatever happened to your sister?"

I was a bit surprised. How did they know I had a sister, especially since neither of them had asked me a thing about my family since I got here, and why would they since they knew I was an orphan? But I figured Sister Euphrasia must have told them something about me.

"Um—she still lives here in town," I said.

"Oh, was she adopted?" Miss Mary asked.

"Yeah, I guess you'd call it that. After my mama died, my sister Jessie's piano teacher, Miss Bergmann, adopted her." I wanted to add that I didn't know why Miss Bergmann didn't adopt me too, other than that she was a mean old thing, but I bit my tongue, knowing no one wanted to hear my sob story.

"Miss Bergmann? What's her first name? We used to know some Bergmanns."

"Thelma Bergmann," I said, hoping to God they weren't friends with her.

"Oh, Karl's daughter," said Miss Florence.

"Yes, that's right," said Miss Mary. "Kathy's niece. How funny."

They were silent for a minute, but I was curious now.

"Why is it funny?" I dared to ask.

"Well..." said Miss Mary, "just that we used to know them and now we know you."

"It's not that funny, Mary. Marquette's a small town," said Miss Florence.

"So even if we don't know someone, they know the people we know."

"But how do you know the Bergmanns?" I asked. I hoped Miss Bergmann wouldn't go and say anything bad to the Mitchell sisters because I was sure Miss Florence wouldn't hesitate to get rid of me then. I wasn't sure I wanted to live and work there, but neither did I want to be losing my position because that old biddy was going around town badmouthing me, and I wouldn't put it past Jessie to be talking about me behind my back.

"Do you see your sister much?" Miss Mary asked in a soft voice, like she was feeling me out or something.

"No," I said. "When I first went to the orphanage, she and Miss Bergmann invited me over a few times, but I don't know—my sister changed after she got adopted, I guess. They don't bother with me now except at Christmas." I almost added "and my birthday" but I realized it was just my birthday a couple days ago and I hadn't heard from them. They probably didn't even know I'd left the orphanage, and they probably didn't care if they did know.

"I'm not surprised," said Miss Florence, with contempt in her voice.

"Oh, Flo," said Mary.

"I just mean that the Bergmanns are stuck up," said Miss Florence. "Thelma went to live with Kathy after her father died, so it must have rubbed off on her."

I didn't know what to say. I wanted to agree that Miss Bergmann and my sister were stuck up, but I didn't feel like I knew the Miss Mitchells well enough yet to trust them with how I felt.

"Lyla, I could tell you a few things about those Bergmanns," said Miss Florence, putting down her knitting and looking me straight in the eye like she was all set to spill the beans about them.

"Oh, Florence," said Mary, "it was so long ago, and they used to be our friends."

"They were your friends," Miss Florence replied, no longer looking down at her knitting but peering over her glasses with fire in her eyes. "They were never mine."

"How were you friends with them?" I asked, thinking this situation was turning in my favor.

"We haven't spoken to anyone in that family in years," said Miss Florence, making it clear she wanted nothing to do with them, "not since Kathy, Thelma's aunt, died, and we barely even spoke to her in the end."

"Kathy was my best friend when we were girls," Miss Mary said. "We were about the same age."

"Oh," I said, not knowing what else to say.

"Best friends," snorted Miss Florence. "Best friends don't act the way she did."

Miss Mary ignored her sister, not explaining what this Kathy Bergmann had done. "Thelma—Miss Bergmann as you call her—" Miss Mary said, "lives in Kathy's house now. When Kathy died, her family sold the house to Thelma."

"Much too lippy, that young lady," said Miss Florence, presumably about Miss Bergmann, "and it's a shame her father died and left her all that money without finding her a husband before he died. It was irresponsible of him to think his sister or her cousins would look after her when she's so addlebrained."

Again, Miss Mary ignored her sister and explained, "Thelma's father was a big logger in the area. He did quite well for himself."

"Only because his logging partner, Ben, had a good head for business," said Miss Florence, "and we all know the truth about him."

"What truth?" I asked, thinking he must have been a crook of some sort.

"Never mind," said Mary. "It's not right to speak ill of the dead, and Ben Shepard was a fine man in many other ways."

"Well, in any case," Miss Florence said, "after Kathy got married, she wasn't much of a friend to you, Mary."

"She had a husband and children to take care of and an aging mother," Mary replied, "and we were still friendly. It's not her fault she got married. If I'd ever married, I'd have been just as busy myself."

"I would have killed you before I would have let you marry a man like the one she did," Miss Florence said.

"Florence and Patrick, Kathy's husband, didn't get along very well," Miss Mary said to me. "That's why we quit being friends."

"Didn't get along well? He insulted me," Miss Florence said, looking at me like she was desperate to win me over to her side. "Why, we used to be members at St. Peter's, but after that incident, I couldn't go to a church that would let such people be members, so we started going to St. John's instead, even though it was farther to walk."

"Oh, Florence," said Miss Mary, "Patrick and Kathy have been dead for years now. Let it rest."

"I don't know why she ever married him," said Miss Florence. "I remember sitting there at their wedding and asking myself that question. I never did like him, not from the first time I saw him. Remember how he acted the first time we met—when we all went ice-skating together."

"I'm sure he was a good husband to her," Mary replied. "He gave her four children, one of whom became a priest—Father Michael McCarey."

"Some women," said Miss Florence, "think they have to have a man if they want to amount to anything. Marriage is for the weak."

"Oh, Florence, you know you don't believe that," said Miss Mary. "You'd have married yourself if the opportunity had presented itself."

"I could have gotten married," Miss Florence said, "but I told him, 'No.'"

"Oh, Florence," laughed Miss Mary.

"I could have," Miss Florence insisted, focusing on her knitting again, "but I knew better. Taking care of you and Roger was enough work. Why did I want to have even more to do? Women just end up slaving away for a man, and if they're lucky enough not to die having the babies, then they die young from all the hard work."

"Well," said Mary. "At least neither of us have died young. And Roger appreciated us and left us well-provided for. We can't complain."

"I'm glad, Lyla, to hear you won't be associating with the Bergmann family," said Miss Florence, looking up at me. "They certainly did know how to put on airs, just because Karl Bergmann was a successful businessman. The rest of the family wasn't much account. Patrick McCarey was a low-bred Irishman—that's the kindest thing I can say about him—and Karl and Kathy's mother was married to a saloonkeeper who died in a barroom brawl. They are not the kind of people with whom decent people like us associate."

I wondered if Miss Florence was including me when she said, "decent people like us." I kind of felt like maybe she was, despite her thinking I didn't look all that useful when I first arrived. I had a sense that Miss Mary meant to take me under her wing and treat me well, and despite Miss Florence's sharp tongue and demanding ways, her having a grudge against the Bergmanns made me feel like we were allies.

When I went to bed that night, I decided I'd stick it out living and working there while I could. It couldn't be worse than the orphanage after all.

Living with the Mitchells wasn't easy. Miss Florence was always on my case about something, but once I realized that, as Miss Mary said, "Her bark is worse than her bite," I learned how to give it back to her when I had to, and I worked real hard for them, so I think she came to respect me. After a month or two, we had fallen into a regular rhythm, and once I basically knew how to do everything around the house, she let me be and even asked me to help her do things I knew she'd rather do herself, but she realized I could do them better or faster. And so I stuck it out for two years with them and probably would have stuck it out longer if circumstances had been different.

It was through the Mitchells that I first met the O'Neills, though they wouldn't remember it, but it's funny that I should meet my last employers through the first ones, though I had several in-between.

The Miss Mitchells were Catholics, old style, what we'd call hardcore Catholics today, and because of them, I kept my Catholic faith. I was so irritated with the orphanage and Sister Euphrasia that, despite that rosary she'd given me, I probably would have quit going to church if the Mitchells hadn't gone regularly. Every Sunday they went to St. John's on Washington Street, even though St. Peter's was closer, all because of that falling out they'd had with Miss Bergmann's aunt so many years ago. And they walked—can you imagine that? Two ladies in their seventies, one of them blind, yet they walked each Sunday to Mass though it was a good twelve blocks and they had to go down a hill and then up one each way. They made it, often even in bad winter weather, Miss Mary with her white cane, and me often hanging onto her arm. I think they only missed Mass once in those years because of a blizzard, though sometimes we were lucky and someone would give us a ride home.

The O'Neills went to St. John's and the Miss Mitchells always said hello to them, so I got to know them that way. At least Miss Mary said hello while Miss Florence nodded, hardly ever more than that.

And then after a couple months, one Sunday afternoon the O'Neills showed up on the front porch and rang the bell. First I saw Mr. O'Neill's automobile, and then I opened the front door and there they were.

"Hello, Lyla," said Mrs. O'Neill to me. "Are the Mitchell sisters in? We've come to pay a call."

As I let them in, Mrs. O'Neill handed me a tray of cookies that Mr. O'Neill said his Aunt Louisa May had baked.

"Oh, Louisa May, she's such a sweetheart," said Miss Mary, and then she invited them into the parlor, even though Miss Florence appeared put out that she didn't know they were coming, and she even grumbled to me, "They could have said something at church about stopping by. I wanted to paint the back porch this afternoon." She wasn't one to rest even on a Sunday.

That was the first time the Mitchells had company while I lived there, and it didn't happen many more times. Since I was the hired help, I figured it was my job just to bring them coffee and plates for the cookies, which I did, but after I passed everything out, and before I could go back to the kitchen, Miss Florence said, "Sit down, Lyla. Don't be rude to our guests by disappearing." And that was when I knew for sure she liked me; that she thought of me as more like family and not just the servant. It was also that day I think I started to understand Miss Florence.

I don't remember much about the conversation that day until someone brought up the Hotel Superior, the big hotel that had once stood at the end of Genesee and Blemhuber streets, just a few blocks up the road from where the Miss Mitchells lived. From what they said, I gathered it was torn down about the time I was born so I didn't remember nothing about it, but the others all seemed to remember it fondly, except Miss Florence, who said, "That was one of the dumbest things they ever tried to pull off in this town, thinking we'd get the tourists they get at Mackinac Island."

"Oh, don't be so bitter, Florence," said Miss Mary.

"But it was such a beautiful hotel," said Mrs. O'Neill.

"It was the result of bad business sense," Miss Florence insisted.

And that's when the trouble started. Miss Mary said to the O'Neills, "Oh never mind Florence. It brings back bad memories for her; that's all."

And Mrs. O'Neill made the mistake of asking, "Oh, like what?"

And Miss Mary, not usually being one to say anything that might hurt someone's feelings, except when her sister was involved—sweet as Miss Mary was, she and Miss Florence sure knew how to push each other's buttons—said, "Florence lost her one true love there."

Surprised, I turned to look at Miss Florence, only to see her face go white and then she spit out, "Don't be ridiculous. I did no such thing."

"Oh, what happened?" Mrs. O'Neill wanted to know, and even Mr. O'Neill, who had been looking bored, sat up on the couch, eager for a good story.

"Nothing much," Miss Florence said, but Miss Mary said, "Florence fell in love with a young man who worked there not long after the place opened.

He told her he was the manager and she believed him, and he got her to meet him in secret and they carried on a love affair for weeks—"

"It was completely innocent," Miss Florence protested.

"And then," Miss Mary said, "one day he finally had the courage to come over to the house. He wanted to ask for her hand in marriage and get Father's permission, only Father just laughed him out the door. The young man had been lying to Florence all along—he was just a bellboy at the hotel, and Father knew it since he'd often go up there to have dinner with some of the railroad bigwigs because he worked for the DSS&A Railroad. He told the young man there was no way his daughter was marrying a bellboy without a penny to his name.

"Well, when Florence found out her young man had lied to her, she didn't want anything more to do with him."

"It's so long ago now," said Miss Florence. "Why do we have to talk about it?"

But Miss Mary insisted on finishing the story. "Florence was so mad she refused to see him when he kept coming by the house, and finally, Father had to threaten to sick the police on him if he didn't stay away."

"Oh, Miss Florence, that's too bad," said Mrs. O'Neill.

"It wasn't too bad. He took me for a fool, and I couldn't forgive him for that."

"The poor boy was heartbroken," said Miss Mary. "He left town soon after."

"Serves him right," said Miss Florence. "He's lucky Father didn't have him arrested for deceiving me about appearances."

"Oh, he was just in love is all," said Miss Mary. "I felt kind of bad for him."

"You would take his side. Mary, why can't you just shut up when you should?" Miss Florence snapped.

"Oh, Flo, calm yourself," said Miss Mary. "We're laughing with you, not at you."

"You'll be laughing when I give you the wrong medicine tonight," Miss Florence replied, and for a minute, I was scared that she really meant it.

"We're sorry, Miss Florence," Mrs. O'Neill said. "But there's no harm done. I'm glad to know you once had prospects, though I don't blame you for choosing to be single. Not everyone can luck out like I did with Robert."

I remember how Mrs. O'Neill squeezed his hand while he blushed a bit.

Imagine that. A forty-year-old man blushing.

Those two, the O'Neills, just seemed a bit too sugary sweet to me, too happy when I first knew them, but while I don't think they remembered me years later when I went to work for them, I never forgot how nice they were to each other. I could see they were truly happy—maybe the only married couple I ever saw who was—so when I went to work for them later, I couldn't help but love them because they had so much love inside them and were even willing to give me a little bit of it.

But anyways, as I was saying, after that, I saw Miss Florence in a different way. Sort of respected her more—maybe her lost love was why she was so crabby. Miss Mary told me that Miss Florence had been ornery since the day she was born, but I don't imagine having loved and lost helped the situation much. I felt a little sympathy for her; well, no, not sympathy because sympathy would make her sound pathetic, but rather, a bit more liking for her. I mean, no one ever seemed to like me much because of my disposition, and sometimes you just can't help being cranky, so I could see how Miss Florence had the same problems—we were like kindred spirits or something, and I could see she wasn't one to tell the world her problems, but rather one to suffer in silence. I was that way too, until the suffering got so bad I'd blow up like she had that afternoon.

I wondered then what other secrets she might be keeping…ones probably no one would ever know.

One day, Miss Florence said to me that it was time to paint the outside of the house.

"What color should we paint it?" asked Miss Mary.

"Just white like it's always been," said Miss Florence.

"Oh, I don't know…" said Miss Mary.

"What color would you like it to be, Miss Mary?" I asked.

"Why would she care?" snapped Miss Florence. "She can't see it anyway."

"I know this house well enough," Miss Mary replied, "that I can see it in my mind. I know every detail of this house, including remembering the day we moved into it, and that's something you can't say Florence because you weren't even born yet."

"You must have been two years old when we moved in. I doubt you remember it either."

"But I do," Miss Mary insisted. "Lyla, what color do you think we should have the house painted?"

"I've always liked blue," I said.

"Only Finlanders paint their houses blue," said Miss Florence, frowning.

"Well," said Miss Mary, "Lyla is part-Finn so it's no wonder she likes blue."

How'd Miss Mary know that? I'd never told them I was Finnish. Hadn't even thought about it in years, really. Maybe Sister Euphrasia had told them, but I couldn't help asking, "How do you know I'm Finnish?"

I saw Miss Florence's nostrils start to flare as she looked at Miss Mary. Miss Mary looked kind of troubled.

"Did Sister Euphrasia tell you?" I asked, sensing something was wrong.

"Lyla Hopewell," said Miss Florence, matter-of-factly, "Marquette is a small town and everyone in it knows everybody else's business."

Dread started to swallow me. No, shame—that's what it was. Shame that my father was a Finlander and he had abandoned my mother and sister and me. My mother's shame that she had married a Communist. I hadn't thought much about my father going to Karelia in years, but now those memories all came back to me, and I understood in a way I couldn't as a little girl the shame my mother must have felt to have her husband abandon us, and how that shame had followed me all these years even without me knowing it. How everyone when they saw me must have thought, "There she goes. The Communist's daughter."

And then tears sprang up in my eyes, and before I knew what I was doing, the shame made me run out of the room.

"Now you've done it, Mary. I told you to keep your mouth shut about all that."

I heard Miss Florence's words as I ran, but I was too upset to do anything but go out to the servant's house and lock myself in to have a good cry. I cried because I was just an orphan, and my own sister didn't love me, and my mother had died, and my father had abandoned me, and I was cursed with being a Finlander and looked down upon for it, and I wasn't even a real Catholic but a Finnish Lutheran just pretending to be a Catholic. And the Mitchells, who I was starting to think at least liked me, didn't really think much of me at all because I was just a dumb Finlander who wanted to paint the house blue.

I cried my heart out like I had never done before. In the orphanage, I had never let myself cry—I'd had to be tough to survive with all the other kids in there, and I wasn't going to act soft around the nuns, but I had started to soften toward the Mitchells, and now to find out that they didn't think any better of me than anyone else just hurt more than I could have imagined. I just sobbed like I hadn't sobbed since Mama died, and then I lay there sniveling and staring at the sky through the window and feeling trapped and lonely and pathetic until I fell asleep from exhaustion.

When I woke up, I looked over at the clock, feeling disoriented. After a minute, I made out that it was seven o'clock, and I remembered how I had run out of the house. But now I felt a panic because I had missed fixing dinner. Even if the Mitchell sisters didn't think well of me, they were all I had, so I knew I better get inside before I lost my position and they sent me back to the orphanage.

I went inside quietly, afraid Miss Florence would be in the kitchen, waiting for me and ready to jump down my throat. After I shut the back door, I gingerly stepped into the kitchen, only to hear them softly speaking in the dining room. Miss Florence must have heard me come inside because she hollered, "Come in and eat, Lyla. The mashed potatoes are getting cold."

They were sitting there at the dining room table, half-finished with their meal. They must have waited a long time for me because I usually cleared away the supper dishes around 6:30.

"Sit down," Miss Florence said when I stuck my head through the door.

"Florence cooked supper since she knew you weren't feeling well," Miss Mary said as I sat down.

"Thank you," I said.

"Do you feel better?" Miss Florence asked. I thought I heard a strain of concern for me in her voice.

"Yes, ma'am," I said.

We didn't say much else but just ate. Then when we were finished, I said, "I'll get started with the dishes."

Miss Florence didn't reply but just got up and went into the parlor.

I cleared the table and brought the dishes into the kitchen to wash them. I was just starting up the dishwater when I heard Miss Mary come into the room and sit at the little breakfast table.

"Lyla, is there any tea left?" she asked.

"Yes," I said. I got her a clean cup out of the cupboard and poured her tea and handed her the cup. Then I turned back to the sink and picked up the dishcloth.

I heard Miss Mary set her teacup on the table, and then she said, "Our mother's maiden name was Hopewell, you know."

It took a second for the comment to register with me, but then I turned around, and it was like everything was in slow motion as I felt my face preparing to form the question on the tip of my tongue; I waited a second for her to say more until I remembered Miss Mary couldn't read my face.

"Hmmph," Miss Florence snorted. I turned around and saw her standing in the doorway. She just turned around and headed out of the room, muttering, "Shirttail relations."

"I don't understand," I finally said.

"Lyla," Miss Mary said softly. "Florence and I are your cousins, your first cousins once removed. Your mother's father was our mother's brother."

That's more than I could quite figure out at the moment. What was more confusing was wondering how they knew this about me, but before I could ask, Miss Mary added, "Florence and I knew your mother. It's a long story, but—well—when Sister Euphrasia mentioned you to us, we guessed right away who you were."

"But," I said, trying my darnedest to understand, "when my mother died—how come...? I'm confused—I don't remember ever meeting you when I was a girl. I didn't even know I had any relatives in Marquette. I—"

"It's a long story, Lyla," said Miss Mary. "Sit down. The dishes can wait a few minutes while I try to explain it all."

I did as she said, wondering what all this meant.

"Our mother, your grandpa's older sister," she said, "didn't really approve, you see, of your grandfather's marriage. She thought your grandfather had married a gold digger since the woman was so much younger than him, a good twenty years or so. I remember when Uncle Roger—that's your grandfather, whom our brother was named after—brought home his bride to meet us. He had never told my mother he was marrying Elizabeth, your grandmother—it had been a rather spontaneous decision—and my mother was not pleased; I hate to admit it, but I think she had hoped he'd leave everything he had to her or my brother and sister and me. Not that he was all that wealthy—he owned a livery stable in town, though, and did a good business, and there had been some talk of Roger taking over the business from him; Roger even worked there at the time; of course, that was right around the turn of the century, and the automobile would have put him out of business in another ten or twenty years.

"Anyway, I remember how your grandfather and my mother had a big fight right here in our parlor, with poor Elizabeth just standing there, not knowing what to say to defend herself. I felt so bad for her, but I had to wonder why she would marry Uncle Roger, who was not that good-looking, and by then, on the wrong side of fifty. Elizabeth was only about twenty, and a good dozen or so years younger than me even at the time. Florence, of course, took Mother's side; Roger took Uncle Roger's side, and I tried to smooth everything over by being caught in the middle, but the end of it was that Uncle Roger sold his business and moved away to Duluth where Elizabeth apparently had family, and Roger then went to work for the DSS&A Railroad like our father did, while Mother and Uncle Roger never spoke to each other again, and what made it even worse was that your Grandma Elizabeth died soon after, following complications giving birth to your mother, Caroline. Elizabeth's obituary appeared in *The Mining Journal*, and when I saw it, I wrote to Uncle Roger to try to reconcile him with the rest of the family, but he never responded, and by then a few years had passed, so I figured if he were ever going to soften, he would have done so by then so I just kind of gave up on it.

"Then your mother grew up and married your father out in Minnesota. He apparently had some Finnish friends who lived here so after your grandpa died, your mother agreed to move back here with him; she later told me she knew from her father that she had family in Marquette, but she didn't know about the argument between her father and my mother. She didn't realize her parents had moved to Minnesota to get away from our side of the family; after all, a lot of people from Northern Minnesota and Upper Michigan moved back and forth between the two places in those days because of the mining work on both of the iron ranges.

"By the time your mother and father did move back here, our mother was dead as well, so I thought it was only right to befriend Uncle Roger's daughter, but Florence, well—"

Miss Mary paused, like she was hesitant to say more, from fear her sister could be listening. I was grateful for the pause because my head was spinning as I tried to follow all of this.

"I'd almost forgotten," I said, trying to catch up, "that my mother had some sort of cousin in Minnesota—must have been my grandmother's side of the family then. That cousin almost adopted me and Jessie, but then he decided he didn't want us. I never knew though that both of my parents were born in Minnesota."

"Well, that's the problem," said Miss Mary. "They weren't both born there—just your mother. Your father was born in Finland, although he'd been in Minnesota since he was a boy, came over with his parents to this country if I remember properly. Anyway, Florence feels bad about it now, but when your mother came back to town, Florence could see that your mother had married a poor man, and worse, a Finlander, and Florence didn't want anything to do with her as a result."

"Oh," I said, trying to imagine what things would have been like if I had known Miss Florence and Miss Mary had been my family from the time I was a little girl—I would have known their brother, Roger, then too.

"You know Florence," said Miss Mary. "She doesn't trust people too well—I think that stems back to that young man who lied to her and broke her heart—she just figured your mother would look to get something out of us and that we didn't need no poor relations around, especially not after your mother confessed to us that your grandfather had died penniless, being heartbroken and having become an alcoholic after your grandmother died. Your poor mother had a difficult childhood, I imagine. She tried not to make it sound so bad, and I think your grandfather gave her everything he could, but his spending was out of control, and not until he died did she realize he had nothing left to his name. So Florence was sure your mother just wanted a handout from us, not really to know her family. And Roger, well, he was a typical man—not that he wasn't a good brother, but you know, men don't have soft hearts like that. He never thought twice about it; didn't seem to care one way or the other if we associated with your mother.

"I always thought it an injustice myself not to have been friendlier toward your mother. I did visit her a few times right after she moved back to Marquette with your father, even though it made Florence angry, but there wasn't much else I could do. By that point, my eyesight was starting to go and I couldn't get around much without help from Roger or Florence. I didn't even know your mother had children, actually, until Florence read her obituary to me. I told Florence then that we should do something for you girls, but she said there wasn't much we could do when we knew nothing about raising children and we were getting on in years ourselves. But when she finally decided it was time for us to get some help around the house, I went with her to see Sister Euphrasia, and when Sister Euphrasia mentioned your name to us, I knew right away you were our cousin's daughter and insisted we take you in. Florence agreed, but only if I promised not to tell you we were your relatives until she knew what kind of a young lady you were. But I think we know you're honest, Lyla, and I do feel some obligation toward you for how we treated your mother and your grandparents. I'm very sorry about it all, Lyla."

Even though she was blind, Miss Mary looked at me with these sorrowful puppy dog eyes, and though I realized how different everything could have been if the Mitchells had just been nicer to my mother and my grandparents, I couldn't take out any frustration on Miss Mary.

"I guess I understand that," I said. I couldn't say much else because I had so many conflicting feelings, and knowing that Miss Florence didn't want to have anything to do with my parents because my father was Finnish didn't make me feel any better. I'd always wanted a family, and I had started to think I might be getting a type of family in these two old maids, but now I'd found out I'd had a family all this time, but they just hadn't wanted to give me the love I was craving. How was I supposed to react to all of that?

Miss Florence never did mention the subject to me of our being relatives, and I never brought it up to her. Once in awhile, Miss Mary would make a comment about it, but I didn't ask any more questions. I kind of felt like it was best just to leave it all alone. We might be cousins of some sort, but what did it really matter? They didn't need a cousin—they needed someone to help them around the house.

But their telling me all this started to awaken memories of my parents in me that I'd suppressed all those years in the orphanage. I had almost forgotten that my last name was really Toivonen and not Hopewell, and that Mother had changed our name to her maiden name after Papa disappeared. I'd been Lyla Hopewell for so long by then that I didn't have any desire to take back my real last name. It didn't really matter to me what my last name was. Not that I felt Hopewell was all that fitting because there wasn't anything hopeful about my life. I figured hope was about the future, and the future only looked bleak to me because I knew I couldn't live with the old ladies forever, but until whatever happened happened, I figured being with them was better than being alone.

Miss Florence stayed pretty cranky with me, but over time, I grew to like and even admire her in a way. She was tough, and she was proud of it; she just wasn't going to give in to admitting she was weak, or to whatever anyone else wanted if it didn't agree with how she saw things, and I was kind of the same way—maybe I got it from that side of the family.

Miss Florence always refused my help unless she absolutely could not do something by herself. She was always busy, always working—I think maybe holding off the bleakness just like me, knowing that the future for her, especially at her age and with a blind sister, could not be very good. I don't know that I understood all that then, but I could see that they needed me. For example, Miss Florence, sometimes when she'd do the dishes, I'd notice that she had missed a spot, or when she ironed, she wouldn't get all the wrinkles out of a dress, so when she wasn't looking, I'd iron it again.

And then one morning, when I'd been living there about a year and a half, I woke up and got dressed just like always, and it being the dead of winter, I put a coat over myself and then left the servants' quarters to go over to the house. I was just fighting with the key to unlock the back door when I heard a loud thumping sound and then a crash. In a panic, I opened the door and turned on the light, and after looking around for a few seconds, I saw, lying at the bottom of the basement stairs, Miss Florence.

I shouted out her name, but I knew before I even got down the stairs that she wouldn't answer. Her neck was twisted in a strange way, and though I felt her pulse and tried to shake her awake, I could see she was already dead—just like that. If I'd only come through the door a few seconds sooner, I might have stopped her or grabbed her when she slipped, or—

"What happened? What's wrong? Florence! Florence! Lyla!"

How could I tell Miss Mary?

I could hear her calling out from the top of the stairs to the second floor. Quickly, I ran back up the basement stairs and through the house to the front staircase. Then I stood there at the bottom of the stairs, looking up at Miss Mary, seeing the fright on her face, but I was afraid if I said anything, she might faint and fall down the stairs herself.

Finally, I called up to her, "Miss Mary, it's Lyla. It's okay. Come on downstairs for breakfast."

She looked uncertain. She looked afraid. She grasped the banister tightly and only took a couple steps before she said, "What is it? What was all that noise? Where's Florence?"

"She's down in the basement," I said. "She just bumped over some old tin cans; that's all."

"Don't lie to me," she said. "That was louder than a tin can."

"Just come downstairs, Miss Mary," I said.

"I don't trust you, Lyla. What did you do to Florence?"

I was stunned. How could she say such a thing? Did she think I would hurt her sister?

"Miss Mary," I cried, putting my hand over my mouth. "Miss Florence—she—I would never hurt her. How could you say such a thing when I know you've both been so good to me?"

"Shh," she said, hearing me crying, and then she slowly came down the stairs. I watched her, my whole insides shaking as I tried to hold in the pain. Then when she was just a step or two above me, I grabbed her around the legs and sank to the floor.

"Miss Mary!" I cried, unable to hold it back. "How could you say that to me?"

"Lyla, I'm sorry," she said, feeling my hair. "It's just—when you're old and blind, you're always afraid. You never know what might happen. I'm sorry, Lyla."

She caressed my hair. I never forgot that. We stood there, my arms wrapped around her legs and nightgown while she stroked my hair.

And then after a minute, I said to her, "Miss Mary, Miss Florence—she fell down the stairs. She's broken her neck. She's—she's—dead."

"Oh," said Miss Mary, and then she tried to take another step.

I got up and took her arm. "Come into the kitchen, Miss Mary," I said. "I'll make you some coffee."

"You better call the doctor, or the police, or—"

"Okay," I said, leading her into the kitchen to the table. "I'm so sorry, Miss Mary. I was trying to open the back door when I heard the fall. If I had only gotten to the house a minute sooner, I could have gone into the basement for her."

"She went down there to start up the furnace," said Miss Mary. "You know how stubborn she was. She didn't want to wait for you because she'd never admit she needed help. Go call the operator. She'll know what to do."

I did so and then came back to tell her the doctor was coming over. The house was freezing because the furnace had gone out, so I went downstairs and got it going. All the while, Miss Florence was lying there on the floor in a crumpled up mess with a broken neck and staring at the ceiling. I think that was the worst few minutes of my life and I couldn't have survived it if it hadn't been for having to concentrate on getting the furnace going. That damn furnace—I blamed it for killing Miss Florence.

By the time I got upstairs, Miss Mary's coffee had brewed, and I had just got it poured and sat down to have a cup myself to help my nerves when the undertakers from the Tonella Funeral home showed up for the body. Neither Miss Mary nor I dared go near the basement stairs while they were down there. I didn't want to see Miss Florence again looking the way she did, and as I turned my head away when they brought the body upstairs, I thought how I was glad Miss Mary was blind.

It was a long grim day for us, but in the afternoon, we finally felt up to talking about it.

"It's probably for the best," Miss Mary said to me. "Florence wouldn't have wanted to live in a world where she couldn't control everything, and she knew that day wasn't too far in the future. It's better this way."

"What will you do now, Miss Mary?" I asked her.

"What do you mean?"

"I mean, you can't live alone."

"I'm not alone, Lyla," she said. "You're here."

I was relieved to hear that. A couple days later, I moved into the house. Miss Mary wanted me to sleep in Miss Florence's room, but the thought of that gave me the creeps so I slept in their brother Roger's room instead.

I was relieved to sleep upstairs with Miss Mary because after Miss Florence died, I could see Miss Mary was failing. "I'm the last one," she would say to me, though once in awhile, she'd add, "Except you, Lyla. You're a Hopewell too." But as time went by, she said it less often.

Before, she had been pretty active for a blind woman in her seventies, but now she didn't do much except get dressed, eat her meals, and then sit in her chair and doze off.

Not long after Miss Florence died, Miss Mary told me to go into Miss Florence's room and find her bank book. It took me a good deal of searching. When I didn't find it in any drawers, I checked under the mattress. In the end, I had to tear the room apart, and finally, I found it inside an old Catholic prayer book. She had carved out half the pages and shoved it inside. It took me most of the day to look for it, but I knew it had to be found. Miss Mary then called her lawyer, Mr. Hampton, to come over and bring with him Mr. Pearce from the Union National Bank and a notary public so they could all witness that she was making me her trustee on the account so I could write checks and make withdrawals and deposits for her. I asked her if she was sure she wanted to do that, and suggested that maybe it should be Mr. Pearce or Mr. Hampton who handled her money, but she said, "No, they're busy men. They can't be here to help me every day and you can. You're the best choice, and I trust you, Lyla." I'm not sure Mr. Hampton trusted me, but he let it be, and Mr. Pearce was always real friendly with me, so it was all settled. That Miss Mary trusted me was all that mattered, and whatever I was, I wasn't no thief, especially not when someone was good to me like she and Miss Florence had been—at least to the best of their abilities; I know that now.

A month or two later, Miss Mary and I were sitting one evening listening to the radio. She would just sit and listen, sometimes humming along or rocking in her chair while I stayed busy with needlework. I still wasn't much good at it, but I did it out of respect for Miss Florence.

We had just finished listening to *The Shadow*, which Miss Florence had thought too sensational to listen to, but Miss Mary loved it, or at least claimed she did; I'm not sure how much she actually heard since she was falling asleep a lot now, napping in the afternoon and the evening. But when the commercial came on, Miss Mary said to me, "Lyla, when I'm gone I want you to have the house. Tomorrow, we'll call Mr. Hampton and have him come over and I'll make up the will so it goes to you."

"I—no, that's not right," I said, not knowing what else to say.

"It is right; you're the only family I have now."

I thought of Jessie; after all, she was related to Miss Mary too, but she'd probably end up inheriting everything of Miss Bergmann's eventually, so why shouldn't I have my own old lady to give me something? And I'd done a good job of looking after my old ladies, other than with what happened to Miss Florence. And once Miss Mary was gone, what else was I going to do? So though I felt wrong about it, I said, "Thank you, Miss Mary" and let it go at that—at least as far as words between us were said, but I never did stop thinking about it.

The next day, Miss Mary was really sick and didn't get out of bed, so she didn't call Mr. Hampton to come over, and a few days later when she felt better, I didn't think it right for me to bring up the subject. I kept trying to think about how I could mention it, but I didn't think it would be right to, so I kept hoping Miss Mary would mention it first, but instead, I think she forgot about it.

Then one morning, I got up and made breakfast like usual, but Miss Mary didn't come downstairs. When I went upstairs and knocked on her door, she didn't answer. Then I knew. I feared it, but I knew. I went in her room and found she had died in her sleep. I was grateful for that—her sweet soul deserved to go that way. But she had left me all alone in the world.

I called the doctor, of course, and he called the undertaker, and they came and took Miss Mary away, leaving me alone in that big empty house where I didn't even belong.

What would I do now? Miss Mary had said she'd change the will, but she never had. I'd have known if she did since I'd have been the one to fetch Mr. Hampton. I hadn't wanted to push the matter, just hoped she'd eventually do it, but I had also thought she would live many more months if not years. I'd had no idea her death would happen so quickly. I was shocked, stunned. Before, when my mother had died, our neighbors and then Miss Bergmann had stepped in and managed everything, and I had just ended up going where I was told. Now my future was all up to me, or rather, nothing was up to me because I had nowhere to go. I sat all night in the rocking chair in my room, staring out at the stars and the moon through the window, wanting to wish on a star, but not even knowing what I should be wishing. All I knew was I was alone and afraid.

In the morning, the funeral home called to ask how I'd be paying for the funeral. So that day I had to walk to the bank to get out the money, and on the way, I stopped at Mr. Hampton's office and told him what had happened and how Miss Mary had wanted to leave the house to me.

"That may be, Lyla," he said to me. "I'm not saying it isn't, but Miss Mary is gone now. It's too late to be changing her will since she can't sign it. Miss Mary, Miss Florence, and their brother, Mr. Mitchell, all had their names on the property, and in their wills, Miss Mary left everything to Miss Florence and Miss Florence to Miss Mary. Since they are all dead now, everything has to go into probate."

"But shouldn't it go to the next living relative?" I asked.

"No. Even if there were a living relative—and Miss Mary and Miss Florence told me they had no other family after their brother died—it would still go into probate. In this case, since there is no family, the property will belong to the state. Everything in that house belongs to the State of Michigan now. You'll have to vacate the property, I'm afraid. I think we can arrange for you to stay there for up to thirty days until you find another position, but that's the most I can do."

"Do you know anyone who needs a live-in-maid?" I asked him.

"No," said Mr. Hampton, "and with the war on, I don't think you're likely to find one. They're looking for workers in other businesses, though, since most of the men are away fighting."

I didn't know what to do. I was young and naive about the world and I had no money, so how could I prove I was the Mitchells' cousin? I didn't even have my own birth certificate, and I'd need my mother's too, and all I knew was she was born in Minnesota somewhere, and it just all seemed so impossible to prove anything. Even if I got the house, I didn't have any money to run it.

So what would I do? I didn't want to go work for anyone else. I didn't want to be anyone's maid, and I sure didn't want to go work in a restaurant or be a clerk at a store where I would have to smile at people all day and be sugary sweet.

So after Miss Mary's funeral, I went home and just sat around the house all day, moping for three weeks, and then Mr. Hampton called to tell me the house would be put up for sale, and if I would clean it out, they would pay me out of the estate for my services so it was ready to be sold.

I figured I didn't have much choice in the matter. I needed the money, so I started cleaning the house. I threw away everything that wasn't of any value, and that was a lot of it—things Miss Mary and Miss Florence had kept forever. If something were broken, they still kept it just in case they could use it for something later. Things were rotting, fading, and rusting down in the basement like you wouldn't believe, and I had to call people to come and take the junk and scrap metal pieces, and all manner of things away. Then there was a big estate sale and Mr. Hampton came over and made sure all the furniture, the lamps, the dishes, everything was sold. I didn't have any money to buy a single piece of all those things that by rights should have been mine. And I hated to see it all go. I knew Miss Mary and Miss Florence couldn't use any of it where they had gone, but I still hated to think of someone else eating off their china, drinking out of their teacups, knitting with Miss Florence's needles—why, they even sold Miss Mary's white cane.

Mr. and Mrs. O'Neill came over for the estate sale and bought a few things. I guess Mr. Hampton told them about it since he was some sort of relative of theirs. I was glad to see the O'Neills since they were the only ones who had bothered to offer me any words of comfort at Miss Mary's funeral, and they had told me that they hoped still to see me at St. John's, but I couldn't bear to go sit in my old ladies' pew again. I started to call them that after they died—"my old ladies." They had been good to me, as good as they knew how, and they had been real ladies despite their eccentricities. Probably just about the last ladies I knew, other than maybe Mrs. O'Neill. So after that, I started going back to Mass at the cathedral, and Mr. and Mrs. O'Neill forgot all about me for another thirty or forty years until I went to work for them.

I tried to think what I might get away with taking from the Mitchells' house since it should have all been mine anyways, but I was afraid to take anything. There was a lot of old jewelry, but I suspected someone would recognize it if I wore it anywhere, and if I brought it to a pawn shop—well, it was a small town, so I knew better.

The only thing I ended up taking were a few photographs. There was one of Miss Mary and Miss Florence as little girls sitting on their Uncle Roger's lap—it said so on the back, and I knew their Uncle Roger had been my grandfather. And then there was another of the sisters and their brother together, which must have been taken about 1920 or so. I figured I at least had a right to those.

I had the house all cleared out, and after the sale, I slept on the floor with just a blanket and a pillow for the last couple days I was allowed to stay there since I'd even had to clean out the little servant's house in the back. Mr. Hampton paid me for all my work, just enough to rent a room at a boarding house for about a month. I hoped I could find work quickly, but I hadn't even looked for any yet. In a couple days, I'd be on my own. It was one of the scariest times in my life, but whatever was going to happen, I figured it would be better than living in the orphanage.

Chapter 10

The next Wednesday when we're supposed to have our women's meeting, I get a call in the morning from Wendy, who tells me the church is having its floors stripped or polished or something so we can't meet there; instead, we're all invited to May's house. She gives me May's address on Wilkinson Avenue, which I don't think anything about until Bel and I turn onto it.

Turns out that May's house is directly across the street from Bill's house. But I don't worry about that because I know Bill's still in the hospital so he won't see me. And I don't see any sign of Alan around, which is fine with me. But that Frank fellow is out in Bill's yard mowing the lawn with his shirt off—apparently trying to show off for the women—and I suppose women like to look at his muscles, but honestly, all he's doing for me is showing how stupid he is because if that lawnmower spits out a branch or a rock, he's going to get cut up.

Bel and I ignore Frank and go into the house. May has seen us coming and opens the door for us.

"Hello, Bel. Hello, Lyla. I'm glad you could come, and don't worry; we'll have privacy here. I live with my grandmother, but she's gone out shopping with one of her lady friends. My daughter is out running around the neighborhood somewhere, and I told her not to disturb us."

I says, "That's fine; thanks for having us," and Bel tells her—before she's hardly even in the door—that she has a lovely home, and then we go into the living room where we find Wendy, Diana, and Sybil waiting for us, so we get down to business right away.

We do the same thing as last time basically. Give our names and then say our spiel. Diana's still feeling guilty about her sex addiction, but not guilty enough, apparently, to keep her from running around on her husband who's leaving her. Wendy's in an upbeat mood if a bit uncomfortable because she's into her sixth month of pregnancy now and it's starting to show. Sybil talks about another date she's gone on with this new boyfriend of hers, and how much she really likes him.

And then May talks some more about how she's worried about her daughter hanging out with the wrong crowd. Only this time, she mentions something about post-traumatic stress and her dad being a Vietnam soldier who was killed. I wasn't really listening until she says that, and then something in my mind clicks and I start figuring things out.

I thought it was kind of weird that May's house was right across the street from Bill's, and now I seem to remember that he was some sort of cousin to the people who lived here. At first, I wonder if May bought the house recently, but she said earlier it was her grandmother's. I seem to remember the grandmother was married to Bill's cousin or something like that. And May's being all Oriental-looking, makes sense to me now. I remember Bill saying to me something about how his cousin's son got a "gook"—that's what he called anyone who was Chinese or Vietnamese or anything Oriental like that—got a "gook" pregnant when he was in Vietnam and they brought the kid back to the U.S. It makes me feel uncomfortable to realize May is some relation to Bill because maybe he said something to them about me—maybe they know more about me than I care to have them know. It's bad enough Marquette's such a small town, but to have him maybe badmouthing me to them, that's more than I want to deal with—I wouldn't come to these women's meetings again if I knew that had happened. I'm just glad he's still in the hospital and not home yet.

"Lyla, do you have anything you want to say?" Wendy asks me when Bel's done talking—I haven't heard a word she said, and that's probably a good thing.

"No," I says. "I'm good."

And then before I know it, the meeting has come to an end. We say that little prayer about serenity and then everyone gets up and starts to leave.

Wendy and Diana leave right away after we all hug. Sybil kind of hangs around for a few minutes before she says, "Goodbye."

I'm more than ready to go myself, but Bel, of course, has to be Miss Social Butterfly so she keeps yakking at May about how the house is decorated, and then when I think we're finally going to leave, she asks if she can use the bathroom, and, of course, May says, "Yes."

I don't want to stand around for five minutes making conversation with May—especially not if she might mention she remembers me because I'm sure I met her once or twice when she was a teenager and I was dating Bill—I kind of remember a Vietnamese girl from back then—so I just says, "I'll wait in the car for you," to Bel and go outside.

As I go out the door, I look across the street, hoping not to see Alan. Frank isn't outside anymore, but I'm not happy to see Alan standing in the doorway with the screen door open. But he probably won't notice me because he's talking to Sybil, who's standing on the front steps.

"What's she doing over there?" I wonder, but before I can give it another thought, I'm startled when someone says:

"Who the hell are you, the Avon Lady?"

"What?" I asks. When I turn around, I find a teenage girl standing by the bushes in a jean jacket. Her skin color makes it clear she has to be May's daughter—the elusive Josie who has her mother so worried.

"What were you doin' in my house talking to my mom? You got something to sell?" she asks.

"No, we were having our women's meeting," I says.

"Oh, I thought maybe you were peddling makeup, or worse, maybe you was one of those Jehovah's Witnesses."

"No, sorry. I'm Catholic," I try to joke.

"Yeah, same thing," says the girl. Then she puckers up her lips, turns to the left, and spits out a giant stream of tobacco juice. I'd be sick from just watching her do it, only I'm distracted because when she turns, I can see the back of her jean jacket, which says, in big bold letters, "Satan's Angels."

"That's fucked up," she says, turning back to look at me.

"What is?" I asks, not knowing what to say to such language coming from a child.

"Being Catholic."

And then it hits me.

"I know you," I says. "You're the girl I saw stealing candles at St. Peter's."

She looks a bit startled for a minute, like she's afraid to be caught. But then she scrunches up her face into this horrible, defiant look.

"So what?" she says. "What the fuck are you going to do about it, Granny?"

I want to slap her mouth, but I'm afraid she'll know karate or something—I mean she is Vietnamese. And she's about my height, but younger and a lot meaner-looking.

"I didn't say I was going to do anything about it," I says, "but I might if you keep talking like that. I'll tell your mother for starters."

"Ooh, I'm scared," she says, rolling her eyes at me. "Do you think my mother cares? She knows I'll kick her ass if she tries any of that discipline crap on me."

"Your mother loves you," I tell her. "She's worried about you too. Don't you think playing this tough, juvenile delinquent role is hurting her?"

"What the fuck do you know about it?" Josie asks.

"I know that in my day young ladies didn't use four letter words like that."

"Who you kidding?" she says. "You ain't innocent. Been around the block more than once from the looks of you."

"When I was your age," I tell her, "the nuns at the orphanage would have washed my mouth out with soap and probably worse for using such language."

"Orphanage? You were an orphan?"

"Yeah," I says.

"That sucks," she says. "I'm practically an orphan. My mother isn't much good at raising me, and I never knew my father. I guess he dumped her because she whined too much. That and he couldn't stand her pansy-assed pretty white girl ways."

I don't know what to say to her. I want to tell her she should appreciate that she even has a mother, but I get distracted when I hear Alan close the screen door. I look over and see Sybil walking to her car. Why was she talking to him? Is he—no, he couldn't be the new boyfriend she's been talking about, could he? But why else would she be smiling like that?

"You got a fag?" Josie asks.

"What?" I says, turning back to her.

"You know, a fag, a cigarette—they call them 'fags' in England."

"No, I—I don't smoke," I says, wondering if Alan really could be—

"I bet you used to," says Josie.

"No, no, I never did," I says as May's front door opens and Bel comes out. "I have to go," I says to Josie, thankful to leave.

"Goodbye," Bel says to Josie even though she hasn't yet had the pleasure of making Josie's acquaintance.

Josie just ignores her.

Bel and I walk to where she parked the car on the road just as Sybil drives off. She looks at us but doesn't wave. I wonder if she's embarrassed that I saw her across the street. But she doesn't know that I have reasons not to like Alan. Wish I could warn her what he's like, but it's none of my business, I guess.

"I'll see ya around, lady!" Josie shouts to me as I open the car door.

"Yeah, maybe at St. Peter's," I says, turning to look back at her. "Only next time, I'll bring my camera so I have evidence."

She gives me this "I dare you to" stare, and then I get in the car.

As I'm shutting the door, Josie shouts, "You don't scare me, you old bitch!"

I don't like being talked to that way, but I realize I'm more worried that Alan will end up hurting Sybil like his father hurt me. But I don't want to stick my nose in her business. Bel's usually the one who does that sort of thing, but I'm not going to tell her who I think Sybil's new boyfriend is.

Bel's unusually quiet on the way home, and when I asks her why, she says, "I'm just thinking."

"That's a first," I laugh, but she doesn't say anything. She's not quick on the comebacks like me.

Chapter 11

"Bill's going to Norlite."

Yes, Eleanor has called me again. I knew she would, though when I didn't reciprocate after the last time, I was kind of hoping she wouldn't. Why does she keep thinking I care any longer? Not that I wish Bill any ill, but it's not like there's any point anymore.

"I hope you don't mind my calling you, Lyla," Eleanor says. "I know Bill wasn't very nice to you when you came up to see him at the hospital, but he was all drugged up and scared and didn't know what he was saying. You're not mad about me calling, are you, Lyla? It's just kind of a shock to me to think of my brother being in a nursing home."

"Eleanor, how could I ever be mad at you?" I says, though I'm definitely perturbed.

"It's just, well, you're young compared to me, Lyla, but you're old enough to know how frightening it is to get old. It's not so much dying that I'm afraid of—it's being left alone, and even though I have my girls, that's not the same as having people who knew you when you were a child. Bill's the only sibling I have left in Marquette. My sister Ada, she's in Louisiana and ninety this year, so at our ages, I doubt we'll ever see each other again. I'm just scared of losing Bill."

"I know, Eleanor," I says. "I never did have any brothers or sisters, at least not that were close like your family is, but I know what it is to fear being alone, though I have been most of my life."

"I hate to think of Bill at Norlite," Eleanor says. "I've known lots of people who have gone there and the staff is just wonderful to the residents, but it's not the same as him being at home."

"What does Alan think about it?" I asks, less because I care about Bill going to the nursing home than that I'm curious what Alan's been up to—does Eleanor know he's dating Sybil?

"He's kind of relieved I think," she says. "He was worried about trying to figure out how to care for his father if he came home."

"Well, he can't be too happy with this dragging on. He probably wants to get back downstate and back to his old life."

"Oh, no. He quit his job downstate. He's decided to stay in Marquette to be near his dad. He says he belongs here. His son, Gil, is up here to visit for the summer, though he'll go back to live with his mother once school starts again."

"Oh," I says. "Is Alan going to live in Bill's house then?"

"Yes, I think so," says Eleanor. "At least for now. His brothers and Bill are okay with it. Well, I have to get going, Lyla; Lucy is going to take me over to Norlite; they're moving Bill there this afternoon. Why don't you give him a day or two to get adjusted, and then you can come visit?"

"I'll think about it," I says—because I'm too darn nice to say, "No," but I mean "No."

"Okay, Lyla. I'll talk to you soon," Eleanor says, apparently taking my reply as a "Yes."

"Goodbye, Eleanor," I says and hang up the phone. What makes her think in that nutty old head of hers that I'm going to go visit Bill? Sure, I feel bad that he can't go home, but I'm not going to go see him. It's not my job to take care of an old man. I already took care of my father, and then there was the Mitchell sisters, and Mr. Newman too. Last thing I need to do is take care of Bill. And he wouldn't be no gentleman like my father or Mr. Newman. Funny, I haven't thought of Mr. Newman in a long while. He was a gentleman. And he'd be just about the right age for me now, though he was something like sixty or seventy years older than me when I knew him. Wish I could find one like him today.

The last day I lived at the Mitchells' house, I was busy finishing up cleaning it since the house was being sold and I had to vacate the premises. As I was washing one of the upstairs bedroom windows overlooking the street, I happened to notice this young couple, a man and a woman, walking down the sidewalk. I was kind of watching them out of the corner of my eye as I continued to wash the window until I saw them stop in front of the house, and then the woman walked up the front walk and before I knew it, she was knocking on the door.

So I hurried downstairs, wondering who they could be. Were they a newly married couple here to see about buying the house? Neither Mr. Hampton or Mr. Pearce had called to say they were coming. And I looked like a mess from having been cleaning all morning, knowing I had to get everything done that day.

But when I opened the door and said, "Hello," I was practically knocked over by the young lady, who threw her arms around me and, squeezing me tight, exclaimed, "Lyla, I've missed you so much!"

"Who the hell is this?" I wondered, looking over the strange girl's shoulder at the young man standing in the doorway and sheepishly looking at me.

"You remember me, don't you, Lyla?" he said to me. "It's Charlie from the orphanage."

"Charlie?" I said. And then it dawned on me who was nearly suffocating me. "Bel?" I said, pulling back from her. "What—what are you doing here?"

"Aren't you glad to see us, Lyla?" Bel asked, letting go of me but leaving her hands on my shoulders to look at me.

"Sure, I'm just surprised," I said. "I haven't seen you in so long that I didn't recognize you at first. Why you—Bel, you've grown up so much."

"I'm fourteen now, Lyla," said Bel. "And I just got out of the orphanage today, so I came over straight away to see you."

I was amazed that she was taller than me by an inch or so and that her chest had developed so much. She was downright beautiful now, and as I looked at Charlie, I could see he was smiling, not at me, but at the sight of her.

"Can we come in, Lyla? We have so much to tell you," said Bel.

"Well, sure, all right, I guess," I said, surprised by the request and feeling uncomfortable—I mean, they were like strangers to me since I hadn't seen them in two years—Charlie even longer than that.

"Is it a bad time?" asked Charlie.

"No, it's just—well, the house is for sale and I was just cleaning it. I have to be out tomorrow. I'm just a bit worried right now. The Mitchells both died and so I need to find other work, and I have to find a room in a hotel or a boarding house or something. I just feel kind of scared is all." I hated the words as I heard them come out, but I did feel scared. What was the point of telling Bel and Charlie, though?

But Bel said, "Oh, that's wonderful, Lyla!" She was beaming like a half-crazy puppy dog. Now sixty years later, she still looked at me that way.

I had no idea what she meant by it being "wonderful." I started to wonder if she'd even heard what I'd said when she announced, "Lyla, Charlie and I have just gotten married!"

"Married?" I said. That was the last thing I expected to come out of her mouth.

"If you let us in, we'll explain," Charlie said, practically giggling. He'd grown to nearly six feet, but he was all lanky and boyish-looking the way he was grinning.

"Um, yeah, come on," I said, leading them through the house and to the kitchen where I found the teapot.

"We're going to be so happy," Bel said, sitting down at the table and grabbing Charlie's hand as he sat down next to her.

"I don't understand," I said. "Bel, aren't you—fourteen now? And Charlie, you're—how old are you, seventeen?"

"I just turned eighteen—it's my birthday today," he said. "We had to wait until today to get married."

In my head, I was trying to do the math. Charlie had left the orphanage two years before me. He would have been fourteen then—we all had to leave at fourteen. So he had left four years ago and that would have made him eighteen now, while I was sixteen and Bel was—fourteen. Married at fourteen? How was that possible?

"I wanted you to come to the wedding, Lyla," Bel said, "but Charlie said it would be more romantic if we kept it a secret, so the witnesses were just people working at the courthouse, but in my heart I pretended you were the maid of honor, Lyla. I didn't know if you'd be able to get away from work anyway since I knew you were working for the Mitchells, and I didn't know where they lived. We asked at the courthouse after the ceremony for your address so we could come over and tell you first of all because I never forgot what a good friend you always were to me, Lyla."

"But—I'm confused," I said. "Tell me what you mean. You're still in the orphanage, aren't you, Bel?"

"Charlie and I bumped into each other one day when I went downtown to do some shopping for the Sisters, and well," Bel said, her eyes looking shy as she kept her head down.

But Charlie wasn't shy as he said, "She was just so fine-looking that I couldn't help myself."

"I—you don't mean," I said, not sure I wanted to believe what I was hearing. Charlie and Bel having—

"I know it wasn't the right thing to do, Lyla," Bel said, "but it's all worked out since we're married now, husband and wife."

"And happy as can be," said Charlie, his eyes adoring her.

"I didn't know you could get married at fourteen," I said.

"Oh, Sister Euphrasia made it right. She knew the judge, and when I told her I was pregnant, she said it was better we get married than I have to give up the baby. I just couldn't do that, Lyla—couldn't give up my baby to someone else, or let it live in the orphanage. You know I couldn't do that."

"No," I said. I don't know that I ever had much maternal instinct, but I wouldn't give up a child either to see it go to the orphanage. "But where are you going to live?" I asked.

"The grocer I've been working for," said Charlie, "well, he doesn't have any kids, so he says I'm like a son to him. Then when I told him I'd gotten Bel in trouble, he said we could live there with him. He has a good-sized apartment above the store, and since he's in his eighties, he has some trouble getting around so I think he's afraid of being alone. He wants us to live there, and he says he'll let me take over the business when he's gone since he doesn't have any kids of his own, and he'll look after Bel in the meantime while I'm away."

"Away? Where are you going?" I asked, wondering how he could be going somewhere when his wife was having a baby.

"Lyla, there's a war on, remember?" said Bel. "Charlie's going to be a soldier, and a hero; of course, he's already my hero."

She leaned over to give him a smooch on the cheek. I was glad when I heard the teapot whistling because otherwise I might have thrown up my breakfast sitting there watching them making puppy eyes at each other.

"Lyla," said Bel, "since Charlie's leaving and you don't have any place to go, why don't you come stay with us? Old Mr. Newman won't mind. Why, he would probably like two pretty women like us to look after him."

"Mr. Newman?" I said. "Who's that?"

"The old man who owns the grocery store where I work," said Charlie. "It's been in his family for like a hundred years or something—his father started it after the Civil War I think he said. He doesn't have any wife or kids of his own. All he's got is a niece who's pretty old and they're not on speaking terms. So he's going to leave everything to me. We'll be rich."

"Well, I wouldn't say he's rich," said Bel. "It's just a little corner party store."

"Yeah, but he used to have a big department and grocery store right on the main street back around 1900," said Charlie. "He sold that when he got older, and now he just has this little corner grocery over in East Marquette, but I bet he's got a bunch of money socked away somewhere. Bel and I are going to have everything our parents and the orphanage never gave us."

"And, Lyla," said Bel, "you can keep me company and help me with the baby. You'll be Auntie Lyla."

I'd just gotten done taking care of two old ladies, and now I was being offered a chance to take care of an old man and a baby. It didn't sound very appealing to me, but where else did I have to go? It at least sounded better than living in a boarding house when I had no money.

"Well, I don't know," I said, so I could think about it a little as I set the teacups down for them. It just sounded too good to be true. I couldn't help thinking about how Miss Mary had said I'd get her house—and she was my blood relative—but it sure didn't work out that way for me. I was wondering if Charlie wasn't just talking big to impress Bel. Since she was dumb enough to let him knock her up, she was probably dumb enough to believe anything he said. How could she have let him take advantage of her like that? He wasn't even that much to look at. He might be tall, but I doubt he weighed more than 140 pounds—all skin and bones mostly. And now that he was going off to the war, he would probably get himself killed and she'd be stuck with a baby. And how much you want to bet, I thought, that I'd be stuck taking care of them both? But even if that did happen, it couldn't be worse than taking care of two old ladies, one blind and one ornery as hell.

"What's there to know, Lyla?" Bel asked. "You need a place to live and I'll need help with the baby."

"I'm afraid I'll be in the way," I said, just to make sure they really wanted me. No one had ever really wanted me before.

"Lyla, you're my best friend. You know that," said Bel. "I need you now more than ever."

Best friend? I hadn't seen her in two years and she was still saying that—well, she must have believed I was her best friend or she wouldn't have been there having tea with me, inviting me to live with her. It was all too much for me. To put off deciding for a few minutes, I said, "Jesus, Bel, I wish I had seen Sister Euphrasia's face when you told her you were having a baby."

"I don't think she was very happy," said Bel, "but Sister Perpetua was there when I told her, and she reminded Sister Euphrasia that a baby is a blessing, and even if I committed sin, God could make good come of it. Then once I told them Charlie was the father, they said I should marry him and they'd sign the paperwork as my guardians to make the wedding happen."

"That's good," I said, "but I still wish I could have seen the look on Sister Euphrasia's face. I bet her jaw dropped to the floor."

"It did," Bel laughed. "She was too shocked to yell. I think she felt guilty that it happened—that one of the girls in her orphanage could have done that under her nose."

"Well," said Charlie. "It was really under Mr. Newman's nose. He was taking a nap while we did it in the storeroom of his grocery."

I didn't need to hear that. I might have been ornery and mouthy, but I'd have known better than to do something that stupid.

"So when did you say you have to be out of here?" Charlie asked me.

"Tomorrow," I said.

"Then we'll come back tomorrow to collect your things and show you where we live," said Bel. "It's all settled."

I hadn't yet said I'd go, but I guess I had no choice. It was something to do until I figured out something else at least.

"I hope you'll be happy," I said a few minutes later when I saw them to the door.

"We'll all be happy together," said Bel. "I'm so excited that we'll be together again, Lyla."

"Well, all except me," said Charlie. "I won't be there."

"The war will be over before you know it," said Bel, "and then you'll be home and a hero to boot."

"Thanks for coming over, and finding me," I said, partly to hurry them out the door so I could finish cleaning and think about all this turn of events, and partly because I was grateful to have somewhere to go, even if I wasn't sure it would work out.

Once they were gone, I had to finish washing the windows, but instead, I went back into the kitchen, sat down, poured myself another cup of tea, and put my feet up on Miss Florence's chair, just to spite her one last time. Then I tried to make sense out of how I'd deal with it all. Bel and Charlie seemed so young and excited about life, but here I was, younger than Charlie, just a couple years older than Bel—only sixteen, sweet sixteen, though I doubted there'd ever been anything sweet about me. After spending two years taking care of two old ladies, I'd started to move at their speed and feel old myself. Was I up to helping to take care of a baby and an old man? If I knew Bel, somehow I figured I'd end up doing most of the caretaking—Bel was just a child herself. I don't know why, but I was pretty sure I had been more mature at fourteen than she now was—at least I hadn't been dumb enough to get myself pregnant. Once or twice when I'd gone downtown to do errands for the Miss Mitchells, I'd seen young men looking at me, but I knew better than to fool around with one and risk losing my place because Marquette was a small town and Miss Florence wouldn't have put up with that kind of foolishness if people started talking. Of course, I ended up losing my place anyways—becoming homeless. But at least I'd have a home if I went to live with Bel and Charlie. Provided this Mr. Newman wouldn't mind. Would he even want me in his house?

I'd just have to wait until the next day to see what would happen. I could always still go to a boarding house if it didn't work out.

That night when I went to bed, I said my prayers, something I hadn't done since leaving the orphanage, despite the Miss Mitchells taking me to church and telling me they had promised Sister Euphrasia that they'd make sure I was raised up a good Catholic girl. I prayed for Miss Mary and Miss Florence and hoped they were in a good place, and I told them how sorry I was that their house was going to be sold and there was nothing I could do about it because they didn't do anything to make it so I'd get it. And I prayed that God knew what He was doing and hadn't forgotten me even though I hadn't talked to Him in a long-time. And I even prayed that God would bless my sister, Jessie, and what the heck, I asked him to bless Miss Bergmann too. For a moment while I was praying, the thought crossed my mind that I could go find Jessie and Miss Bergmann and ask them to take me in—I could work for them just as well as for Mr. Newman. They, or Jessie anyways, were at least family—Bel and Charlie weren't. But Bel and Charlie wanted me, and I guess that made a difference, so I just said, "God, it's in your hands; only this time, could you make it work out better than the orphanage and the

Mitchells did?"

And the next morning, good as her word, Bel showed up. I saw her walking down Jackson Street just as Mr. Pearce pulled up in his car in front of the house. I went out to the street and gave him the house keys, and then I took my bag off the front porch and I walked a few feet up the street before Bel got to the house.

"Are you ready, Lyla?" she asked.

"Yes, I'm ready," I said. I left the Mitchells' house with not much more than I had when I came, other than the family photographs I took, and the one new dress Miss Florence had made me the Christmas before she died.

Bel and I had to walk all the way over to the east side of town where Mr. Newman's store was, but in those days, everyone walked anyways. Mr. Newman had a truck that Charlie always drove to make grocery deliveries, so sometimes he would give us a ride somewhere when there was room, but most of the time, Bel and I would walk. That's actually how Bel learned to drive. She drove the truck to make the deliveries after Charlie went away to the war. I stayed behind to watch the store so I never learned to drive—not that I ever had any yearning to.

Mr. Newman's little grocery store was mixed in with the houses in an older part of town, just a few blocks north of where the really rich people lived on Ridge Street. It was just a corner store; the actual store was on the main floor and upstairs were the living quarters. It turned out to be bigger than what it looked like from the outside, though it was still kind of cramped. Mr. Newman had his own room, and then there was another room for Charlie and Bel to live in. And of course, there was a kitchen that also served as the dining room, and a living room, and a bathroom—I was glad to see that since some people still had outhouses in those days, and Miss Florence had made it clear to me I was downright spoiled as a servant to have my own bathroom. The whole living space at Mr. Newman's was small and cramped compared to what I was used to in the Mitchells' big house, but it was better than a boarding house—at least I'd be living with people I basically liked and who were friendly.

My biggest worry was that Mr. Newman wouldn't like having me there, but he seemed pleased as punch when I arrived.

"I'm eighty-five years young," he said to me as soon as Bel introduced us. "I'm young in my heart, but not in my body, and though Charlie lets me think I'm still useful in the store, I know better, and I sure can't help with a baby at my age, so I'm glad Bel will have you around to help her."

"I hope I won't be in the way," I said to him.

"No, I like having young people around me," he replied. "I was young once myself, you know, and like I said, I'm still young at heart. Young people are the only hope this country has now. You'll carve the new world after this war is over, and after old men like me are gone, though I was once young and full of ideas myself; I never fought in a real war, but I fought hard in the war against Victorian crotchetiness, only I was ahead of my time, and I still see those narrow-minded rigid ways persisting. But I have hope that your generation will know a better world."

"I hope the war is over soon," I said politely, not feeling like I was much hope for the future of the world, or Charlie or Bel either.

"Lyla grew up in the orphanage with me and Charlie," Bel told Mr. Newman.

"Terrible thing to be an orphan, I'm sure," said Mr. Newman, "but the advantage is you don't have anyone expecting anything from you. No family to tie you down or tell you how to behave or make you worry about bringing shame on them. Sometimes, I almost wish I'd been an orphan."

"Do you have any family?" I asked, thinking Bel or Charlie had told me, but I didn't remember.

"My only sister is long dead, but I have a niece who is a materialistic and selfish old woman. She's maybe in her fifties now; I don't know—I've lost track. But she's far older in her ways than me. We don't get along, and she won't get a penny of my money—she wants it, I'm sure, but she doesn't need it. She married the biggest crook in this town; a man who swindled a lot of people out of money under the guise of respectability. So needless to say, I don't have much to do with her or her useless children."

"I see," I said, not knowing what to say to all that. I wondered if his niece and my sister had something in common, but then I remembered I had prayed for Jessie last night so I should be nice to her in my thoughts.

"Lyla," Mr. Newman continued, "I hope you don't practice Catholicism, just because you grew up in that orphanage."

"Well, I—"

But he cut me off before I could finish.

"Backwards. That's what it is. Christianity was well-intended and all, and I have the highest respect for the teachings of Jesus, but organized religion just retards the human race. Holds us back. I believe in Percy Shelley's 'Faith,

Hope, and Self-Esteem.' That's what I believe in. Religion is lacking the self-esteem part, making us think we have to grovel in the mud and be tied down by inhibitions. That's why I quit going to church decades ago. Jesus, now, he believed in freedom like I do, so that's different."

I just politely nodded my head. I wasn't even really sure what self-esteem was, but it didn't sound like something I had.

"I'm a free thinker, you see," Mr. Newman continued. "I don't need any pope or bishop or minister or president or king or anyone to think for me. You're still young and impressionable, Lyla, but because you're young, you can still change your thought-patterns before the religious and political tyrants brainwash you. When you get older, you get set in your ways. Thankfully, I've learned how to think for myself. I suggest you do the same."

"Yes, sir," I said.

"Lyla," Bel interrupted us, "we don't have a separate room for you, but I thought you could sleep on the sofa in the living room, and then once Charlie goes off to the war, you can share my bed; it'll only be a few weeks until then. He only got a short deferment 'cause of our getting married, you know."

"Okay," I said, though I wasn't sure it was okay. Mr. Newman seemed like maybe he had a screw loose what with free thinking maybe meaning he didn't believe in morality or something, but as long as he stayed in his room at night, I'd be okay. If he did try anything, I could probably knock him down anyways since he looked pretty frail. Still, I wasn't used to having men sleeping anywhere near me at night.

Actually, it all worked out real well once Charlie left for the war. I had to endure several weeks of him and Bel acting like crazy lovebirds, but then he was gone, and after she moped around the house for a few days, we got down to running the store for Mr. Newman and doing just fine. Then once the baby was born, Bel mostly stayed upstairs while I looked after the store and kept Mr. Newman company. He turned out not to be a dirty old man at all but a real gentleman, even if an opinionated one. I think he was relieved to come downstairs and sit in the store with me, even though it was hard for him to go up and down the stairs, and I was always afraid of him falling down them like Miss Florence had, but I think he'd rather take that chance than listen to the baby crying all the time.

A lot of the time when things were slow in the store, he would sit and tell me stories about "Old Marquette" as he called it, about growing up there in the years after the Civil War, and how he had left town, frustrated by the narrow-mindedness of people in small towns, and why he eventually came back to be near his family, only to find they'd grown worse than he remembered them, so he hadn't spoken to any of them in years. He seemed a bit broken, like he had been hurt in life and not gotten what he wanted from it, but he was an interesting man, and I wish I'd gotten to know him better. You'd think I would have known him real well from all the stories he told me, but I think his mind was starting to go because he'd talk about people, just using their first names like you knew them too, when you actually had no idea who he was talking about. I remember he talked about a Delia a lot that I think I figured out was his sister, and then there was someone named Roger and a Madeleine, but I don't know what connection they all had to him. Just out of the blue, he'd say things like, "Delia always used to say such and such" and "That Roger; such a snob; my niece is just like him." I tried to ask him who all these people were, but he never would let you get a word in, and once he got going, if you stopped to ask him a question, he'd lose his train of thought, and then he'd get frustrated because he couldn't remember where he was in telling the story. So I finally gave up asking and just nodded and smiled and said, "Uh huh," and sort of half-listened and that kept him happy.

One day, though, he surprised me by asking me about my parents—it happened because a Finnish lady came into the shop asking if we had *juustoa*. It was an odd request since we didn't usually serve Finlanders, but she must have just moved to that part of town. Mr. Newman didn't even know what *juustoa* was, but I told him, "It's Finnish cheese. My mother used to make it for my father."

After the woman left, Mr. Newman looked surprised and asked me how I became an orphan. "I just assumed," he said, "that you had never known your parents since Charlie and Bel told me they never knew theirs." So I told him my story and how Miss Bergmann hadn't wanted me. He thought about it for a little while after that and then he asked, "Is this Miss Bergmann Karl Bergmann's daughter?" I said back, "I don't know," afraid from the way he said it that maybe I had said something I shouldn't have, but I think he was just trying to place her since he seemed to have known the parents and grandparents of everyone in Marquette. But then he said to me, "Don't think about the past, Lyla. It's over. All you can do is live in the present and have hope for the future."

It's been years now since I thought of him saying that, but it all comes back to me now like it was just yesterday. I remember wondering at the time how he could think like that when he was eighty-five with his life all past and nothing to look forward to. But now that I'm seventy-seven, I guess maybe I can understand. I mean, new things do still come your way in life—little surprises and good things—like finding that you like to go out for pancakes in the middle of the night, or being part of a woman's group—well, I wouldn't say that's a good thing yet; the jury's still out, but who'd have thought that I'd ever live in a ten-story high-rise back in those days—they didn't have anything much more than five stories in Marquette back then, and now here Snowberry has been standing for I'd guess more than twenty years.

I can't say the future ever turned out wonderful for me, but neither was it terrible. I don't know that Mr. Newman would think much of the world today, but I guess some things are better than they were back in his day, like how they treat the black people. He wouldn't be happy with me going to church, but even that's better than it was—not so strict anyways. I wonder what he'd think of me even taking time to remember him since he told me not to spend time thinking about the past, but I hope it's okay with him that I remember him, because I did kind of like him. I bet he'd have been a real interesting fellow to know when he was younger. I guess the past isn't so bad to think about anymore—it kind of changes over time. I mean, I used to get angry when I thought about the orphanage and Miss Bergmann and all that, but I'm too old and tired to waste energy on being that angry now. I still snap at Bel and stuff, but I don't have no chip on my shoulder like I used to. I mean, I guess the worst thing that ever happened to me was going to that orphanage. If that's the worst, well, maybe my life hasn't been so bad.

Chapter 12

The Fourth of July weekend—Monday being the Fourth—St. Peter's Cathedral decides to have a bake sale, even though a lot of people will be out of town because of the holiday. Somehow I got on the church bake sale calling list so, of course, I agree to bake, and while Bel is only one of those Christmas and Easter Catholics, she says she'll help me. We decide to bake on Friday afternoon so the cookies and bars will be fresh for Saturday.

I'm thinking we'll make some oatmeal cookies and some date bars, but Bel surprises me when she shows up with a bag full of frosting and sugar and a bag of candy to stick in the frosting.

"I thought we were making date bars," I says as she dumps all her stuff on my counter.

"Lyla, you know better. It's July now."

I know better than to trust the tone in her voice as she says it, and my fears are confirmed when she pulls out a plastic bag full of cookie cutters with shapes like angels, candy canes, and Santa Claus heads.

"It's Christmas in July!" she exclaims.

"Oh, come on, Bel," I says.

"Oh, don't be a sourpuss, Lyla," Bel says. "The kids will love it."

Ever since we saw that *Christmas in July* movie with Dick Powell when we were in the orphanage, Bel has never gotten it out of her head. "It's good luck to celebrate Christmas in July," she always says, "and maybe we'll win the Maxwell House Sweepstakes too."

"It was Maxford," I tell her, referring to the stupid contest in that movie, but she doesn't listen.

Back in the old days, I would have thought Bel was nuts and I would have refused to do anything that would make me look crazy at church, but by now, everyone knows Bel is crazy, so what the hell? I'll help her make her Christmas cookies today, and I can just make my date bars on Saturday morning.

I'd have been okay with the cookies, but it's a boiling hot day and she's also shown up with a video of *White Christmas* to get us in the mood while we bake, even though we've both seen that movie a zillion times. And even though I've told her that every time we watch it, I get ticked off at Rosemary Clooney all over again—I mean, that woman had it all, but then she went and let herself get fat—if I'd had her looks, I'd have done better than end my career doing Coronet paper towel commercials—gee whiz. Some people just don't appreciate the chances they get in life—she was the same age as me too, and here she's been dead for a few years now. I bet less people remember her now than know who that oily looking nephew of hers is. But at least watching *White Christmas* beats having to watch *Meet Me in St. Louis* again. Bel's crazy about that one, but I can't bear to watch it—especially not when Judy Garland starts singing "Have Yourself a Merry Little Christmas." Not that it ain't a pretty song, and Lord knows Judy could sing, but it's that line, "soon again we all will be together" that gets to me. It's something I used to think about in the orphanage—that that kind of Christmas magic was possible, but it ain't. I never could have Mama and Papa back, or Jessie either, I guess—though I keep hoping, but not doing anything about it when it comes to her. I did get back Papa, so I guess like what Bing Crosby sings to Rosemary, I should count my blessings before I sleep. But they sure don't count their blessings in that *Meet Me in St. Louis* film; the whole family's got this giant house and a maid and the biggest problem they've got that they all whine about is moving to New York where their dad's going to make a lot more money. Silly. I bet Judy knew it was silly too—probably part of what drove her to drink and do all those drugs—she realized like I did long ago that life ain't ever going to be like one of those MGM musicals.

So anyways, Bel puts in the movie while I start mixing up the cookie dough. She never is much help. She puts newspaper and wax paper all over the kitchen table, and she finds my giant cutting board and rolling pin, but I do all the rolling because every time Bing opens his mouth, she gets glued back to the television set. I never did figure out what the big deal was about him—he wasn't much to look at. I'd have picked Danny Kaye over him.

Finally, when I have the dough all rolled out and I'm ready for her to start cutting out the cookies, she decides she has to go to the bathroom so she pauses the movie. And by the time she comes back, she's started down Christmas movie memory lane.

"Lyla," she says, forgetting to turn back on the movie as she sits down and picks up a cookie cutter, "do you remember that Christmas when we went to see *Meet Me in St. Louis* at the Delft Theater?"

It's like I brought this conversation on myself by thinking about that movie. I swear, she practically knows how to read my mind after all these years.

"Yeah," I says.

"That was like sixty years ago," Bel starts rambling. "It must be because I remember it came out the last Christmas of the war. I remember how I bawled when Judy Garland sang to Margaret O'Brien. It still chokes me up. I like *White Christmas*, but I think I like *Meet Me in St. Louis* best. I wish I'd grown up in a family like that, with sisters and a handsome brother."

"Yeah, me too," I says. I wish I'd had their troubles too, including a father going to move us all to New York. Instead, my father was going to move us to Karelia and he went without us—those rich St. Louis people had nothing to worry about by comparison. The maid was the only character in that movie I really liked; she was a bit ornery, and I didn't blame her when she had to put up with all those happy-go-lucky young people while she was trying to make dinner and deal with the pigheaded father for a boss.

"We saw it during the war," Bel goes on, "the Christmas when you first moved in and the boys had gone away."

I don't need to ask who she means by the boys. One is obviously Charlie, and the other was his friend, Lon.

"Yeah," I mutter.

"Lon was so sweet on you, Lyla. Remember those sweet letters he used to write to you," she says.

"Yeah," I says. For the first few weeks I lived with them, Bel and Charlie kept trying to fix me up with Lon, but I was never interested in him. I only saw him twice before he went off to war, but for whatever reason, he decided to write to me. I don't know why. He didn't even know me. He hadn't even been in the orphanage with us. But Bel kept scheming to get him to marry me. He must have written me about a dozen letters—I think he thought he'd wear me down by flooding me with letters. I wrote him back the first time to be polite, but when the letters kept coming, I quit writing. I felt bad for him having to go fight in the war, but I wasn't going to encourage him and have him come home thinking we'd get married. And then next I hear, he's dead, killed some place I'd never heard of out in the Pacific, and I have to admit I felt a bit relieved because Bel just about had my and Lon's wedding all planned for when he got home.

And boy did she get mad after she asked me whether I was going to wear mourning for him and I said, "No, it's not like we were engaged or even dating."

"You was in your hearts," she said.

"Bel, I wouldn't have married him if you paid me," I said. "He had buck teeth."

"Like you're such a catch," she had the nerve to say to me.

"Like Charlie's such a catch," I said back, and then she started crying and went in the bathroom and slammed the door. I knew she was worried about Charlie getting killed, so I shouldn't have said that, but I thought, "What the hell do I want to get married for? I don't want any babies, and I don't want some man telling me what to do—I've had enough of people making decisions for me."

Anyways, I haven't thought of Lon in years, but now, suddenly Bel has him in her head again because of these damn Christmas movies.

"I still think about Lon, you know," says Bel. "I often wonder what would have happened if he hadn't died. I know you told me never to mention him again, Lyla, but that was sixty years ago, and I know you really liked him—it just hurt you too much to talk about it after he died. I often think he would have been the one for you, Lyla. Just think, if he'd lived and you'd married, you'd probably be a grandmother now."

Where does she come up with these stupid ideas? I'm about to snap back, "Yeah, and if Charlie hadn't been a drunk, maybe you'd be a grandmother too," but I hold my tongue. She does still know how to push my buttons, but believe it or not, I have gotten better at holding my tongue over the years, so I just ignore her and keep frosting a snowman.

"Lyla," she keeps at it, "sometimes I wonder if that's why you never married—because Lon was always your one true love."

"Jesus Christ!" I says, but then I catch myself and add, "I forgot to take the cookies out of the oven" and jump up from the table. I didn't forget—but I did almost lose it after that comment. For God's sake, I never once had a true love. Never really wanted one. Never saw a reason to after the way most of the men have behaved whom I've known over the years, beginning with her own husband.

I suppose after all these years that I should let Charlie rest in peace, but I don't know how any woman could be interested in being with a man or wishing such a thing upon her friends after what Bel went through with him.

Bel had her baby while Charlie was away at the war. I remember how stubborn she was through the whole pregnancy—in fact, it wasn't proper in those days to go out while showing, but she insisted we go see *Meet Me in St. Louis* anyways. I remember I was so embarrassed to be seen with her. I could care less today, but back then, I guess I still cared what people thought, and she was only fourteen and pregnant, so she looked like a little tramp. I was afraid they'd refuse to let us in the theatre with her looking that way, but the man who sold the tickets at the Delft was kindhearted, and I talked Bel into sitting in the back row where no one would see us.

When she went into labor, I had to run next door and ask the neighbor to drive us to St. Mary's Hospital where Bel had the baby after twenty hours of labor, during which time I could barely get her to let me go to the bathroom because she was so scared and wanted me there with her every minute, even when the doctors and nurses tried to convince her to let me leave the room. And all the while I was worrying about her, I was also worrying that we had left Mr. Newman home alone. I just kept envisioning him falling down the stairs like Miss Florence had. I was always anxious around old people after that. But Mr. Newman made it through the day somehow without us watching him.

When the baby was finally born, it turned out to be a girl, so Bel insisted she wanted to name it Lyla, but I held my ground that I didn't want it named after me—just made me feel too responsible toward it, like I'd be expected to take care of it.

Finally, Bel said, "Well, Lyla, I still want to honor our friendship, and Charlie wanted to name it after me, so I've decided I'll combine our names and call her Lilybelle."

Lilybelle had to be the dumbest name I'd ever heard—sounded like some kind of fairy or a flower, and I told Bel that, though I left out the "dumbest name" comment. I don't even think the name "Lily" is any relation to "Lyla," but Bel had settled on it and there was no changing her mind, so for the next year, I had to listen to her keep cooing, "How's my little Lilybelle, my little fairy baby" like she was some halfwit, which she probably was and still is.

It was only a month or so after Lilybelle was born that Mr. Newman had his stroke. I've always half-suspected that after a month of listening to that baby screaming every night, and knowing it would go on screaming probably for years, he decided enough was enough. Only, the stroke didn't kill him, just left him bedridden. Then he had to have a bedpan, which was pretty disgusting and frustrating for me, and he never could spray straight—not that I've ever known a man who could; even Mr. O'Neill, gentleman that he was, never failed to leave a puddle on the bathroom floor for me to clean up. Anyways, Mr. Newman's sheets always smelled like urine. Maybe I shouldn't say these things about the dead, but any woman knows it's the truth about men.

Anyways, I spent a lot of time in the evening sitting with Mr. Newman in his room, trying to keep his spirits up. During the day, I had to watch the store, but I'd still go up to check on him every hour or so since Bel claimed she was too busy with Lilybelle. I think she just didn't like having an old man in her house—she pretty much acted like it was her house by that point. So a month or two after his stroke, Mr. Newman faded away in his sleep one afternoon. I came upstairs to check on him about an hour after lunch and he was gone. I was glad for it because he deserved a peaceful end.

And then before I knew it, the war was over and we got a letter from Charlie telling us when he'd be home. Mr. Newman had left him everything, and Bel just couldn't shut up about how now we were going to be living the American Dream and be the perfect family—only, I never saw any Norman Rockwell paintings of a happy married couple with 2.5 children and a best friend tagging along. I knew it wouldn't be long before Charlie would want me out of the house, so I started thinking about what else I could do, but I couldn't do much until he got home because Bel couldn't run the store and look after Lilybelle both.

When Charlie did come home, things went smoothly for about three days, and then I could tell he was irritated about a lot of things—especially the baby's crying. A couple times, he and Bel were in their room fooling around when Lilybelle would start screeching, and then he'd holler, "Lyla, can you get her to shut up?"

"She wants her mama!" I would holler back and then go downstairs to tend the store. I wasn't going to take care of no screaming baby while they were having all the fun. It was enough that Charlie didn't have much of a head for business—I sure don't know how he fooled Mr. Newman into thinking otherwise—so I was basically managing the store myself while Charlie drank at night and lay in bed late with a headache, except when he was having his way with Bel. The situation had really started to get on my nerves, to put it mildly.

And then, the saddest thing possible happened. I can't say I felt that fond of Lilybelle, but I did feed her and change her diapers more times than I wanted, and she grew on me, especially when she'd fall asleep on my shoulder, and before she said, "Daddy," and right after she said, "Mama," she said, "Li-a." She was a sweet girl really, despite all the crying. But for whatever reason, she came down with whooping cough. And—

Well, now that I think back on it, it was probably for the best. Just imagine what kind of mental and emotional problems that baby would have had growing up with Charlie and Bel for parents. But then again, if Lilybelle hadn't died, maybe...

Chapter 13

I don't let myself think about Lilybelle any more until after Bel goes home because I know it will upset me and I don't want to upset her. I don't know why it bothers me today except she's triggered something in my memories from talking about going to see that damn *Meet Me in St. Louis* movie that brings back everything to me about the war and after. I should have known better. She doesn't even go to church so why'd I bother to invite her over to bake cookies with me anyways? If I hadn't invited her over, we wouldn't have made the stupid Christmas cookies, and then she wouldn't have brought up that movie, and I wouldn't be thinking about Charlie and Lilybelle. It still gets me angry when I think about it all, but I try to stay calm about it around her. We occasionally mention Charlie's drinking to each other, but not his other problems, and I think Bel is too embarrassed to talk with me about it after all these years.

"I won't allow it," I told Bel. I was practically shouting at her. I'd gone out to church that morning. We had all started going regularly once Charlie came home from the war, only Charlie hated to go, but Bel thought we should behave like a good Catholic family. She thought maybe God would take pity on her then and let her have another baby. She's been trying to get pregnant for months after Lilybelle died.

And then after a few weeks of the three of us all going to Mass, that morning Charlie refused to go, and he told Bel she wasn't going either.

"You can't stop me from going," I told him.

"Maybe not," he said, "but I won't have my family brainwashed by that religion stuff. What good does it do anyone to go to church if God's going to take my baby from me, not to mention all my buddies who got killed in the war?"

I could tell there wasn't going to be any reasoning with him. Not in the state he was in. He'd gone out on a bender the night before and not come home until two in the morning, and then when Bel had tried to get him up for church, first he'd moaned that he had a splitting headache, and then when she kept at him, he had started screaming at her, which probably didn't help his headache any, but then Charlie wasn't smart enough to realize that, I guess. He got so mad that he told her if she went to church, he'd never let her back in the house, so she finally gave into him and said she'd stay home.

"When I get back from Mass," I warned him, "if you've locked me out of this house, you'll be down on your knees praying for your manhood back. And you've known since the first day you met me that I mean it."

Perhaps it wasn't a very Christian thing to say, but then, Charlie wouldn't have known a Christian sentence if it bit him in the ass, even though he had been raised by nuns.

So I went to Mass. And I prayed to God that Charlie would stop drinking and Bel would have another baby.

I was feeling better when I walked home. It was a beautiful sunny, spring Sunday, and I figured I would make us all a nice Sunday dinner to smooth things over after this morning.

And then I got home, and Charlie was out, and Bel was in the kitchen with a steak against her face. I didn't even have to ask, but I made her pull it away so I could get a good look at the bruise anyways.

"Bel," I told her. "I won't allow it. If he ever hits you again, I'll hit him. In fact, I might hit him when he gets home anyways."

"Lyla, calm down," she said as I kept on screaming and threatening to kick him in the nuts. Finally, she let slip out what she'd been keeping from me.

"It's not a big deal, Lyla. He was drunk. He just missed. He's never hit me in the face before."

"What do you mean, he missed?" I demanded, growing wide-eyed. How did I not know he'd been hitting her all this while? When she didn't answer me, I demanded, "He's hit you before when I haven't been home, hasn't he?

You better not lie to me, Bel."

"Well, no, it's more like—"

"Don't lie to me, Bel!" I shouted.

"He just pushed me is all," she said.

"God damn that bastard!" I yelled. "Is this how he treats you after you put up with him going off to war, and you took care of Mr. Newman for him, and had his baby? And he knows damn well how you've grieved over Lilybelle."

"Well, but Lyla, he's grieving too," she said, holding the steak back over her eye again as she tried to pull things out of the icebox for lunch with one hand. She purposely kept her back to me so she didn't have to look me straight in the face. "I think grief is why he's so angry and gets drunk."

"Then he needs to go get help," I said. "Join that Alcoholics Anonymous group that's starting up everywhere or go talk to the priest for counseling or something. You don't hit your wife because your baby died."

"You just don't understand, Lyla," Bel said.

I didn't understand, but somehow that day, she talked me into keeping my mouth shut when Charlie got home. So I just bided my time. A few months later, when I saw a big bruise on her leg, Bel told me she had fallen down the stairs.

"Bullshit!" I said. "More like he pushed you down them."

"I—I can't have any more children; the doctor told me," she said. "That's what happened. He said..." She burst into tears as she tried to tell me, "Charlie said to me, 'What the hell good's a woman if she can't make any babies!' and then he slapped me, and I just happened to be standing by the stairs and I lost my balance. That's all. Lyla, he didn't mean it."

"And I won't mean what I'm going to do to him," I said.

"What? What are you going to do?"

"If I had a gun, I'd shoot the bastard," I said, and I meant it, at least at that moment.

"Oh, Lyla, quit talking crazy like that," she said. "Charlie will be home any minute, and I don't want you two getting into it."

"Well, we're gonna," I said. "I'm gonna make sure he never touches a woman again if I have to turn him into a woman myself."

"Lyla, you're scaring me."

"I'm not putting up with no one hitting you," I told her.

"Oh, Lyla, you've always looked after me, but this is different. He's my husband, the man I love. You can't talk about him like that."

"What the hell are you doing? Defending him?" I asked. "Are you really crazy enough to love the bastard after how he's treated you?"

"He's the father of my child."

"Your child is dead, Bel."

"Not in my heart she ain't. Lilybelle was a beautiful gift, even if I only had her for a little while, and Charlie gave her to me."

I couldn't hold in my temper anymore. I didn't know if I wanted to puke or to hit her for not wanting me to hit him. So I did the only thing I could do, which was stomp into my room—the one that had been Mr. Newman's—and start packing my things.

She must have heard me making a lot of noise because after a minute, she came to see what I was doing.

"I'm leaving," I said.

"Oh, Lyla, don't be overreacting," she said.

"What about underreacting—that's what you seem to be doing, letting a man slap you around."

"But, Lyla. What will I do without you?"

"If you're concerned about that, you'll come with me," I said, stuffing my bras into the old suitcase I still had that Miss Bergmann sent me to the orphanage with.

"Lyla, please. Please, I need you."

And then we heard the door open and slam shut.

"Bel, honey, where are you?" the alcoholic asshole hollered.

"He lives in a four room apartment and he has to holler to find you," I muttered.

"Lyla, please," Bel whispered, but I wasn't calmed down enough to listen to her.

"We're in here, you goddamned bastard!" I hollered back.

In a second, he was in the doorway with a bouquet of flowers.

"Hi, honey," Bel said, hoping to smooth things over between us.

"Charlie, do you think you can beat up your wife and then buy her a few cheap flowers to solve all your marriage problems?" I asked, slamming shut my suitcase and locking it.

He didn't say anything at first. Then he stepped into the room, handed the flowers to Bel, and said, getting up into my face, "You keep your damn nose out of my business."

"The only thing I'm going to put in your business is my knee if you don't get out of my way," I said. "Maybe Bel will let you abuse her, but I sure the hell ain't."

"Get the hell out of my house!" he shouted, moving behind me and giving me a push toward the door.

"Bel, come with me," I begged.

She just stared down at the floor.

"Fine!" I said. "I never wants to see either of you ever again."

And in less than a minute, I was walking down the street with my suitcase, fuming, and so angry I could barely even see straight, and I didn't have any clue where it was I was going.

And I really wished Bel were with me because I hated to think of her being alone with that monster.

I still get kind of down when I think about it, even though it's been nearly sixty years. I wish I'd done something to stop it, but what could I do in those days? The police didn't stop a man from beating his wife back then. There weren't no women's shelters. And I was just a woman. Even if I'd gotten Bel to leave him, he might have come after her and me both and hurt us.

All Saturday, I feel kind of depressed from thinking about it. Bel's always been kind of flaky, but I wonder if maybe she would have been less flaky if I'd done something to help her back then. She found her own strength in time and she's told me I couldn't have done anything for her; that she needed to find it in herself, but I still feel bad about it, like I should have made it up to her somehow.

So when the Fourth of July comes around, I decide I'll be extra nice to her. I call her up Saturday after church, and I don't even bother to tell her no one bought her Christmas cookies at the bake sale—after all, maybe someone will at one of the Sunday Masses. And then I asks her if she wants to go watch the parade on Monday.

"Lyla, you never want to go to the Fourth of July parade. You always say it's too loud and noisy and crowded. You haven't gone to a parade with me in years."

"I know," I says, "but this year I feel like going."

"What made you change your mind?" she asks.

Christ, I'm just trying to be nice to her; I don't need her to grill me about it.

"I just didn't want you to have to go by yourself," I says.

"That's sweet, Lyla. I'd love for you to go with me, and maybe we can go to the Food Fest later too."

"Well, let's not push it," I says. "We'll see how the parade goes first."

So, now I'm stuck going to the parade. That's the problem with me. I think something might be a good idea, might make me feel better, but then it doesn't, and I get into these moods, especially around holidays, where I just feel kind of depressed because I feel like I'm supposed to be enjoying myself, but I'm not, and that just depresses me.

I was actually kind of hoping maybe John and Wendy would call to invite me over again, especially since our talk got cut short on Memorial Day when Alan and that Frank fellow so rudely showed up unannounced. I was just starting to warm up to John and Wendy, but Wendy hasn't even hinted about having me over since. I thought maybe I'd have some new friends— but that was stupid. Why would two young people like that want to hang out with an old biddy like me? No, Bel's the best I can do for company, except maybe if Eleanor calls me to come visit Bill, who I guess must be all situated in the nursing home by now. But I'm not going to go visit him—not even if he asks me himself.

So on the Fourth of July, Bel comes over for breakfast, and I have to admit she tries really hard. I tell her when she gets there that I'm making scrambled eggs, but she says, "No, that ain't festive enough for the Fourth of July." Then she sticks in a video of this silly musical called *1776* that has that bad film look like most of those movies made in the '60s and '70s. And it seems like it's all about Thomas Jefferson's sex life from what little bit of it I actually pay attention to—and she tells me just to sit there and have my coffee and enjoy myself while she makes pancakes. So I says, "Okay," to make her happy, and I drink two cups of coffee and pretend to watch half the movie, and I'm just about ready to keel over from hunger when she finally tells me she's done.

So I drag myself out of the chair and go over to the table and I think, "What the hell did she bake a cake for?" Only, it's not a cake. It's a stack of pancakes, and she's covered the top one in strawberry and blueberry jam and whipping cream so it looks all red, white, and blue, and then she's got a little

American flag on a toothpick attached to it. "I wanted to put in a sparkler," she says, "but I was afraid it would set off the fire alarm, and I didn't think we'd use a whole box of them—they don't sell them separately," she says.

"It's pretty, Bel," I says, "but I don't like whipping cream, you know."

"That's okay. I'll eat the top one—oh, I forgot the candle I bought to replace the sparkler."

And then she grabs two giant birthday candles off the cupboard of the numbers "7" and "6." They're the same ones she used for my birthday cake last year.

"What's that for?" I asks.

"It's America's birthday today," she says. "It's the Spirit of '76. Don't you remember that from history class?"

I remember birthday cakes have candles to represent a person's age, not the year they were born, but I s'pose she couldn't do the math to figure it out—two hundred and...and...twenty-nine it would be—2005 minus 1776.

"Let's eat," I says, but first I have to use the bathroom from drinking all that coffee while I waited.

I go in the bathroom and sit down, and can't help laughing to myself about the pancakes covered in jam with "76" sticking out of them. That'd be one to take a picture of if my Kodak disc camera hadn't broken. I haven't bought a new one—those new digital things are just too expensive as far as I'm concerned. And I don't have a computer to read them on.

Well, we have a nice breakfast. I eat far more pancakes than I normally would, but Bel says we need to eat extra to keep up our strength for walking to the parade. It's on Washington Street, just two blocks from Snowberry, but whatever.

After breakfast, I wash up the dishes while she watches the rest of *1776*. For the rest of the day, I'll hear her humming that song about Jefferson playing the violin.

"We can watch *Yankee Doodle Dandy* tonight, Lyla," she says.

"Great," I think, but I just says, "Okay." Maybe I'll be lucky and fall asleep by then.

"While we wait for the fireworks," she says.

I'd forgotten about the fireworks, but I can see them great where they shoot them off over the old ore dock right from my window. It's one of the few advantages of living high up in a skyscraper—well, at least the closest thing to a skyscraper that Marquette's got.

When it's time for the parade, we put on suntan lotion at Bel's insistence, and we get out our old lady straw hats, and then we take the elevator down to the lobby. We go out into the parking lot to Bel's car where she's got a couple fold-up lawn chairs in her trunk. Then we start up the hill to Washington Street, a bit before the crowd, so we can get a spot in the shade, usually in front of the buildings on the south side of the street between Fourth and Fifth.

We find a good shady spot, right next to a little tree and where we can see up Washington Street where the parade will come down. There aren't any kids nearby to run in the street and grab candy and get on my nerves, so that's a good sign, though it's a good half hour before the parade will start down by Shopko, and probably another half hour after that before it'll get to where we are downtown.

At least we're in the shade so I don't have to listen to Bel complaining about the heat, though it's turning out to be a hot summer, which I can do without. No true Yooper likes hot weather—anything over seventy degrees and I start sweating, and when you spend your life walking back and forth to work and working on your feet all day, it doesn't take much to get you sweating. I'm sweating just from the walk up the hill to here.

I guess a lot of other people must not like hot weather either considering all the guys walking around with their shirts off and the girls in their skimpy shorts and those tank top things that show off their cleavage—well, I'd like to think it was because they don't like to sweat, but I know better. Bunch of tramps is what we would have called these girls in my day. And the guys, they look like babies mostly, they're so young. I admit some of them might be good-looking, but they spoil their looks with all those God-awful tattoos. I can see maybe having one on your arm, but not on your back, chest, and especially on your neck. Just makes me want to puke. And then there are the young teenage boys riding around on their bikes, trying to attract the "chicks," but mostly just making asses out of themselves—only the tramps they'll attract are too stupid to know they're asses. "Male sluts—that's what they are," I mutter to myself as a trio of them go by, trying to do wheelies for whatever girls might be in the crowd.

"What?" Bel asks.

"Oh, nothing. I just don't understand the younger generation," I says.

"Oh, Lyla, how could you? You never were young yourself."

"What do you mean by that?" I asks.

"Here, have your Diet Coke before it gets too warm," she says, pulling two drinks out of her gigantic purse.

I take the pop and crack the cap just enough to let the fizz out so it doesn't explode. I'm not going to ask her again what she means by my never having been young. I was young until I was about ten, but I was never the age of those teenage boys on their bicycles. I never had the freedom to be young like that. I was milking cows at the orphanage and then taking care of two old ladies, and then taking care of a store, an old man, and a woman with a baby and a drunken husband all my teen years. By the time I turned eighteen, I was on my own again, and had my own apartment, but I was busy working constantly so I'd have enough to pay the rent. I had plenty of guys around my age who would try to hit on me when I walked around town, but I just ignored them, and I never went to the bars or anything—I saw what marriage did to people—my father abandoned my mother, or at least that's what we all thought, and I'm sure her heartbreak over that contributed to her death, and then Bel married an alcoholic who beat her, not to mention she lost her child. Why would I want to go through that pain? And then there were the rich ladies I cleaned house for, always fussing over their rich husbands who brought home the bacon, and most of them were scared of their husbands too. What the hell did I want with that kind of a life?

Finally, we see the cop cars starting to come down the street—a sign that the parade is about to start. And then just as the cop cars get in front of us, I see across the street Alan Whitman walking by with that friend Frank of his. Frank looks like he's still one of those silly teenage boys with his sleeveless T-shirt to show off his big muscles. The two of them walk down the street toward the Ramada Inn, looking for a spot to watch the parade, I guess. I hope they don't come back on this side of the street. I don't want to talk to them. I'm glad Bel doesn't notice them. Of course, she hasn't seen Alan but a few times and that was when he was about twenty.

"Are you going to be able to get out of that lawn chair fast enough to catch the candy, Lyla?" Bel jokes.

I don't reply, but I think she's jinxed us because a young couple with two little girls now shows up and decides to stand right by us. Well, those little girls better not try crawling under my lawn chair to get their candy, not that they could knock me over. It's just—well, I don't like kids. I had to deal with enough of them in the orphanage, and I never would take a housecleaning job where there were a bunch of kids. A couple times I was desperate so I agreed if the kids were old enough to look after themselves, but even those kids could get lippy or leave their dirty clothes laying all over the furniture. Guess I just never had a wifely or maternal bone in my body.

"Here it comes, Lyla!" says Bel, all excited as the first float comes along—if you can call any of these things in the parade "floats" anymore. Just a bunch of big noisy smelly trucks and the mayor and rotary people riding around in cars. Hardly a float at all in a parade now. Not like in the old days. Not like the Centennial Year. Now that was a parade to be seen. Not even the Sesquicentennial parade could compare with it.

Someone comes along handing out little flags. They're for the kids so, of course, the two little girls by us get them, but Bel also has to grab two of them. She gives me one to wave, but I don't want it, so she sticks it through the lawn chair webbing behind me. Well, fine. Maybe someone will come up behind me and steal it.

There's some people on horses, and the Marquette Redmen and Redettes trying to play a tune. Then some screeching bagpipe group, and clowns and dogs all dressed up and other silly stuff. Of course, Bart Stupak comes along, wanting to shake all our hands so he can get our votes as state representative or whatever it is he does. And of course, Bel yells out, "There's Bart Stupak! Isn't he cute?" Well, I guess he is kind of good-looking, but he's married and it's not like he'd ever look at her, so what's the difference? Dominic Jacobetti would have been more our style anyways—closer to our age and, not surprisingly, dead as a result.

"I'm so glad you came, Lyla," says Bel during a lull as we wait for some car carrying some dignitary to make its way down the parade route. "Are you having fun?"

"Loads," I says as I watch the little girls run into the middle of the street for a stray Tootsie Roll from the last float that went by. You wouldn't catch me eating that candy after a horse or dog might have stepped on it.

It's getting hotter as the parade goes on, and I'm feeling more annoyed, and a bit hungry. We ate so much for breakfast we didn't need lunch, but now it's the middle of the afternoon and the Diet Coke isn't cutting it; plus I'm afraid to drink it and then have to pee and not be able to make it back home.

I'm so happy when I finally see people down the street starting to move around, a sign the last of the parade is arriving, and in a few more minutes, the police come by to mark the parade's end.

"Wasn't that a great parade?" says Bel. "I think that's the best one I've seen in years."

"Yeah, it was nice," I says, but only 'cause it's a holiday so I don't want to argue with her.

"Are you hungry, Lyla?" she asks as we stand up and collect our lawn chairs. I know you said we could have hot dogs or something, but why don't we go out instead?"

"Where would we go?" I asks. "Is anything open on the Fourth of July?"

"I think Tommy's is," she says, but I can tell from her tone that she doesn't want to go there.

"That would be fine," I says.

"Or, how about we go down to the Food Fest?" she says, which I know is what she really wants.

"Oh, Bel, it's so crowded and—"

"Hi, Lyla! Hi, Bel!"

I turn and find Sybil and May standing behind us.

"Oh, hello!" says Bel.

"Hi," I says.

"Did you enjoy the parade?" Bel asks.

"Oh, yes," says Sybil. "We wanted Alan to come with us, but he had to go up to see his dad. Did I tell you that's who I'm dating? He's May and John's cousin of some sort. I've been kind of quiet about it at the meetings because I don't want Diana to go steal him away from me," she laughs, "but he saw you that day we were at May's for the meeting, so he asked me how I knew you. I just said we were friends and that I drove you ladies to The Pancake House now and then."

"Did he tell you," Bel asks her, "that Lyla used to date his dad, Bill?"

"No, really?" Sybil says.

"I didn't know that," says May.

"Oh, yes," I says. "Wendy knows. I went up to see Bill when he had his heart attack back around Memorial Day and Wendy and John were there."

"Yes, that's right. I think I remember Wendy mentioning that," says May.

"How is Bill doing?" I asks to be polite. "I guess you're related to him too, May. Aren't you a cousin or something to Alan?"

"Yeah, kind of distant cousins. My grandpa was Bill's cousin. He's doing better. He's at the nursing home now and not too happy about it."

"Is he going to be able to come home eventually?"

"No, Alan doesn't think so," says Sybil. "Alan doesn't know what to do. He's thinking about moving back here so he can keep an eye on his dad. He's been here over a month now taking care of him. We wanted him to come to the parade with us, but he thought he should spend the afternoon with his dad. I'll see him later. He'll be coming to the picnic we're having at May's house this afternoon."

I don't say anything about seeing Alan walk down the street before the parade, but somehow I'm not surprised. I always knew he was a jerk. Visit his dad, my ass. But why did he have to lie to her?

"Do you want to come to our picnic?" May asks. "We'd love to have you."

"Oh—" Bel starts to say before I cut her off.

"We'd like to," I says, "but we already have plans to meet some people down at the Food Fest."

"Oh, that's too bad," says May. "Well, come by later if you like. Eleanor is going to come, and her daughters, Maud and Lucy. Do you know them?"

"Oh, yes," I says. "Tell them I said hello."

"Well, Lyla, we could go to the party," says Bel.

"No, no," I tell May. "It's a holiday and you want to spend time with your family and we have other plans."

"I'm not family," says Sybil, "but I'm going."

"You're dating family," May laughs.

"Well, have a good time," I says to end the conversation. "Happy Fourth of July."

"Yes, Happy Fourth of July," says May.

"Happy Fourth," says Sybil. "I'm off work tonight so you better eat your fill at the Food Fest. I won't be able to make any late night pancake runs for you."

"That's all right. We had our pancakes this morning," I says.

"Yes, I made red, white, and blue ones," says Bel proudly.

"Sounds yummy," says May, laughing. "See you later."

As soon as they're out of hearing, Bel says, "Oh, Lyla, it would have been fun to go to the picnic."

"Stop it," I tell her, starting through the crowd and down the sidewalk. "You know you don't want me getting involved with Bill and his family so don't push it."

"Well, no, not with Bill, but Sybil and May and Wendy are our friends," she says.

"They're not our friends," I says. "They're just acquaintances who are being polite. They're young and don't really want to be spending time with two broads old enough to be their grandmothers."

"Oh, Lyla. We're only as old as we think we are."

I force my way through the crowd and ignore her. For a second, I remember how I had kind of wished John and Wendy had invited me over, and I would have gone if it was just them, but I'm not going to a family party at May's house, or ever going to May's house again for that matter—not that Bill would see me if he's stuck in the nursing home now, but—oh, that Alan—he must be a womanizer just like his father, lying to Sybil about going to the parade and then having the nerve to go anyways with Frank—they were probably sniffing around looking for women too.

For a moment, it occurs to me that maybe Alan changed his mind about going to the nursing home, and maybe he was just walking down the street looking for Sybil, but I don't like him, so why should I give him that kind of credit?

"It's too early to eat yet," I says to Bel when we reach Snowberry. "Let's go in and rest for a while and have that lemonade I made up."

We go upstairs to my apartment and take turns using the bathroom. We sit and drink lemonade, and I turn on the TV and we find some music program to watch. Before I know it, I hear Bel snoring. That's okay. I can use a break from all her chatting and the holiday festivities. It's only four o'clock. It would have been nice to beat the crowd at the Food Fest, but if she's going to take a nap, I could take a little one too, just for an hour at most.

I look over at Bel and can tell she isn't going to be up for a while; she's kind of cute when she's sleeping though; looks like a little girl again, like she did when I first met her in the orphanage. She drives me bonkers, but I'm thankful to have her around. I don't want to be all alone in the world, no matter how much some people bug me.

I put up my footrest on my recliner, lay back, and close my eyes. It kind of feels nice to hear someone else in the room breathing. I don't need much human contact, but I need a little. Having Bel live nearby is enough, I guess. I sure don't want to be all alone again. I worry about that—what if something happens to Bel. Then I'll be all alone. That's kind of why I thought it might be nice after all to be friends with John and Wendy—young people give you a little security against being alone since they'll outlive you. I remember how rough it was to be alone all those years...

Chapter 14

It's a good thing I left in a fury the day I stormed out of Bel and Charlie's lives because if I'd taken the time to cool down and then stop and think, which I didn't usually do back then, I probably would have stayed and tried to protect her. And I really do think I would have killed Charlie, in his sleep if nothing else, if I had stayed.

But once I was gone, that life was over and done with for me. I spent many sleepless nights, imagining myself going back, imagining taking Bel away from him, imagining ways I could kill him and not get caught, or just hoping someone would run over him with a car or whatever it took to get rid of him, but in the morning, I would come to my senses and realize there wasn't any way in hell I was responsible for helping a woman stupid enough to stay with a man like that. She'd just have to learn to help herself.

But then I'd go to church and pray that Charlie would quit drinking, or that Bel would come find me or at least find the strength to leave him. I kept hoping for some sort of miracle, like maybe the Virgin Mary would appear to Charlie and tell him he must repent and make up for his sins by going off to Africa as a missionary—and if the pygmies just happened to catch him and make him into stew, well that would be okay too—I mean, they do say that the Lord works in mysterious ways.

For a year or two, I drove myself crazy obsessing about it, but I never once heard from Bel, didn't even bump into her around town. Many times I wanted to go talk to her, but I couldn't bring myself to do it. I don't know if that meant I was a bad friend, or I was just protecting myself from getting hurt, but I just couldn't do it.

That same day I left Bel behind, I found a room to rent just a few blocks from the cathedral. And within a few days, I had a job cleaning house for an old lady down the road, and then that led to another and another cleaning job until I'd go over once a week or so to clean for about a dozen people a few hours each week. I worried a lot about money and not having enough work, but before I knew it, I had more offers than I could keep up with. As long as I managed to keep my mouth shut, I usually got good referrals. I was a hard worker and I could make a floor shine, get all the dust mites and specks of lint out of the rugs, and the spots off the glasses, and I never called in sick or gave my employers reason to complain about my work.

It was a few months before I realized that the house where I rented was only a couple blocks from Miss Bergmann and Jessie. I'd almost blocked them out of my memory by then, but one day, I was walking down the street when Jessie called my name. I didn't even know her at first until she got up right close to me. She asked me how I was and what I was doing and I made the mistake of telling her.

"Cleaning houses, Lyla," she said. "Oh, that's not very good. I'm going to college. I'm halfway now. To Juilliard, the famous music school, only I'm home now since it's summer. But I'm going to become a music teacher I hope."

"That's nice," I said.

"Oh, Lyla. I've missed you. I know we've lost touch the last few years, but I think about you often. You should come to supper some night. I'll call you and arrange that."

"I don't have a phone," I said.

"Oh, well, what's your address? I'll come by and let you know when's a good night after I check with Mother."

Mother? She calls that old lady mother? Miss Bergmann couldn't have been fifty yet, but I'd somehow aged and wrinkled her in my imagination over the years.

I didn't want to, but I gave Jessie my address, figuring I'd think of a way to get out of dinner later.

But I didn't. Jessie came by when I wasn't home and left me a note telling me to come to dinner the next night. I was too embarrassed by my penmanship to write her back, and too afraid to go over to the house to stick a note in the mailbox, so the next night, I showed up at Miss Bergmann's house for dinner.

"Lyla, come in," said Jessie, acting all pleased to see me when I got there, and for just a minute, I thought it was going to turn out all right. But I should have known better.

Miss Bergmann was busy cooking in the kitchen so Jessie sat me down in the parlor and brought me a lemonade. She wanted me to tell her all about everything I'd been doing, but there wasn't much to tell. I just told her I'd been busy doing housecleaning since I left the orphanage. I didn't want to tell her about how much I grew to like the Miss Mitchells, or that they'd been our cousins, or how they'd cheated me out of a house by dying on me before they changed the will. And I sure couldn't tell Jessie how my best friend had married an alcoholic and lost a baby and then I had left her because I couldn't stand to see her abused. I mean, those are the kinds of things you only tell your closest friends or family and Jessie, well, she was only my sister in name. I didn't really know her anymore, and I didn't much trust her either since Miss Bergmann had gotten her clutches on her.

Once we sat down to eat, Miss Bergmann kept asking me about what movies I'd seen. I told her I didn't go to the movies, which was true since I was too afraid of running into Bel there.

"Well, what do you do then?" she asked. "Do you have a young fellow?"

"No," I said. "I think they're more trouble than they're worth."

"Oh, I daresay," she said, "but if they're good-looking like Tyrone Power or Gene Kelly, then well, no amount of thinking otherwise will stop a girl from falling for them. Wouldn't you like to be kissed by Tyrone Power or have Gene Kelly dance with you in his arms, Lyla?"

"Sure," I said to be polite. What kind of a harebrained question was that? The old lady always did make crackpot comments, and she never knew when to shut up either.

I was thankful when it was time for dessert because I thought that meant I wouldn't have long until I could get the hell out of there, but then, as soon as Jessie served the blueberry pie, she said, "Lyla, we have a big surprise for you."

"A surprise?" I said. "What do you mean?"

"Well, Lyla," said Miss Bergmann. "Jessie and I feel we should do something to help you out."

Really? After all these years, they'd finally come to that conclusion. "Like what?" I asked.

"Mother's going to pay for you to go to secretarial school!" Jessie beamed.

"What's that?" I asked, too surprised to understand at first.

"Oh, you know, being a secretary, doing office work," Jessie said.

"You can learn shorthand," Miss Bergmann said. "Then you can write secret love letters to your young man that no one else can read."

"I don't have a young man," I told her again. I held back on pointing out that most young men wouldn't be able to read shorthand so it would be stupid to write a love letter that way.

I was pretty content with cleaning houses, so I don't know why I let them talk me into it. Before I knew it, I was enrolled in a secretarial program.

Well, I know why I agreed to it. Wacky as Miss Bergmann was, she and Jessie had me over for supper a few more times that summer before the classes started. I was starting to think they liked me. I was even starting to convince myself that I would like to be a secretary and learn how to type and take shorthand.

And then I was introduced to the goddamn typewriter. Whoever the hell invented that thing and didn't put those keys in alphabetical order— what the hell was he thinking? And back then, they didn't have any of that fancy correction tape that they use nowadays. I must have wasted a ton of paper those first couple days, and that's all I lasted. I wasn't there even half an hour the third day of class when I slammed my fist down on the damn typewriter and stormed out of the room.

The next day, Jessie showed up on my doorstep. I figured I'd have to face the music eventually; I just hadn't figured out yet what I was going to say to her and Miss Bergmann. I didn't even know if Jessie knew I'd dropped out yet, but when I opened the door, she shouted, "Mother had to pay for that typewriter you destroyed. How could you do that, Lyla? What is wrong with you? Haven't you grown up at all since you were a little girl throwing temper tantrums?"

"I didn't mean to do it," I said. "I just got so mad. Those machines are crazy. It's easier to handwrite."

"You're impossible, Lyla. We're trying to help you, but—"

"Help me? By trying to chain me down to a desk all day with a machine like that?"

"Lyla, you need to move into the twentieth century. Typewriters are the future. They're not going anywhere."

"What do you know, Miss Piano Fingers?" I said to her. "I'd like to see you type on one."

"I type on one all the time," she said.

"Well, good for you," I sneered.

"I don't know what's going to become of you, Lyla. I'm so glad Mama and Papa are dead because they'd be so ashamed of the young woman you've become."

"I'm glad they're dead too," I shouted, although I was breaking into tears, "so they don't have to see what a snot you've become!"

And then I slammed shut the door and just started bawling my eyes out. I ran into the bedroom and cried myself to sleep, and I remember I barely got out of bed for two days. Here I thought Jessie was finally going to act like a sister to me. How could I have been so stupid?

But I was lucky really because I'd quit all my housecleaning jobs and was now out of work, but I went to see this one woman I'd been cleaning for and she told me her friend, a Mrs. Danielle Marshall, was looking for help. Apparently her maid had been hit by a car and killed just the day before, leaving Mrs. Marshall high and dry. Well, I high-tailed it over to Mrs. Marshall's house right away. She had this nice big house on the east side—not one of those mansion-size ones like the O'Neills had, but a really nice home nevertheless. After I told her my name, I said to her, "I'm real sorry to hear you lost your maid like that. I'm sure it was a shock to you, but I bet you're more worried about how you're going to keep this big old house clean by yourself, and you shouldn't let your grief take over the cleanliness of your home."

"Who's that Ma?" a young man hollered from upstairs.

"I hope it's the next maid!" Mrs. Marshall called back.

I had a feeling then that I would like her.

"That's my son," Mrs. Marshall said, ushering me into the house. "He's in college so he's only home visiting for the weekend, but when he is home, he's a handful the way he dirties up the place. Poor Elsie, rest her soul, was always cleaning up after him, and I just can't keep up with him. If you think you can, you've got a job, Lyla."

"I can keep up with him," I said.

I've been cleaning houses ever since then. Was it boring a lot of the time—yes. Was it gross cleaning other people's toilets and bathtubs, sure, but I could do it, and they would pay me to do it so it put food on the table and paid the rent and that's all I needed really. After that, I told myself I didn't need anyone else.

Now and then, I'd see Jessie and Miss Bergmann out in public. Miss Bergmann sometimes would smile at me, but that just made my blood boil. Jessie would just say, "Hi, Lyla," and keep on walking. I didn't care. I knew better than to try to get her back in my life. She'd just walk out on me again like everyone else had.

Those were lonely years for me, and if Mrs. Marshall hadn't been so good to me, I don't know how I would have gotten through them. Mrs. Marshall couldn't afford to pay me full-time—no one could after the war really; not until I went to work for the O'Neills in the end did I have a full-time job, but she kept me busy usually three or four days a week and she had a few friends who'd hire me on and off too, so I managed to make ends meet. I even did more for Mrs. Marshall than she expected because she was good to me.

Mrs. Marshall's husband was long dead, but she was okay financially because her parents had died and left her quite a bit of money, so she didn't have to worry. Her son, Gary Jr., was a bit of a handful whenever he came home from college, but that was only a few times a year and never for much more than a week. In time, Mrs. Marshall told me how her husband had been a drunk and his drinking had killed him. So then I felt I could tell her all my problems about Bel and Charlie and his drinking. She felt bad for Bel, but she told me I'd done the right thing, saying, "Lyla, you can't make anyone do something they aren't ready to do, even if it's the best thing for them." And she agreed with me that you can't trust men. "You can't trust men, Lyla," she would say over and over again whenever the subject came up. Not that she was a man-hater like these feminazis are today, but she knew what it was to be wronged by a man. She told me that was why she had never remarried. "I love Gary Jr.—" she'd say about her son, "and if he ever gets married, I hope he'll be a good father, but honestly, I don't know too many men who make good husbands. You're smart to stay single, Lyla."

I was kind of surprised when she said that. I wasn't more than twenty at the time. I mean, I had kept my distance from men, and after how Charlie had treated Bel, I told myself I was better off without one, but deep down, sometimes I would think about how nice it would be to have someone care about me. I never did go to the movies much after that since Bel liked to go so much and I was afraid of bumping into her at the Delft or the Nordic downtown, but I remembered enough of those tender, romantic Hollywood moments, and Mrs. Marshall was a big listener to the soap operas on the radio. God forbid I should make any noise when *The Guiding Light* came on, despite how silly the love stories were and what she had said about men, and I have to admit, all that romance—well, even if you knew it was all phony, it could suck you in to wishing it was real.

I never did get myself a fellow, though. Not until years later anyways. As I started out saying, those were hard years for me. I was so busy working that I didn't get a chance to meet anyone other than some of Mrs. Marshall's friends who would stop by, and they were too high up in class to be my friends, though I'd go work for a lot of them over the years. I even worked Saturdays a lot of the time. Then I'd come home and feel too tired to go out and do anything, and I didn't have anyone to go out with anyways. And I figured no man would want me with my attitude—I know now I probably had low self-esteem—from thinking my parents hadn't wanted me and blaming them for dying or leaving—and from my sister not wanting me—but back then, I just kind of hid myself away—I guess I was afraid to try getting involved with anyone again from fear I'd get hurt, and I didn't need anyone else to hurt me. My mom, dad, sister, Miss Bergmann, the Mitchell sisters by dying and not leaving me the house, Bel and Charlie—they had all hurt me.

So many times I wanted to go talk to Bel, but I didn't. Sometimes, I'd even look in the obituaries in *The Mining Journal*, having a premonition that I'd read how Charlie had killed her, or I'd look in the birth announcements, hoping she'd had a baby and that would make things better for her. But I never saw any of those things. Maybe once every year or two, I'd catch a glimpse of her somewhere around town, but then I'd go hide before she saw me. I just couldn't bring myself to talk to her. Even Mrs. Marshall had told me I'd done the right thing, but I still felt like I'd been a bad friend.

Sometimes, I felt so lonely I'd have killed myself if it hadn't been for the Catholic guilt the Sisters had instilled in me, making me afraid of God's wrath; and sometimes it was because the priest at Mass would say something—not too often, and especially not when everything was said in Latin and that had been my worst subject in school—but sometimes, I'd hear something out of the priest's mouth, something maybe Jesus had said, like "Blessed are the poor in spirit," and then I'd figure that meant me and I just had to wait and maybe God would make it all right in the end. I had a hard time believing that, but somehow, when things seemed their worst, I could just hold onto that.

A few times I even went to talk to the priest, but then I found myself just complaining about my sister and Miss Bergmann and all, and he just kind of seemed irritated with me, not that I could blame him, but wasn't it his job to cheer me up and listen to my problems? After Miss Bergmann died, I went to see Jessie to tell her I was sorry, but somehow, we just ended up having a screaming match, and I stormed out, feeling terrible afterwards, so I went to the cathedral to talk to the priest, but he didn't do much but roll his eyes at me. That's the last time I went to the priest with my problems or even to confession. After that, I just talked to God. That day, Jessie and I yelled at each other, that was the same day I prayed my rosary and Papa showed up, so to me that was a sign God did listen to me, even if only once in awhile. I figured that meant I didn't need the priest because God could hear me anyways. The bishop might not like my saying that, but I'm too old to care what he thinks now, and I'm older than him by a few years anyways. God's my friend despite what a pain in the ass I can be. It's hard for me to believe, but that's what Jesus said, "No longer slaves. I call you friends." I guess it's good to have a friend, even a friend like Bel.

"Lyla, look what time it is. I'm starving!" Bel exclaims, waking me up. I must have dozed off while thinking about the old days.

"What time is it?" I asks, putting down my footrest and trying to find the energy to get out of my recliner.

"Nearly seven o'clock. We better get down to the Food Fest before they run out of food."

"Yeah, okay," I says, getting to my feet. "Let me just use the bathroom real quick."

After I go, I wash my hands and face, and as I'm washing, I remember how I was just thinking about those long lonely years before Bel came back into my life and then I feel excited that we're going down to the Food Fest tonight—that I have someone to do those sorts of things with.

"I'm ready," I says, coming out of the bathroom and feeling a bit elated.

"Ready for what?" Bel says, looking confused.

"What do you mean, for what? For going to the Food Fest," I says.

She gives me a weird look for a second, then laughs and says, "I was just joking around with you, Lyla."

"You know it's not safe to joke with me when I have an empty stomach,"

I says, but I'm joking around now too. I guess holidays do that to you—put you in a lighter mood.

We go downstairs and get in Bel's car and drive down to Mattson Park.

"Look at all the people," says Bel as we wait for everyone to get out of our way; people are walking across Lakeshore Boulevard in droves to get to the Food Fest, not to mention all the car traffic. "Remember when this was all coal docks and shipping down here?" she says.

"Yeah," I says, "it was a stinky smelly mess."

"Now it's a beautiful park," says Bel, as she pulls into the parking lot. "Funny how things change."

"Yeah," I says, "there's a parking spot opening up."

While we wait for a truck to pull out, Bel puts on her blinker to make it clear she's pulling in there, but just as the truck clears the space, a jeep comes flying in from the other direction and steals our spot.

"Can you believe that?" says Bel.

"Goddamn teenagers!" I says.

"Oh, Lyla, they're just kids."

"They're rude," I says. "We never would have done that—the nuns would have given us a good slap for doing something like that."

Bel drives on and starts to circle the parking lot but not before I get a look at the hoodlums. There's three boys who look like they must be about sixteen or seventeen, and one trampy girl, and I say trampy not only because she's with three boys, but because I recognize her as that Josie, May's daughter, the foul-mouthed, church candle stealer. If I see her in one of the food tents or walking around, you can bet I'm going to give her a piece of my mind.

"I can't believe these kids," I mutter. "What's wrong with their parents?" Nice as May is, she obviously lets that little brat get away with too much.

"Oh, Lyla, don't let such a little thing spoil the evening—look, there's another space right there for us, and it's closer than the other one."

I don't say nothing. Bel likes to pretend she's all above getting angry—says she's learned from going to AA how to stay calm, but I think the truth is she's not in touch with her anger. I heard Dr. Phil say something like that—how we have to get in touch with our anger. Anyone who's had as crappy a life as Bel and never gets angry must be a prime example of that repressed anger stuff. That's one problem I've never had; if anything, maybe I should repress it a little more, but when people do rude things, it just really ticks me off.

We get out of the car and start making our way through the parking lot to where all the food tents are set up. They call this the International Food Fest, but it ain't that international, and it's the same old places selling food every year—one of the Chinese restaurants, Vango's with its Greek food, and a few other places that ain't really international at all. I used to like to come down here to get the deep fried ice cream from Entre Amigos, but they've been closed for years now.

After we buy our tickets, we wander around looking at everything and the prices, which are more than in the restaurants, despite the discomfort of having to sit at rackety old tables in the outdoors with mosquitoes and using plastic silverware, not to mention worrying about your napkins blowing away. Eating outdoors is for crazy people as far as I'm concerned, but I tag along to keep Bel happy.

It's the same old food each year, which is why I haven't come the last few years. Of course, the whole place is packed with young people so you can barely move, and there's tons of people around the beer tent. I steer Bel past there quick. She hasn't had a drink in years, but she tells me you can never be too careful, so I'm not taking any chances.

Finally, I settle on having a gyro from Vango's and Bel does the same. It's good and it's filling, but it's a hell of a mess. I haven't had one in years, but it is the International Food Fest, so what the heck.

It's been a warm day, but there's a bit of a breeze coming in off the lake. The place is crowded and people bump against my chair in the tent. Bel and I find ourselves perched at the end of a table where a bunch of other people are sitting and talking but let us sit down before they go back to their conversation. Bel and I don't talk to each other much while we eat—I think we're both feeling overwhelmed by the crowd.

I'm ready to go home as soon as we're done eating, but Bel wants to walk around, so I agree to make another loop around the tents and the crowd.

Who are all these people? I think everyone in Upper Michigan has converged on Marquette for the Food Fest. I don't see a single person I know.

Well, I spoke too soon. We make our loop and then we're about ready to go when, behind a tent, I see Josie. She's drinking some yellowish brown liquid in a plastic cup that has to be a beer and talking to one of the guys I saw get out of the car with her. Obviously she's too young to drink beer so they're hiding out behind one of the other tents. Even the guy with her doesn't look twenty-one—he must have a false I.D. or something. What is wrong with that girl, drinking beer at her age? When I was her age, I was taking care of the Mitchell sisters. I didn't have time to be drinking beer with older boys.

"What's wrong, Lyla?" asks Bel. I realize I've come to a standstill and I'm staring at Josie, and when Bel speaks, she must hear it because the little brat glares at me. The boy looks slightly scared when he sees us looking at them.

"What would your mother say about you drinking beer?" I asks her. "You're lucky there's no cop around here."

"Piss off!" Josie says.

"Lyla, what—" says Bel, slow to catch on.

"She's May's daughter," I says. "I just caught her drinking beer."

I look at Bel and see her eyes growing wide. She marches right up to Josie and says, "Young lady, you're headed for trouble if you start drinking. I'm a recovering alcoholic and I can tell you that you don't want to get started going down that road."

"It's none of your business," the boy tells Bel as I walk up behind her.

"It is my business. I'm friends with her mother, and I know her mother wouldn't like this," says Bel.

"You don't want me to drink?" Josie says as I see this horrible grin come across her face.

Bel starts to say, "No, you will regret it—"

But before Bel can finish, Josie turns over her cup and pours the beer on Bel's shoes.

Bel stands there, staring at her, but I'm furious and charge toward her, only to step in a hole in the grass and topple over.

Josie and her friend erupt with laughter, and then Josie says, "Come on!" and takes off running with her friend.

"Are you okay, ma'am?" says a handsome young man, who must have seen me fall and is now bending over to try to pick me up.

I have a hard time getting to my feet in the sticky, beer-soaked grass all around me, but he manages to get me to my feet with a little help from Bel, who still seems in shock.

"Oh, Lyla, your pants have a big grass stain on them," she says, wiping at my butt.

"Stop it," I says, shooshing away her hand.

"Can you walk okay?" asks the young man.

"Yes, I'll be fine. Thank you," I says.

The gorgeous, blonde young hunk smiles at me, and for a minute, I wish I were twenty-one again.

"Just be careful, then," he says.

"I will be," I says. "We're heading home now anyways."

I start heading toward the parking lot, trying to look as dignified as possible, with Bel following behind me. I hope the grass stain isn't that bad. It's hard to find decent pants to fit me right, and this pair was my favorite.

"Are you hurt at all, Lyla?" Bel asks.

"No," I says. "Just my pride a little. But I'd like to wring that little brat's neck. I think we should call her mother when we get home."

"Oh no, Lyla. That would ruin their picnic. We shouldn't do that."

"Well, May ought to know. She ought to spank that kid until her butt is black and blue."

"I don't think you're allowed to spank children anymore," says Bel. "If you do, the kids call 911 on you."

"What the hell is wrong with this world?" I says.

By now we're at the car.

"Don't think about it anymore," Bel tells me as we get in the car. "Don't let her ruin your day."

"Did she ruin your shoes?" I asks.

"No, I wiped most of the beer off on the grass. They might smell a little for a day or two, but after that, they won't be any worse for the wear. Let's go get some ice cream to cheer ourselves up. We'll go drive around Presque Isle and get some ice cream there, and by then, we'll feel better."

I don't say anything. All I can see is Josie's snotty face.

"Would you like that?" Bel asks.

"Sure," I says.

We pull out of the parking lot and onto Lakeshore Boulevard and follow it all the way up to Presque Isle. Lake Superior looks calm and graceful tonight. Peaceful, like it doesn't have a care in the world. I wonder why my life isn't peaceful like that. For a minute, I feel like crying, but I get over it by the time we get to Presque Isle and drive around the park. I try to distract myself by looking for deer. We don't see any, but I pretty much have quit thinking about that little snot by the time we get to the Island Store. Bel gets Black Cherry and I get my favorite—Jilbert's Peanut Butter Mackinac Island Fudge. Funny how sugar and chocolate fudge can soothe you.

By the time we get home, it's nearly nine o'clock and I'd be feeling ready for bed if what I ate had agreed with me, but gyros and ice cream don't go together well.

"Should we watch the movie now or wait until after the fireworks?" Bel asks.

"Oh shit," I think, hoping to get out of the rest of the evening. "Well," I says, "won't the fireworks start in about an hour when it gets dark. We don't want to watch just half of the movie. I guess we won't have time to watch it tonight."

"The fireworks don't last that long, Lyla. We can watch half the movie now, and half after."

"All right," I says. "Just let me change out of these pants first."

I go in my room and find a loose skirt to put on so I'll be more comfortable. The pants do have a good stain on the back of them, but I've gotten out worse stains. I'll wash them tomorrow and not think about it anymore.

"Okay, I'm ready," I tell Bel when I come out of my room. "Let's watch the movie." I think I'll be lucky if I'm still awake by the time the fireworks start; I mean, it's been a long day and I was outside a lot and I know all that sun and fresh air isn't good for me, or at least it makes me sleepy, and all that walking around first to the parade and then to the Food Fest besides. But I'll do what I can to stay awake. I know she feels bad about how the snotty girl treated her too, and that I fell trying to defend her, so I figure I might as well let her watch her movie and be extra nice to her.

"Here we go!" says Bel, sticking the tape into the VCR. Then we sit down in our chairs, and before I know it, you'd think I had George M. Cohan belting out a tune in my living room the way she turns up the volume every time a song gets going, and there's like ten zillion songs in this movie. And most of them I never heard before.

"I didn't know Cohan wrote anything other than 'Yankee Doodle Dandy' and 'Give My Regards to Broadway,'" I says. "Who ever heard of these other songs?"

"Lyla, this is the soundtrack of our lives. I love all these songs."

"It's more like the soundtrack of our grandparents' lives," I mutter as some woman starts singing about how Mary was a grand old name. Well, I suppose—I liked Miss Mary Mitchell and Mary Dwyer. But how come no one's ever written a song about Lyla?

"Lyla," says Bel, "you're a Yankee Doodle Dandy at heart and you know it. Think how lucky we are to live in this country."

"Well, I won't deny that," I says, "not after what Papa went through in Russia."

"Shh, Cagney's going to sing!"

And he does, and I sit and watch Bel toe-tapping all the way through it. It's a good thing she's an old lady or she'd have been up and dancing on my coffee table just like Ann Miller in *Kiss Me, Kate*—that's another movie she loves, especially because Howard Keel was in it. Bel told me once she'd have married Howard Keel if she'd had the chance. Good thing for him he's dead now. Not that Bel ever could have competed with the likes of Miss Ellie on *Dallas*.

Well, with all her toe-tapping and singing along, I can't take a nap, so I'm the one awake enough to hear the first big boom, and since she's so into the movie, I have to tell her, "Bel, the fireworks are starting!"

She puts the video on pause and we pull two kitchen chairs right up to the window so we can see the fireworks, which look pretty cool over the roof of the cathedral and courthouse since those buildings are between Snowberry and the Lower Harbor where they shoot them off.

"Isn't it wonderful, Lyla," Bel says, reaching over to squeeze my hand. "Think how many times we've watched the fireworks, but they make me all emotional every year."

"Yeah, I know," I says.

"You feel it too. I know you do," she says. "I know our lives have been hard at times, but I know if we'd been born in any other country, they could have been a whole lot worse."

"Yeah, you're right," I says.

"I wish we knew more about our families," Bel says. "Wouldn't it be something if they fought in the American Revolution or something?"

"I doubt yours did if your maiden name was Archambeau like you think. That's a French name. You'd need an English name or something," I says. But I don't add that my mother's name Hopewell was probably English—it's a possibility my family was here way back then.

And then for just a minute, I wish Papa and Mama were here. I don't have that feeling too much anymore, but I remember them taking me to see the fireworks when I was a little girl, maybe five or six years old, and I miss them.

By the time the fireworks are over, I'm ready for bed, but Bel wants to watch the end of the movie so I says, "Fine."

"Should I make popcorn?" she asks.

"Oh, no, I couldn't eat anything more," I says, but she makes it anyways, and of course, I eat some, and then the girl playing Fay Templeton starts singing about being forty-five minutes from Broadway, and in a lot less than forty-five minutes, I'm out and probably snoring.

When I wake up, James Cagney is tap dancing down the White House stairs and then marching with the soldiers, and I sort of choke up a little. I wonder if the younger generation even knows those old songs and what people did for this country—even people like damn old Charlie. I thought for sure we were going to be goners there a few years back when everyone was saying how the terrorists would get us with biological weapons and that we should put duct tape around our windows and doors—like that would help anything, so I'm glad to see the country's still going. I don't have many years left anyways, so it just has to last until I'm gone.

I hear a noise and look over to where Bel's snoring on the couch. Well, it won't be the first time she spent the night sleeping on my couch. I'm not going to wake her up and make her go downstairs. Tired like that, at her age she might fall in the elevator and break her hip. I get up and go in the closet and find a blanket to cover her up.

"Good night, Bel," I says, turning out the light. "Happy Fourth of July."

I go use the bathroom, and then I put on my nightgown and go to bed. As I lay down, I feel how good it is to let my body relax. It's been a busy day, and I'm not as young as I was—especially not when I have to deal with snotty hoodlums, but...

I wake with a start. Someone's in my room. I don't dare move, but I listen closely, and then, "Aaaaaaaaaaaaaa!" I scream when I feel someone crawling in the bed.

Thinking it's a rapist, I jump up and turn on the light and look around for something to hit him with. Then I realize it's Bel, kneeling on the bed, looking like a deer caught in the headlights.

"Bel, what the hell?" I says.

"What the hell is right!" she shouts back. "What are you doing in my room?"

"This ain't your room, you dumb old broad," I says. "It's my room."

"I—I," she stutters, looking confused.

"You fell asleep on my couch," I says, remembering now.

"Oh, well, yeah...well, can I just sleep here? I'm too tired to go downstairs."

"No, you can't sleep here," I says. "Go back on the couch."

She gives me this ticked off look and grabs my extra pillow. "Fine!" she says and storms out of the room.

"Don't get mad at me," I says. "It's not my fault you couldn't stay awake through the movie."

"Oh, Lyla. My apartment and yours are set up the same, so what do you expect when I wake up in the middle of the night and I'm still half-asleep?" she hollers back. "You didn't have to scream like that and wake up the whole damn building."

"Goodnight, Bel!" I shout back, figuring all the old broads on my floor are hard of hearing anyways. Then I turn off the light and go back to bed. For a minute, I think about getting up to lock the door in case she decides to start sleepwalking again, but then she'd probably walk into the door and break her nose and that would be worse.

When I get up the next morning, she's gone, but the blanket is folded neatly so I figure she left in her right mind anyways. It's after eight o'clock, so I turn on the coffeepot, then go to the bathroom, get dressed, pour myself a cup of coffee, and then sit down in my chair and call her.

"You sure did give me a scare last night," I says after she answers.

"What are you talking about?" she asks.

"You, last night, crawling into my bed. You scared the heck out of me."

"Who is this?" she asks. "Is this one of them pervert calls?"

"No, it's me, you—" I start to say but the line goes dead before I can finish.

"Stupid broad," I mutter to myself, putting the phone back and drinking my coffee. Well, at least I know she got home safely.

Chapter 15

When I next see Bel, I decide it's best not to bring up her sleepwalking episode, just like I try not to remember how that snotty teenager treated me. Seriously, I ought to rat her out to her mother, but I imagine her mother knows she's a hoodlum and doesn't know what to do about it. I'm sure being a single mother isn't easy, especially since May probably worries about her grandmother too, who has to be well into her eighties by now, but still, May should have known better than to go get herself pregnant by an irresponsible guy. Not that my being judgmental will help her any, and God knows, there but for the grace of God go I because the couple times I was stupid enough to get involved with a man, it happened so fast I didn't even think about protection. I'm lucky I didn't end up with a kid.

Anyways, the more I think about that snotty little Josie girl, the angrier I get, and when I'm in a bad mood, I find that cleaning is about the only thing that helps to get the frustration out of my system. In fact, about the only time I clean my place anymore is when I'm angry. Nothing else will motivate me to clean after all the years I spent doing it for a living.

I never did finish cleaning out the refrigerator the day I went over to John and Wendy's, so I decide to finish it now, and while I'm at it, I find myself laughing as I remember the expression on Bel's face when that beer was poured onto her shoes, and then how she was so out of it that she nearly crawled into bed with me, and then how she thought I was a crank caller this morning—it's all hilarious really, and before long, I have to stop and wipe my eyes from laughing so hard.

Dingy as she is, I am glad to have her around. I haven't forgotten those lonely years when I abandoned her with Charlie; I still feel kind of guilty about that. And last night wasn't the first time she's scared me in the middle of the night—she did the same thing when she finally came back into my life after—I don't know—something like fifteen years I guess.

One night I was really down on myself. For the most part, I got by all right from day to day. I mean, I mostly liked my employers even if I didn't like cleaning their toilets, and I got to talk to them about as much as I wanted to, and I had always been a loner anyways, but sometimes, especially on a Sunday evening when I hadn't really talked to anyone all weekend, other than a quick hello to a couple people at Mass on Saturday afternoon, I'd start to feel kind of sorry for myself. I was on the wrong side of thirty by then, and while I had never thought I would want to be married, and I couldn't even say that I had much respect for men, sometimes I wished I had at least one good friend to talk to.

That night when I went to bed, I almost felt like crying myself to sleep, but I just couldn't let the tears out. So I tried to say my prayers, but I ended up giving God a pretty hard time, asking why I always had to be alone so much. I knew it was my own doing, but I just didn't know how to go out and make friends. I liked to blame everything all on Papa going away and Mama dying, and Miss Bergmann turning Jessie against me, and Charlie beating Bel, but well, I knew I wasn't going out and making friends either. But I figured, that's the way God made me, to be a loner, so that was His fault too. "God," I remember asking, "isn't there anyone in the world who loves me?"

I tried to imagine what being loved would be like. Maybe having someone like Tyrone Power take me in his arms and—but no one even half as nice as Tyrone Power would ever want me. Hell, even Ernest Borgnine probably wouldn't look at me.

I must have fallen asleep then because the next thing I knew, I opened my eyes to this blinding light shining through my windows. Scared the hell out of me! For a minute, I thought the aliens were coming to abduct me or something until I realized it looked more like a flashlight.

I didn't usually bother to shut the curtains since my room faced another house's wall and the other house had no windows facing mine so no one could see in unless he walked between the houses. I had an apartment on the downstairs floor of an old house at that point. I couldn't imagine why anyone would bother walking between the houses, but I could tell there was a flashlight and the shadow of someone holding it.

I was debating whether I should get up to call the police or just pretend I was sleeping and hope the creep would go away—I didn't know if this Peeping Tom could see my eyes were open. But then whoever it was started pounding on the window.

"Lyla! Lyla!" It was more a whisper than a shout, but it made me jump.

"Lyla, are you in there?" It was a woman's voice. I got up from the bed, grabbing my robe on the chair and went to the window.

"Who is it?" I shouted through the glass. I thought maybe I was dreaming 'cause I couldn't imagine who it could be.

"It's Bel. Let me in."

The name didn't even register at first.

"Lyla, it's Bel. Let me in."

"Bel," I muttered. Then, "Bel, what the hell are you doing out there?"

"Let me in," she said.

"Go to the front door," I said to her.

I shook my head, thinking "What the hell?" as I walked to the front door. I turned on the living room light and then opened the door to her shining the goddamn flashlight right in my face.

"Bel, turn that off. You're blinding me."

"Sorry," she said, flipping it off. "I left Charlie."

She pushed past me into the house.

"Oh," I said, shutting the door and thinking the middle of the night is a hell of an inconsiderate time to leave your husband if it means waking up people you haven't spoken to in fifteen years.

"You were right, Lyla," she said, collapsing on my couch. "I should have left the bastard a long time ago."

Once she sat down, she was facing me again, so I got my first good look at her; there were big bruises all over her face.

"Bel, he—" I didn't even know how to find the words—I was just so horrified by how she looked.

"It's been worse than this, Lyla. This ain't nothing, but now that he's lost everything, it was pretty bad this time." I could see she was on the verge of tears but trying to hold them back.

She had a cut on her forehead, and there was blood on the sleeve of her blouse. I almost felt like hugging her, but it had been so long that, instead, I just perched on a chair arm beside the couch.

"Are you in pain?" I asked.

"No, I—I drank a half-bottle of whiskey before I got here. I took it. It was all the liquor in the house, and I was hurting so bad, I figured it might make me feel better, and I wasn't going to let him have it—I don't know what I was thinking. He beat the shit out of me, and then the bastard went to sleep, real peaceful like. I thought about killing him in his sleep, but I figured I'd botch it and he'd just wake up and beat me some more, so I took all his liquor and I ran. I didn't even take time to bring my clothes or anything. Can you loan me some, I—"

I was getting over my shock now, and while she was talking, I got up to go in the bathroom so I didn't hear the rest of what she said. I found a washcloth and ran it under cold water. Then I found some Band-Aids and the Mercurochrome and went back into the living room. I sat down on the loveseat with her—it wasn't really a couch—my place was too cramped to fit a long couch—and I started dabbing at her forehead.

"Thanks, Lyla," she said. "That's real sweet of you. You always did take care of me."

And then she just burst into tears, and though it wasn't like me at all, I put my arms around her and let her cry.

"You must think I'm crazy," she said after a couple minutes when she finally quit sobbing. "I haven't talked to you in years, and then I just show up on your doorstep, but you're the truest friend I ever had, Lyla. You have no idea how much it hurt me when you left. I understood why you did it and all, but I just—you were my only friend, so it hurt so bad. Charlie tried to tell me you were a bad influence on me and it was good riddance, and I thought maybe with you gone, he wouldn't be so angry, but it didn't change anything with him. I wish I had left with you that day. So many times I've wanted to come and make things right with you, but he told me if I did, he'd hurt me, and the one time I told him I wasn't scared of him, he beat the crap out of me and even threatened to hurt you, and that scared me more."

"That asshole!" I said. "I'd like to see him try to hurt me. He knows damn well I'd kick him in the nuts just like I did when we was kids. Do you remember that?"

"Yes," she laughed a little, though it made her cough and she had to snort to keep the snot from running out of her nose. I reached over for the Kleenex box and handed it to her.

"You were my hero from that day on," she said between spurts of blowing her nose. "I should have stayed with you. I should have left Charlie when you left. We could have had a life together. We don't need no men," she said. "You don't have a man now, do you?"

"No, I—well, no," I said, though I remembered how I had gone to bed thinking maybe I would like to have one, or at least one close friend, and here Bel had shown up. But she wasn't any solution to my problem—I wanted a real friend, not a basket case, and that's just about what she was at that point.

"I think maybe you should go to the hospital, Bel," I said a minute later as she winced and screamed a bit while I put Mercurochrome over the cut on her forehead. "I can understand the bruises, but how did you get cut?"

"He hit me with a broken beer bottle," she said.

When I heard that, I almost felt like crying myself. I was mad at him for a minute but now I was just worried about Bel.

"We should call the police on him," I said.

"No, they won't do nothing. The neighbors have called the police on him before and they just come out and tell him not to make so much noise. They don't care if he beats his wife."

"It's not right," I said.

"I'll be okay, Lyla," she said. "Can I just stay here with you for a while?"

"Yeah," I said. "I think you should go take a shower though. There's blood in your hair you need to wash out."

When I tried to help her up, she stumbled a bit. "Ow," she said. "I walked around town for a couple hours after I looked in the phone book to see where you lived. It took me that long to get up the courage to come here; I was afraid you'd be mad at me if I showed up, but I didn't know what else to do."

"It's okay," I said.

"All that walking and the alcohol wearing off are making me hurt," she said. "He hit me real hard in the lower back and it hurts like hell."

We got to the bathroom, but she couldn't seem to unbutton her dress, much less her bra. I helped her to undress and get in the shower. I tried not to look at her, but I noticed her whole back was black and blue, and I suspected a lot of those bruises had happened before that night.

"I'm not very attractive tonight, am I, Lyla?" she said. "Charlie used to say I was beautiful when I was naked, but I guess you wouldn't think so now."

"Just get yourself washed up," I said. "I'll go find you something to wear to bed and find you some blankets while you shower."

I let her shower and went to find stuff for her to use for bed. I only had a bed and a loveseat, but she was in so much pain I decided to let her have my bed. The loveseat would be too cramped for her, but I'd manage on it. I didn't know how long she'd stay with me, but maybe Mrs. Marshall or someone else could loan me a cot for a while. I imagined I could trust Mrs. Marshall not to tell anyone that Bel was there with me. From what she'd said, I suspected Mrs. Marshall's husband had slapped her around a few times before he died.

When I told Bel she could sleep in my bed, she said it was wide enough for both of us, but I wasn't going to squeeze in beside her from fear I'd roll over and hurt her in the night since she was so beaten up. I gave her several Tylenol to help with the pain and then managed to get her into bed.

"Thank you, Lyla," she said before I turned off the light. "I love you, Lyla. I don't know what I would have done if you hadn't let me in."

"Shh," I said. "Just sleep now. We'll talk it all over tomorrow and figure out what to do."

The next morning, I woke to the sound of her vomiting all over the floor next to my bed. It had been somewhere around 3 a.m. when I put her to bed, and now it was only 6 a.m. There was no way I could go to work on the little bit of sleep I had gotten, and I was so worried about all the pain she was in, and worse, leaving her alone only to have Charlie maybe show up looking for her; I didn't know if he'd hurt her again, or worse, convince her to go back to him. She'd do that over my dead body. I'd tie her up if I had to so she couldn't.

After Bel got done vomiting and I got done cleaning it up, I tried again to convince her to let me take her to the hospital, but she refused.

"What if you have internal bleeding or something, Bel?" I asked her.

"No, I'll be fine, Lyla," she insisted. "I feel so much better already, mostly from not being afraid. I know I'm safe here with you, Lyla. I think Charlie was always afraid of you, and—I don't know how to explain it—but I knew that was the end of him. He's done for, Lyla. He's ruined his life so much that I think the drinking will kill him soon. We've lost everything. He's in debt so bad that we've lost the store. He'll be out on the street in a couple days. I feel sorry for him, but there's nothing I can do for him now. I'm just glad I got out when I did."

"I am too," I said.

I called Mrs. Marshall at eight o'clock and told her I was sick and couldn't come in. She was surprised because I'd never been sick a single day I'd worked for her, and I felt bad lying to her, but I didn't want to get into explaining everything to her on the phone while Bel could hear me talking about her; I figured I'd make it right with Mrs. Marshall later.

We spent the day laying around the house. Bel said laying around the house was what she did every day—watching soap operas and game shows. I didn't know how she could watch TV that much. I couldn't take more than an hour or two of it before I'd get restless. I especially got sick of all those commercials geared toward housewives for cleaning products, saying things like "Bon Ami, hasn't scratched yet" and "The cleanest clean under the sun is Tide clean." Just thinking of it would make me smell all those stinky cleaning chemicals. When I would have to use that stuff at work all day, you would think on my day off I wouldn't have to think about it, but Bel, despite the bruises all over her, just sang right along with the commercials, "Plop, plop, fizz, fizz, oh what a relief it is!" I preferred the Alka-Seltzer commercials about the blahs because that's what I had after watching all these commercials.

"How'd you watch all this TV when you were helping run the store?" I finally asked her.

"I had a TV in the store," she said. "No one hardly came by anymore, so there wasn't anything else to do. People don't go to the corner grocery stores so much anymore, Lyla. Times are changing."

She was right. Times were changing, and I wasn't sure they were changing for the better, even if President Kennedy thought we lived in some make-believe place called Camelot. I just knew I was getting older, and that bothered me. I was thirty-four then, and until Bel showed up, I didn't have any friends or anything to look forward to in life. The blahs—I guess that's what I had, but somehow I didn't think taking Alka-Seltzer was going to solve it.

It wasn't until that night—after we had chicken soup for supper because Bel didn't think she could keep anything else down, and the time came to draw the curtains and turn on the lights—that I realized that old depressed feeling I usually got at that time of night wasn't there; I remembered how upset I was just the night before, but with Bel chattering away at me, I didn't even have time to feel lonely; in fact, for the first time in years, I felt a little surge of happiness in me.

The next morning, Bel insisted she was okay to stay alone, and since I figured if Charlie was going to show up, he would have the day before, I decided it was safe to go to work. When Mrs. Marshall—I never did tell her about Bel—went out to lunch with her friend, I called to check on Bel and she said she was fine and I could hear a soap opera on, so I didn't worry none about her. When I walked home that night, I actually felt excited to have someone to spend the evening with. I even cooked supper—just spaghetti, but I hardly ever cooked—I'd taken to eating TV dinners more than anything because there was less mess to clean up than if I cooked for just one.

Bel and me got along really well the first few weeks and I was glad to have her there. Once her face healed, she told me she wasn't going to be a burden on me so she went out looking for work. I was afraid to have her leave the house from fear Charlie would get his hands on her, but I also knew she couldn't hide forever. We both wondered what Charlie was doing now. I went by the old store one day and it was all closed up with a "For Sale" sign in the window. There wasn't any sign that anyone was living there even after I went by it a few times. I wasn't so sure Charlie would recognize me anymore, but I was glad not to see him—just wished I knew where in town he might be lurking so I could warn Bel.

Then, just three weeks after Bel came to stay with me, she told me she was moving out. In fact, I came home from work to find she had a bag all packed with things I'd given her, a few clothes, a toothbrush—that kind of stuff—since she had come with just the clothes on her back and a twenty dollar bill she'd managed to steal out of the kitchen cupboard where Charlie kept his liquor money.

"It's kind of sudden, ain't it?" I said after she told me she'd gotten a job as an elevator operator that morning so she'd spent the afternoon looking for an apartment and found one.

"I'm sorry, Lyla. I didn't want to keep it from you, but I have to go and I was afraid if I told you sooner that you'd talk me out of it."

"But why? Why do you have to go? We've been having a good time together, haven't we? It's been like old times."

"I don't want to be imposing on you any longer, Lyla," she said.

"Just 'cause you have a job doesn't mean you can't stay here and save up some money for a while," I said.

"I know, but I just have to go, Lyla," she said again. "Just have to. I'm scared here, Lyla. Scared being with you. I'm not used to someone being nice to me. Not after how Charlie hurt me. I just can't take it. You're too sweet. I love you too much, and I—I just don't trust myself."

"You're not making any sense," I told her.

"I know. I know it doesn't seem like it, but I'm making sense to me, Lyla, and if you understood, you wouldn't like it. I just can't stay. It's safer if I'm on my own."

"But what if Charlie comes back for you?"

"He's moved out of town—the banker told me that. I went to see him yesterday—the banker foreclosing on the store. He was real nice to me, knowing it wasn't any of my doing, and Mr. Newman had left the store in Charlie's name after all. Anyway, he told me that Charlie skipped town, the state police can't even find him so I think he went over the border to another state. I'm sure he's too scared to come back. He always was a coward at heart—that was why he hit me so much. And it's what made me so sad; that I thought I had married a good man, but all he could do is hurt himself with how he behaved. I know he hit me to make himself feel better—so he'd feel he had control over something. Not that it was his fault. The war and Lilybelle dying—that's what did it. If I'd had another child, maybe—"

And then she started crying, and I didn't know what to do. Until she came and hugged me, burying her face in my shoulder and holding me for a long time. I let her hold me for a minute before it got awkward, and then I sort of pushed her away a little and she said, "I have to go, Lyla. I'll talk to you soon."

And before I could say a word, she'd grabbed her suitcase and rushed out the door. And once again, I was all alone.

Chapter 16

A few days after the Fourth of July, Bel and I are out grocery shopping, and on the way home, she turns to me and says, "Lyla, do you ever regret that you never got married?"

"No," I says.

"How can you not?"

"Bel, you know what marriage is like. I'm glad I avoided that mess."

"Oh, I know," she says, "but all men aren't like Charlie."

"Why? Do you wish you'd gotten married again?"

"Well, no, maybe not married, but I'm lonely sometimes."

"Well," I says.

"You never even had a boyfriend besides Bill, did you?" she asks.

I pretend I don't hear her since I don't want to lie, but I never have felt good about Scofield.

"Did you?" she asks.

I've never really told her about Scofield. She met him but didn't know we were fooling around like we were.

"Bill's the only man I ever thought I might marry," I says, trying to avoid answering the question, "and I don't know what I was thinking when it came to that."

"Well, I guess you're better off," says Bel. "That way you don't have any guilt or wondering if you should have done things differently in your relationship."

"Yeah," I says.

But I do have some regret. It all worked out in the end, but what happened between me and Scofield is something I still kind of feel ashamed about.

Back in 1962 or thereabouts I guess it was, when Bel got her own place and started her elevator operator job, she didn't even give me an address or phone number for where she'd be living, and I hadn't thought to ask since she left so sudden, moving in with the few things she had one day while I was at work. For three or four days after that, I worried about her, not knowing how to reach her until one day the phone rang and without even a "Hello, Lyla" or "How've you been?" she asked, "Do you want to meet me at Remie's for a drink?"

Here it had been days since I'd heard from her—for all I knew, she might have run away looking for Charlie, or she could be dead, or that elevator could have crashed with her in it—and here she just calls me up all nonchalant and asks me to go out to a bar with her.

"Sure, I can do that," I said, too surprised to know what else to say.

"I'll meet you there. Half an hour."

"Okay," I said, and before I could formulate any of the dozen questions I had, she said, "Okay, bye."

Despite how all that drinking had made Charlie slap her around, Bel had apparently picked up drinking herself while living with him.

"Bel," I said to her, after we had perched ourselves on stools at the bar at Remillard's, and I'd asked her all about her new job, and she'd ordered her third drink, "how can you still drink after what you saw it do to Charlie?"

"Oh, well, it helps with the pain," she told me, "and I'm not a drunk like him."

"What pain? The pain of him hitting you?" I asked.

"No, the pain of losing Lilybelle, and then—of losing you, Lyla. You don't know how bad that hurt me. I thought it would kill me more than Lilybelle's passing. I mean, I loved my daughter, but she was hardly more than a baby, not my lifelong best friend—at least that's what I thought you were until you left. Part of me thought we'd never see each other again, but deep in my heart, I knew we would always be friends—that you were a true friend because of how upset you were about the way Charlie treated me, and I was right 'cause you took me in right away when I came to you for help. You just—well, you don't know how lonely I was without you."

"Well, I'm here now," I said, "so you don't need to keep knocking back the gin 'n' tonics."

"I just like the taste of them," she said.

Before I knew it, I was going to the bars regular with her. I never drank much—never liked the taste of it. But I was lonely. I wasn't getting any younger; I'd be thirty-five soon and that meant middle-age was upon me and I was starting to feel old. I'd never had a hankering for a baby, and I knew how a man could get you in trouble that way, so I was kind of relieved to think it wouldn't be long before I couldn't have children any longer, but I was lonely and starting to think it might be nice to have a man to go out with once in awhile. That was my roundabout way of excusing the fact that I went out with Bel. I thought, just maybe, some man would show an interest in me, and where else was I going to meet one? And if none did show an interest, well, what else did I have to do except sit around the house? I wasn't much for TV; I liked the music shows like Ed Sullivan, but those family comedy shows just made me sad because they weren't like any real life I had ever known. At least there were real people in bars.

I wasn't sure if Bel wanted to hang out in the bar for the drinking or just because she used to do that with Charlie, or if she was looking for another man too. I didn't ask her because she was easily suggestible and I didn't want her to find some loser or another asshole like Charlie. If that happened, I was afraid I'd lose my only friend to another asshole.

A month or two passed with us going out a few nights a week. Then one night when we were at Remie's, in walked Scofield Blackmore. I knew him the minute I saw him, but I hadn't thought about him in twenty-five years. He had been friends with Jessie just before Mama died and I went to the orphanage. I hadn't known him well, but I remembered Jessie playing with him, and now he was a grown-up version of the little boy I'd known.

Bel and I were sitting at the bar when I saw him come in. The place was pretty empty since it was a weeknight, so Bel saw him right away too; she didn't know him and I didn't tell her I knew him, but the second he came through the door, she made some comment to me about how he was kind of cute. I was surprised to realize that the thought kind of embarrassed me. Was she going to flirt with him in front of me? Scofield had been one of the few nice boys I'd known when I was a girl; never one to tease people. I didn't want him to get mixed up with Bel. I suddenly felt protective of him.

He looked uncomfortable being in the bar; maybe because he was all alone. And Bel was right—he was kind of cute in a sort of weird way; he wasn't good-looking, more what people were now calling a "nerd," I guess. "He is cute," I whispered to Bel. It must have been the beer I'd just had—one was enough to get me tipsy—but then Bel said to me, "Flirt with him," and before I knew it, he'd sat down on the barstool closest to me, and I was leaning over in his direction and batting my eyelashes—God knows where I got the idea to do that—it must have been the beer—and I said, "All alone?"

"Yeah," he said.

I was trying to hold back from giggling, I felt so nervous, and I wondered if his "Yeah" meant he was interested; it scared me to think he might be, even though I guess that's what I wanted, so I said, "My friend Belinda here is looking for someone to go home with."

I didn't really mean it. I just said it to get at her—she never did like being called Belinda. But as soon as the words were out of my mouth, I was afraid it might happen—afraid she'd be dumb enough to jump into another relationship—and more afraid that she'd get her hands on him when I liked him.

Bel smacked me on the arm, and in doing so, she lost her balance and nearly fell off the barstool. She'd already had her share to drink—she'd had a couple even before she came to pick me up to go to the bar. Good thing we had walked there.

The bartender got Scofield a drink, and then Bel asked him, "What's your name, sailor?"

"Scofield," he said, "but I'm not a sailor."

"Nice to meet you, Scofield," I said. "My name's Lyla. I think you used to be friends with my sister when we was kids."

"I don't think so," he said.

"You sure?" I asked. "My sister's Jessie Hopewell. I think you used to come over to our house and play with her. That was before our mother died."

"Oh," he said. "Yes, I remember Jessie."

"Lyla, we better go home while I can still walk," Bel said. "I feel a little sick."

"Go ahead," I told her.

"What do you mean, go ahead? Aren't you coming?" she asked.

"No, I'm busy talking to this gentleman," I said. I wasn't about to spoil my evening just because she wanted to be a drunk. It was the first time I'd talked socially to a man in years—and I was kind of enjoying it.

"Fine. Call me later, Lyla," Bel said, and she went out the door. I could hear in her voice that she was annoyed with me—she always did have a way of being jealous if I talked to anyone else, like I was supposed to be her friend and no one else's.

"What have you been doing all these years?" I asked Scofield, not sure what else to say. I realized I was checking him out. He might have been a bit of a nerd, but he grew on you. He certainly wasn't handsome, but neither was he fat or ugly—kind of tall, sort of thin; the kind of guy you'd like to settle down with actually—a safe guy—not an asshole like Charlie.

"Not much," he said, sipping the beer he'd ordered.

"Where do you work?" I asked.

"At the Red Owl."

"Oh," I said. "I don't shop there much."

He just nodded and kept sipping his beer. He looked really uncomfortable, like he couldn't figure out what he was doing in a bar in the first place, and like he wasn't used to talking to women; I figured that was a good thing—it kind of made me feel braver.

"You ain't married, are you?" I asked.

"Yeah," he said. "I am."

Shit!

"How about you, Lyla? Are you married?"

"No," I said. "Most men just want one thing from a woman, and I'm not that stupid," I said. "This is the 1960s after all. Women have freedoms now that they didn't have when we were growing up."

"Yeah, but some of them have too many freedoms," he said.

"What do you mean?" I asked.

"I mean, I have a wife and a little girl at home, yet my wife thinks she can have a boyfriend on the side. That's one freedom I don't approve of."

Even the bartender raised his eyebrows when he overheard Scofield's angry tone.

I figured marriage problems must have been what drove him to the bar—so he could nurse his anger—or "to help the pain" as Bel would have put it.

"I'm sorry to hear it," I said.

"Sorry, I'm just a bit riled up about it; you understand," he said. "So how's Jessie doing?"

"I don't know," I said. "I never see her. She doesn't want nothing to do with me."

For just a moment, I thought better of saying that—I barely knew him, after all, but he had been Jessie's friend, and he did have his own problems, so I felt like maybe he'd be a sympathetic ear. Before I knew it, I was telling him all about how I had gone to the orphanage while Jessie had gotten adopted, and how Miss Bergmann had paid for her to go to school while I was stuck cleaning houses. And then, he told me all about his wife, Carol Ann, and how screwed up his marriage was.

When we finally finished talking, he said, "I'm sorry to dump all my problems on you, Lyla."

"I think you should go home to your wife and daughter," I told him. "Drinking doesn't help anything."

"No," he said. "I know that. I just needed a night away from her."

"Just be glad you have someone to spend a night away from," I said, although I felt really sorry for him, and wished—it had to have been the alcohol affecting my brain—that I could take him home and comfort him myself. When that thought crossed my mind, I knew I had better get out of there before it was too late.

"Well," I said, "I better get going. It was good talking to you, Scofield. I'll see you around."

I left then, but I didn't really want to. I felt really nervous. My heart was pounding, and I almost went back inside to ask him if he'd like to come back to my place for a while. I knew he was a married man, but I told myself maybe that was a good thing because if I ended up not liking him, he'd go back to his wife and I could stay free, and...it was all irrational, but I was getting old and a bit scared and just couldn't help wondering if, maybe just once in my life...

I probably would have forgotten all about it—in fact, I did really, until a few weeks later when Bel and I happened to be at Remie's again and Scofield came back, only this time with his wife, Carol Ann. Now, I don't usually call people mean names, but "bitch" was about the only word there was to describe that woman—except maybe "spoiled brat" because she did seem more like a child than a grown woman.

When Scofield saw us, he came up to say hello, so Bel, of course, had to say, "Let's get a table" and soon the four of us were sitting down shooting the breeze; well, at least three of us were—Carol Ann sat there, looking sullen and bored. Bel and I both tried to talk to her, but she hardly answered with more than one word replies. I don't think Scofield really noticed—though he was more talkative than before, maybe trying to make up for his wife's attitude. He acted like he was having a good time, but I could see there was tension between them. I also noticed her roving eye, checking out the bartender and turning her head just about every time a man entered the place.

After that night, I felt really bad for Scofield. He was a genuinely nice guy, and I could see he was trying to save his marriage, but you can't save something that never really existed in the first place—that was how I saw it. He deserved better, and I knew, even though they had a baby, she was going to leave him. I don't know what I thought was going to happen. I sure as hell didn't think I wanted to be married, but I started acting like a stupid teenage girl then—probably because I'd never really had the chance to be a silly teenage girl any time before in my life.

Next thing I knew, I was shopping at the Red Owl just 'cause Scofield worked there. I was too shy to flirt with him in public or when he was working, but after a month of going in there a couple times a week, I overheard Scofield tell one of his coworkers, "I work 8 to 4 tomorrow." And so I made a plan. I didn't have a car, so I went grocery shopping every few days 'cause I could only buy what I could carry. I couldn't even afford to waste money on a cab really. So I went back to the grocery store about 3:30 and filled my grocery cart with things I didn't even need and really couldn't afford, but it was worth it because I got to the checkout where Scofield was bagging groceries just a couple minutes before four o'clock. And after I paid for them and he bagged them, I said, "I didn't realize I had so many. I walked here. I'll never be able to carry all of these home." And just like I knew he would with that good heart of his, he said, "I'm getting off work right now. I can give you a ride home."

Now, I didn't ask him to give me a ride—he offered, so I wasn't completely guilty. Maybe he did it just because he was a nice guy, but I kind of thought he was also lonely and he knew he could talk to me about his problems with his wife, and I figured if it wasn't me, it would have been someone else anyways, so it just kind of happened that way. He offered, and I said yes.

He gave me a ride home, and when we got to my apartment, he asked if I wanted him to help me carry the groceries in, so of course, I said, "Yes," and then I said I was starving and asked if he wanted me to make him a sandwich since I was making one for myself. I knew it was too late for lunch and early for supper, but they say the way to a man's heart is through his stomach, and from how skinny Scofield was, I was pretty sure Carol Ann wasn't doing much cooking at home. Not that a sandwich was really cooking, but I knew I could make a better sandwich than that spoiled brat he was married to.

After he thanked me and complimented me on the food, I knew I had him. I don't know what came over me at that point. I don't know what possessed me or how I could have done it, but I told myself it was now or never. I wasn't getting any younger, and he was there so he was available—wedding ring or not; he was hurt and lonely, and I had made my plans and wasn't going back now. So I started the ball rolling by asking, "So how's Carol Ann? Is she behaving herself better?"

It was a rude thing to say, but he didn't blink. When he said she hadn't been going out as much lately, it wasn't exactly what I wanted to hear, so I said, "Well, I hope that'll last, but a young girl like her—it's not likely. When I was her age, I wanted all the fun I could get." Of course, I had wanted fun, but that didn't mean I'd ever had any or even knew what fun was, but wanting him to think I knew about those things and that I wasn't totally pathetic, I told him, "You come to me if she gives you trouble, and then I can give you advice." And then in the gentlest tone I could muster up, I added, "It'll help you to have someone to talk to."

"All right," he said.

I was afraid to push it any farther than that for the moment—I wanted to be—well, subtle—I think that's the word; the important thing was that I'd made it clear to him I was available. Maybe he hadn't read between the lines yet, but I figured I had planted the idea so it would root and become clear over time.

I knew Carol Ann would keep screwing up, and sure enough, a few days later, Scofield knocked on my door, just beside himself because some guy had called the house for Carol Ann. "She's cheating on me," he said. "I didn't want to believe it, but it's true."

"That's too bad, Scofield," I said, and I made him another sandwich, While he ate, I sat down next to him and patted his hand. "You don't deserve that. She's not going to find anyone better than you out there. I've known a lot of men in my time, Scofield, but I've never met one who was as much a gentleman as you are. A girl couldn't do any better. Carol Ann is young and totally stupid if she can't see that."

"What do I do about it, though?" he asked.

"You need to confront her," I said. "Tell her it's you or him."

"I'm afraid of what she'll decide then."

"Scofield, you're a wonderful man. Why do you want a woman who doesn't want you? Lots of women would want you if you gave them a chance. This is 1963. These days, you don't need to stay married to a woman just to keep things looking good for other people. Do what is best for you and your daughter. Maybe what's best is to get rid of her before she makes things worse for you and your little girl. You don't want your daughter to grow up with Carol Ann being a bad influence on her."

As I said it, I realized I was getting myself in deep because he had that little girl—he told me she was four—was I up to mothering her? The thought kind of scared me, but I figured it was a trade-off if I wanted a man.

"Thanks, Lyla," he said. "You're a real good listener."

I told him again that he had to confront Carol Ann if he wanted to save his marriage; I thought how that might make her run then—and then I could have him to myself. I was truly wicked, but determined. God forgive me; it was the only time I ever did anything like that, and I'm thankful it didn't end up worse than it did; thankful I didn't end up getting shot by that crazy woman he was married to, or pregnant by him. Anyways, I convinced him to come back again the next day, promising I'd "think the situation over" and "come up with some solutions" for him.

Sure enough, he was starting to feel he needed my friendship, and I was hoping he'd need something else, something I didn't think he was getting at home any longer.

He came back for lunch again the next day. He said things had been better with his wife the night before, but I told him I thought she was just playing him, trying to make him think things were good so she could get away with more. "You need to confront her directly," I said, and that's when I got lucky.

That night, his tramp of a wife came home with another man. Scofield was furious about it when he showed up at my house. I was hoping maybe he'd use me for what they call "revenge sex" then, but instead, he broke down crying. I admit I was a little put out by that—I realized it might make it easier for me to take advantage of him, but who wanted to seduce a crying man? Still, I was determined to be with a man just once in my life to know what it was like. Scofield was so upset that I felt bad about what I planned to do, but I'd spent days now trying to get him to that point, and for all I knew, this might be my only chance.

So I told him he looked sick and he had better go lie down for a minute. I put my arms around him and kissed him on the cheek and then told him to go rest. I even called the Red Owl and told them he was sick and wouldn't be coming back to work that afternoon—I imagine the person who answered the phone thought I was Carol Ann—you could still get away with stuff like that back then in the days before Caller I.D.

Scofield didn't know how to handle a wife, but I think he was smart enough to know what I wanted, and for whatever reason, he was lonely and hurting, so he did go into my bedroom. He laid down on the bed, but he also fell right asleep. I hadn't thought he'd actually do that, but I thought, "What the heck?" so I lay down next to him and waited for him to wake up; I think I even napped a little myself. It felt good to be next to him. I pressed my body right up against his. He was sleeping on his side so I cuddled up behind him and just held him, stroking his arms and his chest a little, but just a little—I wasn't so forward that I would do anything more than that—not while he was sleeping anyways.

Finally, he rolled over toward me and opened his eyes. For a minute, he looked dazed and confused. I stroked his hair to soothe him and told him how handsome he was and that he deserved a woman who would love him. I told him that I bet he could have any woman he wanted, and then I started unbuttoning his shirt. It was a surreal moment—I could hardly believe it myself, what I was doing—but I let my hands slowly travel down to his belt.

He was too good a man, though. He jumped up and bolted out of the room. I was surprised and hurt, but I quickly got up and went into the living room where he was putting on his coat.

"I'm sorry," I said.

"It's okay," he replied. "It's just, I better get going."

"All right," I said.

I didn't think I'd see him anymore. I was so embarrassed, never planning to set foot in the Red Owl again, but the next day at lunchtime, there he was knocking on my door again.

"Lyla, you've been really good to me," he said as soon as I let him in. "I'm sorry if I gave you the wrong idea. I don't want you to think I've been putting on a pitiful act just to get something from you."

"Oh no, Scofield," I said, amazed that he thought I thought he was trying to seduce me. "I know you would never do that. It's just, I don't understand why your wife treats you the way she does. You deserve something better. Someone who will treat you the way you deserve. If she's not acting like a true wife to you, then, in my opinion, you don't need to act like a true husband to her."

"I have a little girl to consider," he said.

I had no desire to be a mother, but I heard myself saying, "She deserves someone who will actually be like a mother to her." It was probably the meanest lie I could make because I could hurt an innocent little girl, but I said it anyways, and to make it worse, I leaned in and kissed his cheek.

I told him to sit down, and rather than make him a sandwich, I sat down on his lap and kept kissing him, but this time on the lips. He was a bit despondent at first, but after a minute, he gave in, and when I took his hand and led him into the bedroom, he didn't resist. And once I had us fairly undressed, he really got into it. I'd never seen a grown man naked before, and it was quite the sight for me. He might not have been the most beautiful man in the world, but I had no idea how stimulating it would be to touch him, to have his skin pressed up against my own, and he was clearly enjoying himself just as much, probably enjoying having a woman desire him again. I don't think he'd had that in a long time.

I don't know how many times we were together after that, but he came over regularly a few times a week. I worked during the day, but I made sure I was always home in time for lunch when he was available.

Our time together always seemed hurried, though. We had less than an hour, so we usually made love as soon as he walked in the door. I'd have a sandwich made for him before he got there, which he usually took to eat on the way back to work.

All the while he was there, I would feel excited. But the second he was out the door, my spirits would drop. Then I would go take a shower. I would feel dirty and ask myself, "Lyla, what are you doing? He's a married man."

I felt terrible about it all, actually. Felt terrible to think about his little girl growing up in a home where her parents were cheating on each other. I started to tell myself I'd break it off with him, but I kept at it. I just didn't know where I'd find another man if I let him go. I was lonely, and I hoped he really did like me, even if I didn't think he would ever marry me. Oh sure, I fantasized about his wife leaving him and his proposing to me, but somehow, while I secretly hoped he loved me, I sensed he was really just relieving stress by coming to see me. We didn't even hardly say anything to each other—we barely knew each other, so how could I expect that he really loved me? I couldn't. And he didn't. I knew it. I just didn't want to admit it.

I knew I should break if off with him—I just didn't know how. "You can figure it out, Lyla," I told myself. "After all, you figured out how to seduce him." But having a man in my arms, even if it was for less than an hour a few times a week, well, it made it feel like I belonged to someone. And that was more than I'd ever had in my life, the sense that I belonged to somebody. I knew better—I knew I didn't want to be some woman that a man just kept on the back burner for his own convenience. But it was better than nothing. It was like that song Judy Garland sings about how the worst kind of man is better than no man at all.

Now after all these years, it's funny how all those old feelings come back so strong. The guilt more than anything. It took me a long time to get over that. I felt so much guilt that I never even told Bel about it. And knowing Scofield, I'm sure he forgave me before he died—he's been dead and in the grave for years now—died of cancer I think his obituary said. I didn't even go to the funeral—didn't know how I'd explain to his daughter who I was. And our relationship didn't go on for that long really—several months, but that's not long in a lifetime. And I think God forgave me too; I mean, I figure He was looking out for me so I could find a reason finally to break it off with Scofield.

Chapter 17

"Did you see the Finn Fest mentioned in the paper again?" Bel asks me a week or so after the Fourth of July.

"Yeah," I says.

"You're going to go, aren't you?"

"Why would I?" I says. "They had Finn Fest here back in '96 and I didn't go then."

"Yeah, but you're Finnish, Lyla."

"Only half," I says.

"I think you should go—to honor your father," she tells me. "If they had French Fest, I'd go even though I don't know for sure that I'm French—just that my name is Archambeau, and for all I know, the nuns could have given that to me."

"It doesn't really matter what nationality you are," I says, remembering how excited she got over the parade and fireworks. "You're American—that's what counts."

"I know," says Bel. "But I still wish I knew who my parents were. At least you knew that, and you got to spend some time with your parents too. You were a lot luckier than me."

Lucky isn't the right word exactly, but I guess I know what she means. I did have my parents for the first few years of my life, and then those years with Papa later, right after Miss Bergmann died.

"So, the old biddy finally kicked the bucket." That was my first thought—I knew it wasn't a nice one, but I couldn't help myself when I saw her obituary in *The Mining Journal*:

> Miss Thelma Bergmann, age 60, died this past Tuesday following a lengthy illness. She was born in Calumet, Michigan to Karl and Aino (Nordmaki) Bergmann on August 15, 1903. Miss Bergmann moved to Marquette in 1928. She was a well-known piano teacher in the area for many years. She was also a member of St. Peter's Cathedral and active in the Altar Society and Lady Maccabees. Miss Bergmann is survived by a daughter, Jessie Hopewell, and a cousin, Mrs. Henry (Beth) Whitman, both of Marquette. Funeral arrangements are pending with the Tonella Funeral Home.

"What the hell sense does that make?" I asked myself. I felt such a rage come over me, especially because Jessie was named as her daughter—which she wasn't.

And then—then I had a downright stupid thought—with that woman gone, maybe Jessie and me could reconcile, and maybe I'd finally get something. The old woman had had plenty of money. She'd showered Jessie with stuff, and I was the only relative Jessie had. She could share some of it with me—she should. It was the least she could do after her so called "mother" had stuck me in a Catholic orphanage when we weren't even Catholic but Finnish Lutherans.

It wasn't really the money, though, I told myself. It was that deep down I missed my sister. I was too angry and scared to admit it to Jessie straight out, but maybe if I went to talk to her, I'd soften her up and she'd at least admit I'd been done an injustice by Miss Bergmann and we could reconcile—kind of like in the Bible with the prodigal son or something like it.

Jessie'd be stubborn since Miss Bergmann had brainwashed her so well, but if I could have gotten Scofield in bed, then I figured I should be able to convince her to make up with me. I'd make her understand how rough it was for me compared to her.

So I dug in my closet for an old dress; then I walked to Miss Bergmann's house as fast as I could—to get all sweaty—so Jessie'd think I couldn't afford a cab since I'd moved again recently and now lived a good mile from her.

When I reached the old woman's house, I put on a polite smile and knocked on the door.

When Jessie opened the door, she just stared at me for a minute like she didn't know me. Then she finally said, "Hello, Lyla."

"I'm sorry to hear about Miss Bergmann," I told her. "I came to see whether I can do anything for you."

"Oh, thanks," she said, looking kind of in a daze; she let me in without really asking me to come in. I felt like I wasn't wanted, but I went in anyways. I was glad she was alone—I thought maybe there'd be a bunch of people there to console her, but maybe other people didn't like the old lady any more than I did. Maybe she'd realize that now so I could talk some sense into her.

I perched myself on one of the old lady's doily covered chairs. I looked around at her sofa, chairs, end tables, coffee table, the paintings on the wall, the filled china cabinet in the other room. So much wealth compared to what I had. Miss Bergmann must have been as well off as Mrs. Marshall or the O'Neills even. Here my sister had gotten to grow up in all this luxury, while I sat at home with a saggy couch, a secondhand coffee table, and a couple folding chairs, and one cushioned chair that Mrs. Marshall had given me from down in her basement that smelled of mildew, though I'd taken Lysol to it many times.

The least Jessie could do was offer me a cup of coffee, but she didn't. I think she was kind of beside herself; not so much surprised to see me as coping with the old lady's death. I guess I could understand that since the old woman apparently loved her. I just couldn't understand why she couldn't even try to love me. I could have been loveable if she had given me the chance.

"How're you holding up?" I asked her.

"I'm okay," she said. "I kind of expected it since she had multiple sclerosis for years."

"Oh," I said. I hadn't known that, or if I had, I'd forgotten it. That didn't sound pleasant—M.S. I mean. But I wasn't going to feel sorry for her—not Miss Bergmann or Jessie. "And what will you do now?" I asked.

"Move downstate. I was offered a job as a music teacher down there."

That was right; I'd forgotten that too. Jessie had gone to some fancy music college while I hadn't even gotten through secretarial school. Not that she was smarter than me—just had more opportunities, but I couldn't do anything about that now. "Well, now you're free," I said. "I mean, if you took care of her for years while she was sick, now you can have a life of your own."

I was trying to sound lighthearted, but I felt my heart aching at the thought that she'd be moving away—just when I had hoped...

"I didn't mind taking care of her," Jessie said. "She took care of me first."

And then I lost it. I'd been trying to stay calm, but twenty-five years of hurt had been simmering in me just waiting to boil over.

"What right did she have to take care of you?" I demanded. "She wasn't our mother. What right did she have to put me in an orphanage and force us to be Catholics when we were Finnish Lutherans?"

Jessie just stared at me then, her eyes getting wide. I looked for sympathy in her eyes—that's what I should have seen there—acknowledgment of how the old lady had done me wrong, but all I could see was fear from my outburst.

"Lyla," she hesitated, "that was Mama's doing."

"What do you mean?" I said. "It was Miss Bergmann who broke up our family—took our heritage from us."

"Lyla, you know Papa went to Russia—to Karelia—back during the Depression. That was when our family broke up."

"He couldn't help it," I said. "He went to find a better life. He was going to send for us. It's not his fault he was blind enough to believe Communism would be better. Lots of Finns went over there then. He wanted to do what was best for us."

"But it wasn't Miss Bergmann's fault that we never heard from him again," Jessie argued, "and Mama's the one who insisted we use her last name after Papa left; she was ashamed her husband went to Russia. And when Mama died, what else could Miss Bergmann do? She didn't know where Papa was; he was probably dead by then. Miss Bergmann did the best she could to find you a home. She asked lots of people to adopt you before you were sent to the orphanage."

"What right did she have to send me there?" I repeated. "And what right did she have to brainwash us into becoming Catholics?"

"Lyla, it wasn't her fault," Jessie kept saying, but I was too enraged now to listen to her.

"Sure, it's fine for you!" I hollered. "You get all her money, but what do I get?"

Then I saw Jessie's face turn from a trembling white into a bright red rage and I knew I'd blown my chances.

"I wondered why you came," she said. "You think you're going to get money from me. You don't care about her or me."

"Not about her I don't," I said. "I deserve something for how she broke up our family."

"You always were a greedy person, even when we were little girls," Jessie said, getting up from her chair. "You can leave now because I'll never give you a penny."

"I don't want your money!" I said, jumping to my feet. I couldn't stop myself from yelling—it just hurt so much—like it hadn't hurt since I was a little girl in the orphanage. Nothing in my life had ever hurt so much as to lose my parents and then to have my sister leave and turn against me too.

I tried to tell Jessie that I didn't care about the money. I remember stuttering, "I want—I want," but the words wouldn't come out. How could I tell her I loved her and I wanted us to be like sisters again, like when we were little? I could see now that she was so angry she wouldn't believe me if I did say all that.

"I think you better leave," she repeated.

I was afraid I'd say something I'd regret later, only now it wasn't angry but kind words I was afraid I was going to say, only to have her think I was lying and to reject me anyways; that would hurt more than anything so I didn't even try. I went out the door, not saying another word, just trying to hold back the tears springing to my eyes.

Thinking about it now, forty-some years later, just makes it feel like I'm living it all again. I've thought about it so many times. Played that conversation over and over in my head and just wished it had been different. She was my sister. I did love her. I still do. I remember how we used to play together, with our dolls and jacks and stuff when we were kids. I had looked up to her back then. She was always bossy, but I secretly didn't mind. I just wanted to hold my own as well. I was always too proud. Too proud to accept other people's quirks and love them anyways.

I don't know what I was thinking that day. I went to the priest to tell him what had happened, but he barely listened to me. He didn't care. Why would I expect him to care? The only person who ever cared about me was God, and even that had been questionable at times. But the priest told me to pray the rosary, and that made me remember the rosary Sister Euphrasia had given me. I didn't even know where I had put it, but I'd had to recite the rosary so many times at the orphanage that I could just say it in my head, so I did, thinking that at least it couldn't hurt anything. There was nothing else I could do. Until that moment, I had always hoped that maybe I would someday have my sister back, but now I had just blown it. She was moving away, and after that outburst, how could I ever expect otherwise?

And then the miracle happened. It's the only thing I can call it. The only time a miracle happened in my life really. It was such a coincidence, so seemingly impossible, that it had to be a miracle.

I got home and was about to unlock the door when I heard someone behind me. As I turned around, he said, "Miz?" and his voice startled me. He looked like an old tramp.

"What do you want?" I snapped. I wasn't going to feed him. I'd already put myself in the hole a bit between letting Bel stay with me and then giving Scofield all those sandwiches. And I was sure this tramp would want food since he looked thin as a rail.

"Iz yo migir?" he said. I couldn't understand him. He had this crazy accent, but after he kept saying it over and over again, I figured it out when he said, "Lyla, I'ze yo poppa."

"What?" It was all I could say at first. I couldn't take it in. How do you take in someone saying something like that? He started crying and trembling, and then he looked like he was about to hug me, which scared me. I couldn't believe it. I half-thought I was seeing a ghost.

"My papa? How?" I asked. But as I searched his face, behind all those wrinkles, I could see it was him. He was blabbering away in broken English and Finnish. I hadn't spoken Finnish since I was a little girl, but suddenly, I started to understand him, the meaning of those Finnish words all coming back to me from my childhood. Somehow, I pieced together that he'd escaped from Russia. I guess he'd been a prisoner there. I never did get all the details from him. He was too hard to understand, and he seemed reluctant to tell me everything. He—I can only imagine what he went through, and I don't think he could handle talking about it—he tried to tell me none of it mattered now because it was in the past and he was home.

What could I do? I took him in. I wanted to take him in. He wasn't the father I remembered, or the handsome young, strong hero of a father I had built him up to be in my memory and imagination. No, this was a broken old man, in his sixties, but more old and broken than I am now at seventy-seven. So I took him in and I cared for him for eleven years. He wasn't great company, but he was my father. For the first time I belonged to someone.

I told him how Mama had died. I told him I didn't know what had become of Jessie, and I didn't really. He'd shown up the same day I'd had it out with her, so I could have told her, but as I debated what to do, she moved away, and I had no idea where except that it was somewhere downstate. And until then, she'd always had Miss Bergmann. I'd never had anyone, and I secretly didn't want to share my father. And I was kind of afraid of Jessie by then—afraid she'd take Papa from me since she always did get the best of everything; or what would be worse, what if she didn't want anything to do with him—that would have killed him inside I think. Better that he didn't know what became of her.

He was old and tired, and not always all there upstairs. At first, I thought I just didn't understand what he was trying to say because of his accent and the Finnish words he'd throw in, but in time, I realized he was just old and maybe going senile with some kind of dementia or something. After a couple of months, he quit asking me about Jessie and I just tried to block her out of my memory after that.

Papa didn't have much energy anymore. I'd get him to go for a walk or with me to the grocery store, but only because I was afraid to leave him alone. He stayed home in front of the TV all day while I worked. I always came home at lunch time to check on him. In the last few years, I had one of the older neighbor ladies checking on him constantly while I worked.

In a way, he wasn't my father anymore. I loved him, but he was a stranger now. I guess the most I could say is we became friends like a caretaker would become friends with the person she cares for, but he wasn't the father I had dreamt about—the father I used to dream would come and rescue me from the orphanage.

It still felt like a miracle when he came home—just not so much like one in the years that followed. But I guess it had kept him going to dream of coming home to America, and after what he had gone through in Russia—I don't even want to imagine what that was like—that he came all the way back to find only me—to learn that Mama was dead and his other daughter gone God knows where—he had to be disappointed. So, the least I could do was be as good to him as I could.

I dumped Scofield right after that. I didn't want to hurt him, but I had to be firm about it because I knew he didn't have the backbone to break it off with me. I felt bad for him because his wife ran off on him right after that—

from what I heard, she took off to another state with another man, leaving Scofield to care for his little girl all alone. But then, I had a father to take care of. We each have our burdens, I guess.

At least Papa loved me. I wasn't sure how it was going to work out when he first showed up. But I loved him too. He had a lot of love in him. He was always patting my hand, giving me a kiss good night. He tried to help around the house, but he was clumsy and forgetful so I mostly just took care of him. I think he was broken but also maybe a little bit content just to be home. I kind of envied him, that he could just sit in his recliner in front of the TV and take a nap and just look content. He'd been through hell and back I imagine—and yet, in the end, I think he knew how to rest. I never learned how to do that. I've never known how to stop from being busy all the time, or feeling guilty when I wasn't.

Then Papa went peacefully in his sleep one morning in 1974. I woke up and called him for breakfast, but he didn't answer, and a few minutes later when I went to check on him, he was gone.

All he left me were some memories and an old tattered photograph of me as a little girl. He'd kept that photo of me in his wallet and carried it with him wherever he went, even all those years in Russia. He was always taking it out and showing it to whoever would be polite enough to listen to him—the cashier at the grocery store or the neighbor lady. He didn't have any other photos of the family, so I like to think that photo kept him going all those years he was away. It meant, too, that he loved me. That made all the difference to me. Sure, he could be hard to take care of at times, but I tried not to show it. I was glad just to have him, and I still miss him.

After I dumped Scofield, I was so busy caring for Papa that I never got around to looking for another man, and by the time Papa died, I was forty-six and the men my age were all married with kids. And then, after taking care of Papa, the thought of having to take care of another old man, even if he was my husband, didn't really appeal to me too much.

That's the best answer I can come up with for why I didn't marry. The only other man I ever got involved with was Bill, and there was never anything logical about that. I think I was just interested in him for his looks. He was on the wrong side of sixty when I met him, but he still looked good. I'd seen him around Marquette for years and always thought he was good-looking, so when I had a chance with him, I wasn't going to let it slip by.

But mostly, I've been happy to be single. I know I've been better off without Bill too. Look at how he treated me the day I went up to the hospital. I know Eleanor would love for me to go visit him in the nursing home, but I don't see what good it would do anyone now.

When I was young, I used to think people looked at you kind of funny if you weren't married, like there was something wrong with you, but now I guess I just don't give a shit what anyone thinks of me not having a man. I think people who get married are just weak anyways—afraid of being alone. Some of us are just happier with our own company—there's less people to tick you off then. I'd rather be single any day than deal with the crap that Bel or Mrs. Marshall or a lot of other women I've known have had to put up with from their husbands.

Chapter 18

Summer is ridiculously hot this year, and Sundays seem to be the worst. Even with air-conditioning, having my apartment up so high, it's hard to keep the place cool. Bel and I go out for breakfast like usual, but it's too hot to eat much, and when I get home, I end up reading the paper and then laying down for a nap.

I'm probably just tired because I feel awful lonely. Naps do that to me most of the time. I lay down and start to feel lonely 'cause I'm just laying there, trying to fall asleep and not really doing anything. I think I keep myself busy all the time because then I don't have to think about anything a lot of the time, but when you're just laying there to rest, you find yourself thinking about things that bug you, or about what you really want, like maybe someone just to put their arm around you, like when I was a little girl and Mama held me as I...

I've just opened my eyes when the phone rings. I think I drifted off, but it's so damn hot and sticky it's hard to sleep at all.

"Let's go out for a ride to the island," says Bel, "and we can get some ice cream. It's too hot to stay in the house."

"All right," I says. "I'll meet you downstairs in five minutes."

I go in the bathroom to wash my face and do my business and then I find my purse and head downstairs, yawning and still tired. I hate this hot weather. Anything over seventy-five is just too hot for us in Upper Michigan.

I take a minute longer than I said I would, hoping Bel is smart enough to get the car running and the air conditioning going before I get there, but I ought to know better—I should have just thought to tell her on the phone to do that. When I get down to the lobby, she's sitting there waiting for me, chatting to Viola about the weather. Viola's on her way over to the Senior Center to play cards. I never go over there—nothing there but a bunch of old people—and I mean old people. I never did like old people that much, and now that I'm one, it doesn't help matters. I mean, sure I took care of the O'Neills when they were old and the Mitchells too, but being around old people just sort of gets me depressed, reminding me I may not have much time left, so the last thing I need is to waste that time hearing about everyone else's gallbladders and blood thinners and all that crap.

"Hello, Lyla," Viola says to me. I give her a half-smile, which is the most I've ever given her. She's been trying for years to get friendly with me, but it ain't going to work. Not after she tried to blame me for her sister not getting a place in Snowberry, just 'cause my name was on the list one above her apparently, so her sister decided to go live at Lost Creek instead. I have better things to do than listen to that kind of crap. Seems to me Viola's sister probably didn't want to live in the same building as her, and I can't say I blame her 'cause Viola's a snoop from everything I've heard about her, which is why I've kept her at a distance.

"Let's go," I says to Bel.

Bel knows when I says, "Let's go," it means, "Get me the hell out of here now" so she says real quick, "I'll talk to you later, Viola" and follows me outside.

As we walk to the car, I says, "Why don't you just go out for ice cream with Viola since you're so chummy with her?"

"Oh, Lyla, I was just being neighborly is all. You know you're the only one I asks out for ice cream."

Boy, lucky me, I think, rolling my eyes. Of course, when Bel unlocks the doors, the car's hotter than hell inside.

"Turn the air on and let it cool off before I get in there," I says, standing outside and watching the traffic go by while she does it.

After a minute, I get in. It's still hot enough to kill a baby, so I don't know why I don't wait longer. I think about telling her, "Next time, come and turn the air on while you're waiting for me rather than talking to that snoop," but I know better than to think she'll remember next time. It's my fault. I should have told her what to do on the phone when she first called me.

When the car starts up, the radio's playing that twangy WJPD country music, but I turn it off.

"That was Randy Travis," Bel says, like she's all offended.

"You're right—that *was* Randy Travis. He's a has been. That 'Love You Forever' song is older than the hills."

"It is not. It came out in 1987," she says. "I remember because—"

"You can't even remember what dresser drawer you put your bra in most days," I says.

"Well, it's nice you're in such a good mood today, Lyla," she says.

"I will be in a good mood if this car ever cools off."

She's gone up to Baraga Avenue and then drives us straight toward the lake. Lake Superior hardly gets warmer than sixty degrees all year—not that many summers ago, we had ice still floating on it in June—but it sure doesn't look cool today.

"I love the lake," says Bel. "I wouldn't want to live anywhere else. I can't imagine living somewhere like Kansas where there isn't any water."

"Don't worry about it," I says. "You'll never live there."

"But don't you think we're lucky to have so much natural beauty," she says.

"I suppose," I says as we drive around the edge of Mattson Park. "I'm not sure, though, that I care for all these condominiums popping up all along the lakeshore—where do all these people get their money?"

We don't say much else as we go along Lakeshore Boulevard until Bel says, "Look; there's a boat coming in. I always wondered what it would be like to work on one of the ore boats."

"Hard work is what it's like," I says.

"I wonder if the sailors have a girl in every port."

"I wouldn't doubt it," I says. "You wouldn't catch me on one of those boats. With my luck, I'd end up on the next *Edmund Fitzgerald*. No, I'm happy being a landlubber."

We get out to Presque Isle and drive around it. I'm still a bit sleepy from my nap and don't pay too much attention to the scenery, but Bel keeps talking about how beautiful it is, and how much she likes being in the woods—how it makes her feel safe somehow. She's bummed when we don't end up seeing any of the deer they let run loose all over the island. But I always figure that's a good thing because when there's too many, they just get shot anyways.

Finally, we make it to the ice cream stand.

"Let's eat in the car," I says. "Leave it running. If we eat the ice cream outside, it'll melt all over and make a mess."

"All right," Bel says. She leaves the key in the ignition, gets out, locks her door from habit, and shuts it. I knew she'd do that—no brains. I don't say nothing, but I'm smart enough not to lock my door.

We go up to the ice cream stand and I get Peanut Butter Mackinac Island Fudge and she gets Pumpkin.

"That's a weird choice for summer," I says to Bel while the girl makes them.

"Well, I'm kind of tired of Mackinac Island Fudge," Bel says, "and the only other flavor I saw that I like is Rum Raisin, and you know I can't have that—it might make me want to drink."

"Whatever," I says.

"Here you are," says the girl.

"I need a lot of napkins," I says as I pay her before Bel gets her purse open. I don't mind—she's doing the driving after all.

We collect the ice cream cones and napkins and go back to the car.

"Oh no!" Bel screams, trying the lock.

"What's wrong?" I says, trying not to laugh.

"Oh no, I locked the keys in the car and it's running. Oh, I hope the store has a phone so I can call the police."

I don't say nothing, and before I know it, Bel runs back to the store to ask to use the phone.

I just open my car door and get in. When I slam my door shut, Bel looks back. At first, she seems confused, like she's wondering, "Where'd she go?" Then she sees me in the car and comes back. She jiggles her door handle, so I hit the automatic lock so she can get in.

"How'd you get in?" she asks.

"I didn't lock my door," I says as she climbs in. "Give me your ice cream cone. I'll hold it. Drive over by the gazebo so we're in the shade, and do it fast so your ice cream doesn't melt all over me."

She does what I says and finds us a spot in the shade to park the car. We sit there and watch the seagulls and the bikers go by.

"Thanks for buying the ice cream, Lyla," she says.

"Well, you drove us here," I says.

"Charlie always liked pumpkin ice cream," she says.

"Yeah," I says, wondering what kind of ice cream Hitler liked.

"That's why I ordered it really," Bel says. "Today is Charlie's birthday."

"*Was*," I says.

"Well, if he was still alive, he'd be seventy-nine today."

"He's been dead, what, like thirty years now?" I asks.

"Yeah," she says. "But I still miss him, especially on his birthday."

"Bel, it's been thirty years," I says.

"It doesn't matter, Lyla. We were married longer than that."

"Barely," I says.

"You never can give Charlie credit for anything, can you?" she asks.

There's a nasty looking seagull walking around on the grass. He's got a red spot on his beak and a feather hanging off of it. Mean little buggers they are—those seagulls. Only care about themselves. Greedy, selfish bastards.

"There isn't anything," I tell her, "to give Charlie credit for."

"Oh, Lyla, can't you ever have a gentle word for him."

"He was a crappy husband and a crappy father; Mr. Newman trusted him with the store but he ended up losing it because he was a stinkin' drunk," I says.

"Lyla, you know better than that. Alcoholism is a disease and we can't always help ourselves."

"You helped yourself," I says. "You stopped. Why didn't he? He had a lot more reason to stop, too. He had a wife and a business, and—"

"He did the best he knew how," Bel says.

"Well, his best wasn't good enough," is what I want to say, but I keep my mouth shut. Peanut Butter Mackinac Island Fudge is my favorite ice cream flavor—it's better than some pumpkin crap, that's for sure. I'm not going to let her worrying about Charlie, who's thirty years in the grave, ruin a good ice cream cone.

"I thought you and Charlie started to get along in the end," she says.

"We did for your sake," I says. We sure as hell never liked each other, but I knew if I didn't get along with him, I might lose Bel back to him, and I wasn't going to let that happen.

About a year or two after my father died, Bel started acting kind of distant toward me. I thought maybe she was mad at me about something because she didn't call as much as normal—which had been at least twice a night, and on the weekends, the phone would usually ring every couple hours if we weren't together doing something. So, I thought it kind of strange when she was rarely calling me more than once a day, though at first I thought it kind of nice. But then when I didn't hear from her for three days, I wondered what was up with her. Had I done something wrong? Was she mad at me? I felt the old fear of abandonment rise up in me—was she dropping me after all these years—had she been mad at me for a while now but put up with me just because she liked my father or felt sorry for me because she knew how much work it was for me to take care of him, and now that he was gone, she was trying to distance herself out of my life?

But that was downright silly, I told myself. How many times had she told me I was her best friend? And she wasn't one to keep her tongue silent, so if something was wrong between us, I'm sure she would have told me, wouldn't she?

"Well, if she is mad at me, I better call her and find out," I finally decided. "No sense in worrying about it until I know."

Bel called me so much I didn't even know her phone number without looking in the phone book. Maybe that's why she was mad—'cause I never called her.

So I dug out the phone book, found her number, and dialed it.

"Hello," a man answered. I thought I had dialed the wrong number, but when I asked, "Is Bel there?" he said, "No, she's gone to the store.

"Oh," I said. "Will you tell her to call me when she gets home?"

"Sure," he said.

"Tell her it's Lyla," I said.

The phone went dead without even a "goodbye." I didn't think that was so good. What if something was wrong? Who was that guy? Maybe he was just the plumber or her landlord or someone, but—what if he had broken into her house and was waiting to kill her when she got back, or worse, what if he had already done her in?

"Lyla, you're being silly," I told myself. I went and made myself lunch, thinking, "If he's a killer, he's pretty stupid to be answering the phone." But then, I didn't figure most killers are all that smart anyways.

Once I had my sandwich made, and I sat there eating it, I couldn't help but keep worrying. I was just about to pick up the phone and dial it again when it rang.

Grabbing it, I thought, "Please don't let it be the police telling me Bel is dead," before I said, "Hello."

"Hi, Lyla," Bel said.

"Hello," I said, trying to sound all nonchalant-like or something.

"How are you today?" she asked.

"How the hell do you think I am?" I said, losing it at her own nonchalant attitude. "I don't hear from you for three days, and then I call and some strange man picks up the phone who for all I know might be an ax-murderer who's killed you."

"I knew you'd be upset, Lyla," she said. "That's why I haven't called you."

"Upset about what? Bel, don't tell me you did something crazy like marry some guy you met in a bar. You better not tell me that."

"No, you'll probably think this is worse."

"Try me," I barked, wondering what the hell was wrong with her. Was she sick? Was he a doctor or something?

"It's Charlie," she said. "He's staying here."

"What? Are you crazy!" I screamed.

"It's just for a little while, Lyla. It's just—"

"You're out of your cockamamie mind!" I yelled into the phone. "After the way he treated you, and how scared you were when you left him, and—"

"I know, Lyla, but just listen to me."

"What's there to listen to? You tell him to get the hell out of your house right now, or I'll come down there and throw him out with my own two hands. And I'll give him another good kick in the nuts too while I'm at it."

"Lyla, will you shut up for two minutes?" Bel snapped. She didn't do that often. "Just hear me out," she said.

"Don't you go making excuses for him, Bel," I said, calming down a little. "There's no excuse for how he treated you."

"Lyla, he's still my husband you know. We never did get divorced."

"Because he left town and you couldn't find him. What the hell did he even come back for? It's been like twelve years or something now."

"That's what I'm trying to tell you, Lyla," she said, and she started sniffling like she was trying not to cry. "Charlie's sick, and he doesn't have anyone else but me. He's—he's got liver cancer."

Liver cancer? Well, what did he expect after all that damn drinking— that was my first thought. My second thought was—that bastard deserves it.

"He's only got a few months to live, Lyla. He looks so weak. You don't understand. He's my husband. I know he treated me wrong, but—well, he didn't exactly have the easiest life, what with growing up in an orphanage, Lyla. You know what that was like."

"Yeah, I do know what that was like, but you don't see me going around beating up women," I said. The word "cancer" was slowly starting to sink in for me. I'd watched how my father had died slowly, just withering away—that was painful enough, but to have cancer can kill you fast.

"Well, Lyla, you didn't have to go fight in the war, and you didn't have your child die either. You never had to walk in Charlie's shoes. You act like you've had it so rough, Lyla, but you haven't really."

She was sobbing into the phone, but she was ticking me off too.

"I don't need you judging me," I said, but it didn't come out as angry as I intended it. Still, I was glad I said it because it was easier arguing with her than letting this scary feeling get to me that I should feel bad for Charlie.

"He's my husband, Lyla," she told me, "and I'm going to take care of him, and if you can't deal with that, then you can—well, you can just not come over, then."

"Fine," I said. I didn't mean for it to sound all mean-like, but I said it anyways, and then not knowing what else to say, I just hung up the phone. I didn't quite know what I'd meant by "Fine." Had I meant, "I won't come over"? I think that's how I had wanted to mean it, or at least make her think I meant it, but I realized it could have meant I'd accept it.

Still, the thought of her having Charlie in her place just made my blood boil.

I finished eating my sandwich and I waited for a little while. I figured she'd call me back, and then I'd explain to her what I meant—maybe I'd figure it out by then.

When I finished eating, I washed up the dishes, and then I sat and listened to a couple songs on the radio, and then I went and cleaned the bathroom. And then, not sure why, but telling myself I just felt dirty after cleaning the toilet, I went and changed my clothes. I put on one of my better blouses—not one I'd usually wear around the house.

And then I went and sat in my chair to read the paper, but I didn't get past the front page before I said, "Damn it!"

So I put on my coat and went over to the Red Owl and bought a box of doughnuts. I didn't know what else I should buy since Bel had apparently been at the grocery store earlier, but I didn't feel like I could go over there empty-handed—not that Charlie wouldn't have if the situation was reversed. But it was a peace offering I guess. I kind of hoped Charlie's liver cancer made it impossible or at least painful for him to eat doughnuts, but at least I was trying to do the right thing.

And once I got there, I was kind of glad I went. Charlie wasn't more than a couple years older than me. Not quite fifty yet, but when I saw him, he looked more like he was eighty. Most of his hair had fallen out, his face was all wrinkled, and most of the time I was there, he was sitting half-bent over in pain.

"Hello, Lyla," he said when I opened the door and walked right into Bel's apartment without knocking. Bel and I never knocked. He was sitting there in her rocking chair with an afghan over him. He looked pathetic, like a sick dog, but he faked a smile like he was happy to see me—a smile that showed most of his teeth were missing.

"What happened to your teeth?" I asked, knowing it was rude, but I felt like I deserved to get a couple good digs into him.

"I lost them in a bar fight in Wisconsin," he said.

"All at once?" I asked.

"Okay, three bar fights, and one was in Duluth." He grinned, like it was funny, but the only thing funny was the holes in his mouth. I'd have made more fun of him if he hadn't been so down and out.

"Hi, Lyla," said Bel, coming out of the bedroom and looking surprised to see me. What the hell? If she had known me at all, she would have known I'd have shown up. I might get a bit frustrated with her at times, but I don't turn my back on my friends when they need me.

"Hi, yourself," I said, handing her the box of doughnuts. "Here. I brought you some snacks."

"Thanks," she said.

"They go good with milk," I said, hinting that she should go in the kitchen while I asked Charlie a few questions, and of course, going into the kitchen was exactly what she did. Her apartment was in an old house like mine so the walls were super thick and I didn't have to worry about her overhearing us.

"So where the hell have you been, other than the bars in Wisconsin and Minnesota?" I asked Charlie.

"Just around," he said. "Wherever I could find work."

"You lost it all, didn't you?" I said, "The store, your wife, everything."

"Mostly my dignity," he said.

"Yeah," I said, "and you're not going to get it back either by trying to make me feel sorry for you."

"I don't need your sympathy," said Charlie.

"Good. I'm glad we're clear on that. I'm here for one reason and one reason only. Bel is my friend, and when my father was sick and dying, she was a lot of help to me."

"Your father?" he said. "You're an orphan like me."

"It's a long story and none of your business anyways," I said. "The point is that Bel is my friend so I'm here to help her as she needs it. If she decides to take care of you and needs my help, I'll help her because I love her—not that you know anything about how to treat people you love—seems like you messed that up pretty good."

"She's lucky to have you for a friend, Lyla," he said.

"Don't try flattering me," I told him. "You're damn lucky to have a wife who has a lot of love in her and will take you in considering the way you treated her, and don't you think for one damn moment I'm ever going to forget what you were like."

"Trust me, Lyla. I've paid for it," he said, avoiding my eye. "You can't make me feel any worse about it than I already do."

"Maybe not, but I'm going to try once in awhile anyways," I said, half-smiling, and then I thought I saw a smirk on his face.

"Here we are, doughnuts and milk," said Bel, carrying everything in on a tray.

I didn't say a whole lot more after that. Bel was always a TV person, and you could never go over to her place without her having the television blasting. Charlie seemed engrossed in Archie Bunker's antics, but I never could stand that character—he was a perfect example of what kept me away from men.

It's almost impossible for Bel to keep her mouth shut for long, but ice cream can do the trick. When I look over at her, she's eating the last of the cone.

"We should buy some balloons to celebrate Charlie's birthday," I says.

"Why would we do that?" she asks. "We don't even buy them for our birthdays."

"Oh, I thought you would remember how he liked balloons."

"No, I don't remember that," she says.

I don't know how she can forget it; I'm starting to think her memory ain't what it used to be.

"Should we go around the island again?" she asks.

"Sure," I says, finishing up my cone and wiping my hands with the napkins. Then I try to clean up the spot on my blouse where I dripped—but it was worth it; Peanut Butter Mackinac Island Fudge always is.

I can't stop thinking about the balloons—even Chief Kawbawgam's grave looks like a giant balloon to me when we go past it. How can Bel forget about the balloons?

When Charlie came home from the war, Bel bought some balloons to celebrate. Mr. Newman's place was tiny and the balloons were in the way where Bel put them in the dining room. We were all sitting around the table having supper that night when I got up to go fetch something from the kitchen. I bumped my head against one of the balloons, and I just happened to have a hairpin in my hair that hit that balloon just right and...

"POP!"

Scared the hell out of me for a second, popping like that by my head, but when I found a deflated balloon clinging to the side of my face, I couldn't help laughing.

"Charlie, what's wrong?" asked Bel.

I turned and found he wasn't in his chair any longer. I didn't know where he went so fast until I heard Bel say, "Charlie, what are you doing under the table?"

He didn't answer at first so she asked him again until finally he said, "I—I—I dropped my fork."

"What are you talking about?" she said. "It's right here on top of your napkin."

"Oh," he said, coming out from under the table, fake laughing. But he was white as a sheet.

I never forgot that. But I didn't understand it until Charlie was dying.

One night, Bel needed to go out shopping, and I knew she needed a break so I agreed to come over and stay with Charlie for a couple hours. He'd been throwing up on and off for a couple days so I knew she was nervous about leaving him alone, and I knew he wouldn't be around much longer—it was toward the end of winter, late March I think, and the doctor didn't think he'd live to see summer at that point.

Charlie and I still didn't like each other, that was clear, so we hardly said a word to each other, but I think for Bel's sake we kept an uneasy truce. Best thing for us to do was stare at the TV so we didn't have to talk to one another. Of course, that was easier said than done 'cause back in those days, we only got three channels—3, 6, and 13—so it was hard to find anything on to watch. Charlie said he didn't care what I watched, and so I finally settled on *Little House on the Prairie*. It was a corny show, but that Charles Ingalls, what woman wouldn't want to be married to a good man like that—he was the only reason I watched the show, that and I wished my life was sort of more like that.

Anyways, I didn't think Charlie was all that awake, but he must have been. The daughter Mary in the show was doing sewing for Mrs. Whipple, and her son, a music teacher, was giving Mary lessons, but he was also having nightmares from having been in the Civil War. He was really messed up, and snapping at Mary in the show.

And then when the commercial came on, Charlie said to me, "That's like what happened to me in the war." He said it real faint, and at first I didn't get it, so I just said, "Yeah?" to acknowledge him.

"I still have nightmares," he said, and when I looked over at him, I saw tears streaming down his face. "I—I didn't know other people feel that way too from a war."

Now that was back in the days before we knew all about that post-trauma distress—I think people were just starting to talk about it 'cause the soldiers were starting to come home from Vietnam. I sure the hell didn't know anything about it, so all I could say to him was, "Well, I imagine war has to be tough."

"It was horrible, Lyla," he said. "You don't know what we went through. You don't know how lucky you are not to have had to go."

"Yeah," I said. "That damn Hitler."

"You wouldn't even want to know the things I saw happen in that war," he said again. He was making me uncomfortable the way he was saying it.

"No, I don't want to know," I said, hoping to shut him up.

"I saw my best buddies killed; I saw innocent children blown up. I—"

"The show's back on," I said.

But in a little while, I wished I hadn't said it 'cause the character in the show was addicted to morphine and eventually killed himself.

When the show was over, Charlie said, "I should have done that too. I should have done that too."

"Done what?" I asked.

"Killed myself," he said.

"Oh, shush," I said. "Bel will be home in a few minutes and she doesn't need to hear you talking like that."

"I'm just trouble for her," he said. "I shouldn't be putting her through this."

I could think of a million things to say back to him, like how I wished he had committed suicide because then I wouldn't be stuck watching TV with him, but I kept my mouth shut.

"She loves you," I finally said. "So don't worry about it."

"I don't deserve to be alive," he said. "I don't deserve—"

"Shh," I said. "*Cannon* is coming on. If we miss the opening, we won't know what's going on in the rest of the show."

That shut him up. I guess he realized he wasn't going to get any sympathy from me. He'd told me he didn't need any anyways.

Now that I think about it, though, I guess I can see where he was coming from. He must have had that post-trauma problem that other soldiers have. They talk about it a lot more now. Maybe that explains Charlie's drinking and his temper a little—doesn't excuse it by any means, but maybe explains it a little.

As we drive out of the park to head home, Bel says to me, "Lyla, we should go for a real Sunday drive sometime."

"What do you mean?" I asks.

"I mean, we go out for breakfast or we go out for ice cream, but we never do anything that's really like a Sunday drive, like go to Escanaba to go shopping, or go up to Copper Harbor to the little shops there, or anything like that, just for the fun of it."

"With the cost of gas today, that doesn't seem like much fun," I says. "Who needs the junk they sell in those shops anyways? And Marquette's got more shopping places than Escanaba."

"I know, Lyla, but it's just the idea of going somewhere, looking at the countryside, getting out of town."

"My legs get cramped up if I stay in the car that long," I says.

After another minute, she again tries to wheedle me into it.

"Charlie used to go for Sunday drives with me. We used to go up to Big Bay, or to Christmas, or out to Michigamme."

She should know better than to think any argument that starts with "Charlie used to" is going to convince me of anything.

"Good for Charlie," I says. "Was that his way of trying to make it up to you?"

"Lyla, why do you always have to be so down on Charlie? He wasn't all bad; he had his good side."

"What was that?" I asks.

"Lyla, we've had this conversation before. He could be really sweet at times."

"I never saw it," I says.

"Well, you weren't around him as much as me, now were you?"

"No, and you know I had a damn good reason not to be."

She just shakes her head.

"He tried, Lyla. He did the best he knew how. You can be awful ornery yourself, but I don't hold that against you any more than I'm going to hold Charlie's hitting me against him. It doesn't really matter in the long run."

"How do you figure that?" I asks, gazing out at the lake, wondering how she can say such a thing.

"He apologized to me in the end, when he was dying."

"And that makes it all better like it never happened?" I asks.

"Yes, for me it does," she says. "I forgave him a long time ago. It's time you forgive him too. After all, you weren't the one he hurt."

Whatever...I think to myself. I just know Charlie was an asshole. And so was Bill for that matter. I wonder why Bel and me both ended up with pains in the ass for the men in our lives. What did we do to deserve it?

Then I remember that Bill was in the war too—but that didn't give him or Charlie reason to be the way they were, even if, well...I'm not going to tell Bel I kind of understand a little better why Charlie was such an asshole. He would have been one even if he hadn't gone to the war, though maybe not so much of one.

Chapter 19

"I'm Bel, and today is the twenty-ninth anniversary of my husband's death."

For a moment, all the women in our Wednesday group look appropriately sad. I don't feel sad about it. I'd forgotten that Charlie died just a few days after his birthday; back then, I was surprised he'd made it to July, and I had started to wonder how much longer he was going to hang on because taking care of him, especially the last few days when he was in the hospital, really wore on Bel. It was a relief when he was gone; I can't say I ever did feel sorry for him because, despite what he and Bel both tried to claim, I never saw him make any real effort to change his ways until he was desperate for someone to take care of him and had no choice.

But the others in our women's group don't know that. They just look appropriately sympathetic and Wendy even says, "Oh, Bel. We're sorry."

Bel looks like she's trying to catch her train of thought, or maybe hold back some tears—really, after all of these years?—but finally she goes on.

"I can't believe it's been that long—that so much time has gone by. We were married for thirty-two years and had a daughter together, though she died when she was only a year old. If he had lived, we'd have been married for sixty-one years now. Just thinking of that makes me feel ancient, but we got married when I was only fourteen—because I got pregnant, and so the nuns at the orphanage let me marry him. They thought he was reliable. He was eighteen after all and had a job and could provide for me, and we had known each other since we were kids in the orphanage, though he used to be mean and tease me—but later he told me that was only because he liked me and didn't know how else to show it."

I was starting to wonder when she was going to get to the point. I sure was getting sick of hearing about Charlie, but I suppose it was all new and interesting to the others to hear about her screwed up life.

"I still miss him," she says; then she looks at me and adds, "Lyla, I know you won't understand that. You see, everyone, he was abusive and an alcoholic, as I've told you before, and Lyla and I have known each other about as long as I knew Charlie, and she knew he was abusing me and got really mad at me for not leaving him, so mad we quit being friends for many years because she didn't like how he treated me, but I—"

"That's all in the past now, Bel. Don't bring that up again," I interrupt her.

Then, Diana, the trampy one, she kind of glares at me because the rule is that we can't interrupt each other, but I don't think it's fair for Bel to tell everyone how badly I acted back then; I mean, it has been over fifty years now. Sure, I felt guilty about abandoning her, leaving her with the bastard rather than staying with her, but what was I supposed to do? Things were different in those days. The police wouldn't have done anything to help us.

"Okay, well," Bel continues, "I did love him, and I know he loved me. Yes, he beat me and I left him, but he had his reasons, what with being an orphan and being in the war and all, so I kind of understood that, and when he was dying in the end, how could I not take care of him? And I know he loved me because at the end, I thought maybe if I hadn't left him, he wouldn't have gone downhill so fast, so a few days before he died, I asked him if he forgave me and if I had made it up to him by caring for him. I'll never forget what he said then. He looked me straight in the eye and he said, 'Bel, there was never anything to make up for, but if you want to make me happy, give up drinking. Don't let alcohol drive you as crazy as it has me; I know you drink a lot and probably have a problem too, and I'm probably what triggered it. So if you love me, give up the bottle.'"

What the hell? Bel never told me he had said that to her. Not that he had any right to tell her what to do, even if it was giving up the damn bottle, but I'm kind of glad he let her know he wasn't mad in the end.

"It took me a while to do what he said," Bel says, "but I didn't forget. I had to drink my way through his death and the funeral just so I could get through it, but a few days after he was in the grave, that's when I poured my alcohol down the drain, and then that night, I went to my first Alcoholics

Anonymous meeting.

"When you go to those meetings, you learn about the Twelve Steps, and two of the steps, I forget which ones, but they're about making amends to the people we've harmed. Those two have always been the ones that seem to have stuck in my head the most. I realized the best way I could make my amends to Charlie was by not drinking so that's what I've done.

"And so, wherever Charlie is now, and I believe God is merciful so that Charlie's in Heaven, I hope he knows I'll have been sober for twenty-nine years come next week, and I hope he's proud of me. I forgave him, and he forgave me, but the hardest part is forgiving ourselves. Now I think I've done that. That's all I have to say. Thank you for listening."

"Thank you, Bel," everyone says, and then Sybil says, "I'm really proud of you, Bel."

"Thanks," Bel says. She reaches over for my hand, and I let her have it, and when she squeezes it, even though I wish Charlie hadn't been the reason why she quit drinking, I am proud of her that she quit the booze and didn't hold any grudges; I squeeze her hand back for a second—until I feel embarrassed because Sybil's handing me a tissue.

Just as I step in the door, the phone starts ringing. It always rings at the worst possible moments like now when all I want to do is sit down for a rest after driving around in Bel's hot car.

"Hello," I says, picking up the phone.

"Hello, Lyla. It's Eleanor. How are you?"

I'm surprised I'm not cursing in my head when I realize who it is. I guess it's because I'm still feeling kind of good after being at the meeting, so I try to be pleasant as I says, "I'm fine, Eleanor. How are you?"

"I'm not good, Lyla," Eleanor replies. "Bill has taken a turn for the worse. He's been sick for a couple days now, but he refused to go back to the hospital. He wants to stay at the nursing home. But I heard the death rattle in his throat this morning when he was napping. I don't think he has much time left."

"Oh, Eleanor, I'm so sorry," I says, sitting down in my chair and realizing that as irritated as I've been with Eleanor for continually calling me about Bill, the phone calls are almost at an end now, so I should be patient with her—and sympathetic. "Well, he's suffered so much. It's time, Eleanor. I know it's hard, but you—"

"You probably won't believe this, Lyla, but he asked me to call you. He said he wanted to see you, if you'll come. He said if you wouldn't, he'd understand, but he'd like it if you would."

I don't believe it. I know Bill better than that. I don't know what's wrong with Eleanor to keep beating a dead horse, but...well, it must have been all that talk about making amends at the meeting or something because I hear myself say, "Okay, Eleanor. When's a good time for me to come?"

"Anytime," she says and tells me his room number.

Going up there's the least I can do for her if it will give her a little comfort. I've been starting to think she's become delusional in her old age, but if Bill is that sick, he probably won't even know I'm there, and if he does, so what? If Eleanor heard the death rattle, he won't be in any condition to be swearing at me again. I tell myself I'll go for Eleanor's sake; I know how much Bill matters to her, and considering how she's looked after him so well all these past weeks, she deserves a little comforting now.

I kind of tell myself I must not be thinking too clearly, but somehow listening to Bel at the women's meeting has gotten me into a sort of forgiving frame of mind. If Eleanor had called me that morning, I doubt I would have gone. But when I pick up the phone to call Bel for a ride, I can already hear her, despite what she said about Charlie, telling me I'm stupid to go see Bill.

I hesitate for a minute, and then I think maybe I could call Sybil for a ride so Bel doesn't have to know. I don't know Sybil's number—just The Pancake House's—but she must be in the phonebook. And I have a feeling she'll understand better than Bel.

"Sybil, it's Lyla," I says when she answers.

"Hi, Lyla. I knew it was you. I have Caller I.D. What's up?"

And she still picked up the phone, knowing it was me! Amazing.

"I was wondering if you could give me a ride."

"Well, I'm not working right now. You'll need to call The Pancake House."

"No, not to the restaurant. I need a ride to the hospital."

"Oh, are you sick?"

"No, it's—well, it's someone else, an old friend who is dying, and I want to see him before he goes, and I guess they expect him to go any time now. Can you give me a ride? I don't want to impose, but well, I'd rather not ask

Bel for certain reasons I'd rather not get into, but I'd sure appreciate it, Sybil, if you could help me out."

"Yes, I guess I can do that for you, Lyla. I don't have to be to work until this evening so I have a few hours. Do you want to go now?"

"As soon as it's convenient for you I guess."

"I can be there in about ten minutes," she tells me.

"Perfect. I'll be downstairs waiting."

When I get downstairs, I'm glad Bel's window doesn't face the front of the building so she can't see me leaving. And I'm so nervous about seeing Bill that I find myself kind of talkative with Sybil when I get in the car.

"I really appreciate this, Sybil," I tell her. "I know it must have been a surprise to you that I would just call you out of the blue like that, but it's just a strange situation and Bel wouldn't be too happy with me going. See, it's an old boyfriend of mine. He's dying, and I just want to see him one more time. His sister Eleanor told me she heard the death rattle in his throat today, so I wanted to go before it's too late. I just have some things to say to him, things that make sense to me now since we talked about making amends at our meeting today, though I think even Bel would think it's a bad idea in this case."

"Eleanor?" says Sybil, oddly, and then I remember that she's involved with Alan, but it's too late now as she says, "Oh, is your old boyfriend Bill Whitman? That's right, Alan's dad. You told me that at the Fourth of July parade, remember?"

"Yeah," I confess.

"Oh!" she says, "that's funny."

"So you and Alan are still dating then?" I says.

"Yeah," says Sybil. "I mean, I guess we're dating. We like each other—okay, I'm actually crazy about him, but he's had a lot going on with his father being ill so I've been trying not to push it too much. I haven't seen him since last week. I think he's too busy up at the hospital because he didn't call me back when I called him yesterday, which isn't like him."

I somehow doubt it's because he's too busy. What boyfriend doesn't return his girlfriend's phone call the same day? I can't imagine why Alan would play hard to get with a pretty girl like Sybil, but then, I've always known he was a jerk. Somehow, I can't resist suggesting, "Maybe you should come up to the hospital room with me. I imagine Alan's up there now if his dad is as bad as Eleanor says." We've turned onto College Avenue now and the hospital is right in front of us.

"Oh, I don't think so," says Sybil. "He might think I'm being pushy. It's family time. I have to respect that."

"That's just weird," I says, "if you're his girlfriend. I would think now is the time he would want you to be up there with him."

"Well, we have a lot of fun together," she says, trying to laugh it off, but I can see she looks confused. "He told me going out with me was a good way to relax his stress, but half the time he doesn't call me back, and he often has reasons why he can't go out. I—I didn't want to say anything because at the meetings I've been gushing over him, but I just don't know what it is, Lyla. I think he's really special, and I know with his dad being close to death, he's busy and has a lot going on, but I'm starting to think he doesn't feel the same way about me."

"Well," I says, holding back my tongue from telling her how Alan Whitman always was selfish, "I think you just need to give him time. Losing a parent isn't easy. And if he has a brain in his head, he'll realize what a special girl you are."

"Thanks, Lyla. You're right," she says as she pulls up to where she can drop me off at the hospital lobby. "I'll be home until seven o'clock so just call me before then, or else call The Pancake House after that and I'll come give you a ride home."

"Oh, thanks, Sybil. I didn't even think about how I'd get home. Thank you." She really is a sweet girl. I may just have to kick Alan in his business if he hurts her. I bet if I practiced, I could still swing my leg up that high.

And then, before I'm ready, I'm out of the car and going through the sliding doors into the hospital lobby. In a few minutes, I'll be seeing my old boyfriend again, and this time, I'm pretty sure it's for the last time. And still, I'm wondering why the hell I'm doing it. I know it has something to do with our talking about amends at the meeting today, but now I'm so nervous I can't even think what all of that meant.

I walk over to the elevator and take it up to the floor with the skywalk. Marquette General's got the only escalator in Upper Michigan, but at my age, I'm afraid I'll end up losing my balance on the darn thing.

Once I'm out of the elevator, I hesitate for a moment. Then I go across the skywalk and to the next elevator, and up that. And then I'm on the floor. I stand there, just a few steps out of the elevator in the hallway, until one of the nurses looks at me kind of funny, and then so people don't start staring at me like I've finally lost it, I look for the arrows pointing the way to the room numbers and head down the hall to where Bill is dying.

When I reach the right room, I poke my head in the door just long enough to see Alan standing at the foot of the bed. Another man is standing beside him. Then just as I see Eleanor sitting on the far side of the bed and facing the door, she says, "Lyla, oh, I was hoping you were Jason or William. They're both on their way, but I'm glad to see you. Come on in."

The two men turn to look at me.

"Hello, Lyla," Alan says to me. "You remember my friend, Frank."

"Sure," I says to Frank. "I met you at John and Wendy's." I almost say, "You're John's friend," but I guess if Frank's staying at Alan's house, he's friends with Alan too.

"I'm glad you came, Lyla. Bill's just sleeping, but the doctors don't think it will be long," says Eleanor, motioning toward Bill.

I'm too nervous to look at Bill much. He looks awful—pale and shriveled up like an old man—not at all like the handsome man I used to know. It makes me sad to see him like that—and to think what the end is for all of us, no matter how good-looking we once were.

"I'm not sure I should be here," I says. "I don't want to upset him and he didn't like seeing me last time."

"It's okay, Lyla," Alan says. I'm surprised by his gentle tone. "He was never happy unless he was ornery—isn't that right, Dad?"

I realize Bill can't reply. He's got an oxygen mask over his face, part of why he looks so unfamiliar to me.

"Alan, shush. Don't be that way," Eleanor says.

"I'm just joking," says Alan. "I don't know what else to say. I mean, I just can't believe—you always know some day you'll lose your parents, but when it finally happens, I just can't believe it. I—I'm not ready for it. I don't know what else to do except joke."

I guess Alan's only other option is to cry, which he looks on the brink of doing.

"Alan, why don't you guys go get something to drink or a snack," Eleanor says. "You didn't even have any lunch, and I want a few minutes to talk to Lyla. You need a little break. He's not going to leave us yet."

"That's a good idea," Frank tells Alan. "You need a few minutes to gather your thoughts."

Frank places his hand on Alan's shoulder and gently starts to push him toward the door.

"I—I—" Alan stutters.

"Shh," says Frank, his hand moving down to pat Alan on the back. "Come on."

They walk out the door, Frank's hand guiding Alan into the hallway.

"Alan's taking it really hard," Eleanor tells me as I sit down in a chair next to her. "He feels a lot of guilt that his relationship with Bill hasn't been better, but I told him Bill had a way of pushing people away from him, just like he did with you, Lyla. I never understood it. Everyone else in our family was always kindhearted, but Bill just couldn't be a family man like my brother Henry or my father. Of course, my brother Roy never married either, but he was never temperamental like Bill. I don't know what it was that made Bill so different from the rest of the family, other than maybe because he was the baby; I could say he was spoiled and used to getting what he wanted, but other than plenty of love from our parents, my brothers and sister and I never had much when we were growing up, so I just don't know why he's so different. It doesn't matter what he was like, though. He's my brother; that's all that matters. Now I'll be all alone. My sister Ada's alive, but she's in Louisiana and ninety so I'll probably never see her again. I'm just all alone now."

"You have your girls," I says, "and your nephews and nieces."

"Yes, and I love them dearly, but it's just not the same as having your parents and your brothers and sisters."

"No," I says. "I guess not. I haven't had my parents or sister around in years and years, and I admit it gets pretty lonely."

"I guess all we can do is love them while we still have them," Eleanor says.

And then Bill moves his hand a little. It startles me, but Eleanor reaches out to grab it and says, "Bill, can you hear me?"

He opens one eye about halfway; I can just barely see his eye turn toward her. He hasn't seen me yet. I'm afraid if he does, it'll be what kills him.

"I'm here, Bill," says Eleanor. "I'll stay until it's time. Alan is here too, and Jason and William are coming. They'll be here soon. Maybe you want to hang on for them?"

"Who's that?" he mutters, his eye turning toward me.

Eleanor doesn't say anything at first. I don't know what to say. I didn't think he could see me, but either he can, or he heard Eleanor talking to me.

Eleanor looks at me. She raises her eyebrows, silently asking if I want her to let Bill know I'm there. I can't find any words. I'm afraid of upsetting him, but I nod my head just a little.

"Bill, it's Lyla," Eleanor tells him. "She's come to say goodbye to you."

I wait to see how he'll take it. He doesn't say anything at first. Doesn't even blink or scrunch up his face so we know he heard. He looks like maybe he's thinking about what she said though. Then, after a second, he says, in a raspy voice, "Goodbye, Lyla."

And then I can't help myself. I don't know why I'm apologizing to him, but I burst out sobbing and says, "Goodbye, Bill. I'm really sorry about everything."

And then I wait.

"I know," he says.

And his eyes close again.

And it's over, just like that. I don't know what I expected. I don't know what to say—I don't know what to do now. What did he mean by, "I know"?

"He's sorry too, Lyla," Eleanor says like she's some sort of interpreter for him. "I guess he forgives you too. I'm glad you've forgiven him."

That's not really what he said. That's what Eleanor wants to think he meant, but it's not what he said. She reaches out and takes my hand in the one not holding Bill's hand. That's Eleanor all over. Wanting to believe the best. Wanting to make up a happy ending. Is it a happy ending, though? I'm not mad. Bill probably didn't have the strength to say anything else but "I know." But it's a real let down. Even if he meant he forgave me—well, is that what I wanted? I kind of wanted an apology from him too.

"It's too bad you two didn't work out things earlier," Eleanor adds, "but now you can both be at peace."

Bill's eyes are closed now. He hasn't died yet. I can still see him breathing. I don't know if I dare to say anything more to him, if he'll even hear me. Then I realize it doesn't matter. After all these years if "I know" is the best he can do, no matter how much it might have been a struggle for him to say it, if that's the best he can do, then what the hell have I been waiting and hoping for all these years? What a waste of my time and energy to have spent all this time replaying everything that ever happened between us in my head and hoping for a better ending. I had hoped to make my peace with him, and I guess I have, but I also feel angry at myself.

"The hardest part is forgiving ourselves..." Bel's words suddenly come back to me from the meeting earlier that day.

It's time I forgive myself and move on.

"How is he?"

I look up to see another man in the doorway. I don't recognize him, but Eleanor gets up and says, "William" and he walks over to hug her. Behind him is a woman who must be his wife. Yes, the couple who got married the day Bill and I had our big blowout fight that ended everything.

"Eleanor, I better get going," I says before she can introduce me to them.

"I'm glad you came," she says, giving me a hug. I'm glad she doesn't say my name. I doubt William and his wife remember me, and I don't want them to anyways.

"Thanks. I'm glad I came too," I says. And it's not a lie. I am glad because now I feel like I've let it go—the stupidity of it all.

I quickly walk past William and his wife and out into the hallway.

I just want to get out of the hospital. I walk to the elevator and take it down and then find my way back to the front lobby. Then I asks if I can use the visitor phone to call my ride. The woman there doesn't look too willing, but I says, "It's a local call. I just need to call someone to pick me up" so she lets me.

When I call Sybil, she must be able to hear in my voice that I'm upset. She promises to be here in ten minutes. I sit in the lobby waiting for her until I see her car pull up, but I still don't get up. Maybe I'm in shock, or having some of that post-trauma stress disorder like Charlie claimed to have. After a couple minutes, Sybil comes in to look for me and as soon as she sees me, I break into tears.

"Lyla, are you okay?" she asks.

"No, no I don't think I am," I says, not knowing how to explain how I feel. "I just need to get home."

"Come on," she says, helping me up and taking my arm to walk me to the car.

"Do you need to talk about it?" she asks once we're both inside the car and she's helped me with my seatbelt.

"No, there's nothing to talk about," I says.

I want to talk to her, but—well, I never talk to people about my feelings and stuff—not even Bel—and especially not at those screwy women's meetings—so I don't see any point in starting now. It will just make me end up feeling pathetic if I do.

Chapter 20

When I look in *The Mining Journal* the next day, there it is—the obituary:

Marquette—William "Bill" Whitman II, age 85, of 18—
Wilkinson Ave. went to be with the Lord on July 13, 2005.
He had recently been a resident at Norlite Nursing Center
and Marquette General Hospital.

Funeral arrangements are incomplete and will be
announced by the Swanson-Lundquist Funeral Home.

I'm surprised that Eleanor didn't call me. He must have died not long
after I left in order for it to make *The Mining Journal* today. I hope his son
Jason got there in time to say goodbye to him.

For a minute, I wonder whether I should go to the funeral, but what's
the point when he's gone and I've made my peace with him—or my peace
with myself, at least? I'll send Eleanor a nice sympathy card, but it's time for
me to take care of the living, not the dead. I did what I could in the end, and
whether Bill forgave me or not doesn't really matter so much as that I tried.

And I realize there's one person living I can still do something for to
make amends, even if it's just to say I'm sorry. I know I wronged my sister
by not telling her our father had come home, but to tell her that now would
just cause her pain, so I won't say it. I will tell her, though, that I'm sorry
we were never close and that we had a fight right after Miss Bergmann died
when she was full of grief. Maybe after I write to her, we could—no, we live
too far apart to be traveling at our age—last I heard, she lived in Kalamazoo,

which must be about five hundred miles away—but maybe we could talk on the phone or something.

I start writing the letter to her in my head that morning as I eat breakfast and do up the dishes and get dressed. Even when I turn on *Regis & Kelly*, I don't hear a word of it because I'm busy daydreaming about writing to Jessie. Not that I care about *Regis & Kelly*—it's just background noise to keep me company. None of those movie stars they have on there have anything to do with me and my life, so what do I care? And despite what I know some of the other ladies in the building think, Regis isn't that cute—he's kind of annoying, actually.

Bel calls like she does most days to ask if I want to come down to her place for lunch, so I says, "Sure." I wonder if she's seen the paper and knows Bill's dead, but she doesn't say nothing about it on the phone. When I get to her place, though, while she's making sandwiches, she asks, "So are you going to the funeral?"

"No," I says. "I've made my peace with him."

I'm standing next to her, pouring the drinks while she makes the sandwiches.

"What do you mean by that?" she asks without looking at me.

I decide I don't need a lecture from her about my going to the hospital yesterday, and I know Sybil won't tattle on me, so I just says, "I mean, I'm not upset about it anymore. Now that he's gone, there's nothing either of us can do about the past, so I've let go of the pain."

"That's good," she says, but I notice she looks confused. Like she's thinking really hard and just staring at the bread she's buttering.

Since she's not looking at me, I figure it's a safe time to say what I need to.

"Bel, I was thinking about what you said at the meeting yesterday about making amends. I haven't made my peace yet with Jessie. I think I need to do that."

She's still staring at the bread, looking confused. Then she puts the knife back in the butter and spreads more on the bread, like it's going to be a double butter sandwich, but I don't want to rile her up by saying anything about it. Instead, I just says, "Did you hear me? I think I need to make my peace with Jessie."

She sets the knife down, and then she turns around, stares me in the eye, and says, "No, you don't."

"What do you mean I don't?" I asks. "Isn't making amends the right thing to do?"

"Not if it's going to hurt someone," she says. She finally stops buttering and starts in on spreading mayo on the bread. "That's what the Steps say, "Unless doing so will harm others.""

"Who's it going to harm?" I asks.

"Me," she says.

"You! How the hell can it hurt you?" I laugh, though I already know her answer and don't want to hear it.

"You know damn well how," she says, practically slamming her butter knife on the counter and then violently scooping out the chicken salad with a spoon and smooshing it on the bread.

I walk to the table with the glasses of milk and sit down. Then I says, "No, I really don't know."

"No, it figures that you wouldn't," she says, taking a knife to cut the sandwiches in half.

"Well, are you going to tell me?"

"All these years," she says, "you've been whining, 'Oh, Jessie's so mean. She got everything and I got nothing. She never treated me right, and she abandoned me, and blah, blah, blah."

I can't help laughing as she tries to impersonate me, but I point out, "I never said blah, blah, blah."

"I don't care. You've always acted like you didn't have a sister," she says, carrying the plates to the table and then sitting down. "Haven't you figured out after over sixty years that I'm your sister. I'm the one who's always been there for you."

"Yes, Bel, I know you're a good friend," I says, hating when she gets emotional like this, "but Jessie's still my sister."

"What do you need that bitch Jessie for?" she asks, hurt spreading across her face. "Haven't I been a good friend to you? I know I've screwed up plenty of times, but I love you, Lyla. You're my best friend, and yet, you act like I don't even matter to you. It's always about Bill or Jessie."

"But, Bel," I says, trying to think how to calm her down. "I've explained this to you. Remember when I told you about how *The Color Purple* felt like it was about me and Jessie, and that Danny Glover was like Miss Bergmann who kept us apart. You know I want a reunion like that with Jessie."

"So, who am I in the movie then? Oprah Winfrey?"

I laugh, trying to lighten the mood. "I wish you were Oprah Winfrey. Then we wouldn't have to be watching every penny of our Social Security. We'd be living high off the hog."

"Quit trying to change the subject," she says.

"Well, I'm sorry," I says. "You know how I feel about you, but—"

"No, I don't," she says. "You never tell me."

"Jesus Christ, Bel, if you don't know by now, there's no point in my telling you. I'm here eating lunch with you, ain't I? And I go to your doctor's appointments with you, and your recovery meetings, and I go out to eat pancakes with you at three in the morning whenever you wake me up, and God knows how many other things, so just give it a rest already."

"Fine," she says. She bites into her sandwich, and then with her mouth full, she mutters, "I should have known better than to think you'd say it."

"Yeah, you should have," I says before downing my whole glass of milk so I can stare into the glass rather than look at her. Jesus Christ. She's not a little girl in the orphanage anymore. When is she going to grow up?

We sit and eat our sandwiches in silence.

But silence doesn't mean I'm over it. How dare she call my sister, "That bitch Jessie"? I ought to start calling her, "That selfish bitch Bel" since she's so damn insecure she can't understand why I'd want to make things right with my own sister.

I finish my sandwich and then tell her I don't feel very good. That I'm tired.

"You're probably depressed over hearing that Bill died," she says. "He's another one I'm sick of hearing you pine over."

"I ain't been pining over no one," I snap. I stand up from the table, and for just a moment, I consider throwing my plate at the wall, but I doubt I'm strong enough to break it, so I just carry it and the glass over to the counter.

"Whatever," she says.

"'Whatever,'" I mock her. "You sound like one of those teenagers on TV."

"Whatever," she repeats.

"I'll talk to you later," I says, walking to the door. "Thanks for lunch." I hear her start to say something, but I go out the door and slam it behind me to cut her off. I head for the elevator. I'll bet any money that by suppertime she'll have calmed down and be calling me to go out to eat with her.

When I get back upstairs, I decide I'm not going to let Bel's orneriness get to me. I'm going to write to Jessie and that's all there is to it. I sit down at the kitchen table with a piece of paper and try to figure out what to say. I must have written half-a-dozen letters to Jessie in my head this morning, but now what I write doesn't come out sounding as good as the ones in my head, but I write the letter anyways.

July 14, 2005

Dear Jessie,

I don't even know where to begin, but I know I owe you an apology. I don't know why I acted like I did, other than that I was a scared little girl when Papa left for Karelia and then Mama died, and I never got over that. I don't know why I couldn't. I didn't mean to blame Miss Bergmann for not adopting me. I don't even feel angry about that now. I only bring it up cause I was angry about it before. Not even angry so much as just feeling hurt and unloved. I know you had no say in any of it cause you were just a girl like me then. I don't know why Miss Bergmann did what she did and probably never will. But I shouldn't have taken it out on you that day I came over to your house right after she died. That day I wanted to tell you how I wanted us to be like sisters and family again, but I was afraid you wouldn't want that and then I'd be hurt even more. When I heard you say you were moving away, I realized I was losing you and that just made me act the way I did I think. I didn't want you to go.

When I saw in the paper later that you'd gotten married, I was happy for you but I was hurt too that you didn't invite me, and then when you sent a Christmas card that year, I felt so angry I couldn't write you back. By then I felt so much guilt about how I acted.

Anyways, I'm sorry for it all, and I know it's taken just about all my life to find the courage to say so and I'm not doing a very good job now, but I hope you'll forgive me. I'd like to stay in touch with you even if it's just writing letters or talking on the phone.

I don't know how to sign it. I think about writing "Love" but I'm afraid that might be too much so I just put "Lyla" at the end.

I think about writing my phone number after my name, but I'm afraid that if she's mad, she'll call me up and chew me out, so maybe it's better just to put my return address on the envelope and hope she writes back. I can give her my phone number later.

It takes me almost all afternoon to write that letter. I'm just looking for an envelope to put it in when the phone rings, and sure enough, it's Bel.

"Do you want to come down and watch Oprah with me?" she asks.

"Sure," I says. "Just give me a couple minutes."

I can't believe it's already five o'clock, that it took that long to stare out the window and find the right words, but I did it, and I feel better now. I fold it up and stick it in an envelope with my return address on it. I realize I don't know Jessie's address and don't know how to find out what it is, but I'll figure that out later. I stick the envelope in a drawer for now in case Bel comes over and sees it before I can mail it. Then I go downstairs to watch Oprah, but really, to make up with Bel.

Chapter 21

The next morning, I pull out the letter I wrote to Jessie and read it over. I think about rewriting it or rewording it some more. But I'm afraid that if I keep at it, I'll never get around to sending it.

And I need to find out Jessie's address. How will I do that? First, I think about calling information, but then I remember how I heard on *Dateline* that you can find out anything about anyone on the computer—it's called online stalking or something I guess. I imagine Sybil must have a computer. Maybe I'll regret it later, getting the address, but I feel like I can trust Sybil at least since she didn't seem to mind about taking me to see Bill. So I pick up the phone and call Sybil again, hoping she doesn't think I'm becoming a total pest.

"Sybil, it's Lyla. I'm sorry to bother you."

"It's okay, Lyla. Are you calling about Alan's father? I imagine you saw the paper or that his Aunt Eleanor called you?"

"Yes, it's too bad, but it's for the best. How is Alan?"

"I don't know," she says. "I left him a message telling him how sorry I was about his father. I imagine he'll call me later. He's probably busy making the funeral arrangements."

"Are you okay, Sybil?" I asks. "Your voice sounds kind of funny." It sounds almost like she's been crying, but I don't say that.

"Sure," she says. "I was just eating and a piece of food went down the wrong way."

"Oh," I says. "Well, the reason I'm calling is because I was hoping you could look up something on the computer for me. You can get on that online thing, can't you?"

"Yes," she says. "I'm right in front of the computer now. What do you want to know?"

"I need someone's address," I says, "and—well, I don't want Bel to know, but I want to write to my sister—I mentioned her at one of the meetings, how we're, well, estranged, I guess you'd say. I've been thinking about her a lot since we talked about making amends at the last meeting, so I want to write to her. Bel thinks it's a bad idea, but I feel like I should."

"Oh, I think you should," she says.

"I don't know if she'll even want to talk to me," I says, "but I need her address first to find out."

"Sure," says Sybil. "What's her name?"

"Jessie," I says, "and her last name is Goldsworthy I think—that's the man she married, and I only know that 'cause I saw it in the paper back in the '60s so I don't know if she's still married to him, or—"

"Well, do you have any idea where she lives?"

"Kalamazoo I think."

"Okay. Let's see what we get."

I hear her typing away for a minute and then she says, "No, she doesn't come up, but there are Goldsworthys in Kalamazoo. What was her husband's name?"

"Oh, darn," I says. "It started with an E—Edgar or Edmund or something like that maybe."

"How about Eugene?"

"Yes, that sounds right."

"It's the only Goldsworthy in Kalamazoo with an E name," she says.

"It must be him then," I says. "What's the address?"

She gives it to me and I write it on the envelope I'm going to mail. I remind myself to write it in my address book when I'm off the phone.

"Thanks, Sybil," I says. "You've been a great help. I don't know how I would have found it otherwise."

"No problem," she says. "It was easy enough to do. I wish the rest of life were that easy."

"Well, it won't be easy until I see what kind of reply I get from her," I says.

"No, I suppose not," she says. "That's the problem with life. Sometimes we have to wait for other people to decide things before we know if we can be happy or not."

I don't know what to say to that. For a second, I start to say, "That's true" so I don't have to get involved in her issues, but I hear myself instead saying, "Sybil, are you okay? You sound like you and Alan have some real problems."

And then she starts sobbing. Oh jeez, I've had enough crying lately, but I says, "Sybil, are you okay?"

"I'm okay. I'm just being stupid," she says. "Lyla, I don't know what's wrong with me. I'm crazy about Alan, and it doesn't even make sense. I haven't even known him for two months. He's twelve years older than me, and he hasn't even done anything really that would be a good reason for me to fall in love with him, but I am. I feel pathetic or desperate or something to be in love with a man who will barely have more than a ten-minute conversation with me. I haven't even seen him since before the Fourth of July. We've only gone out three times, really, although I've stopped by his house a couple times, but that seems to annoy him. Am I stupid? What's wrong with me?"

"You just want love, honey," I tell her. "There's nothing wrong with that." She's a good girl; she is being kind of stupid considering who she's crazy about, but I won't tell her that. She deserves better than Alan Whitman. That's for sure.

"I think it's that—well, I don't even know that it's about Alan so much as that there's just this void in me that needs to be filled, and I've been afraid to fill it. I kind of thought since he's May's cousin that he'd be safe to fill it. But now I just feel like a stupid lovesick girl chasing after him. I'm sorry to be dumping all this on you when we hardly even know each other."

"It's okay," I says.

"I mean," she goes on, "you don't even know anything about me, really."

"Sure I do," I says. "I know you drive the taxi for The Pancake House, and you write sometimes for *The Mining Journal*, and you help May out in her antique shop, and we go to a meeting together."

"That all makes me sound pathetic too," she says. "I can't even find a full-time job around here, much less a real boyfriend. I don't know why I'm so messed up except maybe that I don't have any family for support."

"That's right; you're kind of an orphan like me, aren't you?"

"Well, I had my grandma until recently, but now I'm all alone. I have some distant cousins in town I guess, but I don't really know them."

"Well, I understand that," I says. "Jessie's the only family I have and we don't even speak to each other." And then I add, though I wouldn't say it to Bel's face, "Bel's the closest thing I really have to a sister."

"I think maybe I like Alan because he's older," Sybil goes on. "I maybe think of him like a father-figure or at least a big brother. He seems safe, even though he doesn't pay any attention to me. I feel like he must be a good man since even though he and his dad didn't get along, he was still here trying to take care of him."

"I'm sure he is," I says. I don't like how he's treating Sybil, but I guess I have to give Alan credit for looking after his dad.

"He hurts too," Sybil continues. "His ex-girlfriend, Sheila—she dumped him, you know, and married someone else and moved downstate with his son, so he had to go down there. He wanted to stay up here but he went to be near his son. Only a good man would care about his son enough to do that. I just think there's so much about him to love and admire, and it doesn't hurt that he's good-looking."

"But he doesn't seem to feel the same way about you?" I asks. I didn't want to stay on the phone this long, but I figure she needs to get it out of her system.

"No, I guess not. We haven't gone out that much. I've tried to tell myself it's because he's worried about his dad, or it's because that Frank who's staying with him is a bad influence on him—he's a player I can tell—but I think I finally have to admit that it's probably more like what that new book *He's Just Not That Into You* is about. Have you heard of it? I think maybe I should read it."

"Yeah, I remember seeing them talking about it on Oprah," I says, "but you don't need to read it. I think you already know he's not that into you."

"I just don't understand why. What's wrong with me? When we've gone out we've gotten along really well. He's funny, and he's handsome, and he's polite, and I just get all tingly when I'm near him, but—"

"But he's just not that into you, right?" I says.

"Yeah, but why not?"

"Oh, honey. It's just the way it is. Maybe he's still in love with his ex-girlfriend. Maybe he feels he's too old for you. Who knows?"

"I just don't understand," she says. "I mean, why can't he just tell me that then? I think it's that Frank that's the problem—I bet he told Alan he can find hotter chicks. I bet he's out chasing the girls and has got Alan doing it too. I don't want to think Alan's that way, but I mean, he does have a child out of wedlock. I know that sounds old-fashioned, but—"

"Sybil," I says, sighing because I feel bad for her and I've learned the hard way that no man is worth hurting over like she's doing. "You ain't old-fashioned. You're just chasing after someone who's unavailable, meaning he's not ready to settle down, and what we call old-fashioned today, we used to call decency in my day, and the truth of the matter is that it's really just common sense. You're too good or too smart to be doing things to hurt people; having kids out of wedlock without a commitment—that's a way parents hurt their children, maybe not intentionally but because they're thoughtless. And if a man can't call you back, he's hurting you. He should have the guts enough just to tell you he's not interested. He might be afraid of hurting your feelings, but we end up hurting people more when we don't state the truth up front. Jeez, listen to me—I sound like I should be on Oprah."

She laughs, but then she's quiet for a moment, trying to figure it out.

"You don't need a man, honey," I finally tell her. "I've never been married, and I've been just fine. Sometimes I thought I wasn't, but I have been." Maybe I'm trying to convince myself more than her in saying that, but she seems to buy it.

"I think maybe you're right, Lyla," she finally says. "In a way, I think I've always known Alan wasn't the one for me, but—I don't know. I think sometimes I seek out unavailable men so I don't have to have a real relationship."

"That makes sense," I says. "That's what I did with Bill. Alan and him probably have the same issues."

"Yeah," she says. "They probably do. Thanks for listening, Lyla."

"You're welcome," I says, thinking I made her feel better enough that I can get off the phone now. "Thanks for giving me my sister's address. I better go get my letter in the mail now before the mailman comes."

"Okay," she says. "I have to go finish writing my story for *The Mining Journal* anyway, but let me know if you hear from your sister, Lyla. I hope you end up building a good relationship with her because you deserve that. You're a very caring person."

"Thanks," I says. What the hell else am I supposed to say? No one ever said I was "a very caring person" before.

I hang up the phone. I don't know how to feel. She talked to me like I was her mother or something the way she confided in me. She's such a sweet girl. If I'd had a granddaughter, I'd want her to be like Sybil. But...I better get my letter in the mail before I chicken out. Besides, if I was such a caring person, I wouldn't have a sister not speaking to me. But now, maybe this letter will change things.

Chapter 22

Once I put the letter in the mailbox, I'm on pins and needles about whether I'll get a reply or not. I try to act all normal, hanging out with Bel, going to church, and eating at The Pancake House at 3 a.m. on Monday morning because Bel can't sleep—I barely sleep either from worrying over the letter. Wednesday we go to the women's meeting again and I don't say anything because I don't want to talk—I don't have anything to talk about anyways except wondering when my sister will write me back. I think if I'm lucky it'll take two days for the letter to get to Kalamazoo, but more likely three, and then two or three to get a response, so I figure that's six days maximum if she writes me back right away, so that could be a letter as soon as Thursday—or Friday—'cause there's no mail on Sunday.

And then on Thursday, there's a letter in the mail with a Kalamazoo return address on it, but no name above the address. It's a really thick envelope, and not regular size but one of those manila ones. Jessie must have written me a really, really long letter. I can hardly contain myself long enough to sit down before I rip it open and pull out a typed letter right on the top, barely noticing there's a photograph and a couple other folded up pieces of paper besides.

July 18, 2005

Dear Ms. Hopewell,

    I received your letter in the mail today. I debated

whether to call you or write you back, but I had so many thoughts that I was afraid I would not be able to express fully on the phone and so I thought it best to write. I was so very moved by your letter, and I know your sister would have been very happy, if surprised, to have received it, but I'm afraid it has come too late.

Your sister, my stepmother—though she was more like a mother to me—went to be with the Lord this past winter. She had breast cancer and although the doctors were hopeful after removing her breast a few years ago, the cancer returned in her other breast, and after several months of valiantly battling it, she passed away on January 9th. I had thought of you several times since then but never wrote because I did not know your address, or if you were even still alive.

I know, as you express from your letter, that there were some hard feelings between you and your sister. She said very little about you when my two brothers and I were children and she was raising us. I was only three when she became our mother and my brothers were eight and five. She became the mother we needed, and she loved us as if we were her own. We could not have asked for a better mother. My father is still with us, but he is just a shadow of himself now, especially since Mother died, and we have had to put him in the nursing home recently.

I cannot tell you enough good things about your sister. She was good to all of us as children and as adults, and she became a wonderful grandmother as well. There isn't a day since her passing that I do not think about her and miss her terribly.

Every once in awhile, she would mention you to us, by saying something like, "My sister and I used to..." and go into some childhood memory of playing in the snow, or what school was like for you back in those days, always to compare our childhood to hers.

It was only when she first came down with cancer that she confided to me how terrible she felt not to have seen you for so many years. She wanted to contact you then, but I think she didn't want you to feel sorry for her because of the cancer. Every few months after that, she would bring up to me the possibility of her writing to you, saying that she felt terrible that she had not tried to stay in touch with you. I encouraged her at those times to write to you, but I guess she never found the courage to do so. I deeply wish now, after reading your letter, that I had sat her down and made her write that letter.

I am so sorry to be the bearer of bad news to you, but there is one bright side to this story I think. In going through my mother's things, I found the following letters. I did not know what to do with them since they were in a language I could not read and I was not sure at all who they were from. Now I am guessing, from what your letter said, that they might have been letters from your father—you will see they are still in the original envelopes and were addressed to a Marquette address and a woman I assume must have been your mother. I don't know if you can read Finnish, which is what I'm guessing is the language they are in, but maybe just having them will comfort you in some way.

I have never been to Upper Michigan, but if you ever come down to Kalamazoo for any reason, please feel free to stop by since I would love to meet you and could show you more of your sister's things, at least photographs of her and such. I am enclosing one I happened to have duplicates for of our family. It was taken Christmas 1970 so you can see we were quite a happy family.

My deepest sympathies on your loss,

Cheryl Goldsworthy Black

The photo shows a family of five—a husband and wife in their forties, two teenage looking boys, and a young girl. The wife is definitely my sister Jessie, though a bit older than I remember her—maybe seven or eight years had passed since we'd last seen each other by that time. She had the pointy framed glasses of that time, her hair up in a bun, and an orange sleeveless dress—not the sort of dress appropriate for a matronly woman in her forties by then, but she looked like she was trying to dress up for what was obviously a family portrait by a photography studio.

I look at the photo for a minute, seeing Jessie's face again for the first time in more than forty years. I realize I haven't even owned a single photograph of her until now. The only photo I had from our childhood was the faded, folded, and creased photo of myself as a little girl that Papa had managed to hang onto during all the years he was in Karelia.

I wonder whether I should cry—after all, I just found out my sister has died. I wait for a few minutes, trying to force the tears, but they just won't come. And then I feel like I'm not very human not to cry, and I start to feel angry that I'm not crying, and then I feel angry that Jessie thought about writing to me but never did. She had always been gentler than me; she knew I was the ornery one, so why hadn't she made the effort?

And then I realize she probably didn't write to me because she knew I was the ornery one—and maybe she didn't think I would write back, or if I did, I would just be hateful with her again. After all, I didn't write for so long from fear she wouldn't write back or she'd just snap at me. I was afraid of pouring my heart out to someone who didn't care. I guess she felt the same way. I don't know why neither of us couldn't get over that fear. And now it was too late.

I set the big envelope and everything in it aside. I see the letters there that Jessie's stepdaughter says are from Papa. For a second, I feel curious about them, but I can't read Finnish, so I don't know what to do with them, and I'm too sad right now to think about it.

I stare out the window for a while, hurting too much to know what to think. I try to force myself to sob, but I just can't.

I don't know what to do. I could go to church and pray the rosary but I don't see what good that will do. God isn't going to bring Jessie back from the dead for me. I could call Bel, but…well, I doubt she would be mean to my face about it, but she'd probably be relieved that Jessie is dead so I can't chase after her anymore.

Finally, hardly knowing what I'm doing, I pick up the phone and call Sybil.

"Hello," says Sybil.

And then the tears break when I hear her voice. I know she'll be kind and understanding. I can barely speak, but I says, "Sybil, my sister is dead. I just got a letter saying she died last winter. I was too late."

"Oh, Lyla," she says slowly, sadly, sounding completely sympathetic.

I swallow, trying to soothe the ache in my throat, and then I says, "My own sister, and I didn't even know she was sick. She died from breast cancer. I always liked to think, if nothing else, that if one of us got really sick, then we'd reconcile, but she didn't even tell me. How can you not tell your own sister you're going to die, no matter how much anger existed between you previously?"

"I don't know, Lyla. I would have killed for a sister," Sybil says. "It's terrible. It's her loss."

"I know I was always a difficult person to deal with," I says, starting to cry again. "But I didn't mean to be. I was just scared. Scared that if I let her know how much I cared, she still wouldn't care so I didn't know how to show it."

"Still, she was your sister," Sybil says. "She should have contacted you, or at least her children should have."

"She didn't have children, just stepchildren—her husband was a widower when she married him. It's my fault. She sent me a Christmas card that first year trying to make things right with me, but I was too stubborn to respond. I wanted to, but I was afraid, and then the time passed, and I just didn't know how she'd take it if I wrote. I just felt like it would be so much work to explain and apologize to her—it's just all been my fault. When I didn't get a Christmas card the next year, I felt so hurt and sad that she didn't send one, but it was my fault because I didn't respond the first time. I just always thought there'd be time to tell her I was sorry, and now it's too late."

"I'm so sorry, Lyla," says Sybil. "I don't know what to say. I guess—well, I guess I do understand how you feel a little, though, about things being left unsaid anyway. There are so many things I wish I could have said to my parents. So many things I want to know about them, questions to ask that never got asked."

"Jessie was the only one," I says, "who knew Mama and Papa when they were young—when we were all together. I mean, when Papa came back, sure other people knew him, but even though I took care of him those years, I didn't really know him. He just wasn't the same then. Those years before Papa left and Mama died, those were the happiest years of my life even if I didn't know it then, and Jessie's the only one who knew about them."

"But once your father came home, didn't she stay in touch with you then?"

"She never knew he came home," I admit, the guilt soaring up in me again. "She actually moved right about the time he got back, and I didn't tell her that he had found me. I told him she'd moved away and I didn't know where she was, and when that Christmas card came, I hid it from him. And then the longer I waited to write to her, the more difficult I knew it would be to explain about Papa and why I didn't tell her right away, but he was so changed, just a shell of himself, not the young strong man I'd known when I was a little girl. He was a shock to me actually. I told myself he'd be a shock to her too, and once I saw her marriage announcement in the newspaper, well, I guess I was jealous. She had found someone else to love her, so I thought I should at least get our father. I—I was so selfish, so childish."

"It's okay, Lyla," says Sybil. "You know better now. You'd do better if you could do it again. That's what matters. I bet she knows all that now."

"All I ever wanted was to make things right with her," I says, trying to blow my nose without making too much noise into the phone.

"What would you say to her if you could?" Sybil asks.

"I don't know. What I said in the letter I guess. But I don't know what I would say in person. I always hoped it would actually be said in person. Did you ever see that movie *The Color Purple*?"

"Yes," says Sybil.

"That's what I always wanted. You know when the sister comes back from Africa and Whoopie Goldberg is so excited to see her and they're running into each others' arms. That's how I imagined my relationship with my sister ending up like—that we'd see each other and forgive and be happy, but I just put it off. I just—"

"Oh, Lyla. It's okay," says Sybil. "Wherever your sister is now, I bet she knows. I bet she regrets it too."

"Yeah, her stepdaughter that wrote said Jessie kept talking about writing to me. She was just afraid to write like I was I guess."

I put the Kleenex on the side table and reach for another one and notice the letters there from Papa.

"See, in your hearts you both wanted to reconcile," says Sybil. "That's almost the same thing, isn't it? Neither of you held a grudge in the end. You can take comfort in that."

I don't know what to say to that. I guess it's true, though. I'll have to think about it, not forget it.

"Are you going to be okay?" Sybil asks.

"Oh sure," I says. "I just needed to get it out. I'm tough you know."

"I know you are," says Sybil. "And I'm glad you felt you could talk to me about it."

"Sybil, do you know anyone who can read Finnish?"

She seems surprised by the question. I asks it though because I've had enough of crying. It doesn't make me feel comfortable.

"Um, yeah, I think so. Why?" she asks.

"Well, Jessie's stepdaughter also mailed me these two letters that I guess Papa wrote to Mama when he went to Karelia. I didn't even know they existed, but Jessie must have taken them when we left our house and she went to live with Miss Bergmann. Only, they aren't much good to me because they're in Finnish so I can't read them."

"I thought you never heard from your father after he left," says Sybil.

"Well, that's what I always thought, but maybe I was just too little to remember."

"I bet we can find someone who can translate them for you. There are plenty of people around the U.P. who can speak Finnish."

"Really, do you think so?"

"Sure, after all, Carl Pellonpaa speaks Finnish on *Finland Calling* every Sunday morning so someone must be watching that show who speaks Finnish, right?"

"I don't know who," I says. "I never watch that show."

"Well, it's been on for something like forty years so someone must," she says. "I'll ask around. You know, with Finn Fest coming up, someone Finnish will be around for sure. I'll find someone for you, Lyla. After all that you and your family went through and your dad being away, those letters will be important to read."

"Yeah," I says. "They won't do me any good otherwise. Thanks for listening to me, Sybil."

I'm too upset over Jessie dying to care much about Papa's letters right now, but maybe I'll feel better about them later. I feel better just to have changed the subject about it.

Sybil says I can call her anytime. Why would she say that except to be polite—especially when she's a beautiful young girl and I'm an old lady, but maybe it's because I let her tell me all about her problems with Alan the other day. When I get off the phone, I realize I was rude not to ask her how things were going with her and Alan. I should call Eleanor too since the funeral is over now. I did send her a sympathy card, but it would be polite to call her and see how she's doing.

But first, I need to think a bit more about Jessie. It'll be weird thinking about her as being dead now. Before, I always had hope that things would work out. Now that she's gone, it's going to take some getting used to.

I don't feel like I can do much of anything right now so I go lay down on the bed and take a nap to let it sink in. As I lay there, I decide Sybil is right—that Jessie and I had both thought about writing to each other to try to make things right between us is almost the same as if we had done so. We'd done it in our hearts and that's what matters I guess. I'm glad Sybil pointed that out to me. I wish I was smart enough to tell her what to do about Alan, but all I really think I can tell her is to dump him because she'll be better off, but somehow, I don't think she'd find that very helpful advice.

Chapter 23

I know I should tell Bel about Jessie being dead, and the sooner the better so she's not upset that I kept it from her. The next day when she asks if I want to go to Shopko with her I figure that's my opportunity. I'll tell her in the car on the way there, and then it won't become some big drawn out conversation because once we get to Shopko, she'll be busy looking around at stuff and not want to talk about it.

It's about a five-minute ride from Snowberry to Shopko so I don't waste any time. As soon as I'm in the car, I says, "So, I sent that letter to Jessie and I got a reply."

"You did?" she says, like she's just waiting before passing judgment.

"Yeah," I says. "But the reply came from her stepdaughter. Jessie died last winter—from breast cancer."

"Oh, I'm sorry to hear that, Lyla," she says.

And that's all she says. We've got the topic done being discussed before we've even reached the stop sign on the corner of Fifth and Washington.

By the time we get stuck at the stoplight on Seventh Street, I says, "Yeah, I'm not sure how I feel about it. I guess it's all for the best—better than if we'd just started fighting again, but it feels weird to know that my sister died and I didn't even sense it or anything."

The light changes. We drive past Harlow Park and come to the stoplight at Lincoln where we have to wait again. She's so quiet I don't know if she's mad or what so I says, "Aren't you going to say anything?"

"About what?" she asks as we start to go again.

"About my sister," I says.

She's still quiet as we go past Kentucky Fried Chicken and Burger King and McDonald's and then through the green light at McClellan and turn into Shopko's parking lot. She looks around for a spot until she finds one, and then finally, as she pulls the car into it, she says to me, "Lyla, I already told you everything I had to say when you told me you were going to write to her." She turns off the engine and adds, "Maybe I shouldn't have called your sister a bitch, but it's no different than the things you say about Charlie. We're best friends; we just want to look out for each other."

"Yeah," I says, undoing my seatbelt and opening the door. I get out of the car and before I can even slam the door shut, she says over the car roof, "I love you, Lyla. It doesn't matter what you do. I love you. I'm not temperamental like Jessie."

I slam my door shut and start walking toward the store.

"Aren't you going to say anything back?" she asks.

"Not in the Shopko parking lot where everyone can hear me," I says. "Come on. I need to use the bathroom."

Once we're inside, she says, "Meet me up front in an hour. I want to browse a little."

"Okay," I says, heading toward the bathroom, wishing I hadn't drank so much coffee this morning, but glad for an excuse to get away from her. I hate when she pulls that sappy shit.

Once I'm done in the bathroom, I find a cart, not that I plan to buy much, but it's handy to lean on if I get tired. I go in search of my hairspray. I also need pantyhose and something else I can't remember at the moment that I should have written down, but if I'm going to be here an hour, that's plenty of time for it to come back to me.

After going down about eight aisles, I finally find the one with the hairspray. I swear Shopko is managed by people on a campaign to keep senior citizens out of its store because every time I come, they've moved everything around again just to confuse us. And every time I come, the hairspray seems to have gone up another ten cents, but what can I do? Shopko beats Walmart, which is too big and too crowded and doesn't carry my brand of hairspray anyways, and Target is too expensive. I don't know why that Target store even opened. Marquette didn't need it. Why would we need a Target when Kmart went out of business after Walmart opened?

Once I find the hairspray, I take my time heading over to the women's clothing to find my pantyhose, wishing I could remember what that other thing is I need. I'm not in any hurry, and if it's something on this end of the store, I'd rather remember than have to walk back over here again so I go along slowly, just browsing, resting on the cart a little.

As I'm going by the music section, all the videotape boxes catch my eye. There's one for The Shirley Temple film collection. We used to watch her movies in the orphanage—they were a few years old by then mostly. But I remember the one time I went to the Delft Theatre to see Shirley Temple in *Heidi*—Mama took me and Jessie to see it; that was probably a year or so before she died, but after Papa had left. I remember that because Heidi was so upset to be taken away from her grandfather. She had to go live with that rich girl Clara, but she just wanted to go home to her grandpa, and I remember thinking how I felt that way—that I just wanted to go home and find Papa there.

Shirley Temple was so adorable, even though she was a bit too chubby in her face. My mother used to say how she should put my hair in curls like that because then I'd look just like Shirley Temple since I have one of those round, Finnish-looking faces. Mama said that on the way home from the movie that day, how I looked like Shirley Temple. I remember that because then Jessie asked, "Mama, do I look like any movie stars?" Mama didn't know what to say to her. She just hemmed for a minute and then said, "Well, there aren't many little girl movie stars." I could tell Jessie was hurt, so I said, "You look like Clara in the movie. Only, without the wheelchair."

"Really?" she said. "She was pretty."

"Yeah, she was," I said, "but I'd rather be Heidi and live in the mountains."

"I think it would be interesting to be in a wheelchair like that," Jessie replied.

"When we get home," I said, "we can play Heidi if you want."

"Okay," Jessie said.

I remember that was the start of many times when we played Heidi together. Jessie would sit in a chair and act like she couldn't walk, and I'd pull her up out of the chair and convince her she could, or we'd pretend we were at the Grandpa's house in the mountains and she couldn't walk and she'd almost fall over a cliff in her wheelchair and then I would dramatically rescue her, even if it was only the bed or the back porch she would really fall off.

We had so much fun playing that game, but the real reason I wanted to play it was because I liked to pretend I was Shirley Temple. I knew Mama didn't have much money to be taking us to the movies, but she promised she'd take us to see the next Shirley Temple movie that came out. But by the time *Rebecca of Sunnybrook Farm* came to the theatre, Mama was already dead. I saw that one later in the orphanage, and on TV too, but it wasn't the same as Mama taking me and Jessie to go see it.

Funny how Miss Bergmann ended up in a wheelchair with her multiple sclerosis when Jessie used to like to pretend she was in one.

I pick up the movie box and look at it. It's got *The Little Princess* on it, which I recognize, but not the other movies; they aren't her better known ones.

Not knowing what possesses me, I go up to the counter and ask the guy, "Do you have the movie of Shirley Temple in *Heidi*?"

He's just a kid—twenty maybe—probably doesn't even know who Shirley Temple is, but he looks in the computer and, after a minute, says, "No, but I can order it for you if you want."

"Okay," I says.

After another minute, he says, "It's only in pre-release now. The DVD won't come out until August 30th, but we can preorder it and call you when it comes in."

"Can't you get it as a tape?" I asks. "I only have a VCR."

"No, they don't make VHS anymore," he says. "You'll have to buy a DVD player."

"I just can't keep up with all that stuff," I says. "Things change too much. I don't want to learn how to use one of them things."

He just kind of stares at me, so I says, "Thanks anyways."

I push my cart down the aisle, figuring I still have to remember that other thing I need so I'll take the long way to the women's department through the hardware, housewares, and the toys.

I probably would have only watched *Heidi* once anyways, but somehow it's kind of cheered me up to think about it. I don't ever really think about me and Jessie playing together as kids. Her stepdaughter said Jessie used to talk about it with her—us playing in the snow and stuff. I remember all that now that I think about it, but it's funny I haven't thought about it in all these years. When I get home, I'll try to remember some other things we did as kids. We must have played together plenty; I mean, I was ten and she was twelve when I went to the orphanage, so really that's most of our childhood we spent together before Mama died.

I pass some duct tape in the hardware section and then remember it's Scotch tape I needed, and I can get that when I head back up front, so I go over to the women's section and find my pantyhose. Then on the way heading toward the Scotch tape, I see some hot chocolate on sale. It's summer so I don't know who wants to drink it—no wonder it's on sale—but I might as well stock up on it now because in another month or so it'll start to be getting chilly. You never know in the U.P. and well, I usually buy the generic brands, but this is Swiss Miss—the girl on the front kind of looks like Heidi, so I don't mind spending a little more—it's less than what I would have spent on the movie otherwise.

When I look at my watch, I see I've been in the store for fifty-five minutes, so I go grab my Scotch tape and then head for the checkout. I get so irritated with those new scan your own item scanners because now they only have one register open that's manned by a real person and I always have to wait. They may be saving money with those scan things, but they're increasing customer frustration doing it that way, not having people to wait on people—just costing people jobs. Hell, I remember when Bel worked as an elevator operator, like you needed someone to do a task as simple as that, and now they've got people doing everything themselves—these young people don't even blink over having to bag their own groceries or pump their own gas. Whatever happened to customer service? But no one at Shopko's going to listen to an old lady like me; they sure didn't listen the time I complained a few years back about how they keep moving everything around because the hairspray wasn't where it was last time I was here.

I don't see any sign of Bel so I go find a chair to sit in. Back in the '80s or so they used to have chairs by the door for the old people to sit in. That was before I was even really old, but they got rid of those too, so now I have to sit in the chairs by the pharmacy, but Bel will know that's where she can find me. I look at my watch and see it's already five minutes later than she said to meet her up front, but she's never on time. I'll just have to wait. She shouldn't be more than another five minutes anyways.

While I'm sitting there, I see a couple old folks I know from Snowberry come to pick up their prescriptions. They say hello to me but I know better than to think they'll stop to chat. I see a married couple from St. Peter's I see in church every week too, but they don't even look my way.

I look at my watch again and see another five minutes have passed, and still no sign of Bel. My stomach starts growling because it's getting close to lunchtime. I suppose Bel will want to stop somewhere to eat since we're out, though I'd just as soon not spend the money. I have to pinch my pennies some, being a senior citizen, and it's not like Jessie left me anything in her will—not that I ever expected she would. And I won't have anything to leave anyone either; she was seventy-nine when she died, so if that's any indication, I probably don't have much longer. Mama was only in her thirties when she died, and Papa must have been maybe in his early seventies I guess, so I've outlived both of them. I'll probably be lucky if I make it to seventy-nine.

What is taking Bel so long? She said to meet her in an hour, which would have been five minutes to twelve, and it's quarter after now.

To make a long story short, I sit and sit and sit and she still doesn't come. I start to wonder whether I should get up to go look for her, but if I do that, that's when she'll show up and wonder where I am. Finally, when 12:20 comes, I go up to the Customer Service desk, hoping Bel will show up while the girl waits on the two customers before me and before I can ask to have her paged. But no such luck.

"Can you page my friend?" I asks the girl when it's my turn in line. "She was supposed to meet me up here half an hour ago, but I imagine she's lost track of time, and at my age, I just don't have the energy to go chasing after her."

"Sure, what's her name?" the girl asks.

"Bel. Bel Greenway."

The girl picks up some sort of speaker thing and says, "Bel Greenway. Bel Greenway to the Customer Service Desk please. Your party is waiting for you."

"Thanks," I says. "I'll wait over in the chairs by the pharmacy if she comes, though she should know I'm there."

"Okay," the girl says.

So I make my way back to the chairs, looking behind me as I go, thinking Bel might have been nearby and heard the message, but no such luck. I'm at the chairs before I see her anywhere, and I sit down and wait for a while again.

After another ten minutes, I'm really getting worried. I think maybe she was in the bathroom and didn't hear the message. But if she's been in the bathroom that long, she must be really sick or something, and I'd see her come out since the bathrooms are right past the pharmacy. Images rise up in my mind of her laying there crumpled up on the floor in some stall, no one having noticed her all this time. I head back to the service counter and tell the girl, "Will you page her again, and if she comes, just tell her I went to the bathroom?"

The girl looks kind of irritated with me, but she pages Bel again as I head for the bathroom.

I go into the women's room but the place is empty. I have to go now anyways—it's been an hour and a half since I went and I did drink a lot of coffee this morning.

While I'm in the stall doing my business, I hear the bathroom door open and wonder whether that's her, but I can't see her shoes from where I am. I figure if it is her, she'll call out for me. I hear whoever it is go into a stall herself while I finish up and flush the toilet. Then I go out to wash my hands, and the other person comes out of her stall, some teenage girl—obviously not Bel.

I smile at the girl and wipe my hands, and then head back to the Customer Service desk.

"Did she show up?" I asks.

"No," says the girl, looking irritated since I interrupt her while she's helping a customer, but what does she expect? I'm starting to get really worried now.

"This isn't like her," I says. "Could someone go look for her for me?"

"We're short staffed today," the girl snaps at me.

"Look," I says, "I don't mean to be a bother, but she's an elderly lady and she's got health problems"—she doesn't really; not any more than any other seventy-five year old lady—high blood pressure and aches and pains is about it, but I need some excuse to argue my case—"so I'd really appreciate it if someone would look for her."

"Just a minute, sir," she tells the man at the counter that she's been waiting on.

"It's okay; I understand," he says. "In fact, I can go look for her while you figure out how to calculate my refund."

"Would you really?" I says to him. "That's kind of you. You're a lot younger than me or I wouldn't trouble you." He looks like he's maybe thirty so I'm sure he could run circles around this store compared to me.

"Sure, what does she look like?"

I give him Bel's description—height, weight, hair color, and the color of the blouse she had on, at least the one I think she had on.

"Thanks. I'll be sitting over here and waiting," I says, pointing toward the pharmacy chairs.

He heads off to the back wall of the store down the middle aisle, and two minutes later, I see him come back from another direction before I lose sight of him again.

I wait about fifteen minutes for him to come back, and finally he does, but he's shaking his head.

"No, no sign of her at all," he says.

"Well, where could she be?" I says. "I don't think she'd have gone home without me. But she has been getting a little forgetful. Is there a pay phone around here? I don't know why it's so hard to find one anymore."

"Here," he says, pulling out a cell phone.

"Oh, I don't know how to use one of those," I says.

"Well, what's her number? I'll call her for you."

I give him the number and tell him to ask for "Bel" and tell her that "Lyla is waiting for her at Shopko."

He dials, and then waits a minute before saying, "There's no answer and there's no answering machine picking up."

"No," I says. "She's old school like me. Doesn't want to bother with those newfangled things."

"Well, I don't know what to tell you," he says. "Do you need a ride home?"

"Oh, I couldn't impose," I says. "You've got other shopping to do."

"Well, I don't want to leave you stranded."

But right at that moment, I see Sybil walk into the store.

"Sybil!" I call to her. "Did Bel send you for me?"

"No-o-o...what do you mean?" she asks.

"She came with me to Shopko, but now we can't find her. We tried calling her at home in case she just forgot about me, but she's not answering her phone. I've been here nearly two hours and she's nowhere to be found."

"Did you look outside for her car?" Sybil asks.

"No, I never thought of that," I says.

"Good idea," says the young man who's been helping me.

"Sybil," I asks, "can you give me a ride home if Bel's car isn't out there?"

"Sure," she says.

"Good luck," says the man. "I hope you find her."

"Thanks," I says. "She probably just forgot about me." I turn to go with Sybil to the parking lot as he heads back to the service counter to have whatever his problem was resolved. I hope the cranky girl at the counter is helpful to him because he's a nice young man.

"Where did she park, Lyla?" Sybil asks me.

"In the back here," I says, going out the store's side door with Sybil following me.

I'm hopeful of seeing Bel's car, though if I do, it'll really make me wonder where in the store she's hiding, but once I get a few steps around the side of the building, I can see her car isn't there.

"She's gone," I tell Sybil, starting to feel despair.

"Are you sure this is where she parked?" Sybil asks.

"Yeah," I says. "I'm positive. But where would she go? Even if she forgot I was with her, she should have just gone home."

"Let's get you home," says Sybil, "and we'll see if she's there. Come on; my car's over here."

"Don't you have to do some shopping?" I asks her.

"I was just going to buy shampoo. No big deal. I can get it later," she says, already walking toward her car.

"It's not like her," I says.

"That's what worries me," says Sybil.

When she gets to her car, she unlocks it and we both get in.

"I hope nothing bad happened to her," says Sybil.

"Me too," I says. "She's never done anything like this before, though she does tend to be flaky at times."

Neither of us says anything for a couple minutes as we head back down Washington Street toward Snowberry. I'm getting really worried, and if it turns out Bel just forgot me, I'm going to be angry, though my being angry will be better than if something bad happened to her, but what could have happened? If she had a heart attack or a stroke or something, she wouldn't have driven off in her car. I suppose it's possible someone could have stolen her car and kidnapped her, but that's a big stretch. You just have to look at her to see she doesn't have any money, and she'd drive any kidnapper nuts in five minutes. If he did kidnap her, he'd probably drop her off on U.S. 41 before he got halfway to Negaunee.

"By the way, Lyla," Sybil says as we turn at Fifth Street to go down to Snowberry, "I found someone to translate your father's letters for you."

"Oh," I says. "Who?"

"*The Mining Journal* wants to do several stories about Finn Fest so I talked to Norma Juntunen yesterday—she's one of the organizers for it. Anyway, she speaks Finnish so I asked her if she'd be willing to translate the letters for us and she said she'd take a stab at it."

"Oh, well, does she charge a lot to do it?"

"She didn't say anything about charging you. I think she's just interested in the letters and wants to help out, but you could probably do something to thank her."

"There's Bel's car," I says as soon as the parking lot comes in sight. "I knew she must have come home without me, but I wonder why she's not answering her phone."

Sybil pulls the car up to the door.

"Do you want me to go in with you?" Sybil asks as I crawl out of the car with my Shopko bags.

"No, she'll just be embarrassed that you had to drive me home," I says. "But thanks for the ride. I hope I didn't mess up your day too much."

"No, it's okay," Sybil says.

"Since you're here," I says, "if you want to wait a few minutes, I'll go upstairs to get those letters and bring them down to you."

"Sure," she says. "But make sure Bel's okay first."

"Okay," I says, shutting the door.

I go inside and up the elevator. I'm not as fast as I used to be, and by the time I get up to my apartment and get the door unlocked and find the letters, I don't want to keep Sybil waiting, so I head downstairs, trusting Bel must be fine, and not wanting to get into an argument with her while Sybil is waiting.

When I get back outside, I go to the driver's window and give Sybil the letters.

"Did you talk to Bel?" she asks.

"Yeah, she's fine. She just forgot," I lie.

"Oh, that's good," she says. "I was getting really worried about her."

"Me too," I says. "Thanks for taking care of the letters, Sybil, and for listening to me yesterday."

"Any time, Lyla," she says.

I walk off, waving goodbye to her, and head back into the building.

I get to the elevator and wonder whether I should go back up to my apartment to call Bel or just go to her place. I have the key to her apartment, so I hit the button in the elevator for her floor and dig in my purse for the key.

When I get off the elevator, I don't see anyone in the hall that I can ask if they've seen Bel so I knock on her door and wait a minute. There's no answer, so I knock again and holler, "Bel, are you in there? It's Lyla."

Still no answer, so I stick the key in the door.

Just as I start to turn the knob, the door's practically jerked out of my hand from the other side.

"Couldn't you wait one minute?" she barks at me.

"What do you mean, wait? I waited nearly an hour for you."

"You did not. You just knocked a second ago."

"I mean, I waited an hour at Shopko for you to come get me so we could go. But obviously you drove home without me. Are you okay? I've been worried sick about you?"

I look her up and down but she looks just fine.

"Can I come in?" I says when she just keeps standing there, staring at me like I'm the one who's daffy.

"Yeah, sure," she says. "I'm just watching the soaps."

"Bel, why'd you leave me at Shopko?"

She goes and sits down on the couch and stares at the TV before she says, "What are you talking about? I've been sitting here all morning."

"You have not. We went to Shopko. You told me to meet you up front at the registers in an hour, which would have been five minutes to noon, but you never came. You obviously drove home without me."

"I don't know what you're talking about," she says, still staring at the TV without even looking in my direction.

"Bel, how can you deny it—are you okay? Did something happen and you had to leave early?"

"No, nothing happened. I never went to Shopko. You're losing it, Lyla," she says, half-laughing, but I know something is up because she won't look at me.

"Bel, I—"

But I don't know what to say. What is her problem?

"Did you eat lunch?" she asks.

"No, I didn't eat lunch. I've been at Shopko for the last two hours."

"Do you want a sandwich?" she asks.

"No, I—Bel, what is wrong with you? If you've been home all morning, why didn't you answer the phone? I called you and you wouldn't answer."

"Oh, I must have been in the bathroom. I thought I heard the phone ring, but at my age, I know better than to try running to answer it; people hang up before I get to it, and I'll just end up tripping or something. If someone wants me that bad, they can call me back."

Shaking my head, I finally says, "Bel, I don't know what's up with you."

"What do you mean?" she asks, turning to look at me for the first time since she sat down on the couch.

"Never mind," I says, shaking my head.

The music comes on for the end of *The Young and the Restless*. She reaches for the remote and turns off the TV.

"So, are you staying for lunch?"

"Sure," I says. I get up and go into the kitchen because just looking at her is starting to irritate me. I open the cupboard and get out the plates. The two of us have been in each other's cupboards for years and we have lunch or supper together almost every day except when there are things going on— which is hardly ever. I don't know what Bel's problem is or what she's trying to keep from me, but she acts perfectly normal as she gets up to pull things out of the refrigerator.

We don't say much while we make the sandwiches, and then we sit down at her table and I says, "I forgot to tell you when Jessie's stepdaughter wrote me back that she sent me two letters from my father."

"Uh huh," she says.

"They're in Finnish but Sybil says she knows someone who can translate them for me."

"When did you see Sybil?"

I almost says, "When she drove me home from Shopko," but instead I just says, "This morning."

"That's good," she says.

"My father wrote them when he went to Karelia. I never knew my mom got them."

"I kind of miss your dad," she says. "He's the closest I ever had to a father myself, and you're the closest I ever had to a sister, Lyla."

"Yeah," I says, wondering why she keeps bringing that up and wishing she'd get over it. Besides, what kind of sister forgets you at Shopko?

Chapter 24

I didn't expect to find out what my father's letters said for weeks, so I was surprised when just a few days later, Sybil called to ask whether she and Mrs. Juntunen could come over the next day to show me the translated letters. Of course, I said, "Yes." And of course, I told Bel they were coming, but since they wanted to come when *The Young and the Restless* was on, she didn't sound too interested, so I just told her I'd tell her about them later. I wasn't so sure I wanted her to be there anyways—ever since the Shopko incident, Bel hadn't seemed very friendly. I wondered if I'd made her angry or she was just embarrassed about having left me and acting angry at me when she was really just angry at herself, and if that was the case, it wasn't my problem. I knew she'd come around in time, just like she had when she got all mad about me writing to Jessie, and then later the same day, she wanted me to have supper with her. Things always work out between us.

I was surprised Mrs. Juntunen didn't just give Sybil the letters to bring to me, but Sybil said she was anxious to meet me. Mrs. Juntunen is some sort of Finnish expert I guess, so she thought the letters and my father's story were fascinating. Sybil told me that she and her husband had gone to Finland many times. She certainly looks Finnish when she shows up at my door with Sybil.

"What an exciting story," she says once we're sitting at my kitchen table and I've poured coffee for everyone. "A terrible and sad one, but exciting, and you obviously have a father to be proud of, both because he had the courage to go to Karelia, and that he was able to escape. I'd love to hear more about him."

"Well, I don't know that much really," I says.

"Lyla, when did your father go to Karelia?" Sybil asks.

"I was just little. Five at the most. I think it was in 1933 that he left."

"Yes," says Mrs. Juntunen. "That's the date on the letters."

"I don't know much else," I says. "Until these letters showed up, I didn't think my mother had ever heard from him, but I guess since I was a little girl, I didn't really know everything that was going on. Sybil probably told you," I says to Mrs. Juntunen, "that my father came back later, in '63, but I never really did understand what happened to him while he was there in Russia. His English wasn't very good by then after years of speaking Finnish and Russian. I knew a few Finnish words that came back to me from when I was a little girl, but I never learned no Russian. Someone told me the Finns were forbidden to speak Finnish; they could only speak Russian in Karelia, so I guess that's why he stuck in so many Russian words when he talked. It kind of embarrassed me when I'd take him places around town and he'd be babbling in Russian and I wouldn't know what he wanted. We talked to each other with our hands as much as anything else. He was just so broken when he came back that I didn't like to ask him many questions. I just tried to make him comfortable in his old age. I was afraid of asking him anything from fear it would upset him; he'd get these looks in his eyes just like he was a zombie or something, and sometimes he just seemed to flip out or be panic-stricken about some little thing. I just realized now as I'm talking that he probably had that trauma panic disorder the veterans get."

"Post-traumatic stress disorder," says Mrs. Juntunen. "Yes, I wouldn't doubt it."

"I remember this one time," I says, unable not to laugh, "it's not really funny, but this one time we saw this policeman when we were in the grocery store, and I thought my father was going to pee his pants from the look on his face. But then when I saw he was shaking, I understood how afraid he was. We left right away then and I brought him home and he went right to bed. He was crying and talking in Finn or Russian—he mixed them so much I couldn't even tell usually what language he was using. I just felt so bad for him that I didn't want to upset him so I just never really did know what he suffered over there, but I imagine it was something awful."

"Stalin did terrible things to the Finns in Karelia," says Mrs. Juntunen, "sending them to places like Siberia. Many of them were murdered. It's almost a miracle your father lived to tell about it."

"Well, he didn't really do that—not tell about it anyways," I says, "but I know what you mean."

"So, Lyla," says Sybil, "Mrs. Juntunen typed up translations of the letters for you so you can read them at your leisure."

"They're very sweet letters," Mrs. Juntunen says, pulling them out of an envelope. She unfolds the ones in my father's handwriting and hands them to me. "They're well worth treasuring," she says. "And here are the translations."

When she pushes the translated ones across the table to me, I don't know why, but I'm almost afraid to look at them. I can't even believe that I have them, or that Jessie's stepdaughter was kind enough to send them to me. They're like what they call a voice speaking from the grave. I mean, I never even thought my mother received any letters from him—we all thought he had abandoned us, or at least that's the impression I grew up with, but maybe I just didn't understand what was going on when I was a girl. I stare at the letters, looking at the words, but they're just words. I can't make no sense out of them.

"We don't want to trouble you, Lyla, if you want to read them in private," says Mrs. Juntunen.

"Oh, no, I want to know what they says. I just ain't sure I can bring myself to read them," I tell her. "I need more coffee. Anyone else?"

Sybil nods so I get up to refill her and my cups. I just need a minute to prepare myself.

"Lyla, would you like me to read them to you?" Mrs. Juntunen asks.

"That's a good idea," says Sybil.

"Yes," I says, coming back with the coffee cups, trying not to spill them.

As I sit back down at the table, Mrs. Juntunen puts on her reading glasses. She picks up the translation and starts reading in a clearer voice than I ever heard my father use:

New York, August 3, 1933

Dear Elizabeth, Jessie, and Lyla,
    I am writing to tell you I made it safely by train to New York City. I can't believe how much this country has changed since I made the journey across it as hardly more than a boy with my parents, or how my life has changed since then.

We came to the United States full of hope but life has been as hard here as it ever was back home and now without my parents alive, I look forward to going back to Finland where I will get to see relatives once in awhile I hope even though we will be some distance from them in Karelia.

It hurt me greatly to part from you. I love you all and cannot wait to be with you again. It will just be a short while that we are apart. I know you understand this journey is for the best. I know you wanted to come with me, but it is better that I go find work and make a home for you and then you follow so you can be comfortable when you arrive. I want only the best for my beautiful wife and precious girls. We will trust in the Lord that we will all be reunited again in just a few months.

I am in good company here having met several other of my countrymen who are preparing to make the journey. We depart on the ship tomorrow so I wanted to make sure to send you this letter so you know all is well. I will write again as soon as I reach Karelia.

My heart is aching for your kisses this night.

Love,
Your husband and papa

Mrs. Juntunen finishes the letter and then looks at me. I turn my eyes down to the table. So many thoughts are going through my head that I can't speak.

"Should I read the next one?" she asks, looking toward Sybil.

"Lyla?" Sybil asks.

I nod my head and then Mrs. Juntunen starts again.

August 10, 1933

My dear Elizabeth, Jessie, and Lyla,

I am still on the ship, but I will mail this letter to you as soon as I find a post office so you worry as little as possible. We are now entering the Baltic Sea and will be reaching

Helsinki tomorrow morning. We will stop there and then go on to Karelia. The journey has been a long but a safe one.

I wish you could have seen us when the boat left New York. We were all crazy with excitement and hope, waving red handkerchiefs and singing "Free Russia." I made friends with many of the men and their families that day. There are one or two cowards on board who feel they made a mistake and say when they get to Helsinki they will get on the first boat back to New York, but all the rest of us are ready to go on our adventure and glad to build a new life and a better world for ourselves and our children. We have already organized ourselves into work groups and await our assignments when we arrive.

We know things will not be perfect when we arrive, but that is why we are going—to help to build a better society, a communist one where everyone is equal and has his fair share and all work for the good of the country, not to get rich and think only of himself like in America. And here we will have a government that truly cares about the people. I cannot wait to become a citizen of this country and forget about the America that did not act like the friend it had promised my parents it would be.

I love you all and cannot wait to be reunited with you. I will probably have difficulty finding time to write once I arrive, but once I am settled, I will write again and send for you as soon as I have the money. I worry about how long that will be but hope it will be next spring if not sooner, and though I miss you all, working for our common good will make the time go by quickly until you are with me again.

Kisses to all my girls.

Love,
Heiki

When Mrs. Juntunen finishes reading, she sets the letter down and says, "That's where he went wrong. He must have become a Russian citizen and given up his American citizenship. Most of the Finns who were able to come back to the U.S. still had their U.S. passports, but once he gave that up, it was almost impossible to get out of Russia."

I don't say anything. I feel choked up and just keep hearing that he said, "Kisses to all my girls." It sounds silly since I'm not a little girl anymore, but...

"Lyla," says Mrs. Juntunen, "I think your father and your story is so fascinating. I understand you never had much to do with your Finnish roots, but I wish you would come to Finn Fest and learn more about them. You could even talk about the experience to people—give a lecture if you want. It's part of your heritage and who you are, after all, and you'd be surprised how many other people in Upper Michigan and Minnesota and Wisconsin are also descended from people who went to Karelia. I'm sure they'd love to hear how it affected you."

"I—I don't think I could do that," I says. "It's too emotional." I don't like to admit that, but it's all I can do not to start bawling in front of this lady; she's kind and all but she's a stranger.

"I understand," she says, "but please come to Finn Fest anyway. Being Finnish is part of your heritage and who you are, and I bet you'd find there are a lot of people there you'd have a lot in common with."

I never really thought much about having a heritage, and as for who I am, I've never really figured that out either. I kind of feel like I want to go to Finn Fest now, but I'm not sure.

"It's not really my thing, but I'll think about it," I tell her.

I've said 'I'll think about it' before and not meant it, but Bel started in on me about going to Finn Fest way back when the summer started, so maybe it wouldn't be such a bad idea. Maybe I could get Bel to go with me so I don't have to go alone.

"Thank you, Mrs. Juntunen," says Sybil. "We appreciate it so much. What do we owe you?"

"Oh no," she replies. "It was fun to do—these letters are quite a fascinating piece of history. I felt like I got paid just by getting to help."

"Thank you again," I says.

She gives me a sympathetic look that makes me uncomfortable. Then she gets up from her chair and says, "You're welcome, Lyla. I should get going, but I hope once this sinks in for you, that you will come to Finn Fest."

"Yes, it has to sink in," I says. "It's like a voice from beyond the grave. I'm just not sure how to take it all in, but I'm glad to know Papa loved us and wanted us with him."

"I'll stay for just a minute," Sybil half-whispers to Mrs. Juntunen as she goes out the door. I should get up and see her out, but I just can't find the strength to get up, and the door isn't far from my kitchen table anyways.

Once we hear the door close, Sybil says, "I should get going too."

But I don't want her to. I'm not feeling so well. I don't know if I should be sad that my father and my family never got to be together again like he wanted, or if I should just be angry at that bugger Stalin, or what I should feel.

"Are you okay, Lyla?" Sybil asks me when I don't reply.

And then I lose it. It ticks me off that I do, but I can't help myself. The sobs come up from my throat.

Sybil jumps up and grabs the Kleenex box next to my chair in the living room; then she comes back and hands it to me.

"I didn't want to cry," I bawl, "but—but I can't help it. I—if I had known all this before. If I had only known—if—I wonder how my life would have been different then? I always felt like he didn't want us; like no one wanted me. Even when he came home, he wasn't all that affectionate toward me, or at least, I wouldn't let him be. He patted me on the shoulder and stuff a couple times, but—why did it all have to happen like that?"

"I don't know," says Sybil.

"All I ever wanted was to be part of a family," I says, finding it hard to believe I'm saying all this but unable to stop myself. "Instead, I've been all alone all my life. I know I'm ornery and all, but I—"

It's too hard to say what I mean.

Sybil just sits there silently, waiting for me to quit crying. After a minute, she says, "You can't change the past, Lyla. I don't understand why, but it was all intended this way for some reason. It's like me with my parents dying when I was young. It's not that different from you losing your parents. God has a reason for it all."

"People say that and it sounds nice," I says, "but no one really knows that."

"Well," Sybil says, "I just basically think that we're put on this earth to learn something. I don't know what you've learned, but I'm sure it's something. You just have to think about what it is now. Or maybe you're not supposed to know the reason for it all, but just to have faith. I don't think we'll know until the next life."

"If there is one," I says.

"There is," says Sybil. "I know that for sure. Maybe someday I'll tell you how I know, but you're too upset and you'd think me nuts if I told you now. That story's for another time."

It sounds like she's going to tell me she's had one of those near-death experiences or something, and if that's the case, then I don't want to know. That's just too creepy for me.

I ball up all the Kleenexes I've used that are laying on the table and then get up to put them in the trash. "Thanks, Sybil," I says. "I feel better now that I got that out of my system."

"You're welcome," she says.

"I do feel better knowing my father cared enough to write those letters; that he didn't really abandon us when we were kids."

"That's good," says Sybil, standing up. "Well, I should get going."

"Okay. Thanks again," I says as she walks toward the door.

She sort of hesitates for a second and I'm afraid she's thinking about hugging me. I don't think I can deal with that right now, but instead, she says, "Lyla, you know, Mrs. Juntunen is right. Your dad's story is fascinating. I think it deserves to be heard."

"Oh, I couldn't get up in front of a group of people and tell it," I says.

"No, I understand that," she says, "but, well, maybe I could write it up as a story."

"What do you mean?" I asks.

"I mean, I could write an article about it for *The Mining Journal*."

I just stare at her for a moment. Me in *The Mining Journal*?

"I think people would find it really interesting," she says, "and we could run it the week of Finn Fest."

"Oh, but what would I have to do? I don't know any facts or dates or anything like that about what happened to my father."

"No, we'll make it a personal interest kind of story," says Sybil. "I'll just interview you and get a couple of quotes from you that I can include. We know enough to make a story out of it. It doesn't have to be that long, and we can put in a picture of you."

I can feel the smile spread across my face. Imagine my picture in *The Mining Journal*.

"Well," I says, trying to hold back my excitement. "If you think people will be interested."

"I do," says Sybil. "Well, I have to get going but I'll call you so we can set up a time for me to come and interview you. How would that be?" she asks.

"Okay," I says. "I'll have myself more pulled together by then."

I can't believe she wants to interview me for *The Mining Journal*. As soon as she's out the door, I feel so excited that I go wash my face in the bathroom sink; then I look at the clock and see *The Young and the Restless* will be over in a minute, so I head downstairs to tell Bel everything.

Chapter 25

When I talk to Bel, she doesn't think it's such a good idea to let Sybil interview me, but Sybil was so excited about the idea that I can't turn her down, so I tell her to go ahead with it. Then Bel wants to come over to listen to me being interviewed, but I tell her, "No." That's the last thing I need, I figure—to have her arguing with me, saying things like, "That's not the way it happened," when I tell Sybil about the orphanage or something.

So a few days later, Sybil comes over and sits down with me at the kitchen table to ask me all kinds of questions, mostly about things she already knows, but she says she has to get my words down "right" so she can quote me properly. She even brings along her tape recorder just to make sure she gets everything right. When we're done, I asks her when the article will be in the paper, and she says it should run a few days before Finn Fest starts, but it just depends on when *The Mining Journal* can fit it in. That means that from day to day, I have to wait to find out when I can see it. She also takes my photograph, and the following Wednesday at the meeting, she tells me it turned out really good, but honestly, how I'll look in the paper is what worries me the most.

About a week after Sybil interviews me, Bel and I call for a ride to The Pancake House and when Sybil picks us up, she tells me the story will be in that morning's *Mining Journal*.

Bel acts all uninterested about the article; she doesn't quite seem herself that morning, even before Sybil says I'll be in the newspaper. I know it's 4 a.m. when we go out, but usually I'm the groggy one until we get to the restaurant and have our coffee. I guess maybe Bel's more tired than she thinks since she acts all sleepy once we get to the restaurant; she can't even seem to find the words to tell the waitress what she wants to order so I have to order her waffles for her.

Then after we place our order, I can't hold it in any longer, so I says to her, "Wow, can you imagine me being in *The Mining Journal*. I'm so excited about this article."

But just to be all snotty, she says, "What article?"

She can be a bit ornery now and then, stubborn is more like it, but rarely snotty, so I don't understand what her problem is. She must be really jealous I guess.

It ticks me off that she can't share in my joy; it ticks me off so much that I don't speak to her again all through the meal, and when Sybil comes to pick us back up, I talk to her in the car rather than Bel.

Once we're back at Snowberry and Sybil drives off, I tell Bel, "I think you better go back to bed; call me when you wake up and make sure you get up on the right side this time."

She just walks over to the elevator without saying anything. I follow her and we ride up and then she gets off on her floor.

"The hell with her," I mutter when the door closes and I go up to my own apartment. The paperboy will leave *The Mining Journal* on my doorstep when it comes, but it's not even six o'clock yet. It'll be hours before it arrives. So I go inside to wait.

All morning I'm nervous about it. Every time I hear someone out in the hall, I go look through the peephole to see if it's the paperboy. When lunchtime comes, Bel doesn't call to invite me over, which is just fine because the paper usually comes just after lunch and I want to be able to read it without her snotty remarks.

Finally, I decide to make lunch, and just as I sit down to eat my sandwich, I hear another noise in the hall. I wipe off my hands and get up to check, but I can't see anyone through the peephole. I open up the door, and sure enough, there's the paper on my doorstep.

The paperboy has it upside down so I can't see where it says *The Mining Journal* or read the headlines, but I quickly bend over to pick it up and bring it inside before someone sees me. What if the story's not in the paper after all, or what if it is and I look awful or sound stupid—though I can't imagine Sybil would let that happen—and everyone in Snowberry will be talking about it in a few minutes?

I don't even dare to flip over the paper until I've got the door shut and locked, and then I carry it over to my chair and sit down and put it on my lap so I still can't see the front of it, and I put up my footrest, and then I breathe a deep breath and says, "Lyla, prepare yourself for good or bad" and turn it over, and there I am, staring up at myself from the front page of *The Mining Journal*. I'm too excited to read every word as I kind of just skim through it the first time and see that it all sounds good before I go back and read it again, this time able to concentrate.

Woman Receives Father's 1933 Letters from Finland

by SYBIL SHELLEY, Journal Staff Writer

When Lyla Hopewell's father left Marquette in 1933 to return to Karelia, Finland, five-year-old Hopewell, now 77, and her older sister expected he would soon send for them and their mother. But Hopewell's father, Heiki Toivonen, never returned and for decades they did not know what had happened to him.

During the Great Depression, many Finnish immigrants and their children were returning to Finland, hoping to find a better life there. But like many others, Heiki Toivonen ended up trapped in Soviet Russia, unable to return or contact his family for thirty years.

Then in 1963, he showed up on Hopewell's doorstep in Marquette, completely unexpected. He spent the final decade of his life being cared for by his daughter. "He was very much a broken man by then," Hopewell said. "The war and his treatment at the hands of the Soviets left him with a broken spirit, his health was bad, and he had forgotten most of the English he knew. We communicated in broken English and the few Finnish words I knew for the rest of his life."

Toivonen was not alone. Many Finns returned to Finland in the 1930s—and many Americans resented them for doing so, calling them Socialists. When no word was heard from Toivonen, Hopewell's mother, who was not of

Finnish ancestry, was embarrassed by the situation, and fearing ostracism and discrimination, changed her and her daughters' names back to her maiden name of Hopewell.

What Hopewell never expected was that thirty years after her father's death, and nearly seventy after her mother's, she found out her father had contacted the family once he reached Europe. Recently, Hopewell's sister, Jessie Goldsworthy of Kalamazoo, died and Goldsworthy's stepdaughter discovered letters written by Hopewell's father and mailed them to Hopewell.

"I had no idea these letters existed," said Hopewell. "They were proof that my father didn't abandon us. He had written us from Finland just before the war broke out, telling us of his arrival." Hopewell's mother had received the letters but never shared them with her youngest daughter.

"When my mother died, my sister and I were separated. My sister was adopted while I was sent to the orphanage. My sister somehow managed to keep the letters, but I never knew they existed." Following their childhood separation, Hopewell and her sister had little communication over the years.

"What is remarkable to me," said Hopewell, "is that these letters show a father I barely remember, a hopeful, happy one. He believed he was doing what was best for his family by going to Russia. These letters now make it feel almost like I have a little bit of him back again through his words."

It was not easy to read the words, however. The letters had been written in Finnish since Hopewell's father had never learned to write in English. Hopewell had to find someone who could translate them. Through a friend, she connected with Norma Juntunen, one of the organizers of Finn Fest 2005. "Mrs. Juntunen was thrilled with the story once she started to read the letters. She's been a great resource to me," said Hopewell.

"Lyla Hopewell's father's story is an example of Finnish *sisu*—the Finnish word for guts or courage," said Juntunen.

"It shows that we Finnish can surmount the greatest odds in the face of adversity." Juntunen notes the irony of Hopewell's name also—"Toivonen is the Finnish name for hope," said Juntunen.

Hope seems to be the story of Hopewell's life. "I was always stubborn," said Hopewell, "to the point that many people thought me difficult, but now I realize that stubbornness was really Finnish *sisu*. For most of my life, I've had little connection with my Finnish roots. Now I hope my story and that of my parents makes people realize how even in difficult times you can persevere."

When I finish reading the article, I'm kind of stunned. I don't remember saying half of that, but I was so nervous that day that I don't remember what I said. Sybil promised not to misquote me, and she said I had done a terrific job, that I had sounded like I gave interviews every day, but I thought she said that just because she was trying not to make me feel bad. Now I realize I did do a good job—especially when it came to what I said about having *sisu* and hope.

But Sybil never told me she would interview Mrs. Juntunen too or what Mrs. Juntunen said. I had no idea that the name Toivonen meant "Hope." I like it though; how funny that both my parents' last names had hope in them. "Hope well." That's what I should do. I should have hope because as bad as I've thought my life was at times, it really hasn't been all that bad. I mean, I'm still kickin' at seventy-seven and that counts for a lot.

I set the paper down and sit there for a minute staring out the window and feeling so wonderfully happy and grateful and like my father's long journey and suffering now has some sort of meaning. I don't think I've ever felt so good in my entire life. Somehow I just feel relieved, like the little ache always in my stomach isn't there, like the heartburn in my chest is gone. It sounds kind of gross, but I feel light, like I do in the morning after I have my coffee and go to the bathroom and before I eat breakfast, when nothing seems to ache in me for about half an hour if I'm lucky.

It's kind of a scary feeling to feel this good, but I do. I'm somehow just glowing inside. I'm in *The Mining Journal*! I'm famous, at least for today, and people will find the story interesting. I feel like crying, but I also feeling like jumping up and down. I feel so good that I almost push myself out of my chair to do cartwheels across the room—there's not much room in my little place to do cartwheels, but I imagine doing them anyways—and I don't even break a hip or throw out my back while doing them.

And then the phone rings—and though in the back of my mind I think "that damn phone," the front of my mind doesn't even seem to mind as I says, "Hello."

"Well, congratulations, Lyla Toivonen," says the female voice on the other end. For a second, I'm confused, wondering who it is—who knows my last name is Toivonen?

"I loved the story in the paper. Did you see it yet? Sybil did a wonderful job."

"Yes, I just read it," I says. "It's very well written, don't you think?"

"Beautifully written," she says. "I'm so glad I had a part in it. Everyone here for the Finn Fest committee is talking about it, and although I've already invited you to come, they insisted I call and invite you again to make sure you come. They all want to talk to you. You're a celebrity now."

By now I realize I'm talking to Norma Juntunen.

"It's kind of weird," I admit. "I'm not used to being famous."

"Oh, just enjoy it," she says. "Come tomorrow, Lyla, please. We would love to have you."

"Oh, I—"

"It's time you meet your Finnish kin. You have a whole family of Finns who can't wait to get to know you."

I don't know why, but to hear that I have a whole Finnish family— something in those words, well, they make me start to tear up. It's just the way she says it, "You have a whole family of Finns who can't wait to get to know you." That's what she said. Is it true? It can't be, but she doesn't let up when I try to get out of going, though I feel that I really want to go—it's just, I don't know what it's like to have a family—it's a scary thought.

"Well, I have a lot going on this week," I start to say.

"Well, just come Saturday then. That'll be the best day. Come in the morning to the registration booth. I'll be there and introduce you to everyone. There'll be so much to see and do, and if nothing else, you have to be part of the world's largest sauna."

I can't help but laugh over that comment. "I've never been in a sauna," I admit. "I don't know if I'll like all that sweating."

"Lyla, you don't know what you're missing. It's time you come and learn how to have fun the Finnish way."

All I can think is that I never learned how to have fun any way, but instead I says, "I normally do my laundry on Saturday, so I—"

"I won't take 'No' for an answer, Lyla," she says. "I think you're just shy, but from what Sybil told me, you also have a lot of 'sisu' like all the rest of us Finns. It's time you meet your people."

"What time is Finn Fest?" I asks, stalling so I don't have to say, "Yes."

"It starts at 8:30," she says. "Come to the University Center at NMU at 8:30—that's where the registration is, and I'll point you in the right direction from there."

"Well, I'll have to see if I can find a ride. I—"

"I'll send my husband to pick you up," she says. I don't like the sound of that. I don't know him. It'll just be awkward.

"My friend Bel will drive me I'm sure. Maybe I'll ask her to tag along," I says, trying to sound enthusiastic, and I realize I do feel enthusiastic.

"Well, if she can't, you call and let me know." She gives me her phone number and then says, "If you don't come, I'll have Sybil hound you and I'll send out a search party to find you."

"Okay," I laugh; no one's ever wanted me to do something so badly before that I can't help liking all the attention. "Okay, you talked me into it."

"Great, see you Saturday," Mrs. Juntunen says. *"On suuri päivä."*

"What?" I says.

"That's Finnish for 'Have a great day'," says Mrs. Juntunen.

"Oh," I says. "Same to you. Goodbye."

"Näkemiin."

I figure that must mean "Goodbye," in Finnish, but I don't try to say it. I just hang up the phone.

Then, before I talk myself out of it, I dial Bel to see if she'll give me a ride on Saturday morning. I even invite her to go with me, and she says she will.

"Finn Fest, here I come!" I think and I almost feel like doing something crazy like those cartwheels I was thinking about.

Chapter 26

As soon as I wake up on Saturday morning, I call Bel to remind her about going to Finn Fest; after all, she's been a bit forgetful lately.

"Will you be ready to go at quarter after eight?" I asks her. "Mrs. Juntunen said to come to the University Center at 8:30."

"Yeah, I'll bring you there," she says, "but I ain't going. I'll just pick you up later."

For a moment, I have flashbacks of the last time she was supposed to bring me home and how that didn't really work out, but I repress them and says, "What do you mean you're not going?"

"It's just not really my thing," she says. "You know, I'm not Finnish."

"So? It's still interesting, and I thought you really wanted to go. Remember, way back at the beginning of summer you asked me if I was going and told me I should since I'm Finnish. You sounded excited about it back then."

"Well, that was months ago, Lyla. Things have changed since then."

"Changed? What's changed?"

She's silent long enough to make me think I lost the phone connection, but then she says, "Never mind…Nothing. I just don't feel like going."

"But Bel, we always do things together and it's important to me." I realize I sound whiny—it ticks me off when I sound that way.

"I know, Lyla," she sighs into the phone. "I'm sorry. I'm just—well, I didn't want to worry you, but I don't feel very good."

"Are you sick?" I asks. Bel's never sick. She has an iron constitution just like me—comes from growing up in the orphanage where you had to learn to be tough.

"I—well, I don't know. I'm just kind of down. I think it's just the heat. It's been such a hot summer, you know."

"Yeah, but we'll be at the University Center and over at the Dome later. That's where a lot of the events are, so it'll all be inside where it's air conditioned—except the sauna I guess."

"I'm sorry, Lyla. I don't think I'll have much fun feeling this way, and I don't want you to worry about me. I'll drop you off and I can come later to pick you up."

"Well," I says slowly, "if that's what you want, I *guess* it's okay." My tone, though, says it's not okay. I expect her to argue with me, but she doesn't. Still, I know she's not sick. I don't know what the hell her problem is, but I know being sick isn't it. "I'll meet you downstairs in forty-five minutes," I says and hang up the phone.

Here I've been looking forward to going to Finn Fest all week, even if I've been pretending I'm not that interested in going. When you've spent your life being disappointed, you learn not to get too excited about things until they happen, and once again, I've been proven right for feeling that way since the only friend I had to go with has to pull this crap on me. Well, of course, there's Mrs. Juntunen—she'll be there, and she said she'd introduce me to some people, but we don't really know each other that well. There's no reason why Bel can't go with me. We always go everywhere together. Cripes, how many times have I gone places with her when I haven't wanted to, like to her doctor's appointments and her stupid Wednesday women's meetings—though, if I hadn't gone to those, I never would have written that letter to Jessie or gotten back Papa's letters, and then I wouldn't be going to Finn Fest at all, so I won't complain about those meetings, but the point is that I only started going to them because she wanted me to, and now she can't even go with me to Finn Fest when she was the one who first suggested it way back when summer started, the day Bill went to the hospital. What the hell is her problem? She's just been getting weirder and weirder lately, and that's saying a lot considering she was weird from the beginning.

As I eat breakfast, I keep grumbling to myself until I'm about ready to call Bel up and tell her not even to bother taking me—I can call Sybil and ask her to drive me. I figure, though, that Bel will just get mad if I do that, so I don't, but the thought of Sybil cheers me up a little; I know she would tell me not to let Bel ruin my day. I've been excited about going to Finn Fest, and there aren't too many things that excite me at my age, so I should just go and enjoy myself. "I just need another cup of coffee and then I won't feel so cranky," I tell myself. "Who said I need Bel to have fun? I did just fine all those years when we didn't see each other. Why am I making such a big deal out of this anyways?"

The old Lyla would have let Bel ruin her day—hell, something less important would have irritated me and ruined my day, like cloudy weather— but that was the old Lyla. I'm going to have a good time today. After all, people want to meet me. I'm a celebrity, and like Mrs. Juntunen said, I've finally found my *sisu*.

When I meet Bel down in the lobby, I don't say much to her other than to ask her if she feels okay enough to drive, which she says she does. I don't know what her problem is. She looks kind of depressed or something, but whatever kind of crap she wants to pull today to get my attention, I'm not letting her wreck my day. When she drops me off at the University Center, I says, "Are you sure you don't want to stay just for a little while?" but she says, "No, just call me when you're ready to leave, about 3:30 so you can go to church I imagine."

"No, I'm going to go to Mass tomorrow," I tell her. "I figured I'd be too tired to go this afternoon, and maybe I'll stay later. *The Mining Journal* said there'd be events going on all day, so if I'm having fun, I don't want to rush myself."

She rolls her eyes, like she's saying, "You won't have fun," but I just ignore her.

"All right, thanks," I tell her and then get out of the car and walk into the building.

After a few seconds, I spot the registration table, and there's Mrs. Juntunen with a big smile and a "Hello, Lyla, I'm so glad you made it." I know she's a nurse or something and her husband's a professor, which means I'm out of her class so her friendliness just makes me feel awkward. Why should she be glad to see me? Already, I feel out of place and I'm regretting that I came.

"I have a nametag for you," she says. "I hope you don't mind that I put 'Toivonen' down as your last name. We're all Finnish today."

"No, that's fine," I says, rather pleased actually. I'm now "Lyla Toivonen"— it has quite the ring to it, though I'll keep using Hopewell for my official last name, but somehow thinking of myself as a Toivonen makes me want to talk with just a bit of a Finnish accent. It makes me feel important—or, maybe that's not the word, but like I know who I am, or at least that I'm someone special—something like that.

"I found someone to accompany you, Lyla, over to Jamrich Hall where some of the cultural activities are, and then I'll be over at the *tori* market at the Dome so I'll see you there later. Make sure you come over there for two o'clock because Sybil told me she's coming, and she has a surprise for you."

"Okay," I says, wondering what I've gotten myself into. I've never liked surprises.

"Here's your day pass," says Mrs. Juntunen, "and this gentleman here is your tour guide." An older gentleman, maybe in his late sixties—I guess that's not older since he must be younger than me—comes up. Mrs. Juntunen introduces him as "Paul Lehtimaki." "Paul is from Minnesota and here just for Finn Fest. He's going over to watch the movie *Letters from Karelia* at Jamrich, and I thought you'd like to see it too."

"Oh," I says, not having known what I would be doing today and afraid I'll fall asleep trying to watch a movie.

"Oh, you'll like it," Mrs. Juntunen adds. "It's about a man who went to Karelia and about some of his letters that were found years later; your father's story actually kind of reminds me of it."

"Oh, okay," I says to be polite.

"My grandpa went to Karelia," says Paul, taking my arm and leading me down the hall; I think he's being too familiar by putting his hand on my arm, so I gently pull it away after a few seconds, but I do go along with him.

"Thanks, Norma!" I says as we leave, trying to get in the spirit and sound cheery.

"Enjoy yourself," she replies. "I'll see you later over at the Dome."

"He came back though after a couple of years, back to Minnesota," Paul tells me.

"Oh," I says. It takes a minute for me to realize what he's talking about—his grandpa I guess.

"Did your father come back?" he asks. "I guess he must have or you wouldn't be here."

"He did," I says, "but not for about thirty years. I didn't go with him. He went by himself and left my mom and sister and me back home. We didn't know what had happened to him all those years."

"Interesting," he says. "Do you want to drive or should we walk? It's over at Jamrich Hall."

"Is that very far?" I asks. I've lived in Marquette all my life, but I've never done more than drive through the university campus—except that one semester I went to a secretarial school, and there's hardly a building on campus the same now as way back then.

"No, five minutes tops," he says.

I wouldn't have said I'd walk if I'd known how far it really is—about three or four blocks. I just don't know where anything is on this campus, and I don't want to get all sweaty walking, but it's actually a pretty perfect summer day. And I guess it's a good thing I've got Paul walking with me or I wouldn't know where to go among all these college buildings. Not that he shuts up once all the while we walk over there; he keeps telling me his grandpa's life story, but at least it keeps me from having to tell all of my father's story, something I'm not comfortable doing, despite all the publicity in the paper. I assume, since Paul's from Minnesota and my father's story was in the paper just before Finn Fest started, that Paul probably wasn't in town yet to read it.

When we get to Jamrich, the movie is just starting. It's being shown in some sort of big lecture hall so I have to be careful trying to find my way down the stairs, and when I'm doing that, of course, is when they decide to turn out the lights, but I manage to find a seat, and Paul sits down next to me. I wonder whether he plans to follow me all day because I'm already sick of listening to him. I hope Mrs. Juntunen doesn't think she's doing me any favors having him latch onto me. I'm not looking for him to be my boyfriend or something.

Fortunately, the movie starts and I can forget about him. I'm not too thrilled at first about the movie because there's subtitles since the main guy is talking in Russian, but I can read them pretty good so it's not too bad.

It turns out I can see why Mrs. Juntunen suggested I watch this movie. The guy speaking Russian is named Alfred, and he's the son of a man named Aate Pitkänen, a Finn living in Canada who decided to go to Karelia about the same time my father did, only Aate never came back to North America, so his son, Alfred, grew up in Russia. Aate wrote some letters home to Canada that never got delivered because he ended up in a prison and the prison warden kept the letters. Again, kind of like my father, except my father's letters got delivered—my sister just never told me about them. The prison warden's son found Aate's letters about the year 2000 and mailed them to the relatives in Canada, and then the Russian man came to Canada to visit his family.

The movie's pretty interesting actually, despite the subtitles. And then as it goes on, I find it makes me kind of emotional. Aate apparently ended up seeing his friends and neighbors taken away in the night by the Communists; they all ended up being shot most likely. I wonder how many people my father knew that were taken away or killed. And then there was the war—I didn't even know Finland was involved in World War II much. I didn't follow the war very well then, just knew the basics—that the Germans, Italians, and Japs were the bad guys and we were the good guys. Poor Finland, though, caught in the middle. Russia was our ally, but it was Finland's enemy so you can't blame Finland for siding with Germany. What a mess it all was, and Aate got caught up in the middle of it until he had to work as a spy for the Russians against the Finns, and the Finns captured him and put him in a prison and later killed him.

It's all a true story, which I guess is what makes me the most interested. And despite everything, it has a happy ending. Happy because Aate's son, Alfred, actually got to reunite with his father's family in Canada. We're both the children of Karelian immigrants—me and Alfred—but Alfred got a happier ending because he had relatives to reunite with—I never had that. Of course, I was reunited with my father in the end, and I was happy for that, happy to be there for him, but he was so broken and confused, and he used to talk in his sleep—I can just imagine how afraid he must have been, living in Russia for thirty years, having to look over his shoulder to wonder what would happen to him. He must have seen his friends taken, probably knew people who were killed, and that he finally escaped and got to Finland and then back to America—well, the whole idea of it is just amazing to me. I don't know how he survived it all. I would have died from all that fear. He told me, I can remember it so vividly, "I come home for my Lyla and Jessie." We, his children, were what kept him alive all those years, but it was like once he came home to find me, it was, well, too much for him to enjoy. I think he put all his energy into surviving and trying to get home, and once he accomplished that, he didn't really have the strength left to start life over in Upper Michigan. I wonder what he expected to find when he came back because so much had changed by then. I mean, he didn't even know my mother had died five years after he left, or whether Jessie and I had stayed in Marquette, or if we'd be married, or he'd have grandchildren, or any of that stuff, but he must have wondered about it. And then he gets home to find just me, all by myself, and that was it. It must have been a disappointment to him.

I must have been a disappointment to him, but after watching this movie, he's not a disappointment to me. At the end of the movie, Alfred says how his father's dream of a better world was betrayed; so was my father's. Obviously, communism didn't work out, but I can understand how Alfred feels, proud, real proud of his father that he was brave enough to go in the first place to try to find a better world; he didn't find it, but he tried. That was something. Something that makes me proud. I couldn't have been that brave. What have I done by comparison that is brave like that?

I've been real lucky in my life. They don't talk about what Alfred's life was like growing up in the Soviet Union—he was a doctor or scientist or something they said, but I can't imagine it was fun. He must have grown up in fear too. I've known fear, but I've know frustration more than anything else. A few times I've feared about where my next meal would come from, but I always managed. I never had much, but I never had to fear for my life like those people under the Soviets had to do.

And then at the worst possible time, the lights in the auditorium come on as I feel the tears start down my face because I realize just how lucky I've been. Lucky that Papa was smart enough not to take us all with him, but to go first and make things ready for us to come later. I can't even imagine what my life would have been like if I had gone over to Karelia with him when I was just a little girl of five. I'd have probably ended up marrying some Russian man, or maybe working on a farm or in the woods, or being shot to death as a Finnish peasant when Stalin turned into a monster and started purging out the Finns. What a horrible life it would have been. Say what you want about Sister Euphrasia, but she sure wasn't no Stalin, and ornery as she was, she made sure all us orphans were fed and clothed and taught and that we had work when we got old enough to leave. It was a big job and must have been wearing on her. Thank you, Sister Euphrasia for being there when no one else was. Thank you, Papa, for caring enough to try to make things comfortable for us before you sent for us, even if it didn't work out. Thank you, God, that it didn't work out that I went to Russia. I've been lucky. I feel grateful. For the first time in my life, I realize how good I've had it. Cleaning people's houses is better than living on a farm or out in the middle of nowhere in Karelia. Having to put up with ornery rich women whose houses I've cleaned is better than seeing your neighbors disappear. And having your father come home, a broken old man you have to take care of, is better than having no father at all.

Everyone in the room starts discussing the movie. I try to listen, but I'm just too overcome by it all, and when Paul, still sitting next to me, starts telling everyone about his grandpa's experiences in Karelia, I have to get up and go to the bathroom because I'm afraid everyone looking at him will be looking at me, and I don't want people to see that I've been crying, and I sure don't want to share anything about how the movie made me feel. They already read about Papa in the newspaper. They don't need to hear anything more about it.

I kind of hide out in the bathroom for a while. I got up early this morning to get ready and didn't get a chance to go to the bathroom like I usually do, so I take my time, figuring the discussion will last a while. I also don't really want to go back and talk to Paul any more or have him start asking me why I was crying. I don't know why Mrs. Juntunen hooked me up with him.

After I finish my business and dry my eyes and look in the mirror to make sure it doesn't look like I've been crying, I go back and find the lecture hall is pretty much emptied out. Now I feel bad, not because I don't see Paul anywhere, but because I wish I had heard more of what everyone said about the movie. In fact, I wouldn't mind watching it again. Alfred didn't even really know where his father was buried, just some grave out in the woods, while I can go visit my father's grave at Park Cemetery anytime I want, and he got to be buried next to Mama. I'm grateful for that. I haven't gone out there to visit them since I put flowers on the grave on Memorial Day. I should go check on it soon.

Papa's been gone over thirty years now. For thirty years he was missing, and then I had him home for about eleven, and now thirty more years he's been gone—thirty-one to be exact. Actually, I think it was thirty-one he was missing too. All these years later, seventy-two since he left me as a little girl to go to Karelia, and there's still pain and hurt.

I know Papa loved me. I know he didn't mean to leave me. I know when he came back he was happy to be with me, but it still hurts after all this time. I know there will always be some hurt, but I also know I had his love. I've spent so much of my life feeling unloved, but I haven't been. I've just felt that way I guess.

I wander back through the halls until I see people going into another room where some children are playing Finnish games. I don't know what else to do. I feel a bit out of energy after the crying, so I just sit down and watch them play for a while. It's more like a dance than a game. I find out later it's called Tikkuristi. I don't really understand it, but I guess they have to dance around these two sticks laid on the ground and try not to step on them, and if you do step on them, you lose. The kids are pretty good at it actually. I doubt I would last as long as them, but then, I couldn't dance that fast either.

I almost feel like I'm in another country listening to this Finnish music they're playing. None of this is familiar to me because I wasn't raised with it, but it's interesting to think about "What if?" What if Papa hadn't gone to Karelia? Would I have grown up knowing all these things about being Finnish? How would my life have been different?

"There you are," I hear before I see him, but I know right away it's Paul. He's found me. He comes and sits down next to me and says, "Are you all right?"

"Yeah, I'm okay," I says, and though I think better of it, I says, "I just got really sad watching the movie. It made me realize what my father must have gone through during all the years he lived in Karelia."

"I know what you mean," says Paul. "My grandpa said that..."

And there he goes again, talking about himself. He obviously has no interest in talking *to* me, just *at* me.

After about ten minutes of my nodding my head and saying, "Uh huh," to him, a man and woman come up to talk to him and Paul introduces me to them as his cousins. They're heading over to the Superior Dome and want to know if he wants to go with them. When he asks me, I says, "Sure," since I don't know how else I'll get over there, and I agreed to see Mrs. Juntunen over there later. Paul's cousins seem nicer than him so I don't mind going over with them if it gives me a chance to talk to someone other than him. It's almost noon and they say they're getting hungry and ask if I want to go over to the Dome to eat with them. They say there's all kinds of American and Finnish foods to try over there. "I'm dying for some *juustoa*," says Brad, Paul's cousin, while his wife, Joan, says she's craving some more *lettuja*.

"I know what *juustoa* is—Finnish cheese—but I never heard of that other thing," I says.

Joan says, "You must not be Finnish then, Lyla."

"I am," I tell her, "but I barely knew my dad and none of his family. I'm trying to reconnect with my Finnish roots."

"Well, we'll help you then," she says. "*Lettuja* are Finnish pancakes, but with fruit in them, more like crepes."

"I love pancakes," I says. "And I haven't had anything like crepes in years, not since the Bavarian Inn in Marquette closed down. I've always wished The Pancake House here had them."

"Well, you won't be disappointed then," says Brad.

Paul says his car is at the University Center, so he'll meet us over at the Superior Dome. Brad and Joan are parked right outside Jamrich Hall so they offer me a ride, and Paul rides over with us to the University Center so he can get his car and then join us at the Dome later.

Once we're rid of Paul, Brad and Joan ask me if I'm having a good time. I says, "Yeah, though it's all a little strange to me."

And before I know it, I find myself telling them all of Papa's story, which I couldn't have gotten a word in about when talking to Paul. They tell me my father's story is remarkable, and Joan says, "Of course, Paul told you our grandpa went to Karelia too."

"Oh, yes, he told me all about it," I says, hoping she isn't going to tell it all to me again. She doesn't, which is a great relief to me. I find I actually like Brad and Joan quite a bit. They say they live up in Virginia, Minnesota, and I tell them that's around where my father grew up before he came to Marquette, so they tell me all about the Finnish population in Northern Minnesota, which I find pretty interesting since it's a big mining area like here in the U.P. and sounds similar.

We have a hard time finding parking at the Dome because the *tori*—the Finnish market—is being held inside, and it being Saturday, even the non-Finlanders are here to check out what Finn Fest has to offer. "It's the biggest celebration Marquette's ever had," I tell Brad when he's amazed by all the cars, and I feel quite proud of Marquette when they tell me how it's a lot bigger than Virginia, Minnesota.

Eventually, we find a parking spot. Joan wants to go inside the Dome to avoid the heat, but the *lettuja* is sold in a tent outside the Dome, so Brad insists we head over there first, and I'm in agreement with him.

The *lettuja* are more like crepes than pancakes, but all that matters to me is that they're delicious. I haven't had such good pancakes since the Bavarian Inn closed. I order one filled with raspberry, and it's so good I have to go back and try the blueberry ones. Brad and Joan both enjoy theirs, and we just stand around eating them and oohing and aahing over the taste while we act like advertisements for them since quite a line forms after we get ours. While we're eating, Paul shows back up. We asks him if he wants to have some *lettuja*, but he says, "No, I'm diabetic and that fruit filling won't be good for me." Well, I guess a person can't help it if he's diabetic, but he could have tried one so long as he's careful with his blood sugar. I think he's just a party pooper. "I do want to get some *juustoa*," he says, "and I was wondering whether they sold blood bread anywhere."

"Blood bread?" I says. "That sounds awful."

"It is," Joan grimaces. "My grandmother used to make it and I could never stand it."

"Where's the blood from?" I asks.

"Oh, they butcher a cow or a pig or chicken to eat I suppose and then use a little of the blood for flavoring in the bread," says Brad. "I guess those farm wives had to bake with whatever they had."

"Paul, I doubt they'll have any blood bread here," Joan says. "I can't imagine it's considered sanitary or healthy. The FDA would probably shut down anyone who tried to sell that today."

"Sometimes I wonder whether it's a good thing I'm Finnish," I says, "when we make things like blood bread."

Paul looks annoyed with me, but that's okay—I said it partly to annoy him.

"When the Finns first came to this country," says Brad, "lots of people thought we were odd; in fact, the Americans thought we were devil worshippers or witches because of our sauna practices, so it's probably a good thing our blood bread recipes didn't get out."

"Let's go inside," says Paul, looking irritated by our conversation.

"You go ahead," I says. "We'll catch up. I want another *lettuja*."

I know better than to have one, but I have no intention of spending the rest of my day with Paul. I plan to avoid him, or hopefully, shake him once we're inside.

Brad agrees to go inside with Paul, while Joan decides to stay outside with me and have another *lettuja*.

"I hear that Norma Juntunen asked Paul to show you around," says Joan, "but I know he can be irritating. I hope you don't mind him too much."

"Oh no," I says as I taste another raspberry *lettuja*, "but my friends are going to meet me here at the *tori*, so I probably won't spend any more time with him."

"I see," says Joan. "Well, then, Lyla, we might as well part ways here and I'll keep him steered in the other direction."

"Oh, I don't mean to be rude," I says.

"No, I understand. Believe me; I understand. He's Brad's cousin, and I actually went out on one date with him before I started dating Brad. In fact, Brad and I met through him, but one date with Paul was more than enough for me. It's all I can do to listen to him at family gatherings."

I'm just about to take another bite when I laugh and raspberry drips from my mouth onto my blouse.

"Oh darn," I says.

Joan has a water bottle with her, so she wets a napkin and gives it to me to clean myself off. I'm not happy about going around with a stain on my blouse, but I don't have much choice now. I would just go home except that Mrs. Juntunen told me Sybil planned to come to the *tori* later. I guess she's reporting for *The Mining Journal* so she'll be too busy to spend time with me, but maybe she can give me a ride home. These Finnish pancakes are good, and I did enjoy the movie, but what do I know about being Finnish?

"Thanks for being understanding," I says to Joan after I get as much of the stain out as I can and we find a trash can for our napkins.

"You're welcome. It's been a pleasure to meet you, Lyla," she says, and she gives me her hand to shake.

"It's mutual," I says. "Enjoy the rest of Finn Fest." And then we both go into the Dome. Within a few seconds, we've gone in opposite directions. Later, for a minute, I spot Paul at the booth where the university is selling Finnish food. If he weren't there, I might have gone over out of curiosity just to see if they had any of that blood bread for sale, not that I'd waste my money on it, but instead, I head in the opposite direction.

I feel a bit overwhelmed by the *tori* at first because there are so many vendors, and an old lady like me with a little apartment doesn't need to be buying stuff she doesn't need or have room for, but I enjoy myself just looking around, expecting eventually I'll bump into Sybil or Mrs. Juntunen. There are bands performing—everything from polka music to traditional Finnish songs, though half the time, I can't tell the difference. It all kind of blurs together as they sing in Finnish, but I find I kind of like it too. It's sort of like being at a wedding where all they play are polkas. I haven't been to a wedding in years, but I feel the festivity of it all.

The *tori* is filled with Scandinavian type clothes and costumes, and needlework and crafts, even dishtowels and rugs and blankets all with Scandinavian colors and such on them. And there are books about Finland and tapes of Finnish music, and all kinds of interesting wooden items carved and painted in white and blue, the colors of the Finnish flag, as well as Scandinavian designs.

I've never been one for crafts, but I have to admit I'm amazed by all of the talented people in the room.

Finally, I see Mrs. Juntunen at some sort of Finn Fest information booth. I don't want to bother her, but she doesn't seem too busy, and I figure I should be polite and talk to her since she was so happy to have me come.

"Hello, Lyla," she says when I come up to her booth. "Are you enjoying yourself?"

"Yes," I says. "That movie was really touching. It really made me realize what my father must have gone through."

I'm being polite, and I did like the movie, but I won't tell her Paul was a bore. I don't know why she hooked me up with him except that she wanted to make sure I stayed today.

"Good. I'm so glad that you've come," she says. "I heard there were a few other people here whose relatives went to Karelia so I figured you might find someone to talk with."

"Yes, there were several there for the movie discussion," I says, neglecting to mention how I ran to the bathroom during the discussion. "I just had my fill of *lettuja* too," I says to change the subject, "and I can't believe everything here in the Dome."

"Have you bought anything at the *tori*?"

"No, I saw a lot of nice stuff, but I'm just not sure who I would give any of it to. It's enough for me just to see everything and feel a part of it all."

"There you are, Lyla," I hear, and turning around, I see Sybil just a few feet away.

"Hello," Mrs. Juntunen and I says almost at the same second.

"Lyla, I brought you a little present," says Sybil, handing me a gift-wrapped box.

"A present?" I says, surprised, as she pushes it in my direction. "What for?"

"We'll just say it's a thank you present for letting me interview you."

"You didn't have to do that," I says.

"Why don't you open it, Lyla?" says Mrs. Juntunen, smiling, like she's in on the joke.

I look back and forth from them and wonder what it could be. It's a long box, like the kind you'd get at Penney's with a shirt or blouse in it, and when I shake it, I fear it's clothes. I don't want to have to wear a sweatshirt that says "Finn Fest 2005" or something that'll make me itch, but I'll feel guilty not wearing whatever it is because it's a gift.

Once I have the box open, I find it's about the last thing I ever would have expected—a blue bathing suit with white trim along the edges.

"Finnish flag colors," says Mrs. Juntunen.

"Bel told me what size you wear," Sybil says. "It's so you can join me in the world's largest sauna."

"Oh, but I haven't worn a bathing suit in fifty years," I reply.

"Well, you just have to, Lyla. I already bought the tickets for both of us. And I have towels for us here in my bag."

"Oh, well..." I says, strangely feeling like I do want to join in the world's largest sauna, but I'm too...

"Go ahead, Lyla," says Mrs. Juntunen. "We Finns don't have issues with showing a little skin. Remember, you're supposed to have fun today."

"Lyla, you only have to stay long enough for us to break the record for how many people can fit in the sauna. That's all," Sybil adds.

"Well, okay," I laugh, "but only because you already bought the tickets."

"Come on; let's go get changed," Sybil says, smiling and leading me toward the ladies' room.

I follow Sybil into the bathroom at the Dome and then into a stall. The bathing suit actually fits quite well and I like that it's Finnish colors. I have to admit I'm kind of excited about the sauna. I've never been in one before, not that I like sweating, but it's kind of like, well, kind of like a party—what am I saying? It is like a party—I may not be the life of it, but I am having fun.

"How are you coming along, Lyla?" Sybil asks me as she opens her stall.

"Good," I says, wiggling into the suit and making sure it fits well, which it surprisingly does.

"Just bring your clothes out," Sybil says. "We'll put them in my bag and leave them with Norma. I tried to talk her into the sauna too, but I couldn't."

I'm surprised since I imagine I'm more of a party pooper than Mrs. Juntunen, but I'm glad someone will watch our stuff.

When I come out of the stall, Sybil says, "Wow, hot stuff! Even if we weren't going into a sauna, you'd make the men sweat!"

"Stop it," I says, afraid to look at myself in the bathroom mirror but unable to stop myself, and though I'm far from having the figure I used to have, I have to admit I look pretty good in a bathing suit for a seventy-seven year old woman. I bet I could pass for sixty-nine. At least I don't have those disgusting varicose veins like so many old people do, people who should know better than to wear a bathing suit—ick!

Sybil has a skirt on around her waist so she says she'll go back into the Dome's main arena to bring our bag to Norma while I wait in the hall for her. She's only gone for a few minutes, but it's long enough for an older man, not much younger than me, to say, "Hey, sweetie. Are you coming to the sauna?"

"Yes," I says. "I'm just waiting for my friend."

"I'll see you there then," he says, and he actually winks at me. As he walks away, I realize he's quite attractive. He's got shorts and a sleeveless shirt on and he looks pretty good in it for a man his age, not all shriveled up like most older men. I figure it's quite a compliment that a man that good-looking, and younger than me too, would even look at me.

Sybil comes back and says, "Lyla, why are you smiling? You have quite the grin on your face."

"Oh, no reason," I says. "Just excited about being part of the sauna I guess."

"Me too," says Sybil. "Let's go get in line. I have our tickets."

"I wish you'd let me pay for my ticket," I says, feeling she's already done more than enough for me.

"No," she says. "It's my treat."

"But why?" I asks.

"Because, Lyla, you gave me a great story to write about in *The Mining Journal*. My editor was super complimentary about it, so it's the least I can do to treat you to a little fun. He even says he's going to nominate me for a Good News Award for it. Now come on before we're late."

We head back outside, past the pancake tent, to join the crowd in front of the entrance to the world's biggest sauna—I'm hoping once I'm inside I can sweat off enough weight that I can go back for more *lettuja*.

Carl Pellonpaa is at the entrance and he's getting the crowd worked up. I always wonder who actually watches his *Finland Calling* show on TV, but I guess there are plenty in this crowd who do. Next to him is Miss Michigan, who's here because she has Finnish blood in her and is from the town of Rock, right here in the U.P. I wonder if she's the only Yooper who ever made it as Miss Michigan. I can see why she did though—she sure is pretty.

"No one's allowed in the sauna who can't pronounce it!" Carl Pellonpaa exclaims. "Let's make sure we all know how to say it properly. I would like to hear this word on the count of three from everybody here," he shouts to the crowd, and then the count begins. "Okay, one, two, three: soooooooooow-na!"

I hate to admit that I would have said it wrong myself, but everyone is there to remind us it's not pronounced like *son-na* but as *sow-na*. The one Finnish word that has become common around America, and yet everyone mispronounces it. I'm glad Carl Pellonpaa straightens it out for us—the Finns deserve a little recognition.

Happy that we all pronounced it correctly, Carl decides we can all enter, and we do. The sauna is a giant tent, and within a few minutes, it's packed with people. The benches along the sides quickly fill up, and since Sybil and I are at the end of the line, we can't find anywhere to sit once we get inside. After a minute of walking down the narrow pathway between the benches, I hear a man say, "There's a spot here."

"There are two of us though," says Sybil to the man, and then I look at him and realize it's the good-looking guy who had called me cutie back in the hallway at the Dome.

"There's room on my lap for your older sister," he says to Sybil.

She turns around, laughing, and looks at me.

"Why not?" I says, then tell Sybil, "You said I have to live a little, didn't you?"

I don't know what comes over me then. I don't think Sybil does either. She laughs as I plop myself down on the hunk's lap while he just roars. For a few seconds, we think it's all a good joke, but then I go to get up and realize he has his arms wrapped around me so I can't.

I wonder whether I should protest, but I like the feel of those strong arms, and then as Sybil sits down next to us, he says, "Can't go now. St. Urho's coming."

And there's St. Urho himself, patron saint of Finland, walking through the tent in his shorts and a purple cape and a Viking hat with grasshoppers perched on the horns.

"No grasshoppers allowed in the sauna," he calls as he walks through, waving the Finnish flag.

Everyone starts clapping for St. Urho, whose saint's day is the day before St. Patrick's—and my birthday no less. Funny, I always knew that, but it never sunk in how funny that I'm born on the Finnish saint's day. The legend says that St. Urho drove the grasshoppers out of Finland—lots of people says the story's made up, but it's fun anyways—I may not know much about being Finnish, but I always do wear my purple on my birthday for St. Urho.

"Well, you know you're in good company when a saint joins you," says Sybil.

"Yeah," says the man whose lap I'm sitting on. "I think I'm in very good company," and he gives me a little squeeze around the waist. "I'm Mike Koski, by the way," he says.

"Hi, Mike. I'm Lyla," I says.

"Lyla what?"

"Oh, I left my nametag with my clothes," I says. "I'm Lyla Toivonen."

"Well, that Miss Michigan doesn't have a thing on you, Lyla Toivonen," he says.

"Maybe not, but I bet she's not sweating as much," I says, the heat now starting to hit me. Later, I'd hear that it got up to 165 degrees in that sauna, though several said they were disappointed that it hadn't been warmer.

"Sweating's good for you," says Mike. "Gets all the toxins out. Especially good for people our age."

"What do you mean 'our age'?" I asks.

"You know, retirees," he says. "I just retired this year, sixty-five and a half."

"Oh, you're just a baby," I says, instantly realizing I may have said something really stupid—he may not want me sitting on his lap if he finds out I'm a dozen years older than him.

"I don't mind a woman a few years older than me. I've always been partial to older women, actually," he says.

"That's good," I says, but then to turn the conversation away from my age, I says, "This is my friend Sybil."

"Hello, I'm Mike Koski," he says, shaking Sybil's hand.

"Glad to meet you, Mike," says Sybil. "I talked Lyla into coming. She didn't want to, but I told her, 'How many chances will you have to be in the world's largest sauna?'"

"Exactly," Mike says. "Are you having a good time, Lyla?" He makes me nervous how he still has his strong arms around my waist—nervous, but happy. I feel like a girl of forty again.

"I'm having the time of my life," I says, and I feel such a high that I almost think I'm going to faint, but I don't think it's the steam. I think it's the hunk that's got me all bothered—who'd have thunk a hunk could do that to me at my age. I almost laugh out loud at the thought and the rhyme I just made up.

Then the woman next to me decides to do just that—faint, so her husband leads her out, and I says once she's gone, "Looks like now there's a seat for me."

"What's wrong with the one you got?" Mike asks in protest as I get up.

Not knowing what's come over me, I says, "Thanks, sweetie," and go to give him a kiss on the cheek, being naughty and thinking I can get away with it. But before I can get near his cheek, he smacks me hard and long on the lips and then says, "It's been my pleasure."

I almost feel like giggling, and I just know the silly grin on my face isn't going to wear away for the rest of the night.

"Lyla, I never saw this side of you before," says Sybil.

"Well, I guess you don't know me very well then," I says, trying to sound more bold than I really am. It must be the heat getting to my brain.

"This is going to make another good story for *The Mining Journal*," she kids.

"Don't you dare," I laugh, and then I explain to Mike, "Sybil's a newspaper reporter."

"Mike," Sybil asks him, "would you like to give me a quote for my story about the World's Largest Sauna?"

"Sure," he says. "You can tell all the readers in Marquette that I saw the prettiest Finnish woman here that I've ever seen."

I think I might be blushing, but hopefully, he'll think I'm just hot from the steam.

"How about you, Lyla?" Sybil asks. "Do you want to give me a quote?"

"Oh, just make up something that sounds good," I tell her.

"Okay," she smiles.

Carl Pellonpaa gets everyone singing now, though the sweat is starting to run in my eyes and I have to keep wiping it away, but I join in with everyone else, not knowing the Finnish words, but going along with the chorus as much as I can to a song about who's going to get the sauna warm.

"It's already too warm for me," says Sybil. "I'm afraid I don't have any Finn in me. All English and German as far as I know."

"Oh well, it's like St. Patrick's Day," says Mike. "Everyone's Finnish at Finn Fest."

Sybil just smiles at him.

The song gets going pretty well with many rollicking choruses followed by a few other Finnish songs I don't know. Mike sings boldly along with everyone—you don't meet too many men who sing, but he's full of energy, and I appreciate that about him. I've always felt an attraction to people who aren't afraid to be the center of attention or have a good time. I guess because I've always been so shy, and to have such a man pay attention to me, well, it's been so long since anyone really paid attention to me, and now this year, John and Wendy treated me like an honored guest, and Sybil apparently wants to be my friend, though I can't figure out why, and Mrs. Juntunen invited me here, and then there was the article in the newspaper, and now this hunk of a Finn is flirting with me—I don't expect it will lead to anything, but—I just wish Bel had come to see it all. She was always better at flirting than me, but then, why would I want her to steal my thunder?

Finally, we all feel too hot to stay in any longer so we walk out of the sauna together.

"I wouldn't have minded if it were another twenty degrees or so warmer," Mike says, "but it's hard to heat up a big place like that."

"I hope we broke the record," I says.

"I need to get home soon," Sybil says. "I have to work later and I should write up my story for the paper tomorrow first. Lyla, do you want me to give you a ride home?"

"Home? Aren't you staying for the banquet?" Mike asks me.

"Oh, I don't know," I says.

"It'll be the nicest part of the whole day," he says, "and I don't have a dance partner."

"Oh, I haven't danced in—"

"Well," Sybil interrupts me, "why don't I take you home to change and shower, Lyla, and then I can drop you back off on my way to work?"

"Yes, why don't you do that?" says Mike, wiping off his big strong sweaty arms with a towel. "I'll go back to my hotel and dress for dinner too and meet you back here."

"Okay," I says. "What time is the dinner?"

"Social hour starts at 5:30, the banquet at 6:30, and the dances at 8," he says.

"I can get you back here by 5:30 or 6 at the latest," says Sybil.

"Thanks, Sybil. I would really appreciate that," I says.

"Great. I'll see you in an hour or two back here," says Mike.

"Where should I meet you?" I asks him.

"Oh, just come on into the Dome and I'll find you; don't you worry," he says, and he gives my cheek a pinch, then asks, "Are you sure you're older than me? You've got such baby smooth skin."

"Oh my God," I says, not knowing what else to say except, "You're such a flirt."

"And you like it," he smiles.

Sybil laughs and pulls me away.

"Goodbye, Mike," I call over my shoulder, and I giggle as Sybil squeezes my arm.

"Oh, I'm so glad you and Mrs. Juntunen talked me into coming today," I says once we find Sybil's car. "And for the bathing suit and everything."

"Oh, our clothes. I'll run back in and get them," Sybil says. "I'll turn the air on in the car for you and then be right back."

"Okay," I says, glad to sit down and be alone for a couple minutes. I feel overwhelmed and over-stimulated by everything that's happened today. I'll have so much to think about for days to come. I don't know what Bel's problem was that she wouldn't come. She's always been so much more outgoing than me. How lucky am I to have a hunk of a Finnish man like that interested in me? Of course, he'll go home to Duluth and I'll never see him again, but it can't hurt any to have dinner and dance with him. I wonder whether I should call Bel to tell her I'm coming back later. "The heck with her," I decide. Then I see Mike walking across the parking lot, and I open up my car window and shout, "Hey, Mike!"

"Hey, beautiful," he says, coming over.

"Sybil went in to get our clothes and then we're running home, but I'm wondering whether you would drive me home later after the dance since it might be too late for me to call my friend."

"Good idea since we might just dance all night," he says. "I'll be happy to."

"Great. Thanks. Here comes Sybil."

"Okay, I'll see you later," he says, and walks off, giving me a nice view of his broad back and his surprisingly tight—

"Norma said she's happy to hear you've been having such a good time," says Sybil, stopping my thoughts from going where they shouldn't.

"That's good," I says. "I just asked Mike if he'll give me a ride home later so I don't have to call you or Bel."

"Okay," says Sybil. "I guess after the banquet tonight, you won't be wanting to go out for pancakes."

"No, not tonight," I says, suddenly realizing that maybe Mike thought my asking him to drive me home was an invitation for something more. Would younger men like him jump to that conclusion? I guess even men my age might. I hope he didn't think that. What will I do if he does?

"Did you have some of those Finnish pancakes?" Sybil asks as she maneuvers the car through the parking lot.

"Oh, they were terrific," I says. "You should tell the owner of The Pancake House to add them to the menu."

Sybil drops me off at Snowberry and tells me she'll be back in an hour for me. Once I get upstairs, I take a shower and then fuss my way through my closet to find something to wear. I only have nice dresses I'd wear to church, and I'm not sure they would be appropriate for dancing, but I have an old pleated skirt that would twirl, and I figure I need the loosest dress possible if I'm going to dance. And then once I'm dressed, I still have about fifteen minutes. I figure I better sit down and rest for a few minutes, and then once I'm plopped into my chair, I think again that I should call Bel, so I do, but the phone just rings and she never answers.

"What the hell?" I think. "She couldn't go to Finn Fest with me, but she can be out running around town."

I wish she had an answering machine because it's a pain in the ass to write her a note, but I do:

> Hi Bel,
>
>   I came home to change my clothes after getting all sweaty in the World's Biggest Sauna. I'm heading back for the banquet and dance and won't be home until late so I found someone else to give me a ride. He said he wouldn't mind. Talk to you tomorrow.
>
> Lyla

Ha! I think. What is she going to think about that message? She'll be shocked just by the sauna part, and I made a point of saying "He" twice. I bet she'll have lots of questions in the morning.

But I do wonder where she is. After what happened at Shopko, I'm a little worried about her, but also annoyed that she wouldn't go with me this morning. I only have a few minutes before Sybil comes, so I take the note and go down to Bel's apartment. I knock on the door but there's no answer, so I manage to wedge the note in the door so she'll see it and then I head downstairs to meet Sybil.

In the car on the way back, Sybil tells me what a great event Finn Fest has turned out to be and how excited she is to write up the story about the World's Largest Sauna.

"Have a wonderful time," she tells me when she drops me back off at the Dome.

"Oh, I will," I says. "Thanks again for everything, Sybil."

"You're welcome. I'm glad you're having such a good time."

"So am I," I laugh, getting out of the car, but then stooping down and putting my head back in the car once I'm on the street so I can still talk to her. "How do I look?"

"Stunning," she says. "Like a blonde bombshell."

"I was never that," I says, "but thanks anyways."

"Have a good time," she says again, and then I shut the door and go inside to find my date.

I don't know where all this confidence is coming from, but I feel like I've been on a high all week, ever since the article in *The Mining Journal* about me and Papa. I wish he had lived to see it, and Mama and Jessie too—it just seems like all the trouble we went through was somehow worth it now; it makes me feel—what's that fancy word they use on Oprah—validated—I think that's it. It kind of feels like all the worrying has been lifted now, and here I am at Finn Fest with all my extended Finnish relatives that I could have been involved with all these years if Papa hadn't gone away, or if I'd just sought out these experiences years ago. Who knew that at seventy-seven, I would suddenly feel again the energy I had as a young woman, and that at least for a little while I would feel that my burdens were lifted, and I actually could have fun.

All these thoughts run through my mind as I walk into the Dome, but once I'm inside, I just feel nervous. The room is full of people talking in groups and having drinks, but I don't see Mike anywhere, or even Mrs. Juntunen or anyone else I know, except—yes, that Paul that bored me all morning. Gosh, I hope Mike shows up before I get stuck talking to Paul again, and then I see Paul is with his cousins, and for just a second, I think that Joan sees me, and I'm about to turn and hide in the crowd from them when I'm startled by an arm wrapping around my waist and a voice in my ear saying, "I can't wait until the dancing starts so I can hold you in my arms."

I turn around and there Mike is, and if I thought he looked good with his clothes off, I was in no way prepared for how handsome he looks in a black suit and tie. Like he could be Brad Pitt's father, with his golden Finnish hair that has hardly a touch of gray in it.

"Hello, gorgeous," he says.

"You're vain," I says, "talking to yourself like that 'cause the only gorgeous one here is you."

"Now I know why I like you so much," he says, stepping to my side to put his arm around my waist and give me a kiss on the cheek. I hope I'm not blushing again because I sure feel like I am. What's happened that suddenly I have a man paying so much attention to me after all of these years?

"You smell good," he says.

"Oh, that's the strawberry shampoo I use," I says.

"No, I don't think it is," he replies.

"Oh, stop it," I says, half-irritated and half-giggling. I'm not sure why I feel irritated except that it scares me a little to think he might really like me, so it's easier to be irritated because I'm not used to feeling happy.

"Do you want a drink?" he asks.

"No, I never touch the stuff," I says.

"Oh?"

"No, I've had some alcoholic friends and it's upset me too much to watch them destroy their lives."

"Okay. Well, I don't drink much myself, but I just thought I'd ask."

He's all cool about it. Not upset with me for saying what I feared sounded judgmental.

Mrs. Juntunen spots me and walks over so I introduce her to Mike, who tells her, "It's a real honor to meet you. Thanks for helping to organize this. I've gone to several Finn Fests in the past, but I never had such a good time before, especially since I met this beautiful woman."

He nods his head in my direction so she'll know who he means.

"Well, I'm glad you found her. She's quite the celebrity in Marquette."

"Why's that?" he asks.

And Mrs. Juntunen goes ahead and tells him all about my father's letters from Karelia.

"That's an amazing story," he tells me when she's done. "Especially that your father was able to escape and come back after all those years."

"Yes," I says. "I still miss him. I didn't realize until today when I watched that movie just how much he must have suffered."

"It's a beautiful movie," Mrs. Juntunen agrees. But then her husband comes over and says she's needed for something, and then I'm left alone with the man I love—how crazy does that sound! How can I love Mike? I've only known him for three hours. Is love at first sight possible? No, not at my age. I know to be careful around men, but it's nice to be flattered a little.

"Should we go find a seat?" I asks.

"I don't suppose you'll sit on my lap again?" he laughs.

"No," I says, half-frowning so he doesn't get too fresh. "It's too hard to eat that way."

We find a table with a couple ladies at it that I know from Snowberry; I don't want to sit there because they've hardly ever said two words to me, but I don't want to make a scene in front of Mike. At first, they don't look too happy when they see me, but then they see Mike and they smile and Minnie says, "Hello, Lyla. We didn't know you would be here. That was quite the story about you and your father in the paper the other day." And then Gloria says, "I still have my newspaper if you want me to cut the piece out so you can have an extra copy." I don't know what possesses me, but I says, "Sure, I would like that," thinking how agreeing to that would give me future contact with them. I know they're part of a knitting group. I never could knit very good, but maybe this will be my in. I could actually start to feel like part of the Snowberry community then for the first time.

Mike makes small talk with them. He's very polite and friendly and he even comments on Minnie's fancy collar that she tatted. He's so attentive to them that I think it a bit strange, and I'm not sure if I have reason to be jealous or he's just been putting on an act. I finally decide it must be an act because I know darn well both Minnie and Gloria are on the wrong side of eighty.

Soon it's time for dinner and more people start sitting down at the table.

A man sits down on the other side of Mike. I made sure I was at the end of the table so I wouldn't have to talk to someone I didn't know, but Mike has no problem talking to people. The man next to him is from Northern Wisconsin, and they get all caught up talking about fishing on Lake Superior at different places. It's kind of a boring topic in my opinion, but I enjoy listening to Mike. He has just a bit of a Minnesota accent—the kind those awful movies *Fargo* and *Escanaba in Da Moonlight* tried to exaggerate to make all of us look like idiots up here in the North. I don't know a single Yooper who wasn't offended by those films. I only saw them because Bel wanted to go, and neither of us liked them.

But Mike has just a touch of that kind of Minnesota/Yooper accent, and I think it's really sexy on him.

"How long have you known Mike?" Minnie asks me when he leaves for a minute to get me something to drink.

"Oh, we only just met here at Finn Fest," I says.

"Well, you're lucky," she says. "He's good-looking. A real keeper."

Gloria asks, "Do you plan to keep him, Lyla?"

"Oh, I don't know. I don't know him that well," I says.

"Well," Gloria says, "you can give him my number if you decide not to keep him."

Like Hell I will! Those two old biddies haven't hardly ever said a word to me or Bel all the years we've lived at Snowberry. Though it would serve them right if I could rag on them about going out with my leftover boyfriends.

The dinner conversation is lacking, at least in my opinion, but the meal makes up for it. The meat is real tender, and I finally get a piece of *juustoa*, that strange Finnish cheese. I can't say I like it too much, though; I remember that Mama used to make it for Papa when I was a girl, but I don't remember what it tasted like then—I probably didn't even like the look of it then and refused to eat it.

I take a minute to look out across the crowd. The Dome is filled, hundreds of people eating away, even a few talking in Finnish, but most in English. It's quite a sight, and again, I'm reminded how we're all one big Finnish family really. It's like we're all children at Mother Finland's dinner table or something.

"Are you both Finnish, Gloria and Minnie?" I asks, suddenly wondering what they're doing here.

"Of course," says Minnie. "My maiden name was Hautamaki."

"And my maiden name was Lehto," says Gloria, "and I married a Seppanen."

"And I married a Nurmela," says Minnie.

"You don't get much more Finnish than that," says Gloria.

"No, I guess not," I says.

"I don't have any dramatic story like you, though, Lyla," says Gloria. "Not about a father who escaped from Karelia. That must have been something."

"Yes, tell us what it was like for your father," Minnie says.

And I do, what little bit I can since I don't know much about it, but I feel real big talking about it, important, like I have something special, something over them. It's kind of a mean feeling to have, but they deserve it. Still, as they keep asking me questions, I can tell their interest is genuine, so eventually, I soften a bit toward them.

When the meal is almost over, I asks them, "Are you staying for the dancing?"

Gloria smirks and Minnie laughs out loud.

"No, I'm too old to dance," says Minnie.

Gloria says, "I have a bum knee, and besides, I don't have anyone to dance with."

"We can't all just hook up with a hunk at Finn Fest," says Gloria, actually winking at me. For just a second, I take that to sound like I'm a cheap tramp, but then I realize they're just joking and maybe a little jealous of me too—which I like.

Finally, Mike stops talking with his fishing buddy and asks me, "Are you ready for some dessert?"

"No, I have to watch my figure," I tell him.

"Babe, you just leave the watching of that figure to me," he replies.

"He's such a flirt," Gloria laughs.

Mike smiles real big at Gloria until she says, "Whoo, I better go, Lyla, before he breaks my heart."

"It was nice to see you, Lyla," says Minnie. "You should come and play bridge with us some time."

"That would be nice," I says, kicking myself under the table. I never learned bridge and don't have any desire to learn now, but it doesn't hurt to be friendly. Maybe they'll still invite me to their knitting circle.

"Well, are you ready to go?" Mike asks. "The dances are over at the University Center."

"Sure," I says. "I need to get up and move anyways after all that food."

It takes us a while to get out of the Dome. So many people are wandering around, and Mike is real friendly so he stops to talk to several of them; later in the car, he tells me he met them all this week at Finn Fest.

"How long have you been in Marquette?" I asks him.

"Since Tuesday," he says.

"And it took you until today to pick up a date for the banquet?"

"Oh, I could have asked lots of girls and had them say, 'Yes,'" he says, "but I didn't see any I really wanted until I saw you."

I can't help but notice that he said, "wanted." Why didn't he say "liked" or "thought was pretty" or something? What does "wanted" mean? "Wanted to go out with" or "wanted" in another way? And here he is going to be driving me home later. That makes me kind of nervous.

But he doesn't try anything once we're alone in the car. A younger man might decide to drive me somewhere else than the University Center so he can have his way with me. At least, that's what I'm thinking when we're pulling out of the parking lot at Presque Isle Avenue. But then, what do you know—he says, "Are you in a hurry? It's so beautiful here. Why don't we drive along the lakeshore and out to the park for a little while. I'm too full from eating to dance right now."

"Um," I says.

"What?" he asks.

"Well, I'm so used to seeing the lake it doesn't matter to me," I says.

"I'm going to miss it here; it's so beautiful," he says. "A half hour or so won't hurt us, will it?"

I don't know what to say. I'm seventy-seven years old and here I have a guy I think wants to take me out to the island so he can make out with me in his car. Or am I reading too much into things? I don't feel so right about it, but I don't object either when he turns north and we head out toward Presque Isle Park.

"Lyla," I tell myself, "at your age, I doubt he wants any of that, and if he does, well, go for it. It'll probably be the last time you ever get any. It might just kill you at your age, but still, it'll be a good way to go—better than the nursing home."

We drive along the lakeshore and then out to the park. There's an ore boat at the big iron ore dock, which serves as the gateway to the park.

"You have such a beautiful dock," Mike says. "Not a big industrial mess like in Duluth, but just peaceful and beautiful."

"Yes," I says. "We get boats in about every day I guess. I don't see them too often though 'cause I don't come to this part of town too often, unless my friend Bel drives me. I don't drive."

"No?" he says. "That's too bad. You're missing out. I thought maybe I'd talk you into coming to visit me, but I guess you can always fly."

"From Marquette to Duluth?" I says. "That would cost something like five hundred dollars."

"Really?"

"Oh yeah, no flights would go from Marquette to Duluth. I'd have to go to Detroit or Chicago or Minneapolis and then to Duluth. That would be like my whole Social Security check just about."

"Oh, come on, Lyla. You must get more than that."

"Well, not enough to go jet-setting around the country and still pay my rent."

"Don't you have a house?" he asks.

"No, I live in a senior citizen home."

"Oh, well, since my wife died, I've been thinking of moving into a place like that myself...but I'll keep driving."

I'd wondered if he'd ever been married. I'm glad he's a widower—that's better than divorced. I wonder if he has kids; not that it matters because they'd be all grown up now, I'm sure. This relationship isn't serious enough yet for me to start asking him a lot of questions, and if I do, he might ask me some too and not like the answers I give him.

By now we're in the park and driving along the lake on the other side of the dock.

"That Dome sure is something," he says, pulling over to the edge of the road and parking where we can see it across the bay. "Let's get out and walk around a little to help our stomachs digest all that food."

"Well, we can do that dancing," I says.

"No, that might just upset my stomach."

"Don't you want to dance?" I asks as he opens his car door to get out.

"Oh, sure. Who wouldn't want to dance with you?" he says. "I just want to walk a little, and spend a few minutes in this beautiful place with a beautiful woman."

I get out of the car, and he walks around to my side.

"Watch out for the geese poop," I says to distract him from getting too romantic. I don't know why I fear romance, but I do.

He ignores me and takes my hand and says, "Let's walk a little bit." And then just as I hear the music, he says, "I think there are bands playing for Finn Fest out here."

"Yeah, over there at the Pavilion," I says, pointing in its direction. "Did you want to go listen?"

"No," he says, "it's kind of nicer just to hear music wafting through the trees. Let's go for a little walk up that hill there."

"Oh, I don't know," I says. "I'm not really wearing the right kind of shoes for walking."

"Lyla," he says, still leading me toward the hill, but turning to look me in the eye, "what are you afraid of?"

How do I say, "That you'll rape me in the woods; that you'll attack me. That you'll find out I'm really not all that experienced with men, even if I do have big boobs, even if—even if I want you to take advantage of me." But I realize all that sounds like some crazy young miss who's never been kissed.

"Nothing," I says. "I just don't want to wear out all my energy walking when we're going to dance later. I'm not that young, you know."

I wish I hadn't said that. Why am I trying to spoil my own fun?

"I've always thought," Mike says—we've now reached the hill and started climbing it; we're just walking along the road, not in the forest where something unsavory could happen—"that you're only as old as you think you are."

"Well, I probably think I'm my age."

"I think you're beautiful, Lyla," he says, and then he pauses and leans over to kiss me, and not on the cheek, but right on the lips. For a moment, my mind goes completely blank until I'm startled by a car horn.

I turn to look and there's a car driving by and hanging out the passenger window is Josie.

"Slip him the tongue, lady!" she shouts.

I'm embarrassed, but Mike just roars with laughter as the car disappears.

"You're making me feel like a schoolgirl," I says. And I turn away my face because I feel embarrassed and a little scared.

"Lyla, I'm sorry; I didn't mean..." he starts to say, his voice clear that he thinks he's upset me.

"No, it's okay; it's just—well, I haven't had anyone kiss me, even pay that kind of attention to me, in years, and well," and then I just start bawling.

He puts his arm around my shoulders and walks me to a park bench.

"What is it, Lyla?"

"No man ever kissed me like that."

"Like what?"

"Like he was kissing me just because he loved me. I've only been kissed by two other men, and one I don't even think knew what he was doing, and the other, well, it was apparent it was just a prelude to what he wanted, but, well, you kiss real sweet, like you just—well, like you're doing it for me, not for you."

"You're funny, Lyla," he says, "and I find it a little sad that you've never been kissed like that before."

He hands me his handkerchief—who still uses a handkerchief in this day and age?—and I use it to wipe my eyes.

After a minute, I says, "It's okay. Now I have been kissed that way. That's all that matters."

I let out a big sigh and hand him back his handkerchief, which he stuffs in his pocket. I see a sailboat going by on the lake.

"Sometimes," I says, "I feel like life is just passing me by and like nothing good is ever going to happen to me. Not that anything bad really has—I used to think everything that had ever happened to me was bad, but today, finally, I realize I'm really very lucky. Still, while my life has not been bad at all, nothing really good happened to me, not until now. The attention I've gotten lately being in the newspaper and then coming to Finn Fest, and now this—it's just so hard to take it all in, to think it could all be so good. It's been a wonderful day."

"I'm glad," Mike says. "I'm really glad. After my wife died, I didn't feel like good would come to me either, but now, just meeting you, I feel like there's hope again. It's been three years now since she died. Three years it took me to start to live again. I don't know what it was, but I just felt like coming to Finn Fest was the thing to do. It just—well, it just felt like a calling or something."

"I'm glad you came," I says. "I never would have come if it weren't for Sybil and then Mrs. Juntunen encouraging me to embrace my Finnish roots and come to Finn Fest."

"Do you think we can work out some way to keep seeing each other?" he asks, taking my hand and squeezing it. "I have to head back to Duluth tomorrow, but I want to see you again."

I want to say, "Let's just play it by ear," or "Let's not ruin today by planning for tomorrow," but instead, I says, "That would be nice. I hope I will get to see you again, and we can figure it out later."

"Yes, later," he says. "You're right. No point in worrying about tomorrow when tonight, we have dancing to do."

He gets up then and we walk back to the car, holding hands, not saying a word, my heart doing flip-flops, my stomach asking questions, or I mean my mind, while my stomach is just nervous. It seems like I'm feeling a million ways at once, and I just don't know how to feel. I've never felt this way before, not with Scofield, not with Bill. I had been with them just to be with someone, but not so much because I really liked them, but I really like Mike. I can't explain it, but I really like him, and I feel I know, without doubting, that he really likes me, and all these flip-flops of my heart and the questions in my mind, they aren't all worries or fear or a panicky need to control the future. They're just the result of excitement, and a bit of disbelief that things have suddenly turned out this way on this day in a manner I never could have imagined.

We drive around Presque Isle and then back to the University Center and to the dance. I admit I don't remember hardly a word we say the rest of the evening. My brain is in overdrive from having memorized the earlier conversations we had, especially at Presque Isle, and I don't think we talk too much the rest of that evening. I think it's enough that we're together, that we have found each other somehow, and now that we have, that's enough for one night.

Finally, around eleven o'clock, I start to feel sleepy. We've danced together at least a dozen dances—slow dances—but also a couple polkas, and now, my feet are sore. When I see Mike let out a yawn, I figure it's safe to tell him I'm ready to go home.

"Me too," he says. "I just didn't want the night to end, but at our age, I guess we can't expect to stay out too late. Let me drive you home."

Once we're in the car, neither of us says anything. For the first time since we were at Presque Isle, I start to feel anxious again. I wonder whether I'll ever see him again, and yet, I'm afraid to say anything and spoil the moment. I give him a couple directions to get me to Snowberry Heights, but that's about all we say until we get to the building and he pulls up to the door.

My hand reaches for the door handle, but then I hesitate. I want to kiss him again, but I don't want any of my neighbors to see me.

"Thank you for today, Lyla," he says as I stare straight ahead, trying to find my courage.

"Thank you," I says, looking at him.

"I had a good time," he says.

Is this where I asks him into my apartment? I can't help wondering, but I feel safe; I feel like I know that's not what Mike wants. He wants me. Just me. I feel more certain of it than anything else I've ever felt before. I want to tell him, "I love you," but that doesn't sound right yet somehow.

So I lean over and kiss him, and it's good. Not as magical as the first time perhaps because it's me kissing him, not as surprising either, but I taste how sweet his mouth is.

Then, before I put it off any longer, I force myself to get out of the car. When I turn around to close the door, he shouts, "*Nakemiin!*"

"What?" I laugh.

"*Nakemiin!*" he repeats. "That's Finnish for 'Goodbye'!"

"*Nakemiin!*" I shout back and wave, and for just a second, or maybe two, I hesitate before going inside, wondering whether I should invite him in for a nightcap—not that I have a drop of liquor in my place.

And then I laugh at myself and go through the front door into Snowberry. "Lyla, at your age," I says to myself, shaking my head, "to be thinking about inviting a man up to your apartment." I laugh at myself as I wait for the elevator and dig in my purse for my key. I had such a wonderful day that I guess it's only natural that I shouldn't want it to end. I doubt I'll ever hear from Mike again, but who knows.

I go to bed with Finnish Polka music going through my head. I think about calling Bel to tell her how the day went, but I don't. I can call her in the morning to remind her about my going to Mass before we go out for breakfast. She obviously wasn't too concerned about my going to Finn Fest or her missing out on it, so there's no reason why I should be too concerned about her and how her day went.

"Don't think about Bel, Lyla; you'll just get yourself all upset about how she acted today," I think as I crawl into bed. I don't want to be irritated after such a nice day. So I decide to think about Mike, how he has those big blue Finnish eyes and that hair that's still blond even though he said he's sixty-five. If he knew how old I was, but, oh well, I can have my fantasy. I can't remember the last time I sat on a man's lap—I don't even think I ever sat on Bill's. Well, it was silly; I'll probably never hear from him again, but it was fun while it lasted.

"Do you want to go out for breakfast?" Mike asks. I had just gotten out of bed and was on my way to the bathroom when the phone rang.

"How'd you get my phone number?" I asks him.

"It wasn't easy since your name's not Toivonen," he says.

"Oh that. I—"

"I spent the last half-hour online trying to find you, Miss Lyla Hopewell, looking through the White Pages at the names of everyone who lives in Snowberry Heights. Anyway, I'm hungry. Are you interested in coming to breakfast?"

"Oh, well, I have to go to Mass," I says, and then before I know what possesses me, I says, "Why don't you come along? At St. Peter's Cathedral. It's a special Finnish Mass anyways. Then we can go have breakfast after."

"What time's the service?"

"Ten o'clock," I says, looking at the clock and seeing it's just a few minutes after nine.

"Well, I guess I can wait to eat until eleven," he says. "I'll pick you up about quarter to ten."

"Okay, see you then," I says, afraid of the excitement I hear in my voice and can definitely feel in my heart.

Those Finnish polka songs are back in my head as I get dressed and make myself presentable. I admit I worry over what to wear, but I only have about three decent looking dresses to wear to Mass anyways, so it doesn't take me long to decide. Then at the last minute, I remember about Bel and give her a call.

"I only have a minute," I tell her. "I'm on my way to Mass."

"Oh," she says.

"I promised this fellow I met at Finn Fest yesterday to go to breakfast with him afterwards."

"Oh," she says with that tone in her voice that makes me want to smack her. "So you're dumping me today?"

"Now, Bel, he's only in town for Finn Fest and he doesn't know anybody else in Marquette. I can't expect him to eat his meals alone, and he's leaving to go home to Duluth today anyways."

"Well, I still have to eat," she says. "I'll come by the cathedral at eleven and we can go together."

That's the last thing I want. I thought she'd understand I wasn't going out to breakfast with her this morning, but I have to admit that while I felt crazy about Mike last night, I'm feeling a little less crazy this morning, and a bit nervous as the minutes tick by before we'll be seeing each other again. Maybe it was just the night and the polka music that got to me, and today, I'll find we don't really like each other as much as we thought we did.

"Okay," I says to her. "I gotta go. See you then."

I don't want to say much more to her; I'm afraid she'll be all argumentative with me like she was yesterday.

In a couple more minutes, I'm downstairs in the lobby waiting for Mike. When he pulls up, he hops out of the car like a gentleman and goes around it to open the door for me.

I barely walk out of the building before he's at my side, kissing me on the cheek. I'm a bit disappointed that it's not one of those kisses on the mouth again, but at the same time, it makes me feel giddy, and I'd be too embarrassed that someone at Snowberry might see us to let him kiss me on the lips.

"Hello, beautiful. How are you this fine morning?" he asks.

"Just fine. How are you?" I says as he opens the car door for me. I silently think of adding "handsome" to what I said, but I'm just too shy to say it.

Once I'm in the car, he goes around to get in on the other side, and then we drive up the hill. "That big church up there is where we're going right?" he asks.

"Yes, that's St. Peter's Cathedral," I says. "Bishop Baraga is buried there."

He must not know who Bishop Baraga was 'cause he doesn't say anything, so I says, "He was the snowshoe priest who walked hundreds of miles to preach to all the Indians around here back in the 1800s. I think he even went as far as Minnesota to preach."

"Really?" says Mike.

"Yeah. They even celebrate Baraga Days all over the country in different places, just like with Finn Fest. He's up for sainthood actually."

Mike doesn't say anything in response—I guess sainthood doesn't really mean that much to him, so I says, "Well, I really appreciate you going with me. I mean, you're not Catholic, are you?"

"No," he says, "but my mom was. Only she agreed to let us be raised Lutheran. Since you were Finnish, how'd you end up being Catholic?"

I tell him about my being in the orphanage, even though I was Lutheran too, and how I used to be mad about it, but I find comfort in being Catholic, and how Bishop Garland had even written in the *U.P. Catholic* this week about how Finland was a Catholic country before the Protestants converted everyone.

"Well," says Mike, "since my mom was Catholic, I grew up around both religions. Half my relatives were Catholic so we went to Catholic funerals and weddings and stuff, and—"

"Oh," I says.

"What?" he asks.

"Well, I just realized. The Mitchells—they, well, they were my mom's relatives. They were Catholic too, so that means my mom was Catholic. She must have decided to marry my dad and raise us as Lutherans just like your mom did. Hmm."

I don't know what else to say, but I store it away for the moment. It means my mom must have really loved my dad to change religions, and it means that I really was Catholic in a way already, kind of like Mike with his mom. It makes me think that Mama probably wouldn't have been so upset that the nuns made me into a Catholic, and I bet Papa wouldn't have been either.

"Well, God isn't Catholic or Lutheran," Mike says. "What matters is just that we all treat each other right, like Christians are supposed to."

"Exactly," I says.

We're at the cathedral now, but we barely find a parking spot. Besides the usual parishioners, I guess a lot of Finns have shown up for the special Mass.

We get out of the car and use the church's side door. Mike takes my hand as we go up the walk. I don't feel right about showing affection in church, especially not here where half the people will know me—not that I ever speak to most of them—but I don't pull away. Once we're inside the main part of the church, Mike stops for a moment and just says, "Wow!" as he looks at the giant pillars, and the stained glass windows, and the altar and the mosaic above it. "It's beautiful," he says.

"Yes, we're all quite proud of it," I whisper. "It's been called the most beautiful sandstone building in the world."

"I can see why," he says.

I lead us down the side aisle and into a pew. He doesn't kneel when I do, but I guess that's to be expected from a Lutheran. Then we sit quietly while he keeps staring at the stained glass windows. When the Mass starts, I'm glad to see he joins in the singing.

I can't say it turns out to be a very Finnish Mass even though it was supposed to be. It's not like it's said in Finnish or anything, but the priest welcomes us all, and Deacon Maki is there, who I know is Finnish at least. I have to admit I don't pay a lot of attention because I'm glad to have Mike there with me. And I'm wondering whether people in church are wondering who this man is who's with me because they're used to seeing me go to church alone or with Bel on holidays. But when we leave, no one says anything to me other than to smile or nod "Hello."

When we get outside, Bel is in her car sitting in the middle of the parking lot. She's blocking other people's cars, but I know she doesn't care.

"Where are we going for breakfast?" she asks, after rolling down her car window when she sees me. She can't even give a nod or a "Hello" to Mike.

"Mike," I tell him, "this is my friend Bel."

"Hello," he says. "It's nice to meet you."

"Hello," she replies. "I was thinking Tommy's for breakfast."

"Sure," I says, then turn to Mike and explain, "since Big Boy burnt down, there aren't too many breakfast choices. And Bel and I go to The Pancake House all the time so we try for some variety on Sundays."

"Sounds good to me," says Mike.

"Okay, I'll see you there," says Bel, and before I can say anything else, she's rolled up her window and is driving off.

I feel like maybe she was a little rude to Mike, but I don't want to apologize to him for her behavior. She's a grown woman and can make excuses for herself.

Mike and I go get in his car and I give him directions to Tommy's. He remarks again about how beautiful St. Peter's is. "It would be a beautiful church to get married in," he says.

That's a strange remark—is he thinking of asking me to marry him? Is that what he meant? I'll wait to see if he makes any more hints and just pretend I'm not catching on for now. Besides, he'd have to convert to get married at St. Peter's. I think he's wonderful, but this is all just happening too fast for me.

We don't say much else on the way to Tommy's other than my giving him directions for how to get there.

When we get inside, Bel has already got a table for us. We've barely sat down and said, "Hi" to her before the waitress comes. We all order coffee. Then I bury my face in the menu, so Mike and Bel do the same, not knowing what to say to each other.

Finally, the waitress comes again and asks if we need more time, but Bel just goes ahead and orders the crepes—I didn't know any place in Marquette had those until now. And then Mike orders a huge omelet, so I get the breakfast special, and then once the waitress is gone, just to break the ice, I tell Bel, "You should have come to Finn Fest yesterday. I had *lettuja*, these Finnish pancakes that are kind of like crepes. You would have loved them."

"Are you Finnish, Bel?" Mike asks.

"I don't know what I am," she says. "That's what happens when you grow up in an orphanage. There isn't anyone around to tell you what you really are."

"Well, your maiden name was Archambeau, so you must be French or French Canadian," I says.

"I s'pose," she says, fiddling with her silverware and looking uninterested.

Mike tries to be friendly by saying, "I think I might have some French Canadian in me too. We're all part of the great American melting pot after all."

"Where are you from?" Bel asks him.

"Duluth," he says.

She wrinkles up her nose and says, "That's such a smelly, dirty town."

"Actually, I think Marquette looks a lot like it, just smaller is all," he says, "and it is beautiful here."

"I wouldn't live anywhere but Marquette," Bel says.

"Mike and I had the best time at Finn Fest last night," I says to change the subject. I describe the banquet and the dance, but even when I mention seeing Minnie and Gloria, it doesn't seem to interest Bel. Once the food comes, she focuses on what she's eating, barely looking at us and just acting bored as we talk. In the end, Mike and I find ourselves talking to each other while Bel stares out the window at the highway. I don't know what her problem is. Is she jealous that I've found a boyfriend? Is he really that?

After we finish eating and wait for the bill, Mike tries again to make small talk. "Bel, you'll have to come visit Duluth some time," he says. "I'll show you around and see if I can change your mind about it being a dirty city. We actually have many nice attractions."

"I have no desire to see Duluth," she says. "Of course, Lyla can do what she likes, but I don't think it would be proper for her to go visit a man she barely knows in a town that far away, and certainly not to stay there overnight."

"Bel, don't be such a prude," I says.

"I'm just looking out for you, Lyla," she says. "You don't really know Mike all that well, do you?"

"Not yet I don't," I says, "but I'm hoping to." I try to sound threatening to warn her to back off. I should just elope and go live in Duluth with Mike the way she's behaving.

Mike says, "Bel, I think Lyla is lucky to have a friend like you to look out for her."

"Well, someone has to," Bel says. "Lyla's always made stupid choices when it comes to men."

"Like you should talk," I says. I know better than to let her get to me, but it's hard not to say anything when she's being so rude. "You know the only steady boyfriend I ever had was Bill. Just because that didn't go so well isn't reason enough to say I make bad choices."

"Even so," she says. "You and Mike need to get to know each other better before you go running off to Duluth, Lyla."

When the waitress comes with the bill, Mike says he'll pay it; I tell him he doesn't have to, but all Bel says is, "Thanks. I'd offer to leave the tip, but I don't have any singles on me."

I just want to slap her. I might just do it too this afternoon after Mike heads back to Minnesota.

"Well, Mike and I are going back to the closing Finn Fest ceremonies," I tell Bel as we walk back out to the car. "I'll see you later."

"Okay," she says and just walks to her car.

Mike looks like he's going to shout after her that it was nice to meet her, but I says to him, "Don't bother."

When we get in the car, I says, "I don't know what her problem is. I guess she's just jealous. We've been friends for so long that she's not used to sharing me is all I can figure."

"Well, I don't blame her. I wouldn't want to share you either," Mike says, starting up the car. He's so mellow about everything. I love that about him, considering I'm usually a ball of frustration. Still, Bel was rude to him, and I'm not going to put up with it. I like Mike a lot, but I know we have a long way to go before we can pretend this relationship is serious, and with us living so far away from each other, I don't expect it will get serious, but Bel can let me have a nice weekend with a special guy—that's not so much to ask from her after she's claimed to be my best friend for sixty-plus years.

Nothing too exciting happens the rest of the day. Mike and I go back to the Superior Dome and just walk around the *tori*, not saying anything too important to each other; we just talk about the things we see for sale. Mike stops to chat with several people, but I don't mind. I have nothing else to do, and I just enjoy listening to him. After a couple hours, I tell him I'm craving more *lettuja* despite having just had breakfast. He says he didn't have any *lettuja* yet, so he's game as well. That's how we while away the afternoon before it's announced that it's time for the closing ceremonies.

Then we make our way to the seats in the Dome. Pauline Kiltinen is there as President of the Finn Fest board to pass the torch off to the chairperson for the next Finn Fest. I'm afraid there'll be lots of boring speeches, but I can see how happy everyone is. When I spot her, Norma Juntunen is smiling like she's about ready to burst. Everyone is so thrilled that the entire event has been such a big success and I kind of feel their enthusiasm.

And there's more music! The Sisu Dancers from Finland do a Finnish folk dance, a bunch of kids put on a short play, and even a Christian rock group from Finland performs. I find I really like this Finnish music. I might just have to start watching *Finland Calling* on Sundays, only it's probably on when Bel and I go out for breakfast. Maybe I can tape it on the VCR.

Finally, when the ceremonies are all done, the crowd claps and cheers, and I get that same feeling I had the day before, that we're all connected, we're all one big happy Finnish family, even though some of us may be Catholic rather than Lutheran, or have English or French Canadian or German or Norwegian or Swedish blood mixed up in us.

"I'm so glad I came," I tell Mike again as we walk toward the door.

"So am I," he says, and then he picks up a beautiful white and blue flower arrangement from the banquet that a woman tells him he can take home. He gives it to me and says, "You've been the flower of the event for me." It's a pretty corny sounding line, but I can't help smiling. I have to smile to hold back the tears over his sweetness and the sadness of knowing he's going to be leaving soon.

Once we get back to the parking lot and the car, I start to feel nervous. It's all over. He's going to drive me back to Snowberry now, and that will be the end of our weekend romance. I feel all these questions bubbling up inside me: When will I see you again? How will I come to visit you? What's your phone number? What's your address? Do you really like me, or were you just looking for someone to have a good time with this weekend?

But I don't ask any of those questions. Bill used to get real irritated when I nagged him like that, and if there's any chance I'll get to see Mike again, I don't want to do anything to drive him away.

He doesn't say hardly anything in the car, so finally, I says, "Mrs. Juntunen sure was happy. She's the one that got me to go to Finn Fest, and I'm glad she did now."

"She seems real nice," he says. "It's got to be a lot of work to help organize all of that."

"She is real nice," I says.

"I'll have to stop and get *The Mining Journal* on the way out of town," he says, "to see if Sybil got her story about the sauna in there."

"Oh yeah, I forgot all about that," I says.

And then, we're back at Snowberry. Mike pulls up to the front door, just like last night, and I wonder what to say or do, but before I can decide, he leans over and gives me another one of those long, wonderful kisses right on the mouth.

"I'm going to miss you something awful, Lyla," he says. "I know I'm going to be thinking about you all the way home."

I'm tempted to ask him to wait ten minutes while I run upstairs to pack a bag so I can go back to Minnesota with him...But I don't.

"Why don't you call me when you get home," I says, "so I know you made it there safely."

"Okay," he says. "I still have your phone number, you know. I wrote it down in my address book when I called you this morning."

Smiling at this news, I says, "Have a safe trip, and thanks for a wonderful time."

"Thank you," he says.

I get out of the car, but then I look back inside and says, "Bye now."

And he says, "Goodbye."

And I close the car door.

I walk to the building's door, but then I turn and wave to him, though I don't know if he sees me since he's almost out of the parking lot.

Feeling a little sad, I go into the building and ride up in the elevator.

I know I'll probably never hear from him again, and even if I do, it won't mean anything. I don't think our relationship will ever go anywhere, but it was nice while it lasted.

When I get to my door, *The Mining Journal* is laying on the doormat. I pick it up and then unlock the apartment door. Once I'm inside, I set it on the counter, and then as I take off my coat, I see the headline about the World's Largest Sauna and the story says it was written by Sybil Shelley. I read it, remembering that wonderful moment when I met Mike, and there at the end is a quote from me. "Marquette native Lyla Hopewell said, 'Experiencing this sauna has been the treat of a lifetime.'" Well, Sybil may have reworded what I said, or I may not remember exactly what I said, but I think what I really meant was that getting to sit on Mike Koski's lap was the treat of a lifetime.

Chapter 27

Mike did call me when he got home, but it was late by then, at least past nine, and we were both really tired after the busy weekend. He had said he'd had a great time with me and that he would talk to me soon, so I said, "Okay," and then I waited.

I didn't expect him to call on Monday during the day, but I thought maybe Monday night. But then I figured he'd been away from home for about a week and was probably busy catching up on things. He'd call Tuesday, I told myself. But when he didn't, I started to get kind of crabby. Okay, I felt like crying, but crying isn't something I do very often. Some guy I only just met wasn't worth crying over, so I bit my lip. By Wednesday morning, I felt kind of angry—I mean, why did he have to be so nice if he was going to be such a jerk and never call me again? I sure wasn't going to sit around waiting on him. I thought about asking Sybil to look him up on the computer so I could get his phone number, but I wasn't about to play desperate either.

Instead, I decided to quit thinking about him and just get ready for the women's meeting.

I'd talked to Bel on Monday and Tuesday briefly, but I didn't get too involved with her those days. Until that morning, I had still been debating about chewing her out for how rude she'd been to Mike, but now I realized there wasn't any point in being mad at her since some guy who couldn't even call me sure wasn't worth getting into a fight over with my best friend. I'd like to blame her, but somehow I didn't think she was the reason he didn't call me back. I figured he was just a flirt, and we'd had fun, and that was it. Life would go on, and I wasn't sure I wanted the complication of a long distance romance. What was I thinking? It had all been fun, but now it was time to get back to real life. So I figured I'd go to the meeting with Bel today and get back into my normal routine.

Somehow, I felt these women's meetings were having a calming effect on me now—after all, it had gotten me to try to make amends with Jessie and look where that had led. And I was starting to think about these young women as my friends too—well, I was still kind of leery of that sex-crazed Diana, but I'd even learned things from her—I mean, I figured after all the problems she'd had with men over the years, maybe I should consider myself lucky that Mike didn't call me.

I decided I wouldn't mention him at the meeting so I didn't have Bel saying, "I told you so." I wouldn't even bring him up around Bel. If I needed to talk to anyone about it—and I didn't—it would be Sybil—she'd understand considering her issues with Alan.

When I call Bel that morning, I ask her how she's feeling since she said she didn't feel good on Saturday and I've been thinking too much about Mike since then to remember to ask her how she feels. But she says she feels fine and she'll meet me downstairs in time to go to the meeting. I'm glad she's going 'cause there's something else I want to tell her, but I'll wait until we're on our way to the meeting so she doesn't have a lot of time if she's going to overreact. Lately, I don't know what's up with her but it sure seems like she's been getting on my case about everything I do.

Bel's in the lobby when I get there. So she doesn't think I'm still mad at her about the thing with Mike, I smile nicely at her and says, "Hello" and she says, "Hello" back and we walk to the car.

Once we're in the car and heading up Fifth Street, I says to her, "I forgot to tell you, but yesterday, Wendy called to ask me if I'd help out with the tours at the O'Neill House."

I hadn't known at first what to say when Wendy asked me. I was silent on the phone until she said, "It would just be for a couple of months, Lyla, and we can just try for a day or two and see if you like it. It's just that you know so much about the house that we wouldn't have to train you like we would some new person. It was John's idea actually. I told him I could work until the day the baby is born but he won't let me. I only do a few tours a week anyway, and we can let you do whichever ones you want—John will be flexible about it. He's just been so busy lately with his writing, and I hate to take that away from him by expecting him to handle all the tours. Truthfully, he can get quite cranky if he doesn't get at least an hour a day to work on his books, and I guess I can't blame him for that. We all need our personal time. Do you think you can help us out?"

I knew I wanted to do it, but I just couldn't believe John and Wendy really wanted me to help out. When I still didn't answer, she must have felt like she still had to keep trying to convince me.

"We were so thrilled with the article in *The Mining Journal* about you, Lyla," she said. "Sybil did such a good job on it, and she told us how articulate you were when she interviewed you. John thought since you know so much about the house that you can tell anecdotes about the O'Neills on the tours. I don't think there's anyone else we could find that would have what you have to offer."

"What I have to offer?" I said, amazed by such words. I had never thought I had much of anything to offer to anyone. This being asked to help like I had something to "offer," well, it felt so—well, like two triumphs in one month. That's the only way I could see it.

"Yes, and the baby will be coming in just a few weeks," said Wendy, "and then I'll need a month or so after to recover, and then I can go back to helping John out. Please, Lyla. The longest it would be is until mid-October when we close the house down from tours for the winter months."

"Okay," I finally said. "I think it sounds like fun, so long as I can sit down for a few minutes after the tours. I can't be on my feet all day."

"Of course," Wendy said. "The tours usually take about forty-five or fifty minutes, so you have time to go to the bathroom or sit down or whatever you need to do in between."

Well, I knew as soon as Wendy asked me that I wanted to do it, only I was a little shy about saying, "Yes," but I said it anyways. I then worried that I'd made a mistake, but the more I thought about it overnight, the more I decided it was just going to be a lot of fun. It might be a little awkward for me at first, but so was going to Finn Fest and I'd had fun there, and who knows—old men like history—so maybe I'd find myself a local version of Mike during the tours.

Wendy wanted me to start on Friday, so I figured today was my chance to tell Bel about it, in hopes she'd give me a ride there on Friday and any other days I'd need one.

But once I tell Bel, she doesn't say anything at first. I start to think she isn't even listening to me until she says, "Oh, Lyla, you're not going to do it, are you?"

"Well," I says, "I told Wendy I would. Why not?"

"But you can't be on your feet like that for hours," she says.

"Oh, no," I says. "It's just until Wendy has the baby and maybe a few weeks after while she recovers. They only have summer hours until early October, and then they're only open a couple days a week after that since the tourists aren't in town anymore. I told her I could help out until then. It's just a few hours a day a couple times a week."

"Well," says Bel, "I guess that would be okay, but I don't want you to wear yourself out, or..."

"Or what?" I says when she doesn't complete the sentence.

"Or, oh, I don't know. I just don't want to miss out on spending time with you."

Miss out on spending time with me? Hell, I talk to her every day and see her almost every day. That's a funny thing to say.

"Well, I wouldn't do it," I says, "if it wasn't for Wendy being about to have a baby. She's due in about three weeks you know."

"Yeah, I know," says Bel.

"Anyways, I was kind of happy that she asked me," I says. "I kind of like the idea of helping out there and feeling useful again."

"You're useful to me," says Bel.

She's turned down Washington Street while we've been talking and gone over to Front, but I haven't been paying too much attention until I realize she's gone past our turn on Ridge Street and we're already blocks past it and going by the Graveraet school.

"Bel, where are you going?" I asks.

"What?" she asks.

"Where are you going?" I repeat. "You went past the church."

"Oh," she says. But she keeps going straight anyways.

"Turn around," I says. "Turn left here and go back."

By the time she turns, we're way down at Crescent Street, but then she slams on the brake so hard the car makes a screeching sound. She's lucky there's no one behind us or they'd have hit her.

"Bel," I says. "You need to use your blinker."

"Quit fussing at me, Lyla!" she snaps. "I know what I'm doing."

She hardly ever raises her voice so I'm surprised by her tone. Is she still mad at me about Mike? Is she jealous or something? Afraid I'm going to move to Duluth and leave her alone in Marquette? That must be it. Well, if I did, it would serve her right the way she acted this past weekend. But I'm not moving to Duluth. Sure, I liked Mike, but who's to say there isn't a guy like that in Marquette? I don't like any of the men at Snowberry, but maybe there's a guy like him at Pine Ridge or Lost Creek or somewhere else?

I get so busy thinking about how maybe I could find me a boyfriend that I only half-notice when Bel turns right again to head back toward St. Paul's where the meeting is held.

We have to stop twice for cars coming the other way so Bel pulls way over because the street is so narrow, but I'm still not paying much attention until Bel says, "Why's everyone being so friendly today?"

"What do you mean?" I asks.

"Well, the people in both those cars that just went by waved at me, and I didn't even know either of them."

I look out her window and see the person in the car approaching her is also waving.

"Bel!" I holler. "They're waving 'cause you're going the wrong way! Don't you know after all these years that High Street is one way?"

"Oh," she says. "Well…" But she doesn't finish her thought. She turns onto Ohio to head over to Pine.

"What are you thinking? Don't you look at the signs?" I says to her.

"Don't get on my case, Lyla!" she says. "I've got a lot on my mind right now."

"A lot on your mind," I scoff.

"Yes, a lot on my mind," she says, pulling onto Pine to head up the rest of the hill. "So much that you're lucky I'm able to cart you around at all."

I wait to see if she's going to tell me what all is on her mind, but she doesn't say anything more. Still, she has a lot of nerve to say she's carting me around when it's her damn meeting we're going to.

We go up Pine Street and then she turns onto Arch and in a minute we're in the parking lot at St. Paul's. I don't say anything more to her as we get out of the car or as we head into the church. But I sure wish I knew what her problem was.

When we get inside, Diana is already there, so we just smile and say hello and act like we haven't been fighting. Not that Diana should be one to say anything—what's driving the wrong way up a one way street compared to sleeping with half the men in Marquette?

Once May and Sybil show up, the meeting starts—Wendy doesn't come 'cause she's got a doctor's appointment today.

I wait to see if Bel is going to tell all of us together what all this "lots on my mind" stuff is, but she doesn't. I wait for her to talk but she says nothing, so I take my turn and just talk about how I had a good time at Finn Fest—though I don't say nothing about Mike.

When I finish, it's quiet for a while, and then Bel finally says, "I don't have anything I want to talk about today, but I'm grateful for these meetings and to realize how far I've come in just the short time I've been coming here, and also going to AA."

That's it. Here I am Bel's best friend and she doesn't even tell me what the "lots on my mind" is. She—of all people—is playing silent when she's the one who always tells me more than I want to know to the point where I've thought about duct-taping her mouth shut before. Finally, I figure she must be wanting me to ask her what's wrong—sometimes she does that—hints at stuff she wants me to ask about. So once we're back in the car, I give in and ask.

"Bel, what the hell's been bugging you? You've been acting so weird lately," I says, laughing like it's no big deal.

"Oh, just stuff, Lyla. You know. I've got all kinds of stuff that I've been working through all these years."

"Yeah, but you always tell me when something's bothering you," I says. "It feels like you're staying silent about it on purpose right now."

"No, I just," she says, "I, well, I just need to figure it out enough that I can even explain it to you. When I'm ready to talk about it, I will."

"Okay," I says. I should probably tell her how she can talk to me about anything, but she ought to know that by now. Hell, I don't think she could ever keep a secret from me, so what's her problem now? I'm so used to having her tongue running all the time that I don't know what to think about the way she's behaving now.

"Okay, so I'll see you later," I says once we're back at Snowberry and she gets out of the elevator at her floor.

I go to my apartment, figuring there's no point in worrying until she tells me what's bugging her.

For a minute, I wonder if Mike will have called me while I was out—I wish I had an answering machine or Caller I.D. just so I would know if he did, but to see he didn't would probably just depress me and I don't need that. I can tell from Bel's mood there won't be any talking to her about it. I think again how I could call Sybil, but I don't want to be some lovesick girl crying on the phone.

A week later, out of the blue, Sybil calls me. By then, I've given up on ever hearing from Mike again, and I've decided I'm not going to talk to anyone about him. But this time, Sybil needs to talk to me. She wasn't at the women's meeting that afternoon, but I'd figured she'd just been busy. Bel and I had just gone out to The Pancake House a few nights before, and she'd seemed fine then, so I hadn't given it another thought.

At first, Sybil just sounds like she wants to make small talk, asking how the meeting went and talking about the weather, but then she finally gets to the point, asking me, "Did you hear that Alan is selling his father's house?"

"No," I says, not really caring.

"He doesn't want to live there," she says.

"I suppose he'll go downstate again," I says.

"No, he wants to stay here. He's a carpenter you know, like his dad and his grandpa were. He got in with the Carpenters Union or something like that. I think he's going to be working on all that Founder's Landing construction down by the lake, or at least, he's hoping to, or something like that."

"Then why's he selling the house if he's staying here?" I asks.

"He said the house has to be sold and the money split three ways between him and his brothers."

"Oh, that makes sense," I says. "They probably all want their share of the money."

"He doesn't want to live there anyway. He's going to buy a cabin on the Dead River—something like that."

"Must be nice," I says. "Waterfront property can't be cheap. I'm surprised he has the money."

"Yeah," says Sybil. "I guess he and...well, never mind."

"What about his son? What's his name? I thought he was living downstate to be near him."

"His son's name is Gil. Alan says he'll come up to visit often."

She seems like she wants to say more—at least that's the feeling I get from her—but she doesn't say more. Finally, I says, "Sybil, you didn't call me just to tell me Alan is selling his father's house, did you?"

"No," she says. But she doesn't tell me why she called. I wait for a while. I got nothing else to do. It's too early to start making supper, so I wait until she finally says, "Lyla, we broke up." Then she laughs nervously and says, "Not that you could ever say we were really a couple anyway."

"I'm sorry," I says. "Are you okay?"

What if she says she's not okay? Is she going to come over here and cry on my shoulder? I thought May was her best friend, or Wendy. Why is she calling to tell me all this?

"Lyla," she says, "I don't mean to tell you my problems, but I wanted to let you know I won't be seeing you much anymore. I'm moving away."

"Moving? Why?" I asks, and I can hear in my voice that I do care. How are Bel and I going to get to The Pancake House if Sybil leaves?

"I just think I need a change," she says.

"Not because of Alan, I hope," I says. "Sybil, he was never worth it anyways."

I hear her sigh, and then she says, "It's kind of about Alan, but it's more about me."

"How's that?" I asks.

"Lyla, I know you're not much of a reader, so maybe you don't remember this, but I mentioned at one of the women's meetings about a book my grandmother wrote, and how Wendy's husband, John, said he'd help me to get it published."

"Yeah," I says, pretending that I know what she's talking about, but I don't really remember it. Books don't interest me much.

"Well, I gave it to John because he knows literary agents and publishers since he's published Mr. O'Neill's memoir, and he's working on getting his own books published. Anyway, it's a strange book.[1] My grandmother wrote it, but she claimed that it was channeled to her by her own grandmother not long after her grandmother died."

"Channeled? What do you mean by that, like written by a dead person?"

"Yes, she claims her grandmother wrote the book through her. Like automatic writing I guess. The funny thing is that when I first met Alan, I thought almost immediately that I'd found my soulmate. That there was something familiar about him that I couldn't place but that drew me to him

---

[1] See *Spirit of the North: a paranormal romance* by Tyler R. Tichelaar, which contains within it the manuscript written by Sybil's grandmother.

instantly."

Has she lost it? Her grandmother's grandmother wrote a book after she was dead? I knew love could break your heart, but not that it would make you so crazy you start to believe in ghosts.

"What do you mean?" is all I can think to say.

"It was more than Alan's looks that attracted me to him," Sybil says. "I don't know how to explain it, except it was like love at first sight, but more than that, I felt like I knew him already the minute I saw him, though we had never met before. I suppose it's possible we had maybe passed each other on the street before, but it was more than that—it was like—like we'd known each other all our lives, and before that even. I know this is going to sound weird, but I think we knew each other in a past life. You know, like reincarnation."

"I don't know anything about that stuff," I says, feeling uncomfortable. This conversation is just too weird for me.

"Well, you know, though, that reincarnation is the belief that we come back and live again—that we can have multiple lives, right?"

"Yes," I says, though I don't think Monsignor Cappo would like me talking about this. "But I don't believe in that stuff."

"It's okay if you don't believe in it, Lyla," says Sybil, "but I do."

"But you're Catholic, Sybil," I says. "You know the Church doesn't believe in that—at least I don't think it does." I'm not even sure why I'm discussing this with her.

"The Church cut Reincarnation out of Christianity because they thought if people knew they had more than one chance to get into heaven, it would destroy the Church's power to make people obey," Sybil explains. "But the Jews believed in Reincarnation. Jesus, I'm sure, understood it, but the Church got rid of it. It's a travesty is what it is, how the Church has denied it just to usurp power."

That's more than I can take in at the moment. I don't like her talking like that, even if I don't always agree with the Church, but I don't want to argue with her since she obviously knows more about it than me, so I just says, "What's your point? Why are we talking about this?"

"Well, because of the book my great-great grandmother channeled to my grandma," she says. "See, in the book she hints that she had some strange experiences where she may have been reincarnated, and she had this sister, my great-great-great-aunt Adele, and Adele was in love with a young man named Ben Shepard, and, well, it sounds strange but I think Alan and I are the reincarnations of Ben and Adele."

I want to say, "That's just crazy" but I don't want to hurt her feelings, and maybe I should be gentle with her since I think the lovesickness has started to affect her brain. So I just says, "Why do you think that?"

"Because Ben broke Adele's heart without ever giving her a reason, and that's what Alan just did to me."

"Well, that could just be wishful thinking," I says. "I'm sure lots of relationships end that way."

"Well, yeah," Sybil says. "That's true, but well, you'll just have to read the book. It's too hard to explain. It's not something I can prove. It's just something I feel—no, something I know—intuitively know to be true. You see, Alan and I are reenacting those events; they say we keep having things repeat in our lives until we learn something from them. I don't think Adele, or I should say, I don't think when I was Adele, I really learned everything I needed to, and so this time, I will. I think she didn't have many choices open to her because of how women didn't have many opportunities back then, but I have opportunities. I don't have to sit around and be lovesick or enter a convent like she did. I can use the pain to be stronger, to find something out about myself. Does that make sense?"

"Yeah, I guess," I says. "So you're not really upset that he broke up with you is what you're saying?"

"I love how blunt you are, Lyla. You make things that seem to be complicated so much simpler. Yes, I am upset, but on another level, I know it was all meant to be, so I'm not going to cry my eyes out for weeks like Adele would have."

"That's good," I says, thinking she can believe whatever she wants, but the bottom line is that she deserved better than Alan.

"It is good," she says. "It means I can free myself from the old attachments. It means I can go on to the next lesson now."

She sounded sad when she first called me, but now she sounds exuberant.

"Lyla, you've made me feel so much better," she says. "I don't know what it is about you, but you're so easy to talk to."

"Must be why Bel keeps sticking around me too," I says.

"You're strong, Lyla. That's why," says Sybil. "You're a no-nonsense kind of woman. You wouldn't have put up with Alan stringing you along like I did."

"I don't know about that," I says. "I put up with his father for three years."

"Well," she says, "I guess we both know better then."

"So, you're really going to move away?" I says.

"Yeah. I need a change. I feel like all these years I've just been waiting for my life to begin. I have good friends and everything around here, and I like working for the paper and helping out May at the antique shop and doing pickups for The Pancake House, but I do have a college degree, you know, and I feel like I should put it to some use."

"Oh, what's your degree in?" I asks.

"Philosophy with a Religious Studies minor."

"Wow!" I says. "I had no idea you were that smart."

"Well, that's what happens when you're a woman who wants to be a priest and you're not allowed to, and you don't want to play second fiddle by becoming a nun—well, that's how I felt about it then, though I understand God wants us to be humble, and the point is to be of service in whatever role we're in, but I found myself questioning too many things while growing up Catholic, especially after my parents were killed in a car accident when I was a girl—and I survived it. That made me think God must have some reason for having let me live, so ever since, I've been interested in studying religion and science and how the universe works and just what God really is."

"That's interesting," I says. And it is, though I'd never be smart enough to go and study it. "So what will you do with that degree?" I asks her.

"I don't know yet," she says.

"Well, where are you going to move to?"

"I don't know that yet either," Sybil says. "I could go anywhere, I guess," she says. "I mean, I don't have any family or obligations, and I've got a little money saved. Enough to travel for a few weeks and try to find out what I want to do."

"When will you leave?" I asks.

"In about two weeks," she says. "I'm going to give my notice at the newspaper tomorrow when I go in, and I already told May, and I'll tell The Pancake House on Saturday, which is the next day I work."

"Oh, well, good luck," I says, not knowing what else to say. I think about saying, "I'll miss you," but the words just won't come out for me.

"Thanks. I'll see you before I go, Lyla. I promise."

"Okay," I says.

When I get off the phone with Sybil, I just plain feel creeped out. I don't know why but it just bugs me to think she and Alan could be reincarnated from some old dead people way back in the 1800s. That's just crazy and it all has to be made up—a figment of her imagination—that's what it is. The priests sure wouldn't like her talking about things like that, that's for sure.

Does it even make sense? I mean, if we're supposed to work out things from past relationships in this life, then how come she and Alan didn't work it out this time either? And maybe that means Bill and I had a past relationship, but then why didn't we work it out this time either—or did we? Maybe how I forgave him, even though he was kind of a jerk with his "I know" comment when I said I was sorry, was our working things out, but if I had to wait a second lifetime just to get that little bit—forget it! Reincarnation is for the birds. Sounds like it causes more trouble than anything else. Sybil is nuts to believe in something like that. Alan's just selfish—that's all he's ever been. Here she spent all that money going to college to study religion and she ends up believing in reincarnation—that's a long-winded and painful sounding way of trying to figure out life. Hell, Sybil could have just watched Dr. Phil and he would have told her what the problem was—that Alan is selfish. That's all it is.

But at least she's free from him now. And off to "find herself." I guess that's what they call it. Funny how relationships affect women. Makes me all the gladder that Mike didn't call me. I'm not going to spend my life trying to "find myself" because of any dumb old man.

Chapter 28

Sybil doesn't actually leave until September 1st. It's a Wednesday so she comes to our Wednesday women's group and hugs us all goodbye, and we all cry—yes, even me. She's still not sure what she's going to do or where she's going. She's put all her stuff in storage that she can't fit in her car and she doesn't have any plans. She says she's just going to get in her car and head for the Mackinac Bridge and from there "go wherever the Good Lord sends me. It might be the Mosque in Detroit," she tells us, "or it might be to visit the Amish—I hear there's a group of them in Shipshewana, Indiana—or maybe I'll try to find some Quakers in Pennsylvania, or who knows—maybe I'll get on a plane and go visit the Holy Land or a temple in India. It's up to wherever God sends me."

"I wish I had your faith," Wendy tells her.

"I wish I had the love of a good man and children like you," Sybil replies. I notice she says, "children" since Wendy is bursting. She can barely walk she's so pregnant now.

Sybil tells us we won't hear from her for a while because she wants time to clear her mind, but she promises to contact us before the holidays. I tell her I'll pray for her, and I intend to, but then I kind of forget about it for a few days because I'm so busy.

That Thursday I have to go with Bel to the doctor. She tells me it's a follow-up appointment to one she had a couple of weeks ago that she went to and never told me about, and she won't tell me why she's going to this one either.

"I just don't want to go alone in case it's bad news and I'm too upset to drive home," she says.

"Do you expect it to be bad news?" I asks.

"Well, at our age, you never know, Lyla," is the most she'll say.

It turns out the doctor is the shrink whose office I went to with her a few months back. I didn't even know she was still going there, but when I asks her, she says, "Yeah, I have been. I just didn't want to worry you."

"Worry me about what, Bel?" I says. "I already know you're nuts. He's not going to tell you anything you and I don't know already."

But when we get to the office, I notice something I didn't the last time—on the door it says "geriatric psychiatrist."

"What's that mean?" I asks her.

"That he's a shrink for old people," she says.

She just seems real weird about it, though. I mean, I went with her years ago when she went to see the codependency specialist, and I went with her to see the alcoholic specialist or whatever they call them. I got to know some of their waiting rooms real well. She never wanted me to go in and talk to any of them, so I'd just sit in the waiting room, but at least she'd tell me all about the appointment afterwards—she was always real talkative about her drinking problems and all her other issues, but today, though she wants me to come, she won't tell me anything about why she's going to see this geriatrics shrink.

"Bel, are you really sick?" I finally says to her while we're in the waiting room.

"Lyla, I—" she starts to say, but then she gets called into the doctor's office.

Something's up with her, but I figure she'll tell me when she's ready. Only by the time she gets out of the office, I have to pee so bad—she's in there for so long that I don't dare go find a bathroom because then she might come looking for me and we'll be wandering around in the Medical Center for an hour trying to find each other—that I'm in no mood for talking to her about her appointment. I mean to ask her when I come out of the bathroom, but sometimes she's cleverer than you'd think, like how she distracts me right away when I come out by asking me if I want to go to lunch at The Pancake House.

"I figure we should get used to going during the day," she says, "since Sybil isn't around to drive us anymore, and I'm not sure I want to get used to a new driver."

"Bel, if we don't go there at night, they'll lose half their business and shut down."

And, I'm sorry to say it, but the place did shut down not too long after, but then the new Big Boy opened back up so we started going there for breakfast.

Anyways, my rumbling stomach makes me forget all about asking her if she's sick until I'm back home again, and then I'm tired, and I just don't feel like calling her—maybe I just don't feel like actually knowing what's wrong with her yet.

Friday morning I'm getting ready to go over to the O'Neill House to help with the tours when the phone rings.

"Damn!" I holler, thinking now isn't the best time for Bel to call to tell me her problems, but she doesn't know that John offered to pick me up this morning since he had some errands to do anyways—and that's fine because I hate asking Bel to drive me over there because she still doesn't seem to like the idea that I'm working there.

But when I answer the phone, it's Eleanor. I thought now that Bill was dead that I wouldn't be getting any more phone calls from her, so I'm sure not expecting the invitation she gives me.

"Lyla, we're having a party on Labor Day and we're hoping you'll come, and why don't you bring your friend, Bel, too—I hear from Wendy that you hardly ever go anywhere without her."

"What's the party for?" I asks, wanting to know before I commit to anything.

"It's Alan's fortieth birthday, so we're celebrating that and kind of having a housewarming for him at his new camp—well, he says it's his house, which I guess it is, but it looks like a camp from what I've heard. Monday'll be the first time I'll have seen it. Anyway, we want you to come. All the family will be there."

"Oh, well, I don't want to intrude on family," I says.

"Lyla, you count as family. You know all of us. John and Wendy say they love you to death, and I understand you know our cousin May, and of course, you know me and my girls and Alan, and John's parents will be there too—Ellen and Tom—I'm not sure, but I think you met them before. I'm going to make my special potato salad. You can't miss that."

"Well, okay," I says, "but what should I bring?"

"Bring whatever you like. We'll be having hot dogs and hamburgers. Tom—that's John's father—will be doing the grilling, and everyone else will just bring a dish to pass."

"Well, Bel likes to make Jell-O salads," I says, "and maybe I could bake some cookies or something."

"Sure, that's fine," Eleanor says. "Do you want to ride with us? We can squeeze both of you in the backseat. Lucy will drive; she and Maud will insist I sit in the front seat since they think I'm getting old, but you and Bel can fit in the back with Maud if you don't mind. I mean, you won't know where the camp is otherwise. We'll pick you up around three o'clock, okay? I'll call you before we leave."

"Okay," I says before hanging up. "I'm looking forward to it."

What the hell? I think when I get off the phone. Why the hell would I want to go to Alan's fortieth birthday party?

But it is on Labor Day, so it's gotta beat sitting at home watching the Jerry Lewis Telethon. Jerry's so fat and puffed up now I can't stand to see him like that—not that I was ever a fan of those stupid movies of his—but you can't help liking someone who cares about helping kids—and that's saying a lot since I don't even like being around kids, but—well, Jerry's a good guy. Still, the telethon gets damn boring with all those corporate sponsors up there handing out checks, and Charro and Tony Orlando and all them just don't seem to be on as much as they used to, and with Liberace, Sammy Davis Jr., Dean Martin, and Frank Sinatra all dead, well…it's just not the telethon it was, and anyways, I can still watch a lot of it in the morning before I go or while I'm baking cookies.

I give Bel a quick call to tell her about the party before John picks me up. Right away, she starts arguing with me about going.

"Well, I don't know what those people like to eat," she says.

"Why don't you make a Jell-O salad?" I says.

"Oh, well," she says, "yeah, I guess I can do that if I can remember how."

"Why wouldn't you remember?" I asks. "You've made hundreds of them over the years."

"Well, I'm not sure where I put the directions."

"Oh jeez," I says. "I gotta go. I'll help you on Sunday with it if you want."

And then I hang up the phone and head down to the lobby so I don't keep John waiting.

I don't have any desire to go to this birthday party for Alan—I hope to God I'm not expected to get him a card or a gift or something because I'm not going to—he'll be lucky if I even speak to him there; actually, he'll be lucky if I bite my tongue about how he's treated Sybil. I'm just going for Eleanor's sake. I can always talk to John and Wendy, and Bel of course.

I am sorta glad that John and Wendy asked me to help with the tours. I've kind of been enjoying them. I've only helped with a couple a day and just one or two days a week, but John says I do a great job, and Wendy says I've been a lifesaver. The doctor actually put her on bed rest the last couple weeks so she's said she doesn't know what she'd do without me otherwise—I don't know either because the last couple times I was there she was laying in bed looking like an overripe watermelon. Makes me glad I never had any kids of my own. I don't know how women do it.

John seems real nervous when he picks me up. "I've been gone almost an hour," he says. "Wendy could go into labor any time now. I don't like leaving her alone."

"There's no reason to worry," I tell him. "Even if she goes into labor, it'll be hours before the baby comes. You'll have plenty of time to get her there."

I sound like I know all about babies, but the only pregnant woman I ever spent time around was Bel back when she was pregnant with Lilybelle, and that was—wow, sixty years ago. Medicine and pregnancy have probably changed a lot since then. It's hard to believe it's been sixty years—that if Lilybelle had lived, she'd be that old now, almost an old lady like me and Bel. What if Lilybelle had lived? What would our lives have been like—would Bel have ever left Charlie? I bet Lilybelle would have gotten married and had kids—heck, she'd probably be a grandmother by now, and Bel a great-grandmother—surrounded by grandchildren and great-grandchildren... and probably too busy for me.

And then I feel awful because just for a minute, it crosses my mind that it's a good thing Lilybelle died because I might be all alone otherwise. No, I try to tell myself—if Bel hadn't always been around, I might have had a chance to find my own husband, but I know that's not true—Bel and I were separated all those years, the prime years for getting married, and I never looked for a man. But if Lilybelle had lived, Bel might have been a lot happier, and maybe Lilybelle and I would have been friends too, or at least I would have been like her aunt—after all, she was kind of named for me, even though I always thought her name was kind of ridiculous.

"Thanks so much for helping out with the tours, Lyla," John says, breaking my train of thought. "It's been a big help and a relief for Wendy and me."

"You're welcome," I says. "I kind of like doing it, though I have a hard time remembering what all that furniture is—I mean what period and all that."

"That's all right," he says. "If you don't know the answer to something, just keep telling people to ask me."

"Okay, I will," I says. That's easy to do since we have a tour every hour and I sell tickets and greet people at the door who come in for the next tour while John's busy giving the current one, and then I lead the next one and we just keep switching off.

"We have a school class coming today," John tells me as we arrive at the house. "A high school interior decorating class coming to see a historic home."

"That's nice," I says.

"The teacher said they're all fourteen and fifteen year olds," he says. "Do you mind leading the tour, or would you rather I did? I didn't know how you'd feel about talking to children."

"Fifteen years old is hardly children," I says. "I was already out working for a living by that age—they sent you out to work when you were fourteen at the orphanage."

"Well, if you're okay with leading the tour, then maybe I can go upstairs for a few minutes to check on Wendy. I gave her a bell to ring, but I still worry about her."

"It's all going to work out just fine," I tell him. "You're going to be a great father."

"Still, I'm glad Neill is staying with my parents for a few days," he says.

"Oh, yeah," I says, having forgotten about Neill, "you're already a great father."

"That's okay," he says. "I'm glad you think so."

As we get out of the car, I realize I mean what I said. He is a great father. I don't have patience for kids, but I admire how I've seen Wendy and John treat their little boy. Maybe I haven't warmed up to that kid yet just because I'm jealous that he has it so much better than I ever did.

Once we're inside the house, there isn't much to do. I usually walk around downstairs and try to straighten up things before the first tour. Once in awhile, I get a dustcloth and clean a little—just can't help it—it's an old habit that's hard to break. Wendy doesn't have much time to clean the house when she's busy with Neill all day and especially now that she's pregnant. John and her have someone who comes in once a week to clean, but these younger girls don't know how to clean like they did back in my day. Modern conveniences like these new vacuum cleaners and dishwashers have made them soft. I bet not one of them has gotten down on her knees to scrub a floor. I hate to think what their bathtubs at home look like.

At the top of the hour, a school bus pulls up and out pop about twenty fifteen-year-old girls and two boys. Most of them are as tall or taller than me—especially the boys. They look bored, but their teacher seems to have them under control. Still, I feel exhausted just looking at them.

I open the door to the teacher while the kids stand all over the front lawn. She says to me, "Hello, is John Vandelaare here? I was told he would personally lead us on the tour." I take one look at her and can see she's what they call one of those "high maintenance" types—any woman wearing a scarf around her neck usually thinks she's something, and I'm too old now to put up with her attitude, so I just says, "I'll go get him for you." She steps into the hall while I go find John, who's in the library. I tell him the teacher wants to see him and I says, "I think you better lead this tour." I don't know if I look worried or if my voice makes it clear I'm not putting up with any high maintenance teachers, but he just says, "Okay, Lyla. I'll handle this one."

I stay in the library for a few minutes as I listen to all the commotion in the hall and the noise the teenagers make. I don't know why, but I feel shy being around all those kids. I never liked teenagers much—never liked kids actually, but especially not teenagers—they just seem like a bunch of spoiled kids if you ask me—hanging out in school and living off their parents when they could be out working like I was at their age.

I can hear John talking to them, but I can't make out the words he's saying. After a few minutes, he leads them into one of the parlors and I hear him slide shut the old parlor doors so I figure I can make my escape into the hall without seeing any of them. Wendy's alone upstairs resting. Neill is at his grandparents, John said, so I don't have to worry about him. I didn't see John go upstairs, though, to check on Wendy, so I figure I should do that and then maybe I can hide out in the private rooms until these kids are out of the house. I'll make it up to John by leading the next two tours.

I leave the library and step into the hall, heading for the stairs when I stop dead in my tracks.

It's that little monster, standing in the hall, by herself, obviously playing hooky from the tour. Her dark hair and complexion make her unmistakable as May's daughter, Josie.

For a moment, I feel trapped. Will she try to assault me? Will she swear at me and embarrass me in front of John? Maybe her teacher has better control over her than that, but I'd find that hard to believe—oh, I bet Josie just loves that high maintenance teacher; what the hell is this girl even doing in an interior decorating class? She belongs in a juvenile delinquent home.

Josie hasn't noticed me yet because she's staring at the giant genealogy chart on the wall—the one that shows the O'Neill family tree, as well as the Hennings who first owned the house and are related to John and Wendy somehow—I never have quite figured out that chart, though I've tried to explain it to people on the tour. Well, I just tell them John and Wendy are related to the Hennings, and if they care, they look at the chart themselves.

The stairs are about halfway between me and Josie. Can I escape up them without her seeing me? I try, but the second I take a step, the old floor creaks. She looks over at me, but I guess she doesn't really see me at first. Instead, she just says, "These people are like relatives of mine somehow."

"Uh huh," I says, surprised at first and then remembering John is related to the Dalrymples—to May, Josie's mother.

"My mother would love this," she says. "See here—this Margaret Dalrymple that married Will Whitman—she was my grandpa's grandma's sister or something like that. That's how we're related—no one in my family ever lived here, but my mother sure likes that we're related to people who did. She's that way—WASPish."

"I thought you were Vietnamese," I says, not sure why I even suddenly feel like talking to her.

I find myself stepping closer until I'm standing just a yard from her; that's when she really looks at me and says, "Oh, it's you."

"Are you interested in family trees?" I asks her—I realize what a stupid comment it is as soon as it's out of my mouth, but I don't know what else to say to her.

"Sure," she says, "about as much as prom dresses, unicorns, and Lawrence Welk." And then she sticks her finger down her throat.

I can't help laughing at the expression on her face; I think she's trying to be funny, not rude, so I find the courage to say, "I'm surprised a girl your age even knows who Lawrence Welk is."

"Are you kidding? Great-Grams watches those old reruns every Saturday night—you'd think it was still 1960 in our house."

"The costumes on that show are kind of out there," I admit, choosing my words carefully, saying "out there" 'cause I figure it's the kind of slang she understands. I feel like I'm talking to a wild dog, like I'm trying to make friends with it, like I'm approaching it slowly, letting it sniff me, letting it see I won't hurt it, and hoping it won't bite me before we become friends.

"Well, Great-Grams is like eighty-something so I understand her watching it, but my mother is only thirty-five. She's too young for that old time shit, but she acts like she's some part of all that Victorian white supremacy era world—before multiculturalism and diversity and good shit like that came along; you know what I'm saying?"

"No, not really," I says, surprised by how smart she sounds despite her foul mouth.

"No, you wouldn't—you're part of that too. I suppose you drink your tea with your pinky up—WASP."

"I don't drink tea," I says, looking around for the wasp—I hate those damn things and I don't know where there's a fly swatter. "I drink coffee."

"Yeah, out of fine china I bet. What the hell? What is wrong with you people living in these old houses and collecting antiques and ignoring that there's a war going on in Iraq and people are starving in Africa. My grandpa died in Vietnam but a lot of good it did. Didn't change you ostriches."

"What are you talking about?" I asks.

"I'm talking about how I'm damn sick of pretending I'm white—of pretending I live in some fucking white lace curtain world—when this world is really all kinds of fucked up. I'm part Vietnamese! Doesn't anyone see that?"

"I can tell from your hair and eyes, I guess," I says, trying to stay calm. I don't want to rile the girl up and wake Wendy if she's sleeping upstairs.

"So are you getting any from that boyfriend I saw you kissing at Presque Isle?" she asks.

I don't know what to say to that—I'd almost forgotten she saw me that night.

"Did you hear me?" she asks. "Are you getting any, lady?"

"My name's Lyla."

"I should have figured—old-fashioned."

"Like Josie's such a great name," I says, getting a bit ticked off. "Sounds like a pussycat."

She fakes a laugh and says, "That's funny—not. But you didn't answer my question."

"No," I says. "I guess we broke up."

"That sucks," she says, scanning my face. I'm afraid I'm showing I'm still a bit hurt that Mike never called me.

"I guess men just suck," I says, trying to use her language and laugh it off.

"No," she says. "They make their girlfriends do that."

At first I don't know what she means until she says, "I gave my boyfriend a blowjob last night. What do you think about that?"

She says it like she's ready to fight me, but I just shrug my shoulders. What am I supposed to think about it? At this point, there's not much she can say to shock me even if I do think she needs her mouth washed out with soap.

"He made me do it," she says, her eyes softening and turning toward the ground. "He told me he'd hit me if I didn't. He hits me a lot."

Why is she telling me this? Do I look like some guidance counselor from an afterschool special?

Finally, I says, "That's wrong."

"He doesn't care," she says.

"Why do you let him?" I asks.

"Huh? You think I like it?" she asks, looking back up at me.

"No, but if you told your mother or someone, it could be stopped."

"I'm telling you, ain't I? I figured if you're out kissing guys, you've been around the block."

"Well, I—"

"What do I do about it? Sometimes I'm afraid he's going to kill me. He gets pissed at me about everything."

Suddenly, I feel the old anger rise up in me.

"Women should never put up with abuse from men," I says. "I kicked a guy in the nuts one time for hitting my best friend."

She lets out a nervous laugh. "I wish you'd kick my boyfriend in the nuts. I wish I could, but he's really tall, and well...I'm afraid of him. He's seventeen and over six feet."

"I don't blame you then," I says. "I'd probably be afraid too."

For a minute there's silence between us. I don't know what more to say to her. Should I call Child Protective Services or something for her?

"Just forget I said anything," she says, turning back to the chart. "I don't know why I did. No one fucking cares about me."

"Your mother cares about you," I says.

"What the fuck do you know about my mother?" she asks, her eyes flashing as she turns to look at me again. "Don't you talk to me about her. She lives in a fantasy world of knick-knacks and white lace. Fuck that. She probably had sex one time in her whole life with my dad and then decided to hide behind antiques and pretending she's a white girl rather than a bastard of the Vietnam War. At least when I'm sucking my boyfriend's dick, I know I'm alive—that's more than I bet she can say."

"You're very vulgar," I says, but not like I'm angry, just sad because of it, which I am.

"Tough shit. What are you going to do about it? Tattle on me to my teacher?"

"No," I says. "I don't think that would do any good."

"You're damn right it wouldn't."

"I'm going to tell you, though," I says, wondering why I'm bothering because it won't do any damn good; what's this hoodlum to me? "That you don't have to do anything you don't want to—not even when someone threatens you."

"You don't know what it's like," she says. "He's an asshole, but he's the only one who pays me any attention."

"I think, Josie," I tell her, "that you're stronger than that. Do you know that you're pretty and you're smart? I can tell you're smart, so don't pretend you ain't. You don't need your boyfriend or your mom or anyone to pay attention to you. You don't need anyone. Not anyone. I never had anyone and I've done just fine by myself."

I don't know if she really hears me, but she's still talking to me anyways.

"My dad didn't care about me," she says. "He left when my mom got pregnant with me. Do you know what it's like not to have your father care about you? Is it any wonder I chase after the first guy who shows an interest in me? I'm not stupid. I know I'm psychologically fucked up—I just don't know what to do about it."

"You still have your mother; talk to her."

"What good is my mother?" she asks.

"She's better than no mother at all," I says. "I know what it's like not to have a father or a mother. I grew up in an orphanage while my sister got adopted. I had nuns raise me and then turn me loose when I was fourteen to support myself. And here I am, still going and doing just fine so you don't have anything to complain about."

"Nuns?" she says. "They're probably worse than WASPS."

"Well, they do have their own way of stinging," I says, wondering why she's so obsessed with insects.

She laughs. "You're all right, Lyla. I mean, you're old and all, but you're a lot cooler than my great-grams at least."

"Well, take it easy on her," I says, half-laughing. "Not everyone can be as cool as me."

"No, I mean," she says, "well, you got mad about my stealing those candles and drinking at the Food Fest, but you haven't blinked an eye while I've stood here swearing."

"Trust me," I says. "I've heard all those words in my lifetime and many more you don't even know."

She kind of scowls, but I don't think it's at me.

"I just get so fed up with all the crap," she says. "And what can I do about it except swear? I can't fight back—not against my boyfriend anyway, and my mom won't understand—she doesn't give a shit about me."

I step closer to her, afraid still that like a wild dog, she'll bite me, or worse, turn and run. But she doesn't do either. I think she's as surprised as I am when I put my hand on her shoulder, but she doesn't shrug it off, and I manage not to pull it away.

"My sister died recently," I says, not quite sure where I'm going with this or how I'll say it. "I never got to make things right with her. I'll regret that for the rest of my life. We let the woman who adopted her come between us. Don't let your boyfriend get between you and your mom. Talk to your mom."

"She won't understand. She'll flip out!" she says.

"Yes, I imagine she will, but...well, so what if she does? Once she gets over the shock, I think I know your mom enough to know she'll do something about it then, whatever you need her to do. She'll be there for you. You know, maybe she needs you too. Her friend, Sybil, just moved away, and she's probably lonely and could use you to be a friend to her just as much as you need her to be your friend now."

Josie looks at me like I'm nuts, but then after a minute, she says, "She did ask me if I wanted to help out in the store—she said I'm old enough now, and I don't think she asked just 'cause Sybil left."

"There, you see," I says.

"But I hate all that old crap."

"Hey, watch your tongue. I'm old crap," I says, trying to lighten the mood.

"Yeah," she laughs, "but you're cool old crap."

"Thanks," I says, "but I bet you could find some cool old crap at your mother's antique shop if you look around."

"I don't know," she says.

"Do you want me to tell your mom about your boyfriend for you?"

"You wouldn't," she says.

"Josie," I says, "I'm not going to let you or any girl be abused by a man. Do you understand me?" I'm surprised, but I mean it. For whatever reason, I like this nasty girl; she deserves better.

She's silent for a minute. She looks down at the ground, like she's trying to decide something, and then finally, she says, "Yeah. I guess so. I've just been afraid is all. I mean, what if no one else ever likes me again?"

"I don't blame you for being afraid," I says, "but your boyfriend doesn't really like you. He mistreats you because he doesn't feel good about himself, not that that gives him the right. And you let him because you don't feel good about yourself, though I don't know why because you're pretty and you seem pretty smart to me."

She looks up at me, like she's not sure whether to believe me or not.

"So," I says, "you're going to tell your mother so I don't have to, right?"

"Well, I—"

I give her the death glare and flare my nostrils.

"All right," she says. "After school, I'll go over to her shop and tell her."

"Promise?"

"Jesus Christ, you don't let up do you?" she says.

The door from the dining room slides open and in a second the hall is filling with teenagers.

"You better go join the tour before they know you're missing," I tell her.

She smirks, but without a word, she starts down the hall. As she merges with her classmates, she sort of looks back and smiles at me. I hope that smile is the promise I was asking for.

In another second, she goes upstairs with the rest of the kids to see the bedrooms.

Damn, I'd like to get my hand on that boyfriend of hers. I wonder if his name is Charlie. I'd give him a good kick in his nuts—that would teach him to keep his dick in his pants.

I go into the library to check if these kids tracked any mud on the carpets. You got to clean it up right away or you'll never get it out. There isn't any mud, but I feel tired. Tense from my little showdown with the wild girl, I sit down in a chair and close my eyes and say a little prayer that Josie will do what I told her—tell her mother what's going on. She doesn't deserve to be on her own in the world at that age like I was. No one deserves that. I guess it doesn't hurt for me to try to help someone sometimes, although you usually just get crap when you do. Still, I'd sure like to beat the crap out of her boyfriend. I start to think about me doing it too, wondering if I could still kick high enough at my age, and as I'm thinking about it, I must drift into a little nap for a minute or two because next thing I hear is a crowd coming down the stairs, and then the house is quiet for a couple of minutes, and then suddenly, I jump up when I hear John yelling.

"Lyla! Lyla!"

He sounds worried. Before I can go to see what's wrong, he bursts into the library.

"There you are, Lyla! Wendy's water broke. I have to take her to the hospital!"

"Oh dear," I says, and suddenly, I feel like a mother hen. "What should I do?"

"Just keep an eye on the house. We're supposed to be open for tours for another two hours. Can you handle it, or should we just close?"

"No, I can handle it," I says. "You go take her to the hospital. Hurry up!"

I've followed John back into the hall, and in a second, I see him practically leaping back up the stairs, two or three steps at a time, and the way he's acting like a maniac when his foot comes down on the steps, I wonder that the old staircase can handle it.

"Wendy!" he screams. I wonder whether I should follow him, but then I hear Wendy yelling, "John, calm down. You're going to make yourself sick. We have plenty of time."

I can hear the upstairs floor creaking a bit as he rushes around collecting things while she appears at the top of the stairs and slowly tries to come down.

I rush halfway up the stairs, almost as fast as John, and I give Wendy my arm.

"Thanks, Lyla," she says. "Are you sure you'll be okay here on your own? We can close down the house for the afternoon."

"No, no," I says. "You just take care of that baby."

"Ohhh!" she screams a little and puts a hand on her stomach.

"Are you okay?" I asks.

Her face is kind of flushed, but she says, "Yes, I'll be fine. I've been through this before. But damn, this better be the last time."

When we get to the bottom of the stairs, John comes bounding down after us, carrying a suitcase.

"Okay, let's go!" he exclaims.

"Thanks, Lyla," says Wendy. I'm surprised when she leans over and kisses me on the cheek. "What would we do without you?" she asks.

I don't know what to say to that except, "Good luck with everything."

"Be sure to lock the door when you go, Lyla," John says.

"Okay," I says. "Call me at home later so I know how things are."

"Okay," John says. "Come on, Wendy!"

"Oh, Lyla, how will you get home?" Wendy asks as she reaches the front door, trying to hide a smirk as she has another contraction.

"I'll call Bel," I says. "It'll be fine. Don't worry about nothing except bringing that baby into the world."

"Thanks, Lyla. You're a godsend," says John.

And then they're out the door.

I go into the dining room from where I can look out the window, and I watch John helping Wendy get in the car. Most men suck, but not John. You can see how excited he is and it's written all over his face that he's crazy in love with his wife. I watch him help her with her seatbelt, and then he runs around to the other side of the car just as the doorbell rings.

"Damn tourists. They can just wait a second," I think as I wait to watch the car pull onto the street on its way to the hospital. And then I go to the front door and find two former Marquette residents on vacation from their home in Maryland; they want a tour, so I gives it to them, being all professional, like it's just any other day at the Robert O'Neill Historical Home.

Chapter 29

"It's a girl!" says John.

"Oh, that's wonderful!" I says. "I prayed all night that everything would go well."

It's 8 a.m. and I'd just gotten up when the phone rang. Bel had wanted to go out for breakfast at five this morning, but I'd told her, "No, I don't want to miss John's call." Though I kind of thought maybe Eleanor would end up calling me. Bel tried to tell me, "He's not going to be so rude as to call you at five or six in the morning," but that only made me wonder why she's always so rude to do it then. But as soon as I heard John's voice, I think how Bel and I can still go out for breakfast since I figure the call will only last a couple of minutes.

"It was a few hours ago she was born," he says, "but I didn't want to call you too early. I hope I haven't."

"Oh no, I was hoping you'd call right away. I've felt so excited. What's her name?"

"Madeleine," he says, "for Wendy's ancestor who ran away from home and never came back to Marquette. We thought it was appropriate."

"It's a beautiful name," I says, and I feel it is. I'm not sure why, but it does feel sort of right to name her Madeleine.

"Her full name is Madeleine Eliza Vandelaare," he says. "Eliza is for Mrs. O'Neill."

"Perfect!" I says. "Mr. and Mrs. O'Neill would be so happy for you and Wendy."

"I hope so," John says. "Mr. O'Neill maybe didn't think about a family being in the house again when he left it in my care, but it seems appropriate. It won't be long before Neill and Madeleine will be sliding down the banisters just like he and Mrs. O'Neill did when they were young."

"I'm so happy for you," I says, and I do feel happy for them.

"I can't wait for you to meet her, Lyla. She's beautiful. We're going to keep the house closed through the holiday weekend—Labor Day's been slow in past years anyway, but Aunt Eleanor says you're coming to Alan's birthday party on Monday at his new house, so you can meet Madeleine then. The doctor said she'll be fine to go out by then. Wendy and her will be going home tomorrow."

"Oh wow! That's fast," I says, "I can't wait to meet her."

I call up Bel after I get off the phone with John, and we go out to breakfast like we planned, and then we go shopping at Econo and buy groceries, including stuff so Bel can make her Jell-O salad for Alan's birthday party. Blueberries are on sale since the season has just about ended so I decide I'll bring a blueberry pie—I don't usually make pies 'cause there aren't enough people around to eat them, but I figure there will be at the party.

"Ain't they having birthday cake?" Bel asks.

"I don't know," I says, "but who doesn't like blueberry pie?" And I'm so excited about the pie that I buy extra blueberries so I can make another pie for myself later, and I buy two half gallons of vanilla ice cream, one for my second pie, and one to bring with me to the party.

"You don't need to bring all that," Bel says.

"I know," I says, "but it's a holiday and you only live once."

She gives me a funny look, but she doesn't say anything. She knows better.

When we get home, I asks her if she wants to go out for supper after I get home from church.

"No," she says. "I'm feeling kind of tired today."

"That's 'cause you got up at 5 a.m. wanting to go out for pancakes," I says.

"Maybe," she says. "I'm going to go take a nap."

"Okay," I says as the elevator stops to let her off on her floor. "I'll check in with you when I get home from Mass in case you change your mind."

When I get home from Mass, I get off the elevator on Bel's floor and go knock on her door. I'm hoping she's changed her mind because I'm starving. I'm wondering if she'll be willing to go to Bonanza. I have a craving for a steak tonight, and it is a holiday weekend, so what the heck.

When Bel opens the door, I can see she's been crying.

"What's wrong, Bel?" I asks.

She just stares at me, her face looking horrible—sticky wet from crying and those puppy dog eyes she has are popping out. But she doesn't answer me; she looks too tongue-tied.

"What's wrong?" I asks again.

She goes over to her chair and grabs a Kleenex to blow her nose; then she gestures for me to sit down, so I do. My feet hurt since I walked to church and back, and I'm a little sticky-sweaty from walking. It feels good to sit down. It'll probably be the only relaxing moment of my day since she's obviously going to dump something on me. I feel my gut tightening as I watch her fold up her Kleenex, then grab another and finish blowing her nose.

"Something's been wrong for a while," I says. "I've kind of sensed it."

"You have?" she says.

"Yeah," I says, real soft-like, and a little scared too.

"I've been feeling kind of weird lately," she admits, sitting back in her chair and looking away from me, out the window.

"Well, you've always been weird; how's that worth crying about?" I laugh to lighten the moment, but I can tell from the look on her face that it's not going to work.

"No, weird, like dizzy-headed," she says. "Well, not dizzy like I'm going to faint, but like I just couldn't put two and two together—at first, last spring, when it started, I thought I was just having one of those senior moments they talk about, but it kept happening more and more."

"Oh," I says. "Well, does the doctor need to change your medication?"

"No, it's more than that, Lyla. I forget things. You must have noticed."

I have a flashback to her driving the wrong way up High Street, and then how she left me at Shopko.

"Lyla, I have Alzheimer's," she says, "and it's only going to get worse."

She finally turns to look at me again.

"I can see how scared you look," she says to me.

I do feel scared—I can feel my eyes getting wider and my heart skipping a beat.

"If you think you're scared, think how I feel," she says.

"Well, but—is it bad—what—can't you take care of yourself then, or—"

"It's going to get worse," she says. "I'm already afraid to turn on a burner on the stove and things like that. I—I'm afraid of being alone anymore."

"Well," I says, wondering what to say—what to suggest—since she does live alone.

"I don't want to end up in a nursing home," she says. "I don't have any kids or grandkids to take care of me. What am I going to do?"

I know what I'm supposed to say and it's crossed my mind before that this day would come, but I thought it was another five or ten years in the future. I know we aren't young anymore, but how could this be happening already? Bel's only seventy-five and I'm seventy-seven, and while I know we're getting up there, it's not like we're eighty or something already.

When I don't say anything, she says, "It's okay, Lyla. I know you can't take care of me. I'd be too much of a burden at our age. I just—well, what am I going to do? It's not easy to get that Dr. Kevorkian to help you these days."

"Bel," I says, stunned by my words but meaning them, "you'll come move in with me when it gets bad. You've got time, though. You aren't that bad yet. You probably have a year or so still of being in your right mind. That's lots of time for us to figure out what to do."

"Us?" she says. She still looks scared, but I can see a little hope on her face now.

"Yes, 'us'," I says. "I mean—you'd look after me, wouldn't you?"

"I—I've been afraid to tell you about this, Lyla, because I don't want to be a burden and I was afraid you'd get mad."

"Why would I get mad?" I says, though I know I can be a crank, but she ought to know by now that I don't mean it most of the time when I snap at her. "It's not your fault," I says. "You didn't choose it."

"And you'd really let me stay with you?" she says. "Won't it be crowded? You only have one bedroom."

"What's the difference? We're at each other's places all the time anyways. We can get someone to come in and help if we need to."

"Thanks, Lyla," she says, looking scared still, like she has more to say to me. I just wait for it until she's ready to say more.

"Lyla, I'm scared. I don't know what will happen. I'm afraid of what it will be like, not even to know who I am or to be trapped in the past or some memory I don't rightly remember, or—"

I don't know what to say 'cause I don't know what it'll be like either, so finally, I says, "I don't know what it'll be like either."

"I was afraid—well, when I was in a bad situation like this before," she says, "with Charlie, you left, Lyla, and I was afraid—"

I can't help but roll my eyes over that one. "Bel," I says, "I left because I couldn't stand to see him hurting you—and I know I shouldn't have done that and I always have regretted it. I won't do that again. In fact, I can make up for it now by helping you out."

Funny. I'm feeling kind of calm about it—hoping this whole "make amends" thing I started on this summer with Bill and Jessie maybe is going to work this time with Bel.

"So," I says, "I came up to see if you want to go out for supper, so let's do that. It'll cheer you up."

Ignoring my suggestion, she asks, "Will you go with me to my doctor's appointments from now on? I don't mean just sitting in the waiting room, but will you talk to the doctor too? I'm afraid I won't even remember what he tells me."

"I will," I says, "if I don't starve to death first. Come on. You'll feel better if you eat something. Go wash your face and let's go. How about Bonanza? I feel like I could eat a huge steak and salad tonight."

"Okay," she says. She doesn't sound very enthused, but she gets up from her chair. "It's just—well, I want to tell you something else too."

"Can't you tell me at Bonanza?" I asks.

"No," she says.

"Is it about your Alzheimer's, or is it something else bad?"

"No, it's—well, it's not about Alzheimer's really, or at least, only a little about it, and it's—it's not bad unless you want to view it that way."

"Can it wait until after supper?" I says.

"Ye-es," she says. "I...I guess so." She doesn't look happy about waiting, but I've had enough bad news before eating my supper. She's just worried—I know that. I said she could stay with me; she's afraid I'll change my mind or resent her or something, but—well, she'd do it for me, I know that. I'll have to get help, though. I can't help her go to the bathroom and stuff when she gets to that point—that might be too gross, but more because I won't be able to lift her; still, that's something I can explain to her later. And it's not like she'll be crippled, just out of her mind. But for now, it's enough that she can feel comforted that I'll look after her.

Eating out doesn't seem to lift Bel's spirits. I get a mini-black gold steak, but all Bel will eat is the salad bar and she hardly eats any of that—doesn't even want ice cream. I eat until I'm bursting—I have the chili, the salad bar, the steak, even have a taco and a little ravioli. I don't have room for dessert, but I got my money's worth out of that meal. You always do at Bonanza—and then some. It's the best deal in Marquette as far as I'm concerned.

I try to be cheery as we eat, but Bel just stays quiet. Well, I guess learning you have Alzheimer's can depress you like that. She admits she's known for a few months now, but it was only after she realized she was starting to forget things, including me at Shopko, that she got scared. I think she held onto her secret as long as she could—she says she doesn't want to burden me—but I have a hard time understanding how she kept quiet about it as long as she did—the whole summer really.

When we get back to Snowberry, I want to tell her I'll see her tomorrow, but she asks me to come over for a few minutes 'cause there's something else she needs to tell me.

I'm about bursting at the seams from eating so much, and I'm going to need a good long trip to the bathroom pretty soon, so I hope it's just something silly she's worrying about, but I agree to go to her apartment for a few minutes anyways. I can always use her bathroom if I have to.

Once we get to her apartment, we sit down in the living room, but then she jumps up to get some root beer and won't sit down until I agree to have some too. I get up because she's so nervous she drops the ice cube tray. I don't what her problem is. She can't have something worse to say to me than that she has Alzheimer's.

When we finally sit down again, she grabs a pillow and clutches it like she needs to protect herself, or at least have a security pillow, before she finally starts talking.

"Lyla," she says after taking a deep breath, "I never told you this 'cause I wasn't sure you'd like it—though I kind of hoped you'd figure it out, and maybe you have—but I want you to know it now, not to hurt or upset you.

I—well, I kind of hope you'll somehow like it, take it as a compliment."

"What is it?" I asks, wondering what the hell she's talking about. That Alzheimer's is really making her odder every day.

She doesn't say anything for a few seconds, but she gets this super weird expression on her face, like her cheeks are caving inward, and then her chest starts heaving like she can't breathe, and then finally, she says, "Lyla, I love you."

I laugh. I can't help it. "That's good," I says. "Yeah, I knew that and you know how I feel."

"No, Lyla, I mean, sure we're friends, even like sisters, but I—well, I really love you. I mean love you like—well, like if I could be with anyone, it would be with you. I mean I'd pick you to, well, I kind of have spent my life with you, only not exactly in as close a way as I mean. I mean I love you, Lyla, and I'm not asking for sex at our age, but just closeness—like being allowed to sleep next to you and hold you at night. To me, you're the perfect woman, the most beautiful, most amazing woman. The person I've always felt I was put on this earth to love. I want to live with you and love you and hold you at night and..."

As she babbles on, I feel like a deer caught in the headlights. And when it really hits me what she's saying, I lose it.

"That's enough of that!" I tell her.

What the hell else can I say to such craziness?

"Lyla, I love you," she keeps on. "You—you know, you—well, like in that Tom Cruise movie—you complete me. You—"

"Shut up!" I says. It's not the words so much as the sick puppy look in her eyes that makes me yell, but I'm yelling anyways. "I've put up with a lot of crap from you over the years," I tell her, "but I'm not putting up with this."

"Lyla, I thought you'd be flattered," she says, a pleading look on her face now. "I don't want to upset you. It could be so beautiful; it—"

"Flattered! You think having a rummy like you wanting that from me— you think that's flattering? How can you say something like that to me? I stood up for you in the orphanage, took care of you when you were so drunk you'd have hurt yourself otherwise, listened to your whining about all your problems for years. You've been a burden on me since day one, and this is how you repay my friendship? Goddamn it, Bel. I'm not putting up with this...this disgusting...lesbian crap. Not after all the crap you've given me. Not ever. This is just—it makes me feel like throwing up. It's disgusting!"

I can see the tears welling up in her face, but goddamn it! How the hell did she expect I'd react to that crap?

I suddenly feel so hot and red in the face that I have to stand up. All that Bonanza chili is doing a number on my stomach—or maybe it's the thought of what she just said that's making my insides churn. What the hell is she thinking?

"Lyla, I just told you I love you," Bel sobs, "and all you can say back is I'm a burden. I say I want to be with you for the rest of my life, and this is what I get?"

"What you get? I'll tell you what you get," I says. "You get to lose a friend because this is just—just sickening—disgusting."

I don't know what I'm doing or saying for a minute, I'm so mad. And then I remember where the door is.

"I'm out of here," I says. "You've come close before, but this time you've really crossed the line."

As I start toward the door, she jumps up, runs to me, and throws her arms around me.

"Get your goddamn hand off my boob, you fucking lesbo!" I holler, trying to shake her loose.

"Lyla, please, I'm sorry," she says, but she does move her hand, though it's on my shoulder. I don't turn around. I stand there, trying to understand how I could have been friends with such a pervert as she keeps rattling on. "Lyla, I can't help it. I've always loved you—since we were little girls. I'd have married you instead of Charlie if it had been possible."

"Get the hell away from me!" I says, turning around and pushing her away from me. "I'm leaving. We're through. I don't ever want to see your face again."

And then I'm out the door. I make sure I grab the doorknob to slam the door behind me, and then I run to the stairwell. I'm not going to wait for the elevator because she'll catch up with me, but by the time I get to the end of the hall, I realize she hasn't followed me. She's probably too ashamed of being seen in the hallway the way she's sobbing.

"Goddamn her!" I keep saying to myself as I climb the stairs up to my floor.

"Just when I thought things were finally getting better," I mutter, as I reach my door and fumble for my key.

I don't feel safe until I'm in my apartment with the door bolted, and by then, my stomach is demanding release so I head to the bathroom, and I sit in there for the longest time and start to cry. She was my best friend. I trusted her. How the hell could she do this to me?

I feel so upset, first angry, but then just depressed. I go into the living room and turn on the TV, but there's nothing on to watch, and I don't feel up to waiting for Lawrence Welk to come on, so I go take a shower and go to bed.

Once I'm in bed, though, I lay there depressed for a long time, wondering how the hell she ever thought she could say those words to me and not expect me to get angry. Did she really think I'd—ooh, gross.

I'm surprised she isn't calling me nonstop, but what would I say to her if she did? I bet she realizes she crossed the line—well, she did cross it. She can go find someone else to take care of her Alzheimer's—I pity the home health nurse who gets her—she'll probably try to make a pass at her. I try to laugh at the image of that, but I just end up crying some more until I finally fall asleep.

In the morning, I'm not awake more than three seconds before I start thinking about it again. "What the hell was she thinking?" is my first thought, but as I get up and turn on the coffeepot and listen to it perk while I go to the bathroom and get dressed, I replay the conversation over and over in my head.

"What the hell?" I keep thinking. After all the years I've known her—sixty-seven years I think it is—you'd think I would have figured it out. You'd think—well, I did know her. I mean, how did she—well, I guess liking girls helps to explain the drinking and her marriage problems—maybe she didn't give Charlie what he wanted in the bedroom because she wasn't that way—but...why now? Why after all these years? Has she been watching that Ellen DeGeneres or *Will and Grace* show or something and it gave her ideas? It must be something she saw on TV because back when we were young, people didn't talk about those things—and I wish they didn't now. Of course, maybe she didn't know she was a lesbian back then—I mean, there weren't any lesbians on TV back then—hell, there wasn't even TV, so maybe she didn't have those ideas back then because there was no one to put them into her head. I guess too, maybe she was scared to tell me until now—

when I said she could live with me because of the Alzheimer's, well, maybe that gave her ideas. Well, she should have stayed too scared to tell me. Hell, remember the 4th of July when she came into my bedroom? If I'd let her live here, she could have done that again and gotten away with it before I woke up. Goddamn, she's lucky I didn't deck her for what she said to me.

"Jesus Christ," I mutter as I pour my coffee and let it cool while I open up the curtains. Then I sit down in my chair and stare out the window. It's just barely daylight. I can feel autumn coming. It's not daylight now when I wake in the morning and I'm getting up a little later each day it seems like. In the summer I'm often up at 6 a.m. as soon as it's light, but now it's not daylight until about 7:30 what with summer being almost over. We're down to about twelve rather than sixteen hours of daylight like we had around the summer solstice.

I'll never get used to this staring out at the sky. The view of Marquette and the harbor is beautiful when you stand by the window, but from sitting here in my chair, I could be a hundred rather than just eight stories up for all I can tell since I can't see the ground below me. Before we moved here, Bel used to say it would make her dizzy to live this high up. Of course, she ended up just a floor lower than me so I don't know that it matters, but maybe she would feel a little dizzier if she lived one floor up. Maybe it would have made more sense for me to move in with her instead of her with me—not that it matters now—but just for the sake of logic, I guess Alzheimer's people probably get more confused when taken out of their homes so it would be better if I moved in with her. I don't know why I didn't think of that when we talked, but—oh, Jesus Christ, it won't ever happen now anyways.

How could she say that to me? Even if she did feel that way about me all these years, she didn't have to tell me something so disgusting. How did she think I would take it? What did she think I was going to say, "I love you too, Bel" or something mushy like that? Did she think I'd start buying her flowers and boxes of chocolates on Valentine's Day or something? That would be just way too weird for me, that kind of gay stuff. I mean, even with a man it can be degrading, and just, kind of gross even, but with a woman, and at our age—nasty!

What will she do, though? She can't be by herself if she has Alzheimer's. She could go to the nursing home, but—well, that—that would be like being sent to the orphanage again. That's all the nursing home is really—the orphanage for old people, where you go when no one wants you—not that it would matter to me that much if I were in the nursing home—no one has ever wanted me. No one except for Bel. If someone did want me, I wouldn't know what to do anyways. I'd probably tell him to get lost because I'd be too old to change how things are now. Even with Mike, while he made me feel good, I didn't really want him—I just wanted him to want me a little.

But what's the point of any of it now? Bel was the only friend I had really. I mean, John and Wendy are nice, but we're not that close, and I don't want to become best friends with Eleanor—she's in her nineties anyways and could drop dead any day—and Sybil has left me.

What's there left for me now? For a little while, everything seemed to be going so well, especially back around Finn Fest. And now, just a few weeks later, everything's fallen apart.

I wonder if Bel will try to kill herself. She'd be stupid enough to do something like that since she's probably afraid of being all alone now. I guess I'll be all alone too, but—ick! It's just disgusting!

What the hell, Bel? Why'd you have to go and say that crap and ruin everything?

Chapter 30

I don't talk to Bel all Sunday, which is good because if she had dared to call me, I would have hung up on her. But I'm still surprised she doesn't call. I guess she realizes she's blown it for good—and good riddance! She's been holding me back all these years—her with her drunk husband, and her damn anonymous meetings, and her 4 a.m. calls to go out for pancakes—I sure as hell won't miss those—I'll finally be able to catch up on my sleep. And she was always such a damn dingy anyways. And she was always poking her nose into my business, and now I know—she's a—well, she's a damn—well, "pervert" doesn't seem like the right word, but disturbed, damn disturbed, that's for sure.

And then on Monday morning, I remember about the big get-together at Alan's camp and how Eleanor will be coming to pick me up and how Bel was supposed to go too, and I wonder if Bel'll be calling me then to worm her way into going still. I don't care if she did make her damn Jell-O salad—I never liked it anyways, and it can rot in hell for all I care. Let her go find a new girlfriend to share it with.

When Eleanor calls, I've got the blueberry pie cooling on the counter and I'm ready to go.

"We'll be there to pick you and Bel up in about fifteen minutes," Eleanor says.

"Bel ain't going," I tell her.

"Oh, why not?" she asks.

"She's sick," I says, thinking that's not really a lie since she's downright sick in the head.

"Oh, that's too bad," says Eleanor. "Well, I'm sure we'll have plenty of food so we can fix a plate for you to bring home for her later."

"Sure," I says, thinking I don't have a problem with bringing home some leftovers—for me.

After I hang up the phone, I wonder how many other people at the party I'll have to lie to about Bel being sick, but jeez, I sure can't tell them the truth. I'll just say she has a bad summer cold—that's easy enough—believable and easy for me to keep straight.

But what am I going to say in a week or so when it'll be long past the time anyone would still believe she has a cold?

I suppose some other people like John and Wendy will be asking me about Bel when they don't see us together anymore—not Sybil, since she's gone downstate—but then, what about those meetings? I won't be going to them anymore; that's for sure. Bel was the one who wanted to go to them anyways, so she can have them. I do kind of like the girls there, but so what? Sybil's gone, and I can stay friendly with John and Wendy anyways, and that Diana's about as sick as Bel, so it's no loss not to see her, and I'll probably see May once in awhile through John and Wendy. So I don't need those meetings. Only—if Bel so much as dares to say one word about what she said to me to those girls at the meeting, why—well, it's anonymous—I mean confidential—so it won't get back to me, but—well, if she has any sense, she won't say anything because she ought to be ashamed of herself saying things like that to me—just disgusting. But then again, she's got Alzheimer's now so who knows what the hell she'll let slip out? Well, just goddamn let her then—if she wants to go around telling people she's a lesbian and that I didn't want to do those disgusting things with her, well, who the hell is going to take her side over mine? I'm not the one who's the pervert.

I realize I'm standing there staring out of the window and obsessing about things. I'm not going to let Bel ruin my day and my fun at the party. I've let her ruin enough things for me over the years.

"Good riddance! Good goddamn riddance!" I shout to myself as I look for a sweater, grab my pocketbook, and the blueberry pie and head out the door.

I end up waiting in the lobby for about five minutes. All the while I wait, I'm afraid one of the other residents will come and talk to me—they hardly ever talk to me, but most of them are kind of friendly with Bel, and whenever I'm seen without her, it's always, "Where's Bel?" If I tell them she's sick, will they go knock on her door to check on her?

Fortunately, I see a car pull up with Eleanor in the front seat before I have to deal with any of the other residents, but I'm going to have to figure out what to say to them later. Could I say we had a falling out, or do I just say that I haven't talked to Bel lately? Whatever I say, those old biddies will figure it out soon enough—maybe not that Bel's a pervert, but that something's wrong between us, and they'll all be gossiping about it; that's for sure. What the hell was I thinking about moving into a place like this full of a bunch of old hens? Maybe I should find a new place to live.

Only, how will I get around? I'll have to hire a cab. Bel won't be driving me anymore—not that she could much longer with Alzheimer's anyways, and Sybil's moved away, so the Marq-Tran bus is about the only transportation I'll have anymore—I can't be affording a cab. Well, I didn't like depending on Bel that much to drive me around anyways—I wanted to take driving lessons that one time, but she told me there was no reason because she could take me places. That was probably just her way of getting to spend time with me. I wonder if she was always checking me out—I bet she was because she was always telling me I looked pretty, and more than once, she said she wished she had boobs like mine. God, how could I have been friends with her all these years and not have realized she was—a—a—well, a lesbian? Ick!

By the time I get to the car, Maud has gotten out of the backseat to open the door for me, and she takes the pie from me until I'm settled. Lucy is driving with Eleanor in the front seat.

"Isn't it a beautiful day, Lyla," Eleanor says. "What a perfect day for a Labor Day picnic."

"It sure is," I says, not noticing until now how sunny it is.

"We couldn't have better weather," says Eleanor. "Days like this make me feel like a girl again."

"I wish I could feel like a girl again," laughs Lucy.

"It's too bad your friend couldn't come, Lyla," says Maud.

"Oh well, I think she needs to rest. She didn't want to be sneezing all over everyone."

"No, if she's sick, she should stay home," Eleanor agrees.

"So where is this camp that Alan bought?" I asks.

"It's out on the Dead River," says Lucy.

"I guess it got damaged quite a bit by the flood a couple of years ago," said Maud, "so Alan got a good price for it, but you know, he has the Whitman carpentry gene so I'm sure he'll be able to do wonders to the place."

"Yes, and his friend Frank will be around to help him," says Lucy.

"I don't think Frank will be much help," says Eleanor.

No one replies, and from her tone, I can tell Eleanor doesn't like Frank.

"It's nice Alan inherited some money from his dad," I says.

"Yes," says Eleanor. "He had to split the money from the house with his brothers, but he's been good about saving all these years. Though I hated to see that house sold. You know, before Bill owned it, it was my parents' place so it's hard for me to see it go."

"It's just a house, Mom," Lucy says. "We'll always have the memories."

"I know," says Eleanor, "but it's hard anyway."

We're just about out of Marquette now, though it always seems to take longer than I expect; it wasn't that many years ago when the Marquette Mall was the end of town—it's right at the city limits actually, but all this strip mall crap has grown up going toward Negaunee for a couple more miles— not that I really mind since Bonanza and The Pancake House are along the way, but that Westwood Mall, and Walmart, and Target, and Menards and all that—I'd like to know who is shopping at all those places? How did Marquette get big enough to warrant all those businesses? I must be getting old when instead of being excited about new stores, I just feel annoyed by them.

Soon we turn down some side road I don't even know the name of— all this part of town keeps changing so fast—and before I can blink, we're going through woods and you wouldn't even know we'd just been in the city a minute ago, but that's how it is in the U.P., just five minutes away from Nature no matter where you live.

I never was that crazy about Nature, though. Since I never learned to drive, about the farthest I ever got out of the city was usually Presque Isle Park. In fact, I don't think I've ever been invited to a picnic that wasn't in Marquette—that said, I haven't been to that many picnics, other than the parish picnics for St. Peter's, and I haven't gone to many of those either— only the ones I could get Bel to go to since I didn't want to go by myself and risk no one talking to me all the time I was there. But now that Bel won't be around any longer, I won't be going to the church picnics either. Oh, so what? I'm going to a picnic today, ain't I, and she's not, and she wouldn't have even been invited if it hadn't been for me. I hope she's at home right now realizing how she screwed up everything between us and crying her eyes out that she didn't get to go to this party. But with my luck, she's probably having one of her memory lapses and doesn't even remember about it today.

I guess that's not so funny though—her memory lapses. I mean, who but me and her doctor know she has Alzheimer's? And what if something happens like she falls and hurts herself or burns the house down—well, leaves the stove on and starts a fire and—and all of Snowberry burns down because of it? I wonder if I should tell the manager at Snowberry about her having Alzheimer's? I wonder if I can get her put in a nursing home where she won't be a menace to herself and everyone else? I mean, I don't care what happens to her now; I just don't want my apartment going up in smoke.

Goddamn it, Lyla! Stop thinking about her. You promised yourself you'd have fun today.

"...did you, Lyla?"

"What?" I says when I hear Eleanor say my name.

"I said, you never stopped loving Bill even after you broke up with him, did you Lyla?"

What the hell! Why can't she drop that?

"Well, I don't know about that," I says, but I know I did still have some feelings about him or I wouldn't have gone up to the hospital to see him at the end.

"Mother, let it go," says Maud. "We should leave Uncle Bill in peace now."

"Yes, you're right," Eleanor says. "I know May will miss having family across the street, though."

"Is Josie coming to the party? I haven't seen her in a while," says Lucy.

"I doubt it," says Eleanor. "May says the girl is just about impossible these days—sassy and all. I don't understand that—even though I was divorced, you girls didn't act that way toward me."

"Times are different now," says Maud.

I don't know about that. I mean Bel was Josie's age when she married Charlie and he must have been about Josie's boyfriend's age. I'd almost forgotten until now about my conversation with Josie on Friday because I've been so ticked off at Bel. I hope that girl talked to her mother by now. I still wonder whether I should tell May what Josie told me about how her boyfriend treats her.

"Here we are; this should be Alan's road," says Lucy, turning onto a dirt path off the paved road.

As we turn onto the path, I see a sign that says: The Best Place.

"That's a nice name for a camp," says Eleanor. "I've heard lots of people say over the years that camp is the best place, but I don't know that I ever heard of a camp actually named 'The Best Place.'"

"It's not a camp anymore," says Maud. "It's a home now. Wait until you see it, Lyla. It's an adorable cabin. I doubt it would have ever been anyone's camp. I don't know how anyone would not want to live there forever."

After a few more seconds, we come around a turn in the woodsy road and there's first a glimpse of the river—I can see the water sparkle in the early afternoon sun, and then there's the cabin to the left, and already a few cars for the party are in the yard. There's no driveway, just hard firm dirt like they have in the woods.

"Will you be able to walk from here, Mom?" Lucy asks.

"I'm ninety-three, not dead," Eleanor laughs, opening her door and getting out like no one's business. She moves faster than I do, and I'm sixteen years younger than her.

Maud goes to take her arm anyways while carrying a dish in her other hand. Lucy opens up the trunk and collects another dish and some plastic silverware. I wait for her, feeling nervous about going into the house. What if there are people here I don't know? I mean, it must not be just a family party if they invited me too—I'm sure not family.

"Can't forget the potato salad," says Lucy, smiling. "Mother insisted on making it and she made tons too."

"I love potato salad," I says.

"I love blueberry pie," says Lucy, gazing with admiration at it, which makes me feel good—at least I brought the right thing—it beats that crappy old Jell-O salad Bel always brings to these kinds of things—well, we don't get invited to these kinds of things—but she always brings it along to the boring old church picnics and potlucks.

The back door isn't very impressive. It just leads into a crowded little mud room, but then I'm surprised when it opens up into a big kitchen-dining room area with a pair of patio doors off the dining room that open onto a deck with the river just below it while a large living room opens up to the left with a loft area upstairs.

The dining room and deck are full of people.

"Let me introduce you to everyone," says Eleanor. Lucy takes my pie from me and says, "I'll find room in the refrigerator for it."

Eleanor walks with me into the dining room and introduces me to everyone. I know May and I can see John and Wendy out on the deck, but I don't know John's parents, Ellen and Tom, or May's grandma, Bea. And there are a few other people who are introduced as family friends that I don't know. One says he went to high school with Alan, but I forget his name right away. And then from a bedroom somewhere comes Alan in just his swimming trunks to give Eleanor a big kiss.

Then he turns to me with a friendly grin and says, "Welcome, Lyla. We're just about to go swimming—do you want to join us? I heard from Sybil that you got a new bathing suit recently."

"No, I left it at home," I says, though for a minute, as I look at how handsome and fine he looks in that bathing suit, even if he's getting a little middle age spread, I almost regret it. For the first time, I can see how much he looks like his handsome father.

"Well, I'm glad you could come anyway," he says, still smiling.

"Thanks," I says, "and Happy Birthday."

"Thank you."

"Alan, aren't we going to eat soon?" Eleanor asks. "Can't you go swimming later?"

"Tom just started cooking the burgers and brats," he says, "so Frank and I are just going to get in a quick swim. We won't be long."

As Alan is speaking, Frank appears, also in his swim trunks, but also wearing a T-shirt that looks about a size too small for him with that huge chest of his. Still, he might be better built, but he's not as handsome as Alan.

"Ready?" Alan asks him.

"Sure," Frank says.

"I should have brought my bathing suit," May says, "but I didn't think it would be warm enough."

"Since I moved in last week," says Alan, "we haven't had a warm enough day to swim, and I suspect it'll be cooling off by the time we're done eating, so Frank and I better go while we can. We won't be long."

"I wish Josie had come," says May as Alan and Frank disappear out the patio door. "She would have liked to go swimming."

"Why didn't she come?" I asks, kind of relieved that she's not there, but hoping she's not somewhere worse.

"She and her friend had to go shopping for school clothes."

"I thought she started school last week," says Eleanor.

"She did," says May, "but she hates high school, so she and I had a long talk and I called up a friend who teaches at that new North Star Academy, and she said they had room still. I have a little money put away so I can afford to send her there. I had gotten her accepted there last year, but then she insisted she wanted to go to the regular high school to be with her friends. She's been such a handful lately, and I'm afraid of her getting into some serious trouble with the crowd she's started hanging around with since she started high school. She seems so miserable and depressed that I thought switching schools might help. She actually asked me if she could when she got home from school Friday so I called my friend right away. We're lucky they could fit her in. And I thought letting her buy some new school clothes might help her get a new attitude and feel better about herself—you know how fashion is all important when you're a teenage girl."

I don't say anything, but I'm glad to know Josie will be going to a different school—I'm sure she asked so she could get away from that boyfriend of hers. I don't know how much she told her mother, but that's okay—at least she'll be out of that situation and safe now.

John spots us new arrivals now and comes inside. He kisses Aunt Eleanor on the cheek and hugs Lucy and Maud. He says hello to me and asks if he can get me a drink. "Just water," I says, afraid of my stomach doing flip-flops if I have the beer sitting on the cupboard.

"Is the baby out there?" Eleanor asks.

"Yes," says John, "she's sleeping, but Wendy is out there with her."

"Is it safe for her to be out in the fresh air like that?" asks Eleanor. "I mean, she's only three days old."

"The doctor said it would be fine to bring her. We asked before we left the hospital."

"Does she sleep good?" Maud asks.

"Oh yes, so far," says John. "She's an angel."

Eleanor is already out on the deck by now to see the baby and Lucy and Maud are right behind her. I wait a minute for John to give me a glass of water as I debate whether I should go outside or not. I'll feel awkward making small talk with these people no matter what I do.

"Hi, Lyla," says a voice. Then I feel my pant leg being tugged on, and when I look down, little Neill is staring up at me.

I'm surprised he even knows my name. This is the first day he's done more than stare at me.

"Hello," I says back to him. "How are you?"

"Good," he says. "We having cake."

"I know," I says. "It's Alan's birthday. Do you like birthday cake?"

He nods his head enthusiastically.

"So do I," I says.

"Come see the new baby, Lyla!" Eleanor calls from out on the porch.

"Okay. Bye, Neill," I says, relieved to escape the kid, though I like that he actually talked to me this time.

I'm not into babies, but I admit I want to see this one. When I get out on the porch, Wendy is sitting with a bundle in her arms, and John is perched beside her, smiling proudly as she feeds the baby with a bottle.

"Hi, Lyla," says Wendy, looking up at me. "Meet Madeleine."

"Hello, Madeleine," I says, and I have to admit, while most babies look like shriveled little frogs, this one is adorable with such fine soft brown hair on her head and an adorable little nose and the tiniest little hands I've ever seen. Bel would have loved her—she looks a bit like Lilybelle. I wish Lilybelle had lived. She would have been like a daughter to me. Maybe she could have talked some sense into her mother. I don't know why she…

"Lyla, you're crying," says John, looking up at me.

"Oh, I'm sorry. I—"

"It's okay, Lyla," says Wendy, smiling at me, "I cried too the first time I saw my little Madeleine. She's going to be a beauty just like her namesake. She's made things come full circle for our family."

I remember hearing how the first Madeleine, Wendy's ancestor, ran away from home; for a moment, I can't help wondering if this one is the reincarnation of that one—sort of like how Sybil thinks she and Alan are reincarnated from someone else. I wonder if Lilybelle was reincarnated—but she didn't live long enough that I would ever recognize her if she was—funny, she could be walking around Marquette now and I might have seen her a hundred times and never known it was her.

Then I get the surprise of my life when Wendy says, "Lyla, I have to go to the bathroom. Would you like to hold her while I go?"

I feel too nervous to say anything, but I realize how much I really do want to hold her.

John tells me to sit down in the empty chair next to him, and then Wendy hands little Madeleine to me, and suddenly my whole body turns warm, and I don't even realize it, but I'm swaying back and forth and loving this little baby girl.

"You're a natural mother, Lyla," says Lucy, stepping out onto the porch.

"You never married or had children did you?" says John after Wendy gives him a kiss on the cheek and goes into the house.

"No," I says.

"Did you ever want to be married?" Lucy asks.

"No, I never met the right fellow I guess," I says.

"It's too bad," Lucy says. "But neither did Maud or I."

"No, it's not too bad," says Eleanor. "We all have our own paths. No matter what happens, God makes them straight."

"That's true," says John. "I know when I thought I was most lost, God was preparing everything to work out in the best way possible for me, and now my life is better than I ever could have imagined."

I hear what they're saying, but I pretend to be too focused on Lilybelle—I mean, little Madeleine. Still, I don't see how God can straighten out this path—not after what Bel said to me. She sure as hell ain't straight.

"Yes, as long as we are open to His guidance," Eleanor keeps on, "it all works out. At ninety-three, when I look back, all I can see is a path to what got me to where I was meant to be."

I wonder where that is—I mean, where the heck is Eleanor anyways? She got married, got divorced, raised a couple daughters, and basically babysat her brother at the end and became an old lady—is that where she was meant to be? And that's more than I ever did just being an orphan, cleaning houses, and also becoming an old lady.

By the time Wendy comes back, little Madeleine is sleeping in my arms.

"Oh, I don't want to wake her up," says Wendy. "Do you mind holding her a while longer, Lyla?"

"No, that's fine," I says. I've stopped listening to the chatter around me. Soon they're all talking to each other, but I'm just watching Madeleine's little chest rise and fall as she sleeps.

At some point, I hear Tom—John's dad—hollering that the food is ready; he's been grilling the burgers and brats out in front of the garage so the smoke doesn't get to us on the porch—and I see through the patio window that he's bringing in plates of brats and hamburgers now into the dining room. And then everyone out on the deck with me starts getting up and heading into the house.

"Do you want me to bring you a plate, Wendy?" John asks.

"No," she says. "I'll come in. Lyla, I'll take the baby and lay her on the bed to sleep so we can eat."

"Is it okay to leave her alone like that?" I asks.

"Oh, sure," says Wendy. "I'll eat fast and she's too young to roll so she can't fall off the bed."

"Okay," I says, starting to feel hungry, but reluctant to let the baby go.

Everyone has gone in now, even John, and it's just me, Wendy, and Madeleine on the porch.

"Can you watch her just one minute longer, Lyla, while I go find a place on the bed to put her?" Wendy asks. "Alan's got so many boxes all over from unpacking still that maybe I need to clear a spot for her."

"No problem," I says. "Take your time."

Wendy goes inside while I stay sitting on the deck with little Madeleine in my arms. It's just me and Madeleine now, and that's just fine with me.

But a few seconds later, Eleanor comes out onto the deck and walks to the railing, then hollers out, "Alan, come in! We're eating!" Then she turns around and asks me, "Are you coming, Lyla?"

"Yes. Just a minute," I says.

Eleanor goes back inside and I sit quietly for a few seconds with the baby in my arms, feeling it pressed against my breast and noticing how calm I feel holding her.

Then I hear some splashing of water, and through the rails on the deck, I see Alan and Frank coming up the ladder on the dock. And then they're standing there for a second. The deck is above the dock, and I can just barely see them between the railings.

"Come on," Alan says, his voice carrying up to the deck. "They've all gone inside. No one can see us here."

"Okay," Frank says.

Okay, what? Are they going to do some drugs? I wouldn't put it past Alan. But then, in the space between the rails, I see Frank lean forward, and then Alan leans in from the opposite direction.

"Oh!" I gasp, instantly hoping they don't hear me, but they're too focused on each other—their lips locked together. "So that's why Alan and Sybil—" I'm shocked as they kiss for what seems the longest time...

When they finally pull back slightly, just an inch or two from each other, I see such tenderness on Frank's face as he places his hand on Alan's cheek.

"I love you," Alan says.

"I love you too," Frank says.

They look so happy. I've never felt happy like how they look...

When they turn toward the deck, I quickly jump up with the baby, who by some miracle doesn't cry. I don't want them to know I saw them, but somehow, I doubt they'd really care.

At that moment, Wendy comes to the door to take the baby from me. As I hand Madeleine over to her, Frank and Alan come up onto the deck.

"Hi, Lyla," Frank says, his biceps and chest glistening with river water.

"Hello," I says, embarrassed to look at him—how can a big man like him be gay?

"I'm glad you could come, Lyla," Alan says to me. "And I'm glad you and my dad got a chance to set things right at the end. Aunt Eleanor says you forgave him for how he treated you."

"Yes," I says, thinking that's not exactly how it all happened, but that Eleanor will interpret it the way she likes.

"That's good," says Alan. "We shouldn't hold grudges in life, no matter what."

"Yes," I says again, wondering if he's trying to tell me he doesn't hold a grudge against me either. I wonder if Sybil holds a grudge—I wonder if she figured it out but didn't want to hurt Alan by telling people, or if she was just embarrassed that he'd dumped her for a man instead. I wonder if Eleanor or the rest of the family knows about Alan.

I feel bad for Sybil, but I know Alan can't help it—I somehow understand that now. I remember seeing it on Oprah—that you're born that way—being gay. That must mean Alan's just always been that way—and I can kind of see now why his father and him always butted heads. No wonder they had a rough relationship...And, Bel—well, she...

"Did you see the cake they got me, Lyla?" Alan asks as we go inside the house.

"No," I says, following him over to the counter where I see a chocolate cake with chocolate frosting, and written across it is, "Happy Birthday, Alan...Life Begins at Forty."

What about at seventy-seven? I wonder. I felt like it was just beginning for me when I was at Finn Fest a few weeks back.

"There's plenty of food over here, Lyla," Tom says, motioning to a plate of brats in his hand.

"Um," I says, "actually, do you mind Alan if I use your phone? Is there a private one in your room or something? I just want to check on my friend,

Bel. She…well, I don't want to say too much while everyone is eating, but she was pretty sick to her stomach this morning."

It sounds gross, but I don't know what else to say. I don't know why— something about the way Frank and Alan looked at each other after they kissed—something about Alan saying not to hold grudges—makes me want to call her. They looked—well, they looked so happy, and I've never felt happiness like that—and now—well, with Bel—I've made a mess of it all. But maybe it's not too late.

"Sure," Alan says. "In my room, second door on the left."

"Be careful not to wake the baby," Wendy says as I head down the hall.

"I'll be careful," I says. "I'll make sure she's okay. I'll just be a minute."

I go into the bedroom and see Madeleine asleep on the bed, perfectly content. I'll be talking quietly, not wanting anyone else to hear, so I won't wake her. As I pick up the phone on the bedside table, I can hear everyone else out in the other room talking as they eat.

"You're just being silly, Lyla—overdramatic, that's what you are," I tell myself, but I also think, "It's been two days since it happened, and I haven't talked to her in all that time, and what if she's so upset that she does something stupid like hurt herself?"

Before I can second guess myself, I dial her number.

After just one ring, I hear, "Hello."

"Bel, why didn't you come to the party?" I asks. "I had to ask Eleanor and her daughters to give me a ride when you didn't show up."

"Oh," she says, pausing—as surprised as I am I guess that I've called her. "Well, I'm not feeling good."

"Your Alzheimer's isn't that bad yet," I tell her. "I thought maybe you forgot to pick me up."

She knows I'm bluffing. I'd have called to ask her where the hell she was if I had expected her to pick me up. But pretending things are okay is the closest thing to an apology she's going to get out of me after the things she said.

"No, I didn't forget," she says, sounding uncertain about what I mean.

"Well, why don't you come over anyways?" I says. "We're just about to eat. You can still make it."

"Lyla, I—" she tries to say, but I'm afraid of what she'll say, so I cut her off.

"And then tomorrow," I says, "we can get started with packing you up to move into my place."

"Lyla?" She sounds surprised.

I don't say anything. I've said what I had to say. I've done the best I could so she better not push me.

"Do you really mean it, Lyla?" she asks.

"Yeah, we're going to eat, so hurry it up and get here," I says, pretending not to understand her.

"Oh, I don't think I should drive much anymore," she says. "At least not when I'm by myself. Do you mind if I don't come?"

"No," I says, realizing she probably shouldn't be driving and she'd just get lost trying to find the place. "Eleanor said we could bring you a plate of food later."

"That would be nice," she says.

"Are you okay until I get home? It might be a few hours. I don't want to ruin the party for anyone, but I think Eleanor will get tired pretty quick at her age so I won't be too late."

"No, I'll be okay," Bel says. "Just be sure to stop by when you get home— to bring me that plate of food, you know."

"I know," I says.

"Lyla," she says, "I'm real sorry about before. It's just—I didn't mean to say things the way it all came out; it's just, well, to me, the best place in the world is wherever you are, Lyla. I—that's all I meant. The only time I really feel happy and safe is when I'm with you."

Safe? I don't think I've ever felt safe in my entire life. And I—well, if I make her feel safe—well, I don't know that I can even imagine what safe feels like, but it sounds real nice. I guess I can give that to her even if I can't have it.

I look out the window, trying to think what to say. There's a beam of sunlight filtering down through the trees onto the river.

"I know, Bel," I says. "I'll see you real soon. I love you."

Be Sure to Read All of Tyler R. Tichelaar's Marquette Books

IRON PIONEERS:
THE MARQUETTE TRILOGY: BOOK ONE

When iron ore is discovered in Michigan's Upper Peninsula in the 1840s, newlyweds Gerald Henning and his beautiful socialite wife Clara travel from Boston to the little village of Marquette on the shores of Lake Superior. They and their companions, Irish and German immigrants, French Canadians, and fellow New Englanders face blizzards and near starvation, devastating fires, and financial hardships. Yet these iron pioneers persevere until their wilderness village becomes integral to the Union cause in the Civil War and then a prosperous modern city. Meticulously researched, warmly written, and spanning half a century, *Iron Pioneers* is a testament to the spirit that forged America.

THE QUEEN CITY
THE MARQUETTE TRILOGY: BOOK TWO

During the first half of the twentieth century, Marquette grows into the Queen City of the North. Here is the tale of a small town undergoing change as its horses are replaced by streetcars and automobiles, and its pioneers are replaced by new generations who prosper despite two World Wars and the Great Depression. Margaret Dalrymple finds her Scottish prince, though he is neither Scottish nor a prince. Molly Bergmann becomes an inspiration to her grandchildren. Jacob Whitman's children engage in a family feud. The Queen City's residents marry, divorce, have children, die, break their hearts, go to war, gossip, blackmail, raise families, move away, and then return to Marquette. And always, always they are in love with the haunting land that is their home.

SUPERIOR HERITAGE
THE MARQUETTE TRILOGY: BOOK THREE

The Marquette Trilogy comes to a satisfying conclusion as it brings together characters and plots from the earlier novels and culminates with Marquette's sesquicentennial celebrations in 1999. What happened to Madeleine Henning is finally revealed as secrets from the past shed light upon the present. Marquette's residents struggle with a difficult local economy, yet remain optimistic for the future. The novel's main character, John Vandelaare, is descended from all the early Marquette families in *Iron Pioneers* and *The Queen City*. While he cherishes his family's past, he questions whether he should remain in his hometown. Then an event happens that will change his life forever.

NARROW LIVES

Narrow Lives is the story of those whose lives were affected by Lysander Blackmore, the sinister banker first introduced to readers in *The Queen City*. It is a novel that stands alone, yet readers of *The Marquette Trilogy* will be reacquainted with some familiar characters. Written as a collection of connected short stories, each told in first person by a different character, *Narrow Lives* depicts the influence one person has, even in death, upon others, and it explores the prisons of grief, loneliness, and fear self-created when people doubt their own worthiness.

THE ONLY THING THAT LASTS

The story of Robert O'Neill, the famous novelist introduced in *The Marquette Trilogy*. As a young boy during World War I, Robert is forced to leave his South Carolina home to live in Marquette with his grandmother and aunt. He finds there a cold climate, but many warmhearted friends. An old-fashioned story that follows Robert's growth from childhood to successful writer and husband, the novel is written as Robert O'Neill's autobiography, his final gift to Marquette by memorializing the town of his youth.

SPIRIT OF THE NORTH: A PARANORMAL ROMANCE

In 1873, orphaned sisters Barbara and Adele Traugott travel to Upper Michigan to live with their uncle, only to find he is deceased. Penniless, they are forced to spend the long, fierce winter alone in their uncle's remote wilderness cabin. Frightened yet determined, the sisters face blizzards and near starvation to survive. Amid their difficulties, they find love and heartache—and then, a ghostly encounter and the coming of spring lead them to discovering the true miracle of their being.

MY MARQUETTE:
EXPLORE THE QUEEN CITY OF THE NORTH
—ITS HISTORY, PEOPLE, AND PLACES

My Marquette is the result of its author's lifelong love affair with his hometown. Join Tyler R. Tichelaar, seventh generation Marquette resident and author of *The Marquette Trilogy*, as he takes you on a tour of the history, people, and places of Marquette. Stories of the past and present, both true and fictional, will leave you understanding why Marquette really is "The Queen City of the North." Along the way, Tyler will describe his own experiences growing up in Marquette, recall family and friends he knew, and give away secrets about the people behind the characters in his novels. *My Marquette* offers a rare insight into an author's creation of fiction and a refreshing view of a city's history and relevance to today. Reading *My Marquette* is equal to being given a personal tour by someone who knows Marquette intimately.

For more information on Tyler's Marquette Books, visit:
www.MarquetteFiction.com

Be sure also to check out Tyler's nonfiction titles

KING ARTHUR'S CHILDREN:
A STUDY IN FICTION AND TRADITION
www.ChildrenofArthur.com

THE GOTHIC WANDERER:
FROM TRANSGRESSION TO REDEMPTION
www.GothicWanderer.com

CREATING A LOCAL HISTORICAL BOOK:
FICTION AND NONFICTION GENRES
www.MarquetteFiction.com

And COMING SOON – Tyler's New Arthurian
Fiction Series Begins!

ARTHUR'S LEGACY:
BOOK I in THE CHILDREN OF ARTHUR series

All his life, Adam Morgan has sought his true identity and the father he never knew. When multiple coincidences lead him to England, he will not only find his father, but mutual love with a woman he can never have, and a family legacy he never imagined possible. Among England's green hills and crumbling castles, Adam's intuition awakens, and when a mysterious stranger appears with a tale of Britain's past, Adam discovers forces may be at work to bring about the return of a king.

For updates on Tyler R. Tichelaar's Arthurian novels, visit:
www.ChildrenofArthur.com

About the Author

Tyler R. Tichelaar is a seventh generation resident of Marquette, Michigan. Since age eight he wanted to be a writer, and at age sixteen, he began writing his first novel, which years later was published as *The Only Thing That Lasts*.

Tyler has a Ph.D. in Literature from Western Michigan University, and Bachelor and Master's Degrees in English from Northern Michigan University. He is the current President of the Upper Peninsula Publishers and Authors Association. He is the owner of Marquette Fiction and Superior Book Promotions, a professional book review, editing, and proofreading service.

In 2009, Tyler was awarded the Best Historical Fiction Award in the Reader Views Literary Awards for his novel *Narrow Lives*. He has since gone on to sponsor that award. In 2011, he received the Barb H. Kelly Historic Preservation Award from the Marquette Beautification and Restoration Committee for his book *My Marquette* and he received the Marquette County Arts Award that same year for an "Outstanding Writer."

Today, Tyler continues to live in Marquette, where the roar of Lake Superior, mountains of snow, and sandstone architecture inspire his writing. He has many future books in the planning.